Praise for
Sinking the Ark

"A tumble through Portland in the mid-seventies, played out in the politically contentious world of a struggling alternative newspaper and the empty pocketbooks of its delicious downtown hippiness. Each character comes brilliantly alive in Tamim Ansary's narration, dope smoking dreamers, radicals, knapsack journalists, idealists, artists, cultists, and so much more. Not just a romp, however. In their personal lives, Ansary's characters are waking to the ills of sexism and in their journalism, the corruption in their town. Packed with humor, this is an easy page turner, a book without brakes. If you missed the era, or lived it, inhale this novel. Steal it if you must."

> — Eric Nalder, winner of two Pulitzer Prizes for investigative journalism, author of *Tankers Full of Trouble: the perilous journey of Alaskan crude*

"Like the best satires, *Sinking the Ark* has a heart of gold at its center, so it roots for the eccentric cast of characters even as it pokes fun at them for their idealism and their contradictions, the bowls of joints on kitchen counters and the copies of *Being and Nothingness* on the nightstands. This is a funny, sharp, yet compassionate look at a singular time and place in American cultural history, down to the last soul-searching detail."

> — Frances Lefkowitz, author of *To Have Not*

"*Sinking the Ark* is equal parts adventure, acid trip, and dramedy. Reading Ansary is like taking a seat by the campfire, the master storyteller catches your eye, you see that knowing twinkle and know that you're in for a ride. *Sinking the Ark* is one of those books that you hope won't end, but you can't put down."

> — Ransom Stephens, bestselling author of *The 99% Solution*

"Before Portland, Oregon, was "Portlandia," before it was the center of the universe, before it was Brooklyn West…it was a really quirky and vibrant place. What a thrill to revisit that moment, brilliantly recorded and yet reimagined by Tamim, in this funny and poignant novel. Makes me wish I'd been destined to be a novelist, rather than an historian."

> — Maurice Isserman, Professor of History, Hamilton College, co-author of *America Divided: The Civil War of the 1960s*

SINKING THE ARK

TAMIM ANSARY

Sinking the Ark

KAJAKI
PRESS

San Francisco

ISBN: 978-0-9982623-2-1

Published by Kajaki Press
www.kajakipress.com
Art by Justin Donica
Cover art copyright © 2022 by Justin Donica
Printed in U.S.A.

Dedicated to my fellow scriveners
Bob Shindleman, Paul Lobell, Nick Allen, Jehnana Balzer,
Phyllis Meschan, Maxine Miller, Maurice Isserman,
and the many others who were my comrades-in-arms
on the Portland Scribe in the Age of Ford

"Wish I didn't know now what I didn't know then…"

BOB SEGER
Against the Wind

Dramatis Personae

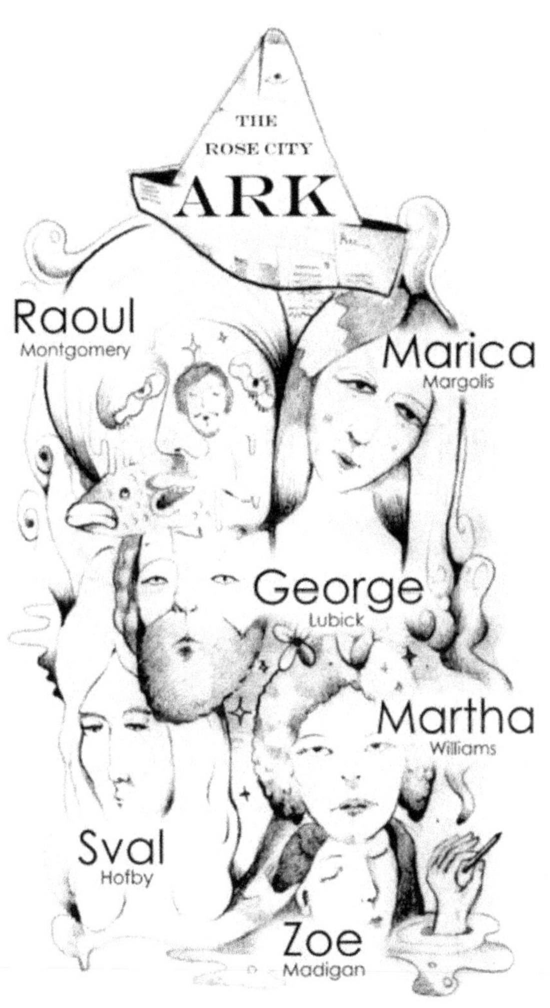

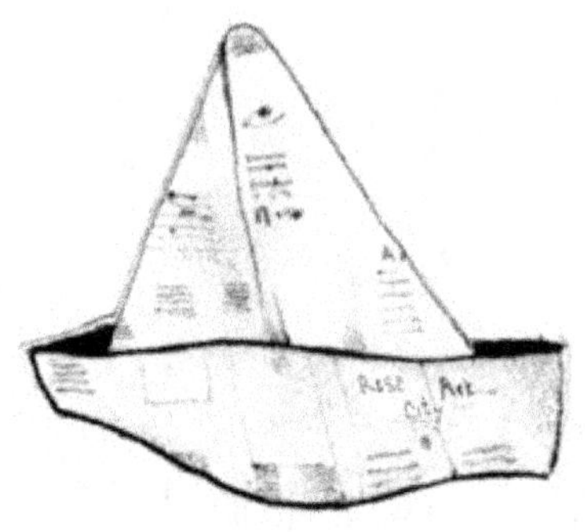

PART ONE
The Proposal

September 1, 1973

The ringing woke Sval in the middle of the night. Shrouded as he was in a web of dreams, he thought it was his alarm clock, and he groped to turn it off, in the process knocking several items off his night table— a half-empty bottle of beer, a half-smoked pack of Camels, a half-read copy of *Being and Nothingness*—waking up finally, enough to remember that he had no alarm clock. It must be the phone.

He got out of bed and wrapped a blanket around his lanky frame. The phone was in the kitchen. So was the big red clock from Goodwill, which let him know it wasn't the middle of the night but six a.m. He picked up the receiver. "Hello?"

"Hofby?" a voice blapped. "Ken here. Singleton. Remember me? Coalition of the Left. We met three weeks back at—"

"I remember you, Ken. Why are you calling me at this frightful hour?"

"I'm calling everyone, man. Spiro Agnew's landing at the Portland airport eight o'clock. Corrupt motherfucker thinks the people are gonna' let him sneak into this burg like he owns it. We gotta' hit the streets, Hofby, give him a taste of the people's wrath. Roust your comrades. Tell everyone."

"Thanks for sharing, Paul Revere. I'll try to be there. But listen, isn't this a little last minute? What kind of crowd you gonna' roust by eight o'clock tonight?"

"Tonight? No, man! This morning! I only just found out myself— don't worry, Hofby, we'll fill the airport all the way out to 82nd Street. I already put the word out to my troops. You just be there."

Two hours later, Sval stood leaning against a fence surrounding the parking lot at the Portland Airport, his face pressed to the cold wires, clutching under his arm a hastily hand-lettered sign that read *Agnew Go Home!* Near him stood Ken Singleton and his "troops," four or five bearded men clad in shapeless workers' slacks and bulky army surplus flight jackets. They had wooden signs but the lettering had smeared in the Portland drizzle, although Sval could make out that Ken's sign had originally read *Agnew = Hitler.* A half dozen Portland cops slouched along a line of construction horses set out as a barrier against demonstrators. They were drinking coffee out of thermos bottles and ignoring the demonstrators, whom they outnumbered.

In the distance, a plane was just pulling up to the terminal and the jetway was rolling out to it. Agnew would go directly into the terminal, if that was even his plane—Sval had to wonder, now that he was here— would the vice-president of the United States really come to town on an ordinary commercial flight?

Ken Singleton took a handkerchief out of his jacket pocket and wiped his wet face. Beads of rain glistened on his beard. "We'll get the bastard next time," he muttered.

Sval looked over his shoulder at the empty parking lot. "You know, Ken, this strikes me as almost counter-productive, coming out in the rain like this."

"What: crying about a little rain?" Singleton sneered. "The revolution is not a dinner party, comrade."

"It's not the rain, Ken. Remember, back in the old days? Every time you went to one of these things, the crowd felt bigger. Sixty-eight … sixty-nine… It didn't matter what the signs or speeches said—the numbers alone sent a message back then. The number alone said, something is happening here, Mr. Jones. Better jump aboard or you'll get left-behind like dog-meat."

"What's your point?" Singleton affected boredom.

"My point? My point is, every time I go to one of these demonstrations now, the numbers have shrunk. The message is still in the numbers, Ken. Every time we demonstrate now, we're telling people, jump off this train before it's too late, you fools, this train's going over a cliff."

Singleton looked at Sval as if he had been watching his lips move but hearing no sound. "Every revolution goes through phases. Right now, the vanguard has to organize the workers."

"The workers be damned. The workers drink beer and watch monster truck rallies. Civilization is crashing all around us and they're part of the problem! We've got to get out of the building before it comes down!"

"You sound like Walter what's-his-name," Singleton spat. "The newspaper guy."

"The Ark? The Rose City Ark? By God, now that you mention it, Ken—yes! That's the sort of thing we need more of now—not demonstrations. Institutions!" Sval crumpled up his sign, "You know what? I'm going to see if the Ark could use another volunteer." Sval retrieved his bicycle and drove away in the rain.

"Marx has a whole chapter on people like you," Singleton yelled after him.

It was September and a light drizzle was coming down the day Sval joined the *Ark*. His schedule was already somewhat crowded at the time. He was volunteering two hours a week at the cash register of the People's Food Store, and he was Mr. Faithful at his neighborhood's community garden every Saturday morning. He also put in time at the car repair co-op even though mechanics, frankly, was not his métier. Sval had served on many an ad hoc steering committee working to build the new society and in a few cases was still serving—but it wasn't enough.

It wasn't enough because serving the greater good felt good, and Sval wanted more of that sensation. The Rose City Ark operated out of two rooms on the fourth floor of the Unitarian Church, both of which were crowded the day Sval arrived to volunteer. He ambled among sociable clumps of workers, introducing himself and making mental notes. Although quiet, he did not go unnoticed. Standing six-foot three in his triple-belted Frye boots, he seemed at first glance to have too many limbs with too many joints, which gave him a gangling look in repose. His embroidered bell-bottomed jeans and waist-length blond ponytail let casual observers know that this man was not and never had been a servile stooge of the corporate state. It took half a lifetime to grow hair that long.

That day, Sval met leonine Walter, the founder, who radiated authority with the quiet ease of a Mount Everest. He met Walter's consort Grace, who was busy directing traffic, her head bound up in a polka dot kerchief from which scribbles of hair escaped. He met Ray Perkins, the lead guitarist of Dr. Rock's Rhythm Remedy, who was also, it turned out, something-or-other here at the Ark, and who let Sval know directly: "I'm carrying this newspaper on my goddamn back!"

And of course he met Marica Margolis. When he first set eyes on her, she was standing in the middle of the large lower room, arguing about something with Ray Perkins. Her black hair fell in ringlets and her green eyes gleamed with an assertive intelligence. She was wearing baggy green jungle pants and a tight T-shirt over sumptuous breasts. Slashing red letters zigzagged across her chest spelling out the words: "DARE TO JUGGLE."

Sval knew who this woman was. He'd seen her on stage, performing with the guerrilla theater troupe whose shirt she wore; but this was the first time he had seen her up close. He watched in fascination as she lifted a book from the table, pointed at it with stabbing gestures, and set it down. Twice she folded her arms so emphatically they thwacked against her body. She was decisive and Sval liked that. But she was also...and his mind groped for the *mot juste*, rejecting out of hand the first few candidates — "gorgeous" —"voluptuous" — "hot" ... well, whatever the word, with such a woman, how could a socially conscious man be sure that his responses were not sexist?

As he was pondering this conundrum, Marica finished up with Ray and bore down on Sval. She subjected him to a quick interview, firing a dozen or so questions in a friendly but challenging voice. He must have given correct answers, for suddenly the sandpaper went out of her voice, and she became his mentor. Guiding him around the room, she pointed out items of interest and discussed the philosophy of the paper *sotto voce.*

"You know," she told Sval, "a lot of people walk in here—men especially, I'm sorry to say—and they have no sense of paying dues. Right away they want page three for their thoughts on imperialism—you know? They never think about lifting a broom or pressing out a headline." She scuffed the floor with her shoe and added in a mumble that seemed almost shy, "You're different, though, Sval. I can tell. You're... a *conscious* man." Their eyes met, and Sval recognized her awkward radiance and his own unsettled heartbeat as "chemistry."

He left the Ark glowing with good humor that day. The news that he wished to volunteer had met with no derision. The people he met had treated him as if he already belonged. Indeed, he might plunge in deeply here: for despite all his commitments, he had the time: his job as a late-night dishwasher at the Genoa Restaurant took up only weekend nights, and this being Portland, Sval's expenses were few. He could picture himself developing one day into Walter's right-hand man. He could picture the two of them in consultation while an anxious staff awaited their opinion: not implausible. Best of all, something might be brewing between him and Marica. He scarcely dared to picture where that might go. He only knew that he had hit a turning point that day and it wasn't even five o'clock yet.

That night Sval went out with a motley assortment of friends, including Zoe Madigan, a pint-sized red-haired woman often on the fringes of his circles these days. Apparently, they had many mutual friends. Zoe had sandy skin and adorable freckles, and her cheeks and lips had a plumpness that reminded Sval, when he got around to noticing her, of a female Huck Finn. Sval didn't know much about Zoe personally, but in the group context, over the months, a pleasing ease had grown between them. He appreciated her opinions on books, her quick tongue, her politics. Best of all, she radiated no sexual charisma. In her company, a man could bring up anything. There were no hidden currents that might lead to awkward waters.

The group herded to the Piccadilly, a favorite old tavern with cracked floorboards, dark walls, and a bar that looked as simple and indestructible as the vinyl booths. A sign above the cash register exhorted patrons to "ask for our world-famous peanut-butter-and-jelly sandwich". The beer was cheap at the Piccadilly, and the fish and chips dripped delectably with grease.

Zoe challenged Sval to a game of eight ball. He followed her into the back room, approving the figure she cut with her derby hat and her hand-painted tie pulled out loose around the collar of her men's dress shirt, which she wore untucked. They carried with them the dregs of a conversation about when and how civilization would collapse. They both agreed that it would, of course, and soon. "We'll be right back to tribal," was Zoe's considered opinion. Sval wanted to talk about the Ark, but when he tried to bring it up, the first topic that sprang to his tongue was Marica. He bit his lips, wondering if it was sexist to feel such gladness at the memory of a woman he had known for less than an hour. In his defense, however, it was not her body per se but the spirit her body expressed that attracted him. Dozens of her expressions fluttered through his mind like snapshots: Marica facing down Ray Perkins, feet apart, hands on hips—the confidence she expressed with that body, the strength. He pictured himself and Marica surviving the collapse of civilization together and planting the human race anew. His mind leapt ahead to the far-flung tribes of their descendants who would remember them as legendary figures, the Great Mother, the Primal Father. He bit his lips again wondering if these thoughts were too intimate to share with Zoe. Voicing them out loud might not be the better part of tact. They didn't know each other well enough for topics so personal.

His voice had run down in mid-sentence but he skated over the awkward moment by setting the table up for eight-ball. Zoe broke. She had a good, clean follow-through and a smooth stroke and sank three balls before giving Sval his first chance.

"So," she said, as he was eyeballing his shot, "you went to Reed's fine college, I hear?"

He missed and stepped back, producing and lighting a cigarette one-handed. "I did," he admitted, "but I dropped out." They were alone in the pool room.

"Then we have two things in common," she said, and executed a difficult bank shot.

"You went to Reed?"

"And dropped out. Many times, in fact. Well, four times. Then they stopped letting me back in. I had to transfer to Portland State. I've dropped out of there three times. Thrice." She proceeded to clear all but the eight-ball and missed this shot, leaving Sval a table so crowded with his own balls that he could hardly fail to sink something just by firing blindly, which he did. She congratulated him and poured another beer. He lit another cigarette and contemplated his next blind effort. "What makes you drop out of school so much?" he asked, "Or should I ask, why keep going back?"

"Well, money. I have trouble staying interested, you see? That's my problem," said Zoe. "But my parents both died when I was 15—same day, two different car accidents—and left me a bunch of money that I can't touch unless I'm going to school. So, I sign up for a semester when I need money and drop out in time to get the refund—with Reed College, that usually got me through to the next registration day. Of course I had to finish a few semesters just to keep up my credibility. My relatives would be shocked if they knew what I'm doing, but I don't think it's wrong, do you?"

"An interesting question for an ethics seminar," Sval agreed.

"No, really," she insisted. "One of my uncles is a farmer, he gets paid by the government not to plant wheat. He says it's the right thing to do because there's too much wheat, and he's keeping the price of wheat up for other farmers. Well, what am I doing that's so different? There's too many liberal arts graduates walking around. Many more get out and a B.A.'s going to be worthless. I'm doing what I can to keep up the value of a college degree."

"By never getting one."

"Exactemente." Zoe sank the eight ball, and Sval put another quarter in the table. She set up the table for another game while he ordered another pitcher. They returned to pleasant speculations about the collapse of civilization, and continued playing. All evening they circled the room with their cue sticks, gauging shots, keeping a table more or less between them, staying on their feet, sharing cigarettes, pitchers, ideas. Each hour seemed no later than the one before as if time had reached where it was going and become a warm, still bath.

Eventually the bartender announced last call and the group, which had shrunk to seven, crowded into Fred's 20-year-old Plymouth. Sval's house was the first stop. There, however, Zoe got out too. She dismissed the others with some vague story about a notebook and followed Sval into the house. She shut the door, and leaned back against it. He turned and found himself standing so close to her that for the first time he realized how small she was. The top of her head came just to his collarbone. The air between them suddenly jelled. One of them would have to say something but Sval didn't trust his drunken brain to come up with the *mot juste*.

She finally broke the thickness with, "It's been fun, huh?"

"Tonight?" he murmured.

"Tonight… last night… the night before. . ."

Hmm. She was right: they'd seen each other every night for ... how long? They were leaning so far toward each other now, she with her face turned up, he bending down slightly, that they might as well have been kissing; so he leaned that last little inch to deliver a friendly peck. How his tongue ended up in her mouth, he was never later able to fathom.

"Let's go upstairs," she gasped.

"Okay," he panted and they bounded up to his room without another word.

Sval's room was in the attic, his bed a mattress in an alcove overlooking the empty street. Zoe headed straight from the door to the bed without pausing to shed clothes yet somehow managed to hit the covers naked. Sval's customary physical grace deserted him on his way across the room: he caught one hand in his sleeve, stubbed his toe on a wastebasket, and only managed to liberate one leg from his pants by the time he slid down beside Zoe. And then physical grace no longer mattered.

Only afterward, as they basked in post-coital satisfaction, with intoxication waning and arousal dead, did Sval pay heed to a still, small voice of nagging dismay murmuring, "What have you done?" This was

Pal Zoe lying next to him—sex had never been on their agenda; their whole companionship was based on that fact. Questions began to bombinate. Just how did he plan to explain to Zoe in the morning that this had been an aberration? How would he tell her that he should have been sleeping with a woman named Marica Margolis this night, it was what the gods had ordained? For that matter, what exactly was that profound spiritual energy he had felt with Marica, that current he had been calling chemistry? In her absence, he saw all too clearly that the word had, alas, merely meant "lust."

"Zoe," he croaked, not knowing what he was going to say, only that something needed to be said.

"Hmm?" she acknowledged after a long moment, her voice thick.

"I'm not—in all honesty—let me make this clear—necessarily committed in a sense. . . to what it might seem we've started here. . ."

Moments passed in silence. He couldn't tell how she was taking it. He lay looking up at the rafters, waiting, feeling her body vibrant with mute tension next to his. Or at least he thought he was sensing mute tension until her even breathing tipped him off that she was asleep.

"Zoe!" He nudged her. "Did you hear me? Hey! I'm not in love with you."

Roused for a moment by his prodding, she murmured, "Hmmm? Uh huh . . . good for me too."

"That's not what I said. We need to talk . . . about how we feel— the significance of this—I, for example, am not in love. . ."

"Me neither. Huh. Interesting. . ." and she drifted off again.

He lay on his side then for a while looking at his friend as she slept. The stripes of moonlight bleached her skin and brought out the freckles scattered across her neck and her small breasts. Gazing at her slender body tangled among the sheets, he could hardly believe that the man he remembered making volcanic love to her less than an hour ago had been himself. Quite possibly he would never feel that way about her again. Sleeping with Zoe had been a blunder. But the demands of honor were clear. He would have to give this relationship a fair trial. He only hoped that when it didn't work out, he and Zoe could still be friends.

The Community

As it turned out, once he joined the Ark, Sval had too much on his mind to think about Zoe. In his second week at the paper, wise old Walter took him aside and asked him to "cover" a neighborhood association meeting. Neighborhood associations were something the city had set up. Nothing much happened at the meeting Sval attended, just some greybeards squabbling over city funding for a sewer project, but out of it, Sval got what Walter called a "think-piece", about the connection between sewer lines and planetary pollution. The issue was the same, was it not? How to get rid of all that shit. Sewers, however, were tangible. About sewers, one could *do* something. The ability to *do* something meant that sewers were empowering. So said Sval, in his first piece for the Ark. Walter ran it without comment on page 5. And a few letters came in complimenting his visionary stance.

The following week, at Monday meeting, Sval buckled up his courage and proposed a new feature for the paper, a collection of nuggets about interesting local projects to save the planet, under the heading "Community Briefs". The proposal passed.

After that he was working on a piece a week, sometimes two. *Right Livelihood*, for example, told about a local Buddhist carpenter who helped homeless people build shelters out of scrap wood and cardboard. *Supply Chain* told of community alternatives to shopping at Safeway. In November, Sval wrote a review of Dare-to-Juggle's performances at Athena Coffeehouse, in which he argued that the beloved local troupe used juggling to express revolutionary social values. That piece got him a chaste hug from Marica—chaste but arousing. Arousing but so what:

there was no next step with Marica. He was with Zoe now. That relationship had yet to run its course.

And there was no telling when or even if it would. An object in motion tends to stay in motion unless it crashes into something, and as far as Sval could see, he and Zoe never crashed into anything. Was this even really a "relationship"? Zoe lived her life, Sval lived his. Many nights they ended up at his house, some nights at hers, but sometimes they didn't see each other for days. Even then, curious ripples seemed to run between them. Once, Zoe took a deep dive into learning magic. Sval as it happened was just then working on a piece about professional Portland magicians. What were the odds? Another time, Zoe got obsessed with researching whether cats dreamed. Wouldn't you know it, Sval was that week working on an essay about history's greatest dreamers. It was almost eerie!

Zoe rarely came to the Ark and never to Monday Meeting. She wrote one short feature about cat-therapy for the paper, but she lost interest in cats after that, and she was never really interested in the *Ark*. She was interested in Sval. And Sval was fine with that. He and Zoe had plenty to share without sharing the *Ark*. One weekend, they took a train to Seattle to see Joe Cocker. Another time, they met a busload of people going to the coast and ended up doing peyote at a 24-hour house party in Cannon Beach. Then, with Halloween coming up, Zoe helped Sval organize a public costume party at the Pythian Ballroom. A few weeks later, he pitched in to help her host a potluck Thanksgiving for 30 people, featuring venison and Wild Turkey. Dare-to-Juggle was there, and some of the Street Stomp musicians, plus various strays who wandered in. Friends of friends. The community.

On the last day of the year Sval and Zoe drove to eastern Oregon to salute the coming New Year in a little-known cave they'd heard about. Even in the dead of winter one could camp in this cavern because it had a hot spring inside: so said rumor. No road sign marked the location of this place; only a select few knew it even existed; but Sval's sources had told him where to pull off the road and how to recognize the beginnings of the path that led to the cave.

The sun was sinking when they arrived, and two feet of snow covered the ground, but did they care? Hell no. They knew about The Cave. They'd be warm soon enough. But just as they were unloading their camping equipment, an Indian police officer pulled up and informed them they were on reservation land. The hot springs were sacred to the local tribe. The cave was off limits to outsiders. The officer was polite but firm. He directed them to the closest campground outside reservation land, which turned out to be a desolate spot in some county park. They pitched their tent in the snow, zipped their arctic sleeping bags together, and spent the whole night huddling and clinging. Naked was better than clothed for keeping warm, it turned out, so nakedly was how they huddled and clung.

By the time they were drinking hot coffee in a warm diner the next morning, that night had become a memory of warming each other with nonstop sex while the wind howled in the darkness outside. Sval saw it as an experience their descendants would transform into myth. Zoe saw it as a metaphorical embodiment of the epic world-story now unfolding in which they two were key figures.

And indeed, those months stretching from late 1973 across New Year's Day into 1974 were laden with the weight of metaphor. Portland was accustomed to drizzle, but that year the rain came down in sheets that lasted for days, the very weather itself announcing the arrival of a winter that went beyond mere weather: the apocalypse was coming. Just as one began to feel the days growing shorter and the nights growing longer, the oil shortages began. In the darkness of mid-December, gas stations started closing around noon. Signs posted on pumps told costumers to come back tomorrow, the gas had run out today, and sometimes, on the morrow, those same gas stations didn't even open.

In the outside world, people were saying the oil crisis was a ripple effect of the Yom Kippur War. Things would get back to normal as soon as the Arabs and Israelis had ironed out their differences. Sentiment in the Community had a different hue. Zoltan the Barbarian nailed it with a blistering article in the *Ark*. Yes, yes, Yom Kippur War, Arab oil, gas crisis—the connections were indisputable, but how was this a source of comfort? Israel/Palestine was right where War III was expected to begin, the nuclear war that could so easily put an end to human life on Earth.

Zoltan's piece sent shivers through the Community—as how could it not at such a time? For in those days, shadows were flickering across the entire country, cast by gigantic figures wrestling on a world-sized stage. The Watergate drama was coming to a peak. The smoking gun had been discovered at last: the Nixon gang, it turned out, had taped their criminal conversations in the White House! Nixon was fighting like a meth-crazed wolverine to keep those secret tapes unheard, but the wrecking ball was already swinging, the momentum of history looked unstoppable, and when the courts did finally pry one tape loose from the clutches of the evil president, it turned out to contain an eighteen-minute gap. *An eighteen-minute gap!* Someone had erased a passage! Who? Why? What was said in those minutes and by whom? It didn't matter: the missing minutes proved that there *had* been a coverup, and the coverup was now the crime in question. For the first time in history an American president was going down. Game over, Mr. Nixon. Oh, this was big!

But Nixon didn't seem to know he was finished. He was sending waves of attack-lawyers into the courts to parry the thrusts coming from every side. His associates were convicted of crimes and hauled to prison one by one, but the glowering gangster of San Clemente hung on. When the curtains opened on the stage that was 1974, he was still fighting to stay in the White House.

Sval wrote local stories mostly, but he felt the flavor of his times. How could he not? Every person on Earth could feel the momentous shift the planet was going through. Sval was sure of this. Every conscious human knew this time would be remembered forevermore as the one that divided all of history into Before and After. Living in Portland at such a time, celebrating holidays at tribal potlucks shared with hundreds, framing the new civilization that would rise from the rubble of the old one now crumbling … if you were part of the community in line to inherit the Earth, there had never been a better time. The darkness was real, but *you*—curled up with good friends in a cozy cabin in front of a blazing fireplace while the blizzard raged outside—*you* could see the sunlit landscape that lay beyond the night. Sval couldn't later remember who came up with that image, him or Zoe, but it didn't matter. Both could see what the other saw and either of them could describe vividly what both of them saw.

One day, after a particularly contentious Monday Meeting, Sval walked to Zoe's house to tell her what had happened. He always did that now: after a contentious meeting he always went looking for Zoe to tell her what had happened. Houses in the community were never locked, so Sval entered without knocking and made his way upstairs. Zoe's door was open, and she was sitting at the table by the window. She brightened at the sight of him but didn't get up, for she was doing something that required great concentration: making an exact replica of Notre Dame Cathedral out of toothpicks. Sval leaned against the doorway and studied her intent form.

A statement was rising inside him. Five months had passed since his friendship with Zoe had taken what he still referred to as "that sudden turn." All these months, he had kept her and the Ark in separate compartments. But Marica was merely a colleague now. *Zoe* was the woman in his life. Perhaps the time had come to trust that he could make his life into a single harmonious whole.

"Zoe," he said.

"Hmmm?"

"How about getting more involved with the Ark? Come to Monday meeting with me this week. What do you think?"

She glanced at him and returned to Notre Dame. "Pass," she said.

Pass? He was inviting her into the most important part of his life and she was saying no thanks? "That's curious. Why? I think you'd find it…at the very least . . . amusing."

"I might," she agreed, "but if I joined the Ark, we'd have nothing to tell each other anymore because we'd never been apart. We couldn't ask each other what we'd been up to because we'd already know. We were both there."

"That we'd lose," he conceded, "but would we not gain expanded opportunities to compare impressions?"

"More stuff to gossip about, you mean?"

"That's one way to put it, I suppose."

"Another way would be?"

"More stuff to share?" he suggested.

Zoe was not impressed. "There's such a thing as sharing too much. People might start to look at us as a couple." She gave him a sharp look. "Which we're not, right?"

"Well, no," Sval said. "Not 'A Couple'', uppercase C, as in 'Unit'. I wouldn't want to see either of us reduced to half of something."

She touched a toothpick to a bead of clear glue and carefully moved it into position. "What are we, though, if we're not a couple?"

The risky question brought him to a pause. Five months of what they'd built together hung on the label he now uttered. "Friends," he declared finally. "Good friends actually. Actually, from my point of view…best friends."

She flashed him a grin. "Best friends who fuck." She rubbed her small hands together. "Best friends who have deep conversations and also do a lot of fucking and sometimes both at the same time. Did relationships like this exist in our parents' generation?"

"They'll be standard after the apocalypse," Sval predicted.

"Well, they'd have to be. After the apocalypse, everyone will have to be more flexible. We don't know what we'll be facing. We couldn't do this and live together though. Could we? I think not," she said—for officially they still lived in separate houses with separate housemates.

"No," said Sval. "I can't see how mingling our dirty laundry and taking out the garbage together would improve the relationship." Breath that he'd been clenching eased out. "Our relationship is amazing as it is. We're really close and yet both completely free."

"Not that we don't already spend five nights together out of every seven," she reminded him.

"Granted. But the other two nights keep the whole thing in perspective."

"A person needs to breathe." Zoe combed her fingers through her short red hair. "Maybe you think we see each other too much as it is?"

"No," said Sval, "as it is feels just about right."

"Just the right amount of togetherness." Zoe began to gather her unused toothpicks and her glue. "That's the goal. Just the right amount of togetherness."

"And we're hitting the mark precisely, I think. What do you think?"

"It's just right. For this moment. Later, it might seem like the wrong amount. Who can tell?" She shut the book and stood up.

"Wrong in which direction?" he inquired.

"Either," she said. "You might start wanting to spend every night with me."

"Or one of us might want to spend less time," Sval allowed.

"Or that," she conceded, "but we have the flexibility to deal with it, whichever way it goes, as long as we're not living together. Our relationship is strong like that. It can bend without breaking."

"Very true," he murmured. "Very true."

Yamhill House

Martha Williams went to a big Halloween party that year at the Pythian Ballroom. Not that Martha was the type to party at the Pythian, but another secretary where she worked knew someone who was going, and they convinced Martha to come along.

It was a public party so getting in cost money. Martha wasn't sure why she rummaged in her purse, she was pretty sure she'd feel out of place inside, but she ponied up, and sure enough, once she got inside, she felt like such a lump among all those long-haired men and all those women without bras dancing wildly, the men shedding their shirts when the room got hot, the women showing off luxuriantly hairy armpits as they waved their arms, anyone dancing with anyone, and some even dancing with no one. She met a man named Sval Hofby that night, and he talked to her for a few minutes, but then a freckle-faced woman with short red hair grabbed his arm and dragged him off. Someone told Martha he worked for the *Rose City Ark*, Portland's "alternative" newspaper.

Martha Williams had never heard of Portland's alternative newspaper. Alternative to what, she didn't know. She didn't even read the Oregonian every day. But she ran into Mr. Hofby again at a place called the People's Food Store. He was behind the cash register. And she saw him again in December, at a little bookstore called Powell's, just a hole-in-the-wall in the southeast. He was buying a stack of books and they chatted for a few minutes, but he was late to a meeting. In February, one of the other secretaries talked Martha into joining a group of women who got together every week to complain about men. Consciousness-raising, they called it. Martha only went a few times but she made a new friend there, Marica Margolis, who also worked at the *Ark*, though not for money, as it turned out. She was a volunteer.

After that Martha started reading the *Ark*, but she did not set foot in the office for another three months. When she did go in finally, one moist March day, it wasn't to volunteer but just to sneak a peek at the classified roommate ads before the paper went out. She thought her friend Marica might help her get away with it.

The moment she walked into the office, she saw Mr. Hofby standing at one of the long tables across the room, bending over some piece of work, his sand-colored ponytail hanging down his back, almost to his belt, a clear sign that he had never held a regular job out there in the straight world where Martha had grudgingly spent so many of her dull days. Martha thought she'd slip in quietly, find the ads, jot down some numbers, and slip out, but her friend Marica spotted her and grabbed her sleeve. "Come here, I want you to meet someone." She pulled Martha across the room to Mr. Hofby and uttered in that always-half-breathless voice of hers, "Sval. This is Martha Williams."

He stood up, a flicker of recognition in his eyes. "Mary. Good to see you again."

"Martha," she corrected him, blushing.

"You know each other?" Marica looked from one to the other.

"We have bumped into each other once or twice," Sval smiled.

"Well, isn't that so typical of Portland!" Marica gushed. "You're always finding out you know someone who knows someone!"

"That's been my experience," Sval agreed. "How've you been, Martha?"

Martha dropped her gaze. "Same old same old." Oh yuck. Why would this man know anything about her "same old"?

"Well, I'll leave you two alone," Marica announced. "Sounds like you have a *lot* to catch up on."

Martha threw a desperate glance after her friend, but Marica bustled away without a backward glance. Meanwhile Sval was standing there, waiting for her to speak, his eyes expressing courtesy and attention, nothing more. Martha knew what he must be thinking. She remembered how she'd looked in the mirror that morning.

"Marica's been nagging at me to come to the Ark," she said. "She keeps telling me the paper needs volunteers, but don't worry, that's not why I'm here. I just wanted to look at roommate ads. I quit my boring job, see. And now I can't afford the place I'm renting. I was thinking I might look for a roommate situation. Would it be cheating, do you think, to look at the classifieds before the paper comes out? I don't want to break any rules."

"What rules? This is the Ark, ma'am. We don't believe in rules here."

Martha buckled up her courage. "Well, Marica keeps saying there are lots of jobs here for a volunteer, like ordering supplies and stuff. I don't need to be paid. If there's anything I could do around here, just to help."

"Jump in, there's tons to do. Anyone can join the Ark, this is after all the community paper. From each according to her ability."

"I'm not really part of 'the community'," Martha admitted.

"Nonsense. We're all part of the community. You wanted to see the classifieds? Let's see if they've been typeset. In fact, if they have, why don't you lay them out? I'll find someone to show you how. I'm not an expert, I fear."

"If I can," said Martha, smoothing her gingham skirt over her belly. "If it would help." She spent the rest of the afternoon laying out the classifieds, and that's why she was the first to see the ad placed by the people at 1253 Yamhill Street, seeking a roommate.

The house on Yamhill Street was planted atop a knoll and went three stories up from there. The front door could not be seen from the sidewalk. A deep porch ran the width of the house, and most of it was screened off by bushes. Two huge oak trees blocked out the entire second story. All Martha could see from the sidewalk was the top story, a jagged skyline of gables.

She unclenched her fist and read the damp scrap of paper one more time. "Eight-plus women and men seek person to share LARGE house on quiet street." LARGE was correct anyway, and the street did seem quiet, but that phrase "eight-plus" worried Martha. Too late to turn back, though. She hitched up her skirts and started climbing. As soon as she passed through the bushes and onto the porch, she heard the wail of rock-and-roll shaking the windows.

A slight figure in rumpled clothes opened the door and blinked out. His eyes were large and round, and his black bush of curly hair made his head look oversized. He had the look of a bewildered night creature caught in a blaze of headlights.

"Hi," she said. "I'm Martha."

"Hi," said he. "I'm the Golem. You looking for El Dorado?"

"Umm…no. I came about the room?"

"What room?"

"Let her in, Raoul. Jeez." The music turned down suddenly and a woman with braids came flopping out from behind a curtain. "Howdy. You must be Martha. Don't mind Raoul. He's the Golem. You called about the room?"

"Are we renting a room?" Raoul exclaimed.

The woman swept him aside affectionately. "I'm Susan," she said. "Come in."

Martha stepped gingerly into a living room filled with stereo equipment. The amps seemed built into the walls. The polygon-shaped speakers loomed like spaceships from a distant galaxy, but the music coming from them was the familiar *Abbey Road*, the good side. There must have been at least 500 record albums on shelves made of vegetable crates. The only furniture consisted of enormous pillows and a hatch cover resting on cinder blocks.

"Let me give you a tour." Susan led the way to a room dominated by a huge butcher block table, the top of which was littered with art supplies, books, beer cans, and ash trays. Three walls were papered with paintings, drawings, and magazine clippings tacked up randomly as if on a bulletin board. Against the fourth wall, ice cream barrels stacked up and held in place by a wooden frame made a honeycomb of makeshift pigeonholes. All but one of them were stuffed to overflowing. Martha peeped into the empty barrel and saw a photograph of Ike Eisenhower, leaning through a window, grinning and waving. A dialog balloon pasted to the photo read, "Hi there. I'm still dead."

"We call this room the kindergarten," Susan apologized.

"Greatest goddamn room in all of Portland," Raoul boasted. "I'm an artist, you know."

Martha followed Susan through the kitchen which looked, thank goodness, fairly clean. "Excuse me," she ventured as Susan started upstairs, "Do people play music really loud around here?"

"It's only good if it's loud," said Raoul.

"The third floor is pretty quiet," Susan assured her

She led the way up two flights of stairs to a large square hall. The room for rent opened off the right. It had a slanted ceiling, finished wood walls, and an alcove that terminated in a large dormer window facing south over a panorama of rooftops, treetops, and ribbons of streets, upon which moved toy-sized cars and people.

"This is lovely," Martha breathed. Then she strolled back into the hall. "Are there three rooms on this floor?"

"No. Just two."

"This is a closet then?" She opened the third door off the hall and fell back with a shriek. A bald man was sitting cross-legged in the small dark space. His heavy-lidded eyes snapped open to deliver a stern glare.

Susan stepped forward quickly and shut the door. "That's Zack, our Zen Buddhist. He doesn't live here, he just uses the closet."

"That's a good sign, you know, if you're worried about noise," said the Golem. "Zen Buddhists don't like to meditate where it's noisy. I can get pretty noisy myself: I'm an artist, you know. Artists make noise! But my laboratory's down in the basement."

Susan rolled her eyes and gave Raoul a friendly nudge. "He calls it a laboratory. It's not really a room but it's space. He pays a little extra." She led the way back down to the kindergarten, where six of the eight-plus roommates had gathered to grill her.

"Well," said Susan. "This is probably all that's coming. Should we start? This is always so awkward." She giggled, and then, getting serious, suggested: "Why don't we just go around the room and everybody tell a little bit about themselves. I'll start. My name's Susan—you know that already. I've lived in Portland for a year. I've got a coffeeshop gig, but really I write poetry."

Martha smoothed her blouse and folded her hands in her lap. When Susan was finished speaking, a man named Joe began. He worked the graveyard shift at the post office but his real love was his dirt bike. The speeches went on and on. Martha tried to listen carefully, but little more than the names sank through—Hank… Mindy. . . Shirley. . . Somebody wanted to live in the country. . . somebody liked chocolate ice cream better than fruit flavors. . .

Raoul had a notebook in his lap and seemed totally absorbed in doodling.

"And it's an okay job as jobs go," Hank was saying. "They let you wear your hair as long as you want. Heck, if I went back to Moscow, Idaho looking like this, they'd string me up quicker'n you could say jackrabbit."

A silence followed.

Finally someone said, "Raooooo-ul."

"Huh?" Raoul looked up from his sketch pad. "Oh. My turn? Oh. My name is Raoul. . . I live in this house. . ."

"She knows *that*, Raoul."

"Oh. Okay. Well. . .let me think. I'm an artist … I work with glass…"

"Tell her about your job. He cleans windows on skyscrapers," Susan confided. "He's one of those guys you see fifty feet above the sidewalk, standing on a platform."

"Well, I guess that's working with glass," said Martha, which provoked chuckling around the room.

"That's only what I do for money," Raoul declared indignantly.

Martha regretted offending him. She tried to make up for it. "What kind of artist are you?" she inquired.

"The only kind," he said grumpily. "There's only Art. All the rest is technical. You know? I'm building this aquarium—"

"He's been talking about his aquarium for as long as we've known him. But no one's ever seen it."

"They *can't* see it yet, it's not finished!" Raoul protested. He glanced around the room from face to face, looking for cues, it seemed—could he shut up now? Had he said enough? Martha felt sorry for him, but she couldn't help him. She felt nervous enough on her own account. And then came the dreaded question.

"What about you, Martha?"

"Me? Oh." Martha tried to keep her hands still. "I've never lived in a house like this before, so you'll have to be patient if you let me in. I don't know what you're supposed to say in an interview. And maybe I should tell you—I've never lived with a whole bunch of people either. So maybe I'm not the roommate you'd be looking for. I don't know what else to tell you about myself. What do you want to know? Ask me questions."

"Where you from?"

"Estacada. But I've lived in Portland six years. I moved here in '68 to go to school—"

"What school?"

"Oh—" She colored and waved her hand. "Just Portland Community I never finished. I was taking night courses, working days. . . I had this filing job, see."

"How come you're looking for a room?"

"Well, I quit my job, and then I couldn't pay the rent at my old place. So I got evicted. So here I am."

This drew a moment of respectful silence. Eviction gave her some prestige.

Then Joe tapped the ash off his cigarette. "We've only advertised in one place, and the Ark hasn't come out yet. How'd you hear about the room?"

"I work for the Ark."

At once she felt a quickening of interest around the circle.

"The Ark?" Raoul woke out of his absorption with his sketchbook. "You mean the newspaper?" He was all big inquisitive eyes. "What do you do there?"

"Nothing very glamorous, I'm afraid. This and that."

"Who can get a job there? Do they need an artist?"

"There's no jobs, exactly. Most everyone is a volunteer. The Ark pays a few people for jobs no one wants to do. Well, I guess, Walter and Grace pull a salary. And the typesetter, but he loves typesetting, he'd do it for free, only people said—"

"I'm not talking about *money!*" Raoul was exasperated. "Could somebody walk in and get them to publish his cartoons?"

"They might, if somebody wanted to ask."

The Golem stared at her for a moment. "Could he draw what he wanted? Or would they tell him what to draw?"

"It might depend on what they needed—"

"I knew it!" He gave her a gloomy nod and subsided into his thoughts.

When the interview ended and Martha stood up, she noticed Raoul's sketch pad lying open on his vacant chair. The page was filled with deft caricatures of the people in the room, among whom she had no trouble picking out herself: the plain, plump face with the hair tied back in a prim bun, the tight smile bracketing her lips: a maiden aunt already at 23. Oh my: did it show so clearly? She left the house depressed.

Monday Meeting

Raoul studied the back of his new roommate's head, trying to read her brain waves by means of extra-sensory vision. No reading. Rats.

"Hey Martha."

She turned from the sink. "Yes?"

"You want to go downstairs and see my aquarium?"

She stood drying her hands on her apron, her eyes gleaming with bright uncertainty. "Me?"

"Sure, come on." He led the way down to his laboratory: a portion of the basement that he had walled off with Indian bedspreads and sheets of corrugated tin. On the makeshift door hung three signs, each smaller than the one above. They read:

Keep Out!
The Golem is Not In
Don't go away mad, just go away

He turned the middle sign over to expose the side that read "The Golem is Home." Inside, he flicked a switch, and instantly, several dozen powerful lights placed at strategic angles erased every shadow. The room was long and thin and had no windows. Miscellaneous equipment covered a solid work bench. Tools and gadgets hung from the walls.

Raoul pointed toward the corner where a dozen or so cardboard boxes and at least that many lengths of heating duct lay piled in an untidy heap. "There it is." he declared with pride.

Martha gulped. "That's an aquarium?"

Raoul flushed. "Just a model, for crying out loud. You can't build something like this without a model."

"I see."

"Let me put it together. Then you *will* see." He picked up a half-smoked joint from the edge of the table. "Here. Take a few tokes. It'll help."

"It's a little early for me—" but Raoul paid no attention to her. He was scuttling around his space, hauling boxes and tubes hither and thither while Martha scrambled to keep out of his way. He set one box on a shelf, one on the work bench, and two on the floor across the room from each other. He suspended several from the ceiling and hooked a few to the walls. The boxes were of various sizes and shapes and each one had holes, enabling Raoul to plug them together with lengths of heating duct. Within a few minutes he had reassembled the boxes and tubes into something like a large tinker toy construction wedged snugly between the four walls, the floor, and the ceiling, creating a maze of tubes and boxes within the room.

"There!" he declaimed. "Now! You gotta' picture all these parts made out of glass and filled with water... with a landscape inside them— bridges and castles and little villages and trees and canyons and stuff— that's important. Villages and canyons. Hidden lights'll go here and here...and here—all kinds of fish will be in it, you know; swimming through the grottos—the colors'll be amazing...like the astral plane...rainbows and mother of pearl...even yellow—"

"I don't quite—"

"Don't you see? It'll fill a room. You'll have your couches and stuff built right in. *You'll* be the one living underwater, *you'll* be the one in the bubble, not the fish. See?" He gazed at her, shining his fervor, eager for the light to dawn in her eyes too.

"It seems like a big project," she offered.

Raoul turned away in disappointment. She was not The One. Not that he ever really thought so, but this just proved it: if she couldn't look at cardboard boxes and see glass, she wasn't The One. "Well. It'll take years to finish."

"And then what? Will you try to…sell it?"

"Sell it! You can't sell art. I'm building this for my girlfriend. Zara's her name."

"Oh. Does she live here? I don't think I met her yet."

"She's on the East Coast right now." Abruptly he began dismantling the cardboard aquarium. The show was over.

After she left, Raoul sat on his bench and stared at the floor. Sometimes he wondered about people. Were their eyes made of wood? How long had he been laboring on his masterpiece without one iota of appreciation? But then, all the great artists had gone through this sort of thing. In fact, the world's indifference might just be an early sign of his genius.

Then a terrible thought filled him with dread. What if Zara came to town today or tomorrow—what could he show her? Cardboard boxes and heating ducts? What if she acted the same way as Martha and all the others? Impossible that she would, but what if she did? Raoul began to chew his fingernails, panic mounting in his chest. He had to impress Zara, when she came to Portland. He had to become famous before she arrived. The aquarium was taking too long. He had to activate plan B: cartooning.

He dropped the box he was holding and scurried up the stairs. "Martha! Hey! When are you going to the Ark? You work there, did you say? Take me along next time. Okay? I gotta' go to the Ark."

Martha was washing dishes, but she stopped to listen to him, her hands dripping into the sink. Then she nodded. "I'm going there in half an hour for copy meeting. You want to go today?"

Raoul could breathe again. His career was back on track. He would soon be a famous cartoonist. Not that he was quitting on the aquarium, but a man had to be practical. As he turned toward the kindergarten, one of the other roommates went by with the day's mail. "Letter from Zara," she said, handing Raoul an envelope.

Raoul frowned at it like an art dealer studying a possible forgery, then pocketed the letter and headed upstairs to his room. His eyelids were really beginning to feel sandy now. He was entering his 23rd hour awake, part of an experiment to see if sleep was the thing that was stopping him from busting up to the next level. From his closet he extracted a shoebox labeled SOULMATES. The top showed a pair of shoes walking side by side. The shoes had arms and faces added by Raoul, and were holding hands. The box was filled with letters from Zara, in chronological order.

Raoul set the box on the orange crate by his mattress, then sat by the window cross-legged and took out the letter that had arrived today. He read it with scrupulous attention, his eyes brimming with tears. When he had finished reading the letter he put it into the shoebox in its correct chronological spot and wiped his cheek.

Boy, he felt terrible. He stretched out fully clothed on his mattress and sank almost immediately into a deep sleep. He dreamt that Time Magazine had selected him as its Man of the Year because of his aquarium. The eulogy inside said that no man in history had done so much to "bring these two great races, people and fish, together." A picture showed him cavorting with a school of voluptuous, bare-breasted mermaids, every one of whom had Zara's face. In his dream the real Zara was flipping through the magazine when she saw the picture, and she cried out with jealousy and helpless longing. The picture moved for Zara, like an image on a TV screen. She saw Raoul, sporting gills and scales, the embodiment of all her fish fantasies, equally at home in water as in air, capable of passing in and out of marine worlds with ghostly ease.

At that moment, Raoul was awoken by a banging on his door. It was Martha. "I'm going to the Ark," she called out. "You coming?"

The copy meeting was about to start. Martha pointed out the various luminaries to her housemate Raoul. "That's the founder over there, his name's Walter. Right next to him, that's his wife or whatever." Her voice dropped to a whisper. "And the man next to Walter? See him? That's Sval Hofby, the writer."

Raoul had never heard of Sval Hofby the writer. The man in question had a lean, calm look and sand-colored hair down to his butt. His suede vest was sliced into fringes at the bottom, and his bell-bottomed jeans had paisley patches on both knees. He was at least six feet tall, and looked gangly until he moved, and then his fluid grace reminded Raoul of a pelican in flight. He was leaning casually against a table, listening to Walter. Once in a while he nodded politely and jotted a note.

Raoul looked away from Sval Hofby and his heart double-pumped. Perched on a table across the room was the most remarkable Zara look-alike he had ever seen, except that her hair was black and curly, not canary-colored like Zara's; and her eyes were green, not brown; and her features were sharp and smart, not round and sleepy like Zara's. Also, she had a more athletic build and was probably somewhat taller than Zara. And whereas Zara always wore short dresses and mini-skirts, this was a large-breasted woman wearing baggy green jungle pants and a tight T-shirt across which blazed the slogan "DARE TO JUGGLE."

Otherwise, the resemblance was staggering.

Martha noticed Raoul's distraction. "What's the matter?"

"That woman——" he choked out.

"That's Marica Margolis, you ought to meet her too. Hey, Marica!"

"No," Raoul protested weakly, squirming back from a confrontation with the Goddess, but a wave of fresh arrivals swept him further into the room. Martha grabbed his hand and bustled him forward.

"Marica, this is Raoul, one of my new roommates."

Marica turned, still smiling from another conversation. Her black hair framed a face just askew from classic beauty. She brushed the hair back from her face languidly, a gesture that cut through Raoul like a razor—the narcissism of Zara revisited! She put her hand out to shake his, saying "I'm glad to meet you, Raoul," but Raoul just stood there. Shaking hands with such a divinity would have been too audacious.

"Raoul draws cartoons," said Martha. "You should see them, Marica. He's got a real knack. He wants to do cartoons for the paper."

"I see." The smile on her face hardened slightly. She gestured to the long-haired man. "Sval, could you come here?"

The lean man detached himself from Walter and came ambling over.

"This is Raoul. He lives in Martha's new house. He wants to do cartoons for the paper. What do you think, could we use cartoons?"

Sval looked tactfully blank. "Sure, man, that would be great. What kind of cartoons?"

"Exactly. What *kind* of cartoons?" said Marica. "We do not want S. Clay Wilson in the Ark."

"We had a little trouble last week," Sval confided. "A guy came in with a regressive portfolio—lots-of-genitals-and-chopped-up-body-parts: the S. Clay Wilson school of art, if you know what I mean. What kind of work is yours?"

Raoul's entire digestive tract puckered up. He'd sketched a few genitals in his life—so what? Here was the inquisition he had feared. Why had he ever let Martha talk him into coming to this place and exposing himself to these barbarians? Who needed this kind of Third Degree? What kind of cartoons indeed—great ones! He tried to frame an answer but nothing got past the fist of guts plugging his throat.

Fortunately, Martha came to his rescue in the only way possible. She thrust a pencil at him, "Draw," she said.

Raoul knocked out a 20-second sketch of Sval, three lines that caught the bemused mouth, the calm eyes, the long jaw. Sval smiled and handed the drawing to Marica, who nodded agreeably.

"Quite excellent, compeer," said Sval. "Listen. I'm doing a story about the Ark itself next week, a human-interest piece—the faces behind the bylines kind-of-thing. Why don't you catch a few faces during the meeting? We'll see about running them with my story. Could you do that?"

Raoul nodded eagerly.

"Get one of Walter for sure... and Grace...and Ray Perkins over there—"

"Gross! Do you have to include Ray Perkins?" Marica made a face.

"He's part of the collective," Sval reminded her.

Just then Walter cleared his throat and all the conversation died away. People scrambled for chairs or for places on the floor. Raoul found himself jostled into a seat across the room from Marica and Sval. Walter settled upon a high stool and asked if anyone had any criticism of last week's issue. A storm of complaints broke out, mostly about typos and technical errors. Several people raged about a misplaced headline, "Piggin' Out on Pogo," which was written for a recipe column about possum soup made from road kill but had accidentally ended up above an article about the grand opening of the Men's Feminist Awareness Center.

Each quibble dinned along until Walter cleared his throat, whereupon the noise died away and everyone waited in silence for Walter to pronounce. Each time Walter spoke, he had the air of a plain man puzzling through complex issues and making common sense of them as best he could. Everyone had raised good points, Walter would say; and he would summarize those points. By the time he finished, only one conclusion remained possible, but Walter himself never drew it. He let someone else dot the i. Raoul sketched Walter as a majestic, bearded lion peering out of the sky: he was Aslan.

Then, about fifteen minutes into the meeting, the pattern was broken. Just as Walter cleared his throat for one of his summaries, Marica jumped into the silence ahead of him. "We're wasting time," she said. "Week after week, we argue about typos. We never talk about the real issues at this paper, and we do have some real issues, folks." She waved a copy of the latest Ark like a flag. "How come we don't run more stories written by women?"

"Oh Gawd," Ray Perkins erupted at once. "Are we going to start a quota system around here? What the hell difference does it make who writes which stories? All that matters is the stories—are they good?" He gazed around the room, looking for approval.

"What difference does it make?" Marica countered. "What difference? Well, let me—"

"Hear me out! Will you let me finish?" Ray shouted. "What are you saying, Marica? We should run just any story, as long as some woman wrote it? I say, forget who wrote it—man, woman, or dog, don't even look to see!"

"Woman *or dog*?"

"Goddamn it, let me finish," said Perkins. "Look at the story, not who wrote it! All I'm saying. Standards, people! If we have space for ten stories, let's run the ten *best* stories—this isn't rocket-science, folks. Quality is all that counts. And why am I the only one who gives a damn about quality here?"

Two men broke into applause. One said "Yeah!" Raoul sketched Perkins as a big hyena surrounded by smaller hyenas, all of them with bloody jaws.

"Quality?" Marica sniffed. "What an *interesting* thing to say. So you think women can't produce quality writing. Is that how you explain it?"

"Explain what?" said Perkins. "You haven't—"

"Explain the fact that 80 percent of this paper is written by men!"

"*Is* that a 'fact'? Has anyone actually taken the time to count? Or are we just kinda' sorta' 'goin on our feelings' here?"

"Well, let's just look at this week's paper, shall we?" Marica opened her copy of the Ark. "Page 2, letters from the readers—"

"Page 2 doesn't count!"

"Well, my, my, my!" Marica persisted. "Eight letters from readers and not one of them from a woman. Is it just my silly female intuition, or is that unbalanced? Page 3? Big surprise, 'The Struggle Goes On,' written by a man. Page 4, two stories, both by men. The Watergate Seven Convicted? Why couldn't a woman have written that? Page 5 and 6—"

"All right, we get the point. But—"

"In fact, the first full-fledged piece by a woman isn't until page 16 and you know what that one is? It's the *recipe* column! About how to cook *possums*!"

In that moment, Raoul saw an actual light shining from Marica's silhouette. He almost saw her wings. He sketched her as an avenging angel: Joan of (the) Ark. "And oh my God," she was saying. "Oh my God, look! Even *this* one's running under the headline PORTLAND MEN GET IT TOGETHER! *Portland men get it together?* I mean, people! Twenty-one pieces and only three by women! Come on! The Ark is supposed to represent—"

"Statistics," sneered Ray. "There's lies, there's damn lies—"

"What lies? You count 'em, Ray. What's wrong? 'Girls can't count?' Is that what you're saying? Go ahead then, you count."

Now at last Walter stirred and cleared his throat, most emphatically. Into the silence, he said sternly, "I have never counted articles, Marica, but you do make a good point: it seems there *has* been some imbalance at the Ark. But Ray makes a good point too: there is no barrier to women writing for the Ark, never has been. The process is open. So, I'm not sure we need to beat ourselves up over the ratio. Granted, some pieces never get published, but only because there isn't room, and if you count those pieces, I think you'll find that 80 percent of *them* were written by men too. In other words, you've put your finger on a problem, Marica, no doubt about it, but it is not a problem that begins at the Ark, and it's not a problem we can solve here at the Ark. It's a problem in the culture."

Then came the customary beat of silence, but Sval cut this one short. "Excuse me. Walter?" Heads turned. Sval was frowning. "I guess I'm not following you. This problem we're dealing with…It's…" His frown deepened as he groped for the way to articulate this thought. "Sexism, isn't it? Do you mean we have to wait until sexism has been eradicated from American culture before we can begin to deal with it here at the Ark?"

"Ha! Good question," a heavy-set bristle-headed woman belted out: Raoul rendered her as a bear.

Walter measured Sval with a look. In another moment, he might have made a reply, but Sval spoke first. "Just to finish the thought. I wanted to say, Walter, I agree with you. The process is open, and that's good, and we shouldn't sell ourselves short on the credit we deserve for that. But if 'open' isn't working—and it *isn't* working, is it? I mean, 80 percent of the paper is written by men. If that's our fundamental objective fact, then the facts say it isn't working. In which case, our task, it seems to me, would be to change that fact. I only report how it looks from where I'm standing."

He glanced around the room. Marica wore a fond look, Ray a puzzled one. "Because this isn't just a newspaper," Sval said solemnly. "This is one of the seeds of a new civilization. We're building a new world in the shadow of the one that's about to collapse. We have to start living like citizens of that new world already, because that's the only thing that's going to make it real. And we have to set up our own way of doing things, new ways, because we're living in the last days of the old civilization. We all know it. And once it collapses, it will be too late to work out the kinks." Walter was gazing thoughtfully at his fingertips. Raoul drew Sval as a Galahad: young, and brave, and noble, and pure.

"Thank you, Sval, I couldn't have put it better myself," Marica breathed. "And don't all of you see *why* women aren't writing for this paper? It's because we don't see the Ark as serving our needs. Because anything we make reflects how we made it, how we do things, and here at the Ark, how we do things isn't balanced. It's dominated by masculine energy. It just is."

"I would like to offer a tentative suggestion," Sval put in. "Why don't you, Marica, write the page three story for next week? After all, you haven't written anything in the five months I've been here, and I know you can write."

Marica was startled. "I would…" she sighed, "but time is a problem. My commitment to Dare to Juggle… And besides, I'm more performance-oriented. Words are too rational for me—" She whipped around to face Perkins. "Don't say it! Don't you dare."

"Say what?" he smirked.

"Or else undertake to solicit something from the women's community," Sval broke in, gazing into Marica's eyes.

She gazed right back at him. "All right," she vowed, "I will, but if I do all that, what will you contribute, Sval?"

"I will contribute unlimited support," vowed Sval.

"Hmmm." Marica subsided from that. Ray looked thoughtful. Walter's lips were pursed.

After the meeting Raoul took his drawings to Sval who studied the menagerie of angels, beasts, and superheroes with amusement, then handed the cartoons back to Raoul. He put his hand on the smaller man's shoulder and said: "Excellent, comrade. Hang on to these. We'll run them someday."

"Someday? What about today? Why not next issue? Don't you like them?"

"I like them too well. You see—" Sval glanced around, then pulled Raoul aside and dropped his voice. "At the moment, this collective's full of factions and frictions. Walter and Grace are holding things together but if they ever leave—and they will, my friend, you can smell it coming. They'll leave and this place will explode. Follow me? I don't think it would be good politics just now to run my story with illustrations showing Marica as an angel, for example, and Perkins as this mad dog hyena-thing. Not that you've missed, mind you." Sval's eyes twinkled. "You've hit the nail on the head too squarely, comrade." He spotted Marica, and said, "Pardon me," to Raoul. He and Marica ambled away, quietly discussing something.

Martha came up just then. "Ready to go, Raoul?"

"Huh? Oh sure...I was just looking at ... Sval and Marica make a great couple, don't they?"

Martha's jaw muscles bulged slightly. "They're *not* a couple," she said. "Sval's got a girlfriend, her name's Zoe. She doesn't come to the Ark much."

New Day Coming

Marica waited till the crowd thinned out before heading for the door, only to find Perkins tagging along behind her. Where had he come from? She whirled on him. "What?"

"Thought we might have coffee somewhere," he grinned.

"Do we have something to discuss?"

"C'mon, Marica. It won't kill you to be nice."

Her downturned lips registered distaste. "I'm perfectly nice. It's just weird is all, you asking me out for coffee."

"Why? We've been out before."

"That's when I didn't know you."

"Okay, look, maybe I rushed things a little. I couldn't help myself: you're just too hot. Ouch!" He mimed burning his fingers. "Come on, now, don't put on that frown, it's a friggin' compliment, okay? Look, I fucked up a little that first time, is that what you want to hear? I'm sorry, how's that? Just coffee, get to know each other. We'll take it slower."

"What's the point, Ray? We already know we've got nothing in common."

"Scared of me?" He rolled his eyes and mugged a leer.

"Humph. You give yourself too much credit." She eased through the doorway.

He hustled alongside her. "I'll walk you down to the street."

"It's a free country. You can walk wherever you want."

At the second-floor landing, he took up his argument again. "What have you got against me, anyway?"

"Your nineteenth century attitudes. Isn't that enough?"

"Why? Because I treat you like a red-hot chick? It scares you, doesn't it? You're not ready for a 1974 romance. What a waste!"

"I am not a chick, Ray! Jesus! Do you know how to say 'woman'?'"

She stopped to scold him but before she could launch her lecture, he seized her hand, pulled her close, put his arms around her waist, and pinned her to the wall with his weight. "You and me, babe, nothing else makes sense. Just accept it. Accept it and enjoy." He kissed her on the lips and held the kiss as if the contact would melt her. She pushed him away, her indignation at a boil.

"How dare you?"

He wiped his lips, laughing a little. By then she was all the way to the first landing. "Hey," he called after her, "You got a problem, you know that?"

"You're the one with the problem," she hurled back.

"Frigid bitch!"

"Pig!"

The slammed door clipped his voice short. Marica hurried south on Ash, breathing hard, her skin so flushed that the mild chill of the afternoon could not touch her. What was this impulse to cry? She bit it back. "Frigid!" she muttered. Life was so unfair. Had she asked for this body?

Damn it, she wasn't going to let Ray spoil *this* day. Today she had spoken out at the paper. Today, she had established herself as a voice in the community. She wanted to celebrate today, share her triumph with someone.

She crossed Taylor Street and took off her shoes to cross Colonel Summers Park. She loved the feel of wet cool grass against her bare soles. Just as she reached the banks of busy Belmont Street, a bus came honking to a stop right in front of her. Its door squiggled open. "The bus driver leaned to look at her. "Getting in?"

There was something mystical, Marica thought, about this great vehicle stopping just for her. It was not, of course, the personal kindness of the bus driver, and yet there was a kindness in the system here, coming from some greater force. Humanity had built a world in which a bus would stop just for her—this was wonderful. Especially because this bus went right to Martha Williams's house. Marica could recognize a cosmic sign when she saw one. She jumped aboard.

Martha's little room in her new house was cozy, but then Martha could make any living space cozy. She had that knack. Actually, it was more than a knack, it was a sort of genius: what she could do with cheap items she'd found in thrift stores. The women sipped tea together and talked about the copy meeting. Marica longed to hear Martha's review of her outburst. She wanted to know: had she sounded masterful? Or shrill? She wanted to hear, but she didn't want to ask. She wanted Martha to bring it up herself.

Martha, however, had something else on her mind. She seemed distracted at first and then finally she came out with it. "Marica, there's something you should know."

"Yes?"

"Walter's going to quit."

"No. Quit the paper? What do you mean?"

"He's getting a job in New York with some magazine. It's called *New Times* or something like that."

"Oh, people are always saying stuff like that about Walter. They were saying it six months ago when I first started coming. You can't believe everything you hear."

"This time it's true."

"How do you know? You've only been at the paper, what: two weeks? and already you know things I don't know? Who have you been talking to?"

Martha took a sip of tea and cradled the cup in her palms. Her cheeks dimpled as her lips pressed together. "Well, Walter asked me to type a letter for him. He told me not to tell anyone yet—so don't tell anyone, okay?"

Marica felt a surge of energy. "My lips are sealed." She could not help but lean forward. "Tell me about the letter. Who was it to? What did he say? I won't tell anyone."

"He was saying yes to the job. He doesn't know if it's final yet, that's why he doesn't want to tell anyone. But I saw what they wrote to him: it looked final to me."

"Wow. Oh my God, Martha, this is so big. Are you absolutely for-sure sure? Because who's going to take his place?"

"I don't know. He'll pick someone, I guess."

"Well, I know who thinks he'll get picked. And we've got to block him, Martha. We cannot let that happen."

"Ray Perkins?"

"Of course Ray Perkins. For some reason, he's Walter's golden boy."

"Well, he does do good graphics. He sells a lot of ads. He does a lot of stuff for the paper, he really does, whatever you think of him personally."

"Oh, pish!" Marica's agitated fingers made her cup rattle when she reached for it. "Everybody sells ads. I sold one myself, last week. To the Wishbox Collective. I know those folks and they know folks. I bet they brought in at least three more ads." She spilled a little tea and burned her fingers and then sucked on the tips of them. Through Martha's dormer window she saw fluffy clouds in the sky. "He thinks he's carrying the paper on his back. Mr. Big Ego. I do a lot more production than he does. Don't let him fool you. That's what's wrong with most men, big bloated egos. That's what I like about your friend Sval Hofby—I don't mean attracted. Oh God, no," she cautioned. "In fact, that's just it. Sval is sort of…sexless in a nice sort of way. Sort of neuter. In the good sense of the word."

"I don't think he's so neuter," said Martha.

"Well, I meant it as a compliment."

"Oh." Martha sipped her tea. "So what do you think, is something going to happen?"

"If I have anything to say about it, you bet. Sval as managing editor? In a heartbeat. Honestly, we should get some of the women together and caucus about this, before Walter makes the announcement—just to be ready."

"I meant between you and Sval?"

"Between me and Sval?" Something in the woman's voice made Marica cautious. "Oh, good heavens." She studied her friend's face. Could it be…Could her feelings be…? Well, why not! Wasn't good old Sval the one man who could appreciate Martha's legion of good qualities? Now that Marica thought about it, wasn't Sval just what Martha needed? Well, if there was any chance…any chance at all—why, then, in the name of sisterhood, Marica would cheerfully put aside any thoughts she might have had about Sval—not that she'd ever had any.

"I'm going downstairs now," said Zoe. "You staying tonight?"

"I could," he agreed. He didn't want to intrude where he wasn't more than abundantly welcome.

"I want you to," she said, and she left him to fetch something from the kitchen.

"Well then, I will. Grab me a beer while you're in there, huh?" He followed her down to the humid warmth of her basement boudoir, a room ankle-deep in discarded clothing and personal effects. Zoe lit a candle by the bed and turned off all the other lights, creating a bubble of warmth. Sval shed his clothes and crawled between the sheets with a sigh. Zoe slipped in next to him, naked. They hugged and rubbed bodies and kissed sporadically.

"Want a back rub?" she asked.

"Mm." He turned over and relaxed under her palms and fingers.

"Anything historic happen at the Ark today?" she asked idly.

"Mm. Well, Marica made a forceful statement. Quite forceful, about women's input at the paper. Sure you won't change your mind about getting involved?"

"Marica is an interesting girl," said Zoe. "I saw the two of you talking at the barbecue this weekend. You have a closeness, don't you?"

"We have a partnership you might say. At the Ark, she's part of my gang, no doubt. It's true."

"When you talk, you lean toward each other. That's always a sign."

"A sign?" he stammered.

"Relax." She squeezed his shoulder muscles. "I know you're attracted to her. It's okay."

"How do you know?" His voice cracked.

"Girls know these things."

"Women," he corrected her reflexively.

"I said relax." She pushed down, and one of his vertebrae made a noise like corn popping.

"Ouch."

"Don't say ouch. This is good for you. Say ahh. Last night, for example, when you were sitting next to Robin from Clinton Street? She turned you on—"

"Gad," he said. "Could she tell, do you think?"

"What if she could?" Zoe laughed.

"I don't want to be obnoxious."

"No one thinks you're obnoxious, Sval. It's only me you can't fool. You ask how I know? I look at you when Marica comes into the room and I see steam." She continued to knead Sval's back in silence.

"Well," he admitted finally. "There's always been a certain chemistry between Marica and me."

"Chemistry, huh. Made any compounds together?"

"You mean, have we slept together? Of course not."

"Why 'of course'?"

"Because the day I met her was the night you and I took that ... sudden turn."

"Ah. That sudden turn." Zoe stopped rubbing him and lay down. Side by side in the half-lit room, they stared up at vague shapes along the dark ceiling: heating ducts, floor beams.

"Actually, that's why I wanted to talk to you that day." He felt better as soon as he'd released those words. "I was dying to talk about Marica."

"You did seem excited. I thought it was about us."

They listened to each other's ragged breathing. "It wasn't about Marica. It was the whole package," he said. "I see that now. My life changing—it was thrilling. Marica, yes, but also the Ark, also all these new ideas sprouting up—this whole sense of new beginning. You'd become the one person in the world I had to tell. That snuck up on me,

Zoe, I didn't even realize it until that night. You'd become the one person I just had to talk to when something happened. Something good, something bad, didn't matter. It was you I wanted to tell."

"It's snuck up on me too, how *good* we are together, it keeps sneaking up and sneaking up."

"It does," he admitted. "In fact—there's a place in my life where there's only me and you. It's come down to an inner circle of two." He marveled at the ease of making this unprecedented declaration. "You are my primary relationship."

"I know," she said, "You're mine too. And yet somehow, we're still not A Couple. That's like a miracle. This thing we have, it's incredible. That's why I was wondering. About Marica, for example, with all this sizzling chemistry, now come on, don't deny it."

"Is that what we mean by not-a-couple," he wondered.

"Is *what* what we mean," she said. "When you say 'is *that* what we mean', what do you mean by '*that*?' Say it, Sval."

He paused, then stated carefully, "If we're talking about what I think we're talking about, jealousy would be the central issue, wouldn't it."

"Jealousy is a primitive emotion," she said. "If you want to know my opinion. It's part of that whole thing we're trying to outgrow, isn't it? You're free, I'm free, we're good people, we trust each other, don't we? I trust you, Sval. That much I know."

"So jealousy would not be an issue, you're saying?"

"I don't see how we could square it with everything else we believe in, you and me. I can't promise I would never get jealous. I might, it's human, but that's the risk we have to take if we want to do this. There's always going to be a difference between what you believe and how you feel. We've never talked about that, have we? Our assumptions. Are we monogamous? Is that our assumption?"

He gave her question long consideration. She was not trying to jerk a particular answer out of him, she really wanted to know. He found himself peering into darkness. "I don't know," he hedged. "Is it?"

"I don't know, but if it is, we should say so." She paused. "And if it isn't, that's what we should say. I mean, look. If you want to know how I would feel, I think I could handle it. How about you?"

"Handle what, exactly?"

"Us having a relationship that's open. We don't own each other. We don't limit each other. We pick our way through the world, each of us, we do not tell each other what to do. We're mostly with each other, but we might be with other people sometimes. If it happens that way that's the way it happens. If it feels right, we do not resist."

"Hmm," he said. "Well." Affection flooded him from head to toe: this Zoe! No matter what happened, he wouldn't lose her, she was saying. What a woman. Marica came into his imagination like fireworks. Vistas of gardens. "Yes," he declared "I could handle it, I *think.*" The bed became a boat and they were lolling in the tropics. What could he have done to deserve a woman like Zoe? "We have to be very supportive of each other, though." He took her in his arms. "That's the only way it's going to work. Because whatever happens I don't want to lose..."

But he couldn't bring himself to utter the word "you". It would have been accurate but the word was too sentimental. Too aggressive, perhaps. He searched his vocabulary for an acceptable synonym."

"This incredible thing we have together," he said finally. "You and I."

"Me neither," she said. "I don't want to lose it either, this thing we have. You and me."

That week Sval started working on *One and Only, the Myth of Romantic Love,* in which he theorized that the idea of romantic love was invented by industrial civilization and implanted by the corporate state, as a mechanism for creating nuclear families—because what corporate industrial society needed were nuclear families as its units. In a tribal post-industrial society such as the one now taking shape in Portland and would one day be the society of the world at large, the nuclear family was going to be an anachronism. The myth of romantic love was best consigned to the cabinet of historical curiosities, wrote Sval.

The Women's Candidate

Sval stood in his kitchen, rapidly gobbling peanut butter and jelly sandwiches. By God, he was glad to have sloughed off the academic persona. Sval Hofby, philosophy student, gone forever—he'd never really existed. *This* was the real Sval Hofby, this vital journalist with rolled-up sleeves, wrestling with real issues amid the hurly burly of life itself. Sval quaffed a beer to finish his meal and hurried to his desk. There amid the jumble of overflowing ashtrays lay his latest journalistic effort for the Ark: *The Concept of Bread in Myth and History.*

He slipped the manuscript into his briefcase and left his house. A feather-light rain made his bicycle tires hiss on the wet asphalt. Street lights and porch lights floated by, fuzzy halos in the haze. He crossed Morrison at the light and took back streets to the church. The windows on the first three stories were dark, but light blazed from the fourth floor. Sval took the stairs in long bounds, collecting himself into an exclamation mark at the office door before stepping inside.

Two unknown scruffies were pecking out stories at the typewriters in the corners. Martha hunched at her station behind the IBM composer. Marica was standing over a layout at one of the long work tables, a pot of melted wax bubbling at her elbow.

Sval flipped his hat onto a table and strode across the room. His boot heels clicked on the green-and-black slate tiles. Martha's cheeks quivered with delight. "Sval—is that your story?" She came out of her seat, hands outstretched. Sval relinquished the manuscript carelessly while unwrapping his scarf and unbuttoning his jacket. Marica favored him with a glance.

"Oh, Sval," Martha chortled. "I don't *believe* it! 'The Concept of Bread in Myth and History?' Is this really about where to get day-old bread in Portland?"

"Well…there's only one place, turns out, so I had to dress it up a little."

Marica pushed back her heavy black hair. "No. That title's got to go. 'The Concept of Bread?' Bread isn't a *concept*, my dear, it's a *thing*! Not to mention Myth? And on top of that, History? What are we, elitists?"

"It's a joke," Sval explained, pained.

"Oh please! Spare me the joke. Let's call it…" Marica paused for a moment, and then said: "The Bread Also Rises…?" She considered her own suggestion, and then agreed with herself. "Yes. The Bread Also Rises. Good head." She dropped her attention back to her layout.

Sval edged next to her, gazing at the ringlets of hair obscuring her face. "Yes?" she demanded gravely. "Is something interesting?"

Sval colored. "Thought I'd see what I could learn about layout."

"You know perfectly well how to do layout," she scolded.

"Not really. I've never gotten involved much in production."

"Oh? Too mundane for Mr. Concept-of-Bread? I bet you never wash dishes at home either."

"Actually," he protested, "around my house I'm known as Mr. Kitchen. But production…seems so…technical. Layout, for example…"

"Nonsense, it's very intuitive. You just have to let your body get into it and keep your mind out of the way." Her body undulated then illustratively. He nodded and felt comfortable moving closer, eager for instruction in this concept of getting his body into it. "You see," she said, "you just cut the copy up in columns, wax the back and lay 'em down. Just a thin coat of hot wax. If you do it right, the paper will still feel warm against your palm. Then if you've got space to fill, you put in a graphic. Tell you what, get some copy and I'll show you what to do."

Sval trotted off and came back happily with a column of paper, fresh from the typesetter: the gardening column. After his lesson, the office was silent except for the counterpoint of typewriters, as Sval and Marica worked side by side. Sval kept his eyes trained on his hands, but he could see Marica at the edge of his circle of vision. It struck him that of course she knew he was "with" Zoe, she thought of him that way: as part of a couple. He wondered how she'd react if he let her know about the thrilling new development in his life with Zoe, their decision to "open" up their relationship. Was there any way to raise the topic without sounding…sleazy? Marica put down her scissors, wiped her hands, yawned, and arched her back, cracking several vertebrae, her leotard top stretching smoothly over her unencumbered breasts, the fabric defining her nipples. Sval quickly dropped his gaze to the layout board and pursed his lips as if in deep consideration of some problem in design.

"How are you doing?" she asked.

"I think maybe this one's done."

She glanced at it. "Oh, that looks fine. Yes, it does, Sval. You never cease to amaze me." Then she turned her gaze directly upon him and said, "You want to go someplace? I absolutely *neeeed* to get out of this office."

Sval's heart thumped and whumped and bumped. He had never been alone with Marica. He checked his watch. "Eight thirty," he murmured. "Well, I suppose it's too late for that one anyway."

"What one?"

"Oh…" He waved. "The Friends of the Environment were meeting tonight, but I guess it's too late. Might as well have a beer somewhere."

"Listen, if you've got a meeting to get to—"

"No, no," he said quickly, "it's too late, I might as well—"

"Really, Sval, don't humor me. If you've got someplace else—"

"It's too late for that. I mean it. Let's have a beer."

She paused, her green eyes resting on his face. "Are you sure?" she cooed.

"Absolutely." Sval felt like a light bulb, visible for miles. If anything happened with Marica tonight, the gossip would be incendiary. He could sense Martha and the two scruffies gawking as he followed her out. They carried a pregnant silence between them, all the way down the dark stairwell and through the massive double-doors, into the falling mist. They had strolled about half the distance to Belmont Street before she blurted "Did you hear?"

"Excuse me?"

"About Walter and Grace?"

"Oh, that they're leaving? Yes. Walter got some kind of magazine job in New York, I heard."

"Not that," she said, "Everyone knows that. I mean about Ray Perkins."

"What about him?"

"That he wants to be Managing Editor. That he's going around talking to people about it already."

Sval released his breath. "I hadn't heard. But I guess he's got as much of a right as anyone to—"

"Please, Sval. This is no time to be a liberal. If Ray Perkins takes over the Ark, the community is going to lose its paper. The Ark won't be the Ark anymore. I'm sorry, but that's the way I feel."

"Hmmm." It was a hmmm that could be taken for agreement. "But can Perkins get it just because he wants it? Has he really got the support? Every staff meeting seems to end up as a shouting match between him and the collective."

"Yes but...but he does have a kind of energy. Give the devil his due."

"If you're trying to talk me out of voting for Perkins, you need not bother. I wouldn't dream of it."

"Oh, I know. That's not what I was thinking."

Sval stumbled on the curb and regained his balance under a shabby little awning jutting out from the shack-like structure of the Brooklyn Diner. He held the door open for Marica and followed her into the humid warmth. A horseshoe counter filled up most of the long narrow room, with a row of weathered geezers in Levis and plaid shirts arrayed around it. Squeezed in along one side of the room were booths of dark red vinyl patched with duct tape, occupied mostly by clumps of younger folks in their twenties and early thirties, dressed in colorfully-patched thrift store castoffs, square-shouldered striped suits from the 40s,

Navajo hats, silver and turquoise jewelry, and hand-painted ties four inches wide. A battered jukebox, loaded with a mix of country hits and rock and roll classics partially blocked the narrow aisle near the entrance. Behind it squatted a sleek new cigarette machine. Marica led the way around to a booth in the back. A plump waitress rolled up to them with a damp cloth. Marica ordered coffee, Sval a slice of cherry pie and a beer.

"Okay," he said, now that they were settled. "I give up, tell me. What's on your mind?"

Marica leaned forward on her elbows and gazed at him. "I was thinking, Sval Hofby for Managing Editor."

He kept his gaze steady, but allowed himself a grin and cleared his throat.

"Wouldn't you like to run?" she said. "Your name came up at the women's caucus last night. I thought you should know. The women's caucus would support you."

Sval shifted in his seat. "Why me?"

"Because..." Her breasts flattened against the Formica tabletop as she leaned forward.

"Yes?" he urged, leaning toward her like a wire to a magnet.

"The Ark," she said, setting four fingers lightly on his arm, "*needs...*" and here she paused to search for the appropriate phrase, settling at last for: "A nonsexist man as managing editor."

Those four fingers touching Sval's skin scared up a bristle of arousal. He met Marica's eyes, although at the lower margins of his circle of vision he could see how her breasts were pressed against the Formica, the flattening making them bulge against her arms. "Why not a non-sexist woman?" he inquired blandly.

She withdrew her hand. "Why, Sval!" she laughed. "How politically correct of you to say that!"

"Well. If I'm campaigning for the women's vote, after all."

"You better be," she warned him. "No one is going to take Walter's place without support from the women of the Ark."

"Granted. Which brings us back to the question. Why me? Why not you?"

Marica leaned back, sucking on the tip of a finger. "It's so complicated," she sighed finally. "It has to be someone who can get support from both the men and the women. And that's you. Anyway, I don't really have the time—I do have another commitment, you know: Dare to Juggle."

"I know." He tapped a Camel out of his pack. "When are Grace and Walter pulling out exactly, do you know? When is their last day?"

Shortly after Sval got home, Zoe called. She wanted to come over and hang out. She arrived looking like a little boy, bundled up in a brown down jacket, a long woolen scarf, and a tasseled ski cap, with only her freckled cheeks showing and her small nose ruddy from her ten-block walk through light rain. Sval gave her a firm hug and helped her unbundle. She shook her red hair loose and stretched her arms back, cracking her shoulder joints. She was wearing a man's dress shirt untucked, with the tails hanging down loose over her mottled jungle pants. On Zoe it was oversized, and it made her look impossibly cute.

Sval wanted to blurt out the big news at once, that the women of the Ark wanted him to be the new managing editor but some thread of loose emotion tied his tongue. Here he was, a rising star at the Ark, admired by Marica Margolis, soon to be her lover perhaps—not that it would change anything between him and Zoe—but he couldn't be careless now: what were Zoe's needs? Their relationship might be entering the rapids. He would have to be careful.

Zoe showed him the six-pack she had brought along and went to the refrigerator. "Where are the roommates tonight?" she called.

"I don't know, out somewhere."

"Good. That means we can sin together on the living room couch, doesn't it? You know us lapsed Catholics. We just looove to sin." She moved restlessly through the dining room and into the living room.

"What are you looking for?"

"Produce," she said. "I had a rough day."

"In the dope chest." He pointed and then got himself a beer. "I had a rough day myself. Found myself face to face with a tough decision."

"What decision was that?"

"Oh..." He flung it out casually. "Apparently there's some sort of groundswell at the Ark to draft me for Managing Editor."

"I can see how that would make for a tough ethical choice."

"Uh huh. Do you?" He had assumed—hoped—she would be at least a little impressed. "What issues do you, um, see?"

"Well. You're always complaining that the Ark isn't a true collective because two people make all the decisions—and isn't that what a managing editor does? Make all the decisions?"

"Am I always saying that?"

"Well, you've had your criticisms. 'Government by guru' you said one time. That phrase! You really nailed it, Sval. Government by guru. Walter's too rooted in the Sixties, you said once. Leadership's something we have to learn to share. That's what you always say."

"I do, don't I?" Sval was recognizing his own language. He sipped his beer. "I wonder though—might I be in a better position to push for that kind of change if I went ahead and ran for the position—?"

"And yet, just by running, you'd be making a statement that betrays what you believe." Zoe shook her head, sympathizing fully with his ethical dilemma. "This one's tough, Sval. You'll really have to get this one right."

"Exactly. Too true. And yet—labels aside: here's the rub, you see: if the position exists by whatever name, *someone* will fill it. I'm just concerned that it'll be this fellow Perkins. If he takes over, that'll be the end of the Ark as an organ of the community. It just won't be the Ark anymore. He'll turn it into a slick rag with lots of music listings. You'd never hear another story about the lettuce boycott, or hunger right here in Portland or overturning the values of corporate America or draft resistance or outsider art or—I'm sorry, maybe I'm being pessimistic, but that's how I feel."

"It sounds like, what you have to do..." She had finished rolling a joint and now paused to light it and to take a long puff before concluding, "you have to change the structure after Walter and Grace leave so that the position doesn't exist anymore. By any name. That's allowed, isn't it? Getting rid of all these roles and titles and stone-age shit? *Nobody* for managing editor, that's what you have to propose."

"Nobody for managing editor," Sval murmured, trying out the sound of the phrase. "You turn a pretty phrase yourself, Zo. That would be radical."

"Can you do that? Propose a total change like that?"

"Anyone can propose. But only the collective can dispose."

"So talk them into it," she said. "You know how to talk people into things. Look at some of the things you've talked me into." She flashed him a look, then rolled off the couch and crawled to the stereo on her hands and knees to look for a record, incidentally offering him a view she knew full well he liked.

"That would be a legacy all right," he mused, gazing at the view he liked. "Bringing honest-to-God visionary anarchy to the Ark. You may be right. Better than anything I could do as managing editor. Hmm." He turned the phrase over in his mind. No one in charge. No one telling anyone else what to do. All important decisions made by consensus. The group gathering to discuss until agreement was reached. A fully democratic paper, open to the community. Not some product peddled to the passive masses. What would happen if it took root here? Other institutions would want to try similar experiments. No telling how far the ripple effects might spread. He might be called upon to consult, give advice. Offer his thoughts on the pitfalls and possibilities—could his busy schedule take the extra load? Ah, well, if it would help the community evolve into the post-apocalyptic age, he would simply have to make the time. He began nodding his head, unconsciously responding to the liquid sounds of a late Van Morrison album pulsing out of the speakers. "I should dip into my Bakunin tonight," he remarked aloud, and then, becoming aware of the music, "What is this? It's pretty good."

"It's Van." Zoe plopped on the couch next to him and turned into his arms for a kiss; which he returned; and as the kiss lingered Sval felt the nature of her tenderness changing. Her lips parted and her warm sweet breath filled his mouth, as her tongue began to flicker against his lips. He slid his hand under her shirt. The phone rang.

"Damn." Sval groaned.

"Ignore it," Zoe advised, but Sval Hofby had never ignored a ringing phone and wasn't about to start now.

"It could be important." He trudged dutifully to the kitchen. The phone was on a packing crate filled with old copies of the Ark, the Worker's Guardian, and Rolling Stone. He sat on a footstool and picked it up. "Hello?"

"Hello!" a voice shouted. "Hey, Izzy, pal, it's good to hear your voice!"

"If you mean Isaac Bernstein, this isn't he," said Sval stiffly, "It's one of his roommates. Can I help you?"

"George Lubick here—George. Lubick! Friend of Izzy's. Where is he?"

"He's not here just now. Can I take a message?"

"Yeah, tell him I'm in Forest Grove and I'll be there in half an hour."

"You'll be here?"

"He knows I'm coming. It's cool."

"Well..."

"Listen, I've got your address here, but how do I get to it? I'm on I-Five."

Despite a swelling reluctance, Sval found himself providing directions to his house. He returned to Zoe with a glum look.

"Forest Grove," she said, "is a long ways off. We've got time for lots of things we'll regret in the morning." She took his hand and tugged at his belt.

"Yeah, I guess you're right.," and he sank back down beside her but felt ill-at-ease. Street sounds kept distracting him as they kissed. "Was that a car door?"

"Relax. It can't be him yet." Zoe caught his face between her palms. "Give me some tongue, lover." She began to fumble with his zipper.

"Umm...but is it wise to...plunge into this too deeply," Sval said, "with a visitor expected?"

"I'm not sure, Professor." She undid the top three buttons of her blouse to expose her breasts. "What would Schopenhauer say about it?"

Sval hesitated, considering the Schopenhauer question. "Well, in *The World as Will and Idea*," he began, but Zoe pulled him in and smothered his discourse with her breasts. Against her warm skin, Sval felt the furrows melting from his face.

A car pulled up someplace within a block of the house and a door distinctly slammed. Sval's head instantly snapped to attention.

"Will you quit? He's still miles away." Zoe pulled him back and Sval closed his eyes, again relaxing on a warm tide of desire—

—when suddenly a tremendous clatter exploded at the front door. Sval jumped to his feet, zipping up his fly, and even Zoe began languidly to button up.

"George Lubick," said the man on the dark porch. He thrust out his hand. His face looked like something hewn from granite with a few swift clean strokes of a rock hatchet. He had a massive pack on his shoulder and as he came forward, he gave such an impression of momentum that Sval stepped aside as he would have for a rolling boulder. Lubick swung the pack off his shoulder one-handed as if it were a purse and dropped it with a noisy sigh of relief. The floor trembled. He wiped shining black hair back from his high forehead with two flat, powerful-looking hands. Then he noticed Zoe and bore down on her with an outstretched hand, thundering, "George Lubick." She allowed her hand to be crushed. He turned to Sval.

"You must be the guy I talked to on the phone. What's your name again? Zorba? Gall Bladder?" George spoke with a thick New York accent.

"Sval Hofby. I'm Zack's roommate."

"Zack, huh? It was Izzy back in Yonkers. Hey, listen, nice place you got here. Big!" He stood in the middle of the living room, surveying the framed prints and squares of ornamental cloth covering the walls. "How many you got sharing here? Three, huh? Nice, nice. Spacious. Say, what do they gouge you for a place like this in Portland?" And upon hearing the rent, he said, "No shit? Maybe I'll stick around this burg for a while."

Sval followed the newcomer into the dining room and then the kitchen, and watched as he flung open the refrigerator door, knocking the chart of kitchen duties to the ground. "Got anything to drink in the house? Good cognac? Liqueur? Decent wine? Anything at all? Huh, just beer. Not even good beer. Horse piss. Well...I'll stoop." He yanked a beer out of the six pack and popped the top off with his thumb, catching it behind his back with his other hand, then firing it off one-handed, landing it squarely in the waste basket. He grinned happily, his every feature turning exactly upside down, as if his face had only two modes, gloom and radiance. "Nothing but net and fouled on the play," he chortled. "Chance for a three-pointer."

Sval had no idea what he was talking about.

Lubick took a long greedy suck out of the beer bottle and slapped it down on the table, wiping his mouth. "Jesus, that's good," he allowed. "That's good. I'm tired. Christ! Driving all the way up from L.A. non-stop, let me tell ya'. That's murder on the back. Wha'd I say on the phone, Forest Grove? Turned out to be Tigard. That's closer, huh…"

"Considerably," Sval glowered.

"Well, anyway, I'm here. What's this?" George snatched up a copy of the Ark and flipped through it.

"Paper I work on."

"Yeah? I didn't know this burg had a hippie rag. Portland's looking better and better. What's the deal there? Three or four paid staff, coupla' hundred volunteers?"

"Something like that."

"I know that scene, man. Been there. Berkeley, L.A. I worked on RAT in New York—of course. Who didn't? You guys got room for a photog? I've got some great stuff on Chile. I've been in South America for the last year or so. I was there when the coup went down." George grimaced in pain. "Jeeeeesus, my back's killing me. Where do I crash? It's got to be flat and hard."

"How about the floor," Sval responded. "That's as flat and hard as we've got."

"Yeah, fine. Show me where."

Sval escorted him to Zack's room and then returned to Zoe, who rolled her eyes and chuckled. "How long you going to be stuck with that character?"

"He didn't say."

"*He* didn't say? Was it his to say? Don't *you* get to say? Isn't this your home?"

"True, but there's the hospitality issue. One must be a good citizen. Still, suggesting a three-day limit might not be outside the bounds. I'll have to check with Zack."

"And then what? He's not going to find a place of his own in three days."

"Hmm. And then," Sval said thoughtfully, "maybe we can send him over to that house Martha Williams moved into. Sounds like a zoo over there, they can probably absorb one more animal."

Gone Fishin'

George's exile to Yamhill house was easily achieved, but like the cat in the folk song he came back every other day around dinner time. To his credit, he often brought groceries and cooked for the whole house: invariably a heaping platterful of stir-fried hippie hodgepodge swimming in olive oil and soy sauce.

Then one Monday he broke his pattern by showing up in the morning, this time with cream cheese, lox, and bagels. He announced that after brunch he was going to the Ark with Sval. He brought along a tattered cardboard suitcase, which Sval eyed uneasily. At the Ark, he broke every elementary rule of good behavior for a newcomer. He should have spoken only when spoken to, kept his opinions to himself, offered his services without strings attached, and allowed other people to tell him where he might fit in. Instead, he abandoned Sval at the front door and strode around the room, blaring at anyone he could corner: "George Lubick, photog, here—let me know next time you're running down a hot story, huh? You need pix, I'll get you pix." Worse, in response to all queries he pointed to Sval and said, "I'm with him."

When the meeting started George flung open his battered suitcase and dealt out his photos of South America, over 100 contact sheets, trumpeting that he was prepared to do an eight-page layout. "Just tell me what you want. Peasants? You want peasants? Got 'em. Guerrillas? I got 'em." Within minutes, he had managed to offend everyone in the room and yet the discussion ended with a commitment by the paper to save the whole middle spread in the upcoming issue, two full pages, for George's photo spread on Chile during the coup.

Sval felt some odd proprietary concern for George, as he might have for a deranged relative. After the meeting he tactfully drew George off to a nearby tavern to let him know about his social errors. If someone doesn't have a clue, you can't judge them for upsetting the apple cart. You have to let them know what the culture is in these parts. Give them the tools they need to find their place. But the meeting had left George in a roaring good mood and in no mood for instruction. He toasted the Ark, bought round after round of beer, and told Sval that he was "a righteous dude, 100 % full of all right." He never seemed to catch on that Sval was trying to engage him in a little criticism/self-criticism.

About a week after he broke into the Ark, George showed up at Sval's doorstep with his roommate Raoul, the cartoonist. Both men were clad in rubber overalls, T-shirts, and identical shapeless canvas hats. "Get your boots on, Sval," George boomed. "We're off to fish the Sandy."

"Uh...thanks, but I don't have a fishing pole," Sval demurred.

"Never mind that, I'm lending you a rig."

"But the weather doesn't look too good."

"Are you kidding? Perfect day for fishing, come sunset."

"It's about to rain. There won't be a sunset."

"Only amateurs fish when it's sunny. Come on, we'll catch a mess of rainbow trout that'll call you Dad. Raoul can tell you. I took him out last weekend, right Raoul? Had a good time, didn't you?"

"Well," said Raoul.

"Well..." said Sval. "I really don't have much expertise in this line, as it were..."

"Time to learn," George declared cheerfully. "I'll teach you the basics. I gave Raoul the basics last time and he caught three big ones, right Raoul?"

"Yeah."

"Your skin's whiter'n fish belly, Hofby. We're getting you out from under the light bulbs, pal. Act of charity. Come on."

"Well, I'd like to go with you, but I've got this meeting—"

"No you don't, you malingering bastard," George roared. "Get your boots on, get your ass in the car."

"Oh, all right," Sval grumbled, his voice masking a guarded gratitude. He liked getting out of the city, but he only did so under the aegis of somebody else's relentless bullying; and most people were too polite to bully. He donned appropriate garb and joined the other two outside. George's brown-and-tan Ford looked somewhat like a Buster Brown shoe. George drove east on Stark Street. The houses thinned down on either side of the road, giving way finally to truck farms and hilly pastures where occasional cows grazed in clumps. The hilltops were covered with dark green patches, fir trees rising out of pools of blue shadow. Past the Portland city limits, the road became narrower, winding down around the hillside in a gentle descent. Farmland gave way to ever thicker forest, a mixture of pine and fir, until the greenery bulged and bristled into the road on both sides. They were driving in a green tunnel now, pervaded by the sound of unseen water trickling over rocks. Finally, George turned off the paved highway onto a dirt road.

"You'll want to stay on Stark," Sval informed him politely. "It goes right to the Sandy River."

"Uh huh, right to Dabney State Park and six zillion families," George snorted. "I'm taking you fishing, city boy."

"Do fish shut their eyes when they sleep?" Raoul wondered.

"You handle that one, Sval," George said.

"I think they have eyelids," Sval murmured, keeping his gaze moving between the road and the speedometer.

"Yeah, but do they dream?"

Sval smiled. "How would anyone know?"

George took both hands off the wheel to flatten his hair back, then grasped the wheel again but with only one hand, leaning back in a casual way that made Sval nervous. "Say, listen, Sval, what's this I hear about a route you've got. You deliver the Ark?"

"Uh huh, to stores and bars and whatnot."

"You make money outa' this, or is this another volunteer deal, service to the greater good and all that bullshit?"

"There's money in it," Sval said diffidently. "A nickel for every copy sold is my take. The bar gets ten, the Ark gets ten. I've got about 100 outlets so it comes out to maybe thirty, forty, dollars a week."

Raoul mused, "Maybe none of us are real. Maybe we're all in somebody's dream. Or maybe characters in a movie but we're such good actors we don't even know we're acting. Or maybe none of us exists except in some guy's imagination."

"That's not exactly a new idea," Sval informed his friend. "Such a 'guy' has been posited in the history of ideas. Technically speaking, he's known as 'God'."

"God!" Raoul whistled in awe. "I never thought of that. But sure! It makes sense. That *would* be God, wouldn't it?"

"Bishop Berkeley, for example. Eighteenth Century England," Sval said, falling into his pedagogical tone. "He said—"

"Berkeley didn't know shit," George blapped, steering around a dead possum. "The world exists, all right. That's the trouble with the world. Ask that possum. So listen—about that route—"

"You've read Berkeley?" George didn't seem like the type.

"The Comics Illustrated version," said George. "How long does it take?"

"To read Berkeley?"

"No! Your route! Your route!"

"Oh. Five, six hours every Friday."

"Whoaza! Five hours, you pull down forty bucks? I want a route," George declared. "How do I get one?"

"Well, first of all, you work at the Ark longer than you have," Sval said, his voice thin with disapproval. "Quite a bit longer."

"Yeah, yeah, sure." George brushed away this trivial precondition with some irritation. "And then what?"

"And then you happen to be in the right place at the right time. I got mine from the guy before me, when he had to leave town in—"

"So these puppies are inherited?"

"Basically. Yes."

George sighed. "Christ, I could use one little steady under-the-table gig like that. That and the census five, six hours a week, I could do Portland."

"How can a man of your world-weary sophistication contemplate living in Portland?" Sval said. "After Paraguay and Upper Volta, it must seem like nothing much happens here."

"True," said George. "But nothing's better than something. Anyway, I figure, why not?"

"Weak reason."

"Bah! There's no difference between one reason and another. They're all excuses."

Sval smiled and shook his head. "My tendency, I guess, is always to probe for deeper justification."

"Oh help! Brrrrr! Don't say that. The enduring chill! What do you do about the Abyss?"

"The Abyss?"

"Yeah, yeah, the Abyss. The Big Nothing. You know, the Nada. What you hit if you go deeper. Don't tell me you're one of them high-on-God grunts?"

"Please." Sval looked offended. "You mean, perhaps, the problem of Despair? I'm familiar with it, of course. I've struggled with it a bit in my time."

"Yeah? So what's the answer, professor?"

"Blame it on the weather. In Portland, thank heavens, we always have the rain."

"That's an answer?"

"Sure. It turns Despair into another trivial seasonal affliction, like the common cold, the stuff of small talk. You meet someone and say whatchoo been doing lately and they say oh, struggling with Despair, and you both just nod and move on to some other topic."

From the back seat, Raoul, who had thoroughly bundled himself in a horse blanket, exclaimed suddenly: "The Ministry of Strange Desires. Good title."

"Nice trick if you can make it work for you," George shrugged. "Myself, I never found anything that worked except fishing and the world series. And college basketball, *maybe*. Here we are." The smell of the wet gravel banks was suddenly in the air. George steered the car over a hump of dirt and skidded to a halt under a tree. By the time Sval and Raoul had climbed out of the car he was already in the back, pulling poles, bait, gear, and beer out of the open trunk.

"Try not to make noise as we go down to the banks here. The fish'll hear."

"Fish can't hear," Sval scoffed.

"Hell they can't," George insisted. "Hear, smell, see, the works. To catch a fish you gotta' sneak up on it. You know how to cast?" He raised his eyebrows at Sval.

"I guess I do, now that you mention it. My uncle took me fishing a few times, him and his sons. They were into it."

"Good. Come on." George picked up his own rig and started toward the river. Sval followed. Raoul brought up the rear, gazing appreciatively at the surrounding trees, firs and a scattering of elms, and sniffing the air happily as he trotted along like a puppy.

Sval said, "Anyway, George, you were right about the weather, it's clearing up."

"Sssh. We're coming up to the river. Do you know where to cast?"

"Does it matter?"

George gave him an exasperated look. "Your hook has to land where the fish are! Okay, listen. Here's a rule of thumb to get you started. Cast where it's deep, see? But moving. Got that? Good rule for anything, actually. Where it's deep but moving, that's the place. Like an undercut river bank—see that spot there? Cast upstream, let your bait drift down, then start reeling in. If one spot doesn't work for you, try another. Right behind that boulder's going to be good, but that one's tougher. I'll start there. Raoul—"

"I'll go down the river."

"Good idea. Sval, you try that river bank."

"Wait," said Raoul. "Let's do this before we split up." He took a joint out of his shirt pocket and snapped his fingers for a match, which

George provided. The three men stood in a close circle passing the joint around until it was down to a tar-soaked stub, which Raoul swallowed, declaring, "Waste not."

"Okay," said George. "Let's go."

Raoul started picking his way downstream along the river bank, humming. The sun was drifting across a patch of open sky between two bright clouds. The air was soft and a slight breeze played against his skin. He felt the glassy clarity of vision that marijuana gave him in the first few minutes after he got stoned for the first time each day; and he felt satisfaction. The field of gravel ended, but Raoul waded without hesitation into the jungle of moist foliage that came up to his chest. It parted with snapping, sliding sounds. Small insects fled at his approach, skirring through ribbons of sunlight. Their gossamer wings were rainbow-colored and delicately ribbed like tiny panes of leaded glass.

Raoul looked up at the broader view of hillside green with Douglas firs, and the fairy tale beauty of it staggered him. He had emerged from the underbrush onto a path that curved away from the open hillside, deep into the green shade, and back out for breathtaking vistas across sun-washed scrub oak. Huge flowers bloomed by the side of the road, slender green stalks holding aloft clusters of red petals, or soft mounds of white fluff.

And then he saw the tree. From ground level it looked like a charred stump. Raoul couldn't say what made him stop and look up unless it was that dramatic gash where lightning had scooped clean through the wood, leaving only a layer of gnarled bark. But that sliver of bark, he found, supported a whole tree, for starting about twelve feet above the ground, the trunk was intact; and way up, hundreds of feet up, where the top emerged into sunlight, *this tree still had leaves.* The trunk was in a somber shaded world, but the leaves were living up there in the sunlight! Looking up and shading his eyes, Raoul could vividly imagine being one of those leaves. What a view he would command—of hillsides covered with greenery, rolling from horizon to horizon. And straight up overhead the blue depths of space itself. And at night, the blackness pierced a million times by stars. And that's when it hit him: the analogy was blindingly precise. Zara had struck him the way lightning had struck that tree, blasting out his feelings and leaving him looking dead; but as with this tree, deep inside his gnarled bark were channels of sap. His body was only a vessel running life-sustaining juices up to the part of him that lived outside the shaded realm of this Gothic world, the part of him that stirred in sunlit breezes, commanding vistas of rolling hillsides and limitless space—the part of him that was…the Dream Navigator.

Sval caught no fish, but he didn't mind. Sitting by the river all that long and placid afternoon was not a waste. Isolated from distractions, he was able to work out his ideas for the proposal much better than he could have done in the city. Fortunately, he had his micro-notebook along, and a ball point pen, so he was able to jot down thoughts— although deciphering them later would be a problem; weeds and gravel didn't make the most efficient desk. When the light finally faded, he collected his equipment and went to find the others.

George had caught five good-size fish and strung them on a stick. He commiserated with Sval about catching no fish and assured him that he would bring him out to try again, possibly the very next day. Dusk was falling fast by then and the mist was growing heavy again, and Raoul was out of sight. Sval and George put their gear in the car and walked downstream, assuming that they would run into their friend eventually. But after ten minutes they realized something had gone wrong.

"Where could he have gone?" George wondered.

"I don't know, we couldn't have walked past him," Sval said. "Maybe he ducked into the bushes to empty his bladder."

"Yeah, I gotta' pee myself. Let's walk back."

"We'd better call out to him," Sval suggested.

"Good idea. Hey, Raoul, ho! Raouuuuul! Hoooo!"

"Raoooooul!" Sval echoed.

An answering cry came to them across the surface of the slurping river. "George! Sval!"

"Raoul!"

"George!"

"Where are you, man?"

George and Sval could see nothing at all in the darkness among the trees where they were anxiously looking.

"I'm over here—in the water."

They turned and now, indeed, in a pile of brush and logs jammed against a boulder in the middle of the river, they did see an indistinct wriggling mass.

"What the hell are you doing out there?"

"I'm stuck."

George and Sval exchanged glances. "You need help?

"Yes."

"I better get the flashlight out of my car," George said. He returned with not only the flashlight but his plastic fisherman's trousers and a rope. "You hold the light," he said to Sval. With Sval directing the beam at his feet, George stepped from stone to stone. Sval watched from the bank. The heavy camper's flashlight threw a broad spot of light over the struggling Raoul. A few minutes later, George and Raoul were both on their way back. When they got to shore, Sval saw that Raoul was almost completely wet.

"Good heavens, what on earth happened?" he demanded.

"I fell down and got my ankle caught under that log."

"But what were you doing out there?"

"My hook got caught in that old tree."

"Couldn't you just pull it out?"

"It wouldn't come out," said Raoul. "I was afraid it was going to break and I'd lose the hook."

"What the fuck, so you lose a hook—that's not a tragedy," George exclaimed.

"Really? It was your hook. I didn't know. I didn't want you to be mad at me."

"Well, that's noble, I guess. Where's your rig?"

"You mean my pole and everything?"

"Yeah."

"I must've dropped it in the river when I fell," Raoul admitted humbly.

"Oh my God! You lost a rig to save a hook? I don't believe it! How long ago did this happen?"

"Maybe an hour..."

"But we were right down river—why didn't you call out to us? One of us could've come and helped you."

"You said not to make any noise. You said it would scare the fish. I didn't want to scare any fish."

George was silent much of the way home, and his eyebrows were drawn together like a clenched fist.

Everybody in Charge

Sval strolled down the block to Marica's house, whistling the Hendrix guitar lead from *All Along the Watchtower.* Sunlight, bright and thin as gold foil, fell on a pavement glittering with mica. All the leaves were dripping and twinkling from the morning's rain. Grass, poking up through the many cracks in the uneven sidewalk, looked translucently bright and new in the sunlit mist. Marica in her back yard, wearing Osh Kosh B'gosh overalls and a straw hat, also looked fresh and new, some adman's corny but delicious image of Spring itself. "I'm putting in a community garden," she chirped. "Want to help? There's an extra shovel in the shed."

"Sure." Sval jumped the fence and set his briefcase down on the broken bit of deck that passed for a back porch here. Business could wait, he decided. Fetching a shovel, he set cheerfully to work across the yard from Marica. She had already dug up a patch near the south end of the garden and was spading randomly around the edges to expand it. Sval began at the north end and dug rows methodically back and forth.

"Listen, Sval," she panted out, "I've got a bone to pick with you. That guy George Lubick? Honestly! Where did you dig him up? And how could you bring him to the paper? That dinosaur! I hope he's not going to make the Ark his regular habitat!"

"As a matter of fact," Sval admitted, "he took pictures for my story this week, my overview of Portland collectives. He's not so bad once you get to know him. Pretty good photographer."

"Another vote for Perkins!" she said bitterly.

"Not so, Marica. His politics are solid, believe it or not. Even if his personal flavor is a bit...strong."

"With a guy like that, his personal flavor and his politics are the same thing," she sniffed. "But maybe you'd have to be a woman to understand that."

"Well, no, I think I do in a sense understand."

"Well, my God, that day at the Ark, imagine! Him walking in right away with his 'Gimme' eight pages.' I know Chile's important, but honestly! This newspaper's supposed to serve a whole community! And the way he argued about it, cutting people off right and left." She started shoveling again with a fury.

"He does tend to flatten everything in his path," Sval agreed, "but a lot of that, I think, is just restless energy."

"Are you defending him? That tactless...juggernaut?"

"No," said Sval, but he said it reluctantly, for he did feel a strange compulsion to defend George. With a squeamish feeling that he was squandering his credit with Marica to no good purpose, he found himself pressing on: "It's just that his putative tactlessness is really—a kind of spontaneity. He's like a force of nature. One doesn't call a hurricane tactless just because it flattens everything in its path."

"I'd rather not be flattened, thank you."

"No. Of course not." Sval recognized the futility of the argument. "Can we move on for a moment, beyond George Lubick? I'm not his keeper, you know. He walked into the Ark by himself. If we're really committed to an open paper, though, we're going to have to deal with an occasional George Lubick. I mean there's a principle involved."

This touched a button. "I guess you're right," Marica relented. "That's something I have to work on."

They gave themselves over to simple labor, then, and felt a communion of sweat and muscle. He continued digging rows, advancing his column of spaded earth toward Marica's ever-widening circle. His nostrils filled with the smell of moist soil. As he came close to Marica, he could hear her panting breath. He started on the last sliver that separated his patch from Marica's. Just as his hands slipped on the shovel, Marica said, "There!"

He wiped his forehead and stopped to look. Their sections had merged. The garden was fully spaded. Marica stood surveying the black loam. "Looks fertile enough, doesn't it?" she said thoughtfully. "What should we plant?"

"How about tomatoes?" Sval could picture sinking his teeth into a round, ripe, juicy one just now.

"Mmm, yes. Tomatoes sound good. And zucchinis," she mused.

"Zukes are a must," he agreed. He walked back to the shade of the house and picked up his briefcase. "Here's what I came about, actually." He drew out a sheaf of papers. "I wrote up that proposal we were talking about. To get rid of the managing editor position and make the Ark a real collective. You want to read it over if you have time? See if you think the wording is okay?"

"Sure. Thanks, Sval. I will."

"The extras are for anyone you think might be a vote for our side." As he gave her the papers, his fingers grazed against hers. He thought he heard her breath quicken; but maybe it was his own. "Let me know what you think," he said, and when she merely nodded, he turned and nonchalantly walked away.

Raoul glanced up from his sketch book. Had someone knocked? He shuffled to the front door and pulled it open. On the porch stood a bearded man with fine brown hair that flowed over his shoulders. A hand-tooled belt with a silver buckle held up his perfectly flared and faded bellbottom jeans. Raoul recognized Ray Perkins, bass player from Dr. Rock's Rhythm Remedy but also a leading member of the Ark Collective.

"Hey man," Perkins flashed a blazing smile.

Raoul felt himself shrink into hiding. He stepped aside and Perkins ambled into the house. Raoul followed the man, wondering what he wanted. Perkins strolled through the front room and into the kindergarten, pulled out a chair at the butcher block table, paused to gaze at the hundreds of drawings covering the walls, and then sat down.

Perhaps he had sensed the genius in Raoul's work and wanted to experience the artist in his atelier, Raoul thought. And then he thought, nah.

"Man, you're a genius," Perkins uttered warmly.

"A genius?" stammered Raoul.

"The way you caught Ivancie last week—those City Council drawings—ouch! Masterful." Perkins' gaze roved over the big table and spotted the glass salad bowl filled with sifted marijuana. "Oh my God!" he exclaimed. "Dope?"

"TNT," Raoul boasted. "Shall I roll one?"

"Bombs away," Perkins smiled. "Like I was saying, man, your drawings—you are hot, dude! You're what the Ark has needed for a looong time—a real, professional quality illustrator—I'm not going to insult you and call you a cartoonist: your work has too much range. Where'd you learn to draw like that?"

"Where did a bird learn to fly," said Raoul. "I'm just like that tree." He handed Perkins a perfectly rolled joint with both ends twisted to points. "You should see my aquarium."

Perkins puffed the joint to life. "Smells good. Columbian?"

"Oaxacan Red."

"Yum. Anyway, like I was saying, it hurts me to see work like yours next to some of the crap we put in the Ark. I'm not blaming anyone, but just between you and me this open-door policy eats shit. Let's face it, we've got a morale problem on this staff. A lot of people feel they're going nowhere with this paper, and they don't like it. What about you?"

"I like going nowhere."

"Well, look, I can understand if you're depressed. There was a time when the Ark could have been a contender, know what I mean? It was out there on the runway, ready for takeoff. Then all these nit-picking nitwits came aboard, dragging along their negativity and here we are. Take Margolis, for example—this crap about women-writers—God! That's why Walter and Grace left, you know."

"Walter and Grace left?" Raoul was startled.

Perkins cocked his head at him. "Don't put me on—you were there. And if you think Walter quit because he got some fancy job offer in New

York—well, I've got a bridge I'd like to sell you. He built this paper with his two hands, you think he's just going to walk away? Truth is, he burned out. That's an open secret. But let me tell you something, Raoul—*I* don't think the Ark is a hopeless case. I think it can be saved! Now I'm not saying I should run the show, but who's stood up for quality from day one?" He paused.

Raoul panicked because Perkins was acting like he was supposed to know this one. "I dunno," he confessed.

"Me, for crying out loud! Thing is, Raoul, what we need is vision. Where are we going, what are our goals? Take circulation for example: I can see doubling it—three months max. Imagine that. Eighteen thousand people seeing your cartoons every Thursday. How does that sound?"

"Huh?" Raoul's attention had been wandering.

"Circulation. I'm talking eighteen thousand."

"What about it?'

"How does eighteen thousand sound, compared to nine thousand?"

Raoul frowned. "It's more."

"You're damn right, and more is better! Right?" Perkins took off his jacket and started in again, about circulation, ad rates, and the like. Raoul smiled and nodded, but he wasn't listening. He was floating in empty space three feet above his own head. He could see his body leaning forward listening and Perkins gesturing and yapping. He could see through the walls that surrounded them. He could see what surrounded the walls, above and below, and on all sides, extending forever: nothingness. Emptiness pressed in on that bright little bubble of a scene from everywhere, trying to swallow up the bubble. Darkness was trying to suck the light out of this bubble. How lonely it was out there in the dark without his body, only the sight through the keyhole of his eyes for company: two men at a table smoking dope and chatting inconsequentially about nothing. Yes, he could feel the vacuum now, sucking at him in earnest, the old familiar terror, and he had to cling to that keyhole with all his might, had to pour his attention into the room and ignore the emptiness; he forced himself to pay attention to this man gobbling about something, forced himself to pretend it had some importance, until at last the keyhole became his eyes again, and he was able to reel himself back into the illusion that he was sitting in a room, and that Much existed instead of Nothing. Phew—that had been a close one!

"Is it a deal?" Perkins fixed bright eyes and a big smile on him.

"It's a deal," said Raoul, liking the important-sounding resonance of that phrase. It felt good to be someone who was making a deal. He stood up because Perkins stood up, and they shook hands as if they had really made a deal of some kind. It was actually an enjoyable movie, Raoul found.

After Perkins left, Raoul spent two hours etching a detailed map of Atlantis with pen and ink. Around sunset, Sval Hofby came over, looking for "George." He meant the dragon.

"He's asleep," said Raoul. "Should I wake him?"

He didn't really want to and was relieved when Sval said, "No, I just dropped by."

"Sit down." Raoul gestured to an empty chair. "Smoke some dope."

"No thanks. The Association for the Future of Oregon is meeting at five." Sval glanced at his watch, then set his briefcase down and pulled out a sheaf of papers. "I brought over a copy of this proposal. Read it and see what you think. A few of us are going to offer it at Friday meeting."

"Well...okay." Raoul reluctantly accepted and read what Sval gave him. "I see," he concluded when he handed it back. "You don't want to be the Managing Editor and you don't want anyone else to be either."

"Well—that's perhaps one way of putting it. But that's only the whiskers of the beast. Raoul, my friend, we're proposing to abolish everything—every title, every position. We propose running the paper as a free-flowing totally democratic collective from now on. No bosses, no barriers, no gurus, no fixed roles—tear down the walls and let the paper breathe like an organism, we say. Some people are going to call this a proposal for anarchy, but *I* call it libertarian socialism."

"But you don't want anybody to take Walter's place. Is that right?"

"I think the whole collective should take his place. Yes. What do you think?"

Raoul wriggled shyly. "I don't know. Perkins was over here talking about the circulation. He said we could double it if we could get a new leader."

"It's a point to consider," Sval pursed his lips. "But the way I see it—look. I live in a house with three other people. We have to work together on a lot of things, like keeping the kitchen clean and whatnot, and we do it without electing one of us leader. Do you have a leader in this house?"

"Gee, I never thought of it that way. But could it work like that at the Ark? Would the paper come out every week if no one was running it except all of us?"

"No one running it except all of us. Nice phrase. That could almost be a slogan. No one running it except all of us." Sval took out a small notebook and jotted it down. "Would the paper come out every week? Good question. I don't know the answer." He put his notebook away. "Corporate America says that the pyramid is the only way to organize work. Perkins agrees. I happen to think—and Marica and a lot of other people—that the circle can get the job done just as well. That's why I'm going to support The Proposal. I always think it's worth a small risk to accomplish something truly amazing."

Raoul felt a surge of light, such as often came with cosmic insights. "Me too," he said eagerly. "Like, I'm working on this art-piece—an environment, you see—a room that's got an aquarium woven into the space. A place where fish and people can mingle."

Sval gazed at Raoul with affectionate amusement. "Where fish and people can mingle? How, pray tell, did you arrive at that objective?"

"It came from my—from Zara, my girlfriend on the East Coast. Fish were her favorite animal—she's that kind of person, you know, she has a favorite everything. A favorite color, a favorite movie, a favorite vegetable—broccoli, I remember. And when it came to animals, it was fish. She had a whole wall of them. A Paul Klee painting, a photo of her dad on a fishing boat holding up a shark. She had a dress with fishes on it, I remember. It was so beautiful. And she always ordered fish in a restaurant—oh, she liked them all different ways. And she had aquariums, but they were just boxes. So when she left—I mean, when I left and came here—I decided to build something that would truly amaze Zara. And I've been working on it ever since."

Sval nodded thoughtfully. "I've heard about your aquarium, and I believe I get the gist of it. This proposal, Raoul, this is *my* aquarium. Can it be? Only if we believe in it. So, what do you think—you gonna' vote for it."

"Sure!" Raoul said cheerfully. "If it's your *aquarium*, of course I'll vote for it."

Sval stumbled into Zoe's house feeling drained. The proposal was out of his hands now, scattered to the far corners of the community, and only the collective could decide its fate. The living room was empty, and he didn't know who was home, but he put on a Santana album and dropped onto the couch. Where was the satisfaction he was supposed to feel in a job well done?

Zoe came in from a back room, her hair wrapped in a towel. He could smell her clean, fresh animal smell, and the jitters faded out of his stomach. He followed her into the kitchen. A man with a red beard was sitting there eating the last of an apple. He stood up when he saw Sval and said to Zoe, "I'll be going then."

"Okay, bye," she said and followed him out of the room to show him to the door, which was a bit odd. When she came back, she set to work wordlessly, making two cups of hot chocolate.

"Dark out tonight," Sval remarked.

She handed him a steaming cup. "Feeling okay? You look a little dazed."

"Worn down by the day's labors. I've been getting the proposal out."

"I know," she said. "I saw you 'getting The Proposal out' to Marica Margolis."

"What do you mean?" His mind scuttled to remember how he'd acted with Marica, today, how he had touched her. He couldn't remember touching at all except for that graze of finger tips.

"I was visiting Corrine on Taylor Street," said Zoe. "Her bedroom windows look out over Marica's backyard. It's a small world, huh? You helped Marica spade up her garden, I noticed."

"Well, it was a good day for working with the earth. And then I went to the Morrison Street House. I've been all over town today, getting the proposal out."

"Poor guy," said Zoe. "Why don't we take you and your hot chocolate downstairs and tuck you into bed? You can get the proposal out to me."

"Or into you," he said, "as the case may be."

He followed her downstairs to her lair. Whatever was or wasn't happening with Marica had nothing to do with Zoe, he had to remind himself. From her, he had permission. What a woman.

Breaking News

Friday morning arrived with a great drumroll of thunder from the weather, followed by slashing rain, as if all the elements knew that on this day the Ark would gather to consider Sval's seminal proposal. The hammer of heavy raindrops on the roof woke Sval up at four a.m., and he couldn't get back to sleep. Driving rain in March would simply have been weather, but in April? Here it was again: weather as metaphor. Today was not to be just any day.

He left Zoe breathing softly under the covers and poured himself a glass of milk in the kitchen to settle his stomach, then sat at the cable-spool table to go over the language of the proposal once again. There was nothing to correct, so he settled on the couch in the living room with headphones and lulled himself with that gentle masterpiece, *American Beauty Rose*. By the time Zoe and the roommates woke up, the house stank of nicotine and coffee. Sval used breakfast, the newspaper, and Spinoza to pace himself through the morning. At two o' clock he finally permitted himself to drive over to the Ark. The meeting would not begin for three hours, but he wanted to savor the political currents. Halfway up the stairs, however, he ran into Marica.

"Oh, Sval," she gasped, "I'm so glad you're here! Did you hear the news? Do you have your car here? It was on the radio—some man took a bunch of people hostage at the food stamp office. It's happening right now! Could we get a story on it, do you think? It would be like, wow, fast-breaking news, almost!"

"But the meeting," he spluttered. "The proposal—"

"Oh, go," she scolded, shooing him toward the stairs. "The meeting's not for three hours yet."

Sval permitted himself to be herded. She was right, of course: he'd be better off keeping busy until the meeting. On the freeway, however, halfway to the Hollywood exit, he felt a peculiar thump and then heard a savage, metallic scraping. Suddenly, he spotted a wheel rolling on ahead of his truck and a moment later recognized it as his own! He couldn't savor the humor of the image just then because his Old Red Chevy was skidding into the left lane, making cars on that side of him squawk and flurry like chickens. Sval jerked the steering wheel, and the truck fishtailed far to the right amid fresh screams of tires and horns, sliding between two Cadillacs before it scraped the guardrail for fifty feet and came to a halt.

In the stillness that followed, Sval's ears and eyeballs tingled. A split second ago he was going to die. Instead, now, he was alive. Climbing out of the cab, he felt holy. But the traffic thundered by, indifferent to the miracle of his survival. Every eyewitness to the miracle had hurled on, and these new drivers pouring past saw nothing but some guy with a broken truck. The pleasant surprise of being alive gave way to mundane dismay about his situation: stranded on a busy freeway in the rain with a truck that had only three wheels. He would have to call someone, but it couldn't be a towing company because a commercial tow would cost him his life's savings. As he walked down from the freeway, Sval ran through a list of names in his mind. Yamhill House, he decided: Martha would help him. Good old Martha.

But it was George Lubick who answered the phone. "Hello!" he shouted. "Sval, that you? Who do you want? Martha? She's not here. Bye."

"Wait—um. What about you—do you have a functioning vehicle?"

"A car that works? Sure. What's the problem?"

"I'm stranded on 80 going east. It's kind of a dangerous spot."

"Yeah?"

"Yeah. My truck broke down. It's pretty close to an off ramp. If you could give me a quick tow, perhaps. I've got a chain."

"Sounds like you've got a problem all right," George conceded, "but look. Truth is, I was about to take a nap. I've been working at this fucking bookstore for four hours, and my back is killing me."

Sval felt angry blood rush to his face. Where was this man's sense of community? But it would not do to lecture. "My car," he uttered through clenched teeth, "is in a pretty tight spot, George. I'm just over a blind curve—I would not balk at calling this a life-or-death situation. But I know I have no right to impose on your right to nap. Perhaps there's someone else in the house—"

"All right, I get it," George broke in. "Crisis. Where are you?"

"About half a mile up from the Hollywood exit. Best to get on at 12th Street heading east. You'll see me."

"I'll be there, probably."

"Probably?" Sval demanded, his voice cold.

"Ninety percent chance. Ninety-five, even. Listen: here's what I'll commit to 100 percent: If I don't come out, I'll try to get someone else."

Sval's mind spun for a moment, then found a hook. "Bring your camera, if you come. I was on my way to cover a fast-breaking story."

"Yeah? Something juicy?"

"Succulent as roast suckling pig."

Twenty minutes later George stood beside him on the freeway. "What the hell happened here?"

"One of my wheels fell off."

"What?!" George bent down to examine the studs. "How come? These do-hickies didn't break off, and they've still got their whatchemajiggers."

"Evidently, I didn't tighten the nuts enough," said Sval sullenly.

"Where's the tire?"

Sval gestured vaguely east.

"What: it rolled right down the freeway? My God!" George slapped his forehead. "This is the worst fuck-up I've ever heard of. How could you be so dumb? Don't you even have a spare?"

Sval blinked. "Of course I've got a spare. But I can't just put it on."

"Why not?"

"Because the other one fell off! The nuts are gone. Scattered."

"Scattered where? They must be right around here somewhere."

"Anywhere within half a mile. You can't look for nuts on a busy freeway. Just give me a tow home, sirrah. It's not far."

"Home? You're on your way to cover a story, boy! What the hell was it about, anyway? Not some goddawful new collective opening up, I hope."

"I've lost my energy for that." Sval muttered, glancing at his watch. The meeting was set to start in one hour and twenty minutes. At this moment, there was an actual chance that he would miss it. No story was worth a risk like that.

George slapped him on the back. "Come on, where's that old journalistic spirit? Hey, look!"

George flung his bulk out into the freeway and leapt back just before a truck flattened him. He was holding up a piece of metal. "One of your bolts," he crowed. "Get your spare out."

"You spotted that little thing in the lane?"

"Are you kidding? I've got the eyes of a photographer. Get the spare out, and tell me about this story we're rushing to cover."

"Some guy's taken some clerk hostage at the food stamp office, but—"

"All riiight! I've often wanted to club a few of those petty bureaucrats myself. What's the word on this guy, is he political? Just crazy? What?"

"What's the difference? We can't get there in time."

"Course we can, get out your spare."

"One bolt, George!"

"Three," George said impatiently. "We'll borrow a bolt off each of your front wheels. Give me the whatchoocallit—"

"Lug wrench."

"Yeah. That."

They got Sval's car off the freeway and parked. Then Sval got into the Ford. George drove like a madman, but looked perfectly at ease, steering one-handed, putting on bursts of speed at each straightaway, braking for corners, accelerating into the turns. At each red light, he nosed into the intersection to check for cops and traffic, then shot through.

"You drive with panache," Sval gasped, clutching the dashboard.

"Bronx style," came the short reply. "Here it is." George screeched to a halt and jumped out.

Sval grabbed his notebook and followed. Inside the building, the familiar smell of sweat and old clothes enveloped him. Five lines of people stretched across the room, looking as dazed as travelers on a three-day bus ride. Behind the long counter, rows of bureaucrats bent over Formica desks, scratching on forms. The fluorescent lights gave the whole place the cast of a wax museum. There was no sign of any disturbance. Indeed, it took a second to realize anyone was moving.

"Looks like we missed the excitement," Sval murmured.

"Let's make sure. Hey, you." George strode up to a gap-toothed man with matted hair. "Been here long? What happened with the hostage crisis?"

The man flinched. "I been standing here two fuckin' hours."

"Yeah, yeah, what about the hostages? That thing?"

"Been here two fuckin' hours."

George moved impatiently to the next line and the next, shouting and gesturing, but nobody seemed to know or care about the hostage crisis. Then George's eye lit on a sign labeled *information* . He swept aside the woman whose turn was just coming up and stuck his head through the window to crane at the clerk. "Hi, hey. You must've been here when it happened. Right? The guy that took the hostages. Yes? Is that a yes? Get over here, Sval, we got a live one. We're the press," he explained to the terrified clerk.

Behind her in the vast room, other clerks had risen from their nests and now stood staring at the disturbance in a variety of frozen postures. One of them was speaking to someone on the phone, Sval noticed.

"George," he muttered tactfully, tugging at George's elbow.

George shook him off. "Here, Sval. Talk to this one while I get some pictures." George already had the lens cap off and had fallen into a photographer's crouch. He backed up to get a good angle on the shot, compressing the row of people behind him. But the row decompressed suddenly and violently, shooting George forward like a cannonball. His shutter clicked as he lurched and caught his balance. Behind him, pushing and shoving erupted up and down the line. "Quit pushing," someone shouted. Cloth ripped. Someone's fist landed on someone's face—and then suddenly a melee was raging from wall to wall.

Sval got a fingernail scratch down one cheek. He tripped backward, landing on the floor. At that moment, three policemen entered through the far door. They paused for a moment, sizing up the situation, and the fighting died away.

"That one, officer, he started it," sobbed the clerk, pointing at Sval.

"What's the big idea, buddy?" said one of the cops.

"Me! No, it was—I'm sorry, officer, it's all a misunderstanding. My friend and I are reporters. We're here to cover a story."

"Reporters, huh? What newspaper you work for, fellas?"

"The *Rose City Ark*."

"Never heard of it."

"It's a people's newspaper," Sval replied with dignity.

The cop's lips curled. "Hey, Frank, you ever hear of a 'people's newspaper' called the Ark?"

"Yeah," the other admitted. "It's that dope-rag with the sex ads: the hippies used to sell 'em downtown. They got 'em in boxes now."

"The Ark does *not* carry sex ads," Sval declared indignantly.

"What story you covering here?"

"The hostage crisis. The radio said some man took hostages at the food stamp office—"

A derisive laugh cut Sval short. "That was downtown, Jimmy Olson. You're forty blocks off and about two hours late. They booked that man, it's over. Now get out of here and let these people work. Go on back to your people's newspaper."

"You should try reading it sometime," Sval inserted suavely, "It's not what you think. Home subscription costs $10 a year."

"I get the Oregonian," the officer snapped.

"The Oregonian," George hooted. "Owned, written, and read by pigs."

Sval felt his blood gel. Even George lost the laugh off his face as the three cops turned in unison.

"What? did? you? say?"

"I called you a pig. What're you going to do? Put me in jail? It's not against the law."

Two of the cops lunged at George, but the third one held them back. "Say again?" he scowled.

"Pig. You can't arrest me for saying that word, I know my rights. There's no law against expressing an opinion."

"Or, for that matter, an incorrect fact," Sval noted anxiously.

"Come on, buddy, we're going to the station." The cops grabbed George's arms and hustled him toward the door, Sval following along behind, inquiring, "What's the charge? Could I get some clarity? Excuse me, what's the charge?"

"I can't believe this!" George slapped his forehead, even though two cops were holding that arm. "Incredible. This isn't America, it's Nazi Germany! Here, Sval!" Even amid his shouting and ranting, he managed to get his car keys out of his pocket and drop them on the floor where Sval could pick them up. "Bail me out," he called, as he was dragged around the corner. Sval could still hear his voice— "My back's killing me—I worked four hours in a goddamn bookstore today—" before a door slammed shut.

Sval drove back toward his own car in a daze. He passed under the freeway near the place where he lost his tire. The freeway curved just at that point and a gas station perched just at that curve. The building faced the freeway and had three windows, but the glass in the middle window had a jagged hole, through which Sval could see a candy machine lying on its side. "What happened there," he asked the attendant, as he bought fifty cents worth of gas.

The attendant shrugged and spat. "Some punk threw a tire through it."

Sval pulled out of the station with a leaden conscience. As soon as he got home, he called Zoe, and together they charted a plan to collect bail for George. Just as he hung up, the phone rang. "Sval?" George's voice exploded. "Get a pencil, pal!"

"George? Where the hell are you calling from?"

"Downtown city jail. This is my one call, let's not blow it. Got a pencil? Get this down. The guy's Chicano, 35 years old. Name's Guillermo. I got the whole story. The man pulls into town broke and they won't give him food stamps 'cuz he doesn't have a kitchen. Rich, huh? But listen. He's gone now, they've put a new guy in here with me, heavy dude. A biker. Hope you're gettin' all this, 'cuz I might be too beat to write it up when I get home. Or maybe too beat up. Anyway, you're the writer."

"I didn't get a thing. Listen, George—"

"Okay, okay, we'll hammer it out together, soon as you spring me. You working on bail?"

"Yes, but I'm trying to tell you, it's 5:15 now, and I'm late for the meeting at the Ark—"

"Meeting at the Ark!" George exploded. "You're going to run off to some petty goddamn collective meeting and leave me locked in a jail cell with a goddamn killer Nazi biker?"

"It's not petty, George. My Proposal—"

"Your Proposal! I don't believe this. I come get you out of a life-or-death crunch on the freeway—life or death, didn't you say? You wouldn't balk? And now you—"

"Please, George. Be rational. The meeting'll last three hours at the very most. After that I can take up a collection—"

"Listen, if they want your proposal, they'll vote for it," George interrupted. "You don't have to be there. You're just one vote."

"I'm not just a vote. I'm a voice," Sval mustered the dignity to declare.

"A voice! They'll have fifty people in there screaming their goddamn heads off. You think they're going to need another goddamn *voice*! Meanwhile I'm in here with this chain-swinging homicidal Cossack biker maniac."

"Okay, George, you've made your point. Maybe you're right." Sval's guilt caught up with him. "I'll raise the money in the neighborhood and be there soon—probably."

"Probably?" screamed George.

"I'd put the chances at ninety percent," Sval replied with grim satisfaction. "Maybe ninety-five, even."

Victory

Sval arrived at the Ark just in time to see the meeting breaking up. But who were all these women coming down the stairwell, all these strange faces? He recognized a few from the Athena Coffeehouse, and two from the Shoebox Collective, and one or two from Family Vaudeville but the rest...? Spotting Martha and Marica, he rushed to the comfort of their familiar faces. "What happened?"

"Sval," cried Marica, her face aglow with pride. "Where've you been?"

"It's a long story. What about the proposal? What happened?"

"We won, my friend! It's in."

"Hallelujah! How——?"

"Long story," she laughed, just as Raoul came bouncing up. "What do you say we go somewhere and exchange long stories?"

"Over libations, by all means," Sval agreed, and so they all strolled down to Euphoria. "Tell me all," Sval begged, once they were settled.

"Well, there's not so much to tell," Martha bubbled. "I guess most everybody was already in favor of Marica's proposal."

"Marica's proposal?" Sval repeated.

"Oh, it's not my proposal," Marica chided her friend. "It's *everybody's* proposal. A lot of people put their ideas into it. I just read it to the collective is all." She glanced at Sval, who was swirling his beer and guarding a wry smile.

"Oh, sure, as if," said Martha. "She's always like this," she confided to Sval. "She just refuses to take credit." Martha went on to recount what happened at the meeting, setting forth each argument in detail: she had the memory of a tape recorder. "Here," she concluded finally. "I've got a copy of the proposal, if you want to read it." She began fumbling in her purse, but Sval waved her off.

"I'm familiar with the major points," he said in his driest voice and raised his glass to Marica. "Congratulations."

"Oh, it's you that deserves congratulations," she assured him.

The next hour slipped by as the group relaxed and the conversation turned personal. Martha took her leave shortly after eleven and Raoul finally drifted off at a quarter to midnight. That thinned the group down to just Sval and Marica: it was their third time alone together.

"So," he said, and he rearranged his body in his seat. Any small awkwardness about the Proposal was gone. What kind of person would he be if he wanted to claim personal credit? The proposal belonged to the Community.

"So..." she responded dreamily, gazing into the air.

He considered taking her hands. Would it be too much of a move?

"Well." He slapped his hands together.

"Well what?" she said, looking up.

"What else is on the agenda for tonight?"

"Bed," she said.

"Bed," he agreed blandly. "Uh huh. Bed is good."

"It's been a long day." She made no move to get up. "Why are you looking at me like that?"

"I was just..."

"Go on. What?"

The signals were unclear. She was waiting. How to broach this delicate subject? "I was trying to imagine your bedroom."

"Pardon me?"

"Your bed." He retreated from the warning in her voice and regrouped. "The furniture upon which you, um, recline."

"It's brass," she said. "I have a big brass bed, like in the Dylan song."

Sval could hear the lyrics in his mind: *lay, lady, lay...* "Mine is a mattress on the floor," he admitted.

"Ew." She wrinkled her nose. "That doesn't sound very nice."

"Oh, yours is more comfortable, I'm sure. The superior choice if one were obliged to choose."

She stood up. "Good heavens, look at the time! I need to lie in a bed, not talk about one." She fumbled in her purse for change.

"Going already?" he faltered.

"What do you mean, already?" She sounded upset and looked impatient as she continued searching for change. "It's late, Sval. It's very late. I have to go home. I have to go home now, and so should you."

He couldn't think of any way to stem the tide of departure. "Well, so good-bye," she said, and her eyes warned him not to say anything but "Good-bye," in return. She was frightened, and he didn't blame her: sleeping with Marica would be a blind launch into a vast unknown. Not a line to cross lightly.

After she left, he jogged to Zoe's house because it was closer than his own, and though he was a little drunk when he started, the night air and the rain restored him. He arrived with his face cool and wet and entered her house without knocking. Zoe was sitting in the dining room with some dark, Latin-looking man. The table between them was littered with dirty dishes, and the smell of marijuana hung in the air. Candles provided the only light.

"Hi, Sval. This is Anthony. Friend of Mark's. He's passing through Portland, crashing for the night. He's going to work on the pipeline up in Alaska."

Sval shook hands with the stranger. "The pipeline, eh? No judgment here. We all do what we must to survive. The Long March cannot be a straight line, alas." He sat down, and poured out the story of his evening, omitting only his final encounter with Marica. But he had interrupted a conversation about the Patty Hearst case, which revved up again as soon as his voice ran down. Sval was in no mood for this topic. "I'm up to speed on this one," he broke in abruptly. "Whole thing started as a Steve Canyon strip, etc. I've heard it. Nice meeting you, Tony. Good luck up there in Alaska. If you'll excuse me now, I'm tired." He stood up. "Zoe? I'm bushed. I'm going to bed."

"Okay."

She gave no indication of whether she meant okay go home, or okay stay here. He waited for a sign. Then he lost patience. "What`s your plan, Zoe?"

"I'm operating without a plan," she smiled, but she understood what he needed and gathered up some dirty dishes to take to the kitchen, where they could speak privately. He followed her gratefully.

As Zoe stacked the dishes in the sink, he put his arms around her from behind and rested his head against her warm nape, feeling the soft hairs brushing his nose. She leaned ever so slightly back into him.

"Your body feels good," he whispered.

She finished with the dishes and turned. "Yours too. Tired, huh?"

"Just emotionally. I was alone with Marica at the end there. It was one of those molten situations—"

"I don't want to hear about it."

"No, wait. Nothing happened, that's what I wanted you to hear."

"I can't be your confidante about this, Sval. Anything else, yes, but if you have to share this story, it can't be with me."

"Uh huh, okay. But really?" Disappointment welled inside him like a blister. "Are you sure that's the best way to deal with this thing? It creates a locked door, could a locked door ever be good for a relationship?"

"Sval."

"Okay. Respect. I just thought we might talk about it rationally."

"Go to bed," she said.

"Here?"

"Here."

"You coming down soon?"

"I'm going to smoke one more joint with what's-his-name. Give me a kiss. I'll be down later."

Sval lurched down the stairs, his head a swirl of fleeting thoughts. He crawled between the sheets of Zoe's bed and fell asleep within minutes, cradled in the gratitude of having such a place as this for refuge and such a woman as Zoe to call his Primary Relationship.

The Kitchen

As soon as Martha closed the door to her little room, the euphoria drained away. Now she had to get some sleep. She had a job interview at 10:30 tomorrow morning and she couldn't afford to blow it: twenty hours a week of filing medical records at five bucks an hour—it seemed almost too good to be true.

She set her clock for 7:30, got under the covers, and closed her eyes, hoping to cheat her way into deep sleep before insomnia even knew she was in bed, but it didn't work. A rafter creaked. A fly started dive-bombing the window. She noticed the hissing of the rain . . .Would the interviewer be a man, she wondered? Would her dress be right? A drop of something fell somewhere. The outer world bled into the clangor of her thoughts, which segued subtly into dreams even more exhausting than insomnia.

She was on her way to her job interview already. She had forgotten to wear shoes. "Your feet are too big! Heee-yah!" jeered the man pulling the rope attached to the ring through her nose; and he swirled her to a halt in front of a desk surrounded by people on chairs. She stood facing a featureless man in a suit, beside whom cringed her obsequious father, smelling of liquor and whining, "Shall I lay her on the desk for you, boss?"

A pair of scissors were thrust upon her. Suddenly a great racket broke out, of people sawing their chairs in half. But where was her chair? And how could she be expected to saw wood with a pair of scissors? "It's not fair!" she cried, but the noise drowned her out. Martha clapped her hands over her ears, but the noise cut through. She struggled to wake up, but the sound only gained intensity and volume, until at last she realized she was fully awake and the sound was real: somebody was sawing wood outside her door.

She glanced immediately at the clock: 5:30 a.m.

She jumped into a robe and poked her head out of her room. Raoul stood in the hall with a saw in his hand, leaning over a door laid flat across a couple of sawhorses.

"Huh?" He turned around, blinking and peering.

"Just what do you think you're doing?"

"I'm sawing my door in half. Why?"

"Do you know what time it is?" she snarled. "Do you have any idea?"

He glanced at his watch. "It's ten past nine."

"Ten past nine?" Martha plunged back into her room to look at the clock and found that she had kicked the cord out of the wall in her sleep. "Oh—" she was about to say 'shit' but caught herself in time: "—fiddlesticks!" Less than an hour and a half left to get ready! She grabbed her clothes and hurried to the bathroom to receive another rude shock: she had gained a pound in her sleep! What a time for the scales to screw up!

She showered quickly, dressed, and hurried downstairs. Only one thing could save her now: a good breakfast—nothing else could kill this crabgrass of bad mood. A poached egg on toast with two strips of bacon. A steaming cup of hot milk with chocolate dusted on it. A napkin, matching silverware, and the special dishes she kept hidden from her goopy roommates.

At the threshold of the kitchen, however, she stopped dead.

The cupboard doors hung open and empty shelves gaped out. Bags and cans of food were strewn all over the countertops. Jars of peanut butter and jelly stood open side by side, with knives stuck down their gullets and gobs of their innards clinging to their lips. A rank smell of leftovers hung heavy in the air. Dirty dishes stretched across all the available counter space and out of the sink rose a great pyramid of dishes, the top of which was actually wedged under the long, swinging arm of the faucet.

The hope of breakfast died away in Martha's breast. The urge to kill rose up.

Raoul was halfway done sawing his door in half when Martha popped out of her room and shouting wildly, "Do you know what time it is?" Very odd. The incident set off in Raoul a train of thought that traveled so far, so fast, he had no idea where it was going until it stopped dead in the middle of a great idea: speaking of trains, why not train a houseplant to double as a lampshade?

He dropped the saw and hurried downstairs to record the brainstorm. In the kindergarten the current resident crasher George Lubick sat slumped at the big table. Crasher was the right word for George this morning. His hair pointed in all directions and his eyes had the blank look of a battered fighter. The sight brought Raoul up short with a serious oops.

The night had been one of fiery invention, a night when Raoul's skull felt literally in danger of blowing up from the pressure of ideas. In the wee hours, he had achieved the impossible—painted in total darkness, thereby busting through an artist's worst trap, the urge to repeat what worked before. He craved to tell someone about his great breakthrough but the sight of George wilted him for a moment. George was a dragon: he roared and knocked things over when he turned, like dragons do with their big tails. Dragons were too big and energetic for indoors. With such creatures, Raoul tried to avoid notice altogether. But George was the only pair of ears around, so Raoul sat down. He decided to ease into conversation slowly with a little small talk to break the ice.

"Say, George, how far would you say light travels into a body?"

"Howzat?"

"Light. We're made of atoms, you know—and atoms are mostly empty space, right? So, light must go through that space. But how far in does it go? Could you take a photograph in someone's stomach? And if it doesn't go all the way inside a person, how come? What stops it?"

George yawned. "You been up taking weird drugs, haven't you."

"All night," Raoul agreed happily. This was good. The dragon was talking. He and the dragon were making friends. "How about you?"

"Ditto," George groaned. "Couldn't catch a wink down there behind the furnace with all the racket going on."

"In the basement?" Raoul exclaimed, astonished. "Behind the furnace?" Why, behind-the-furnace in the basement was just about the quietest corner of the universe. Raoul knew, because for some reason he could hear absolutely everything down there through the heating duct in his bedroom. Then he realized that the opposite must be true as well: in the basement, one would be able to hear any noise in Raoul's room—such as the sound of a door being sawed in half...or of Raoul chanting from the Bhagavad-Gita...

The noise that kept George awake must have been the noise Raoul was making. Raoul sat in stricken silence, waiting for dragon fire.

But George's scowl slowly gave way to the friendly glower of an old warrior noticing a boy. "You weren't the worst of it, pal. That damn furnace clicking and banging—it's like sleeping in a goddamn boiler room down there. I've got to get out of this place, Raoul. I haven't slept in days. Got to find a place to lay my head."

As he said these words, George laid his head on that morning's Oregonian. Then he pulled back and sat up straight, ogling. "Ha!" he declared and picked the paper up for a closer look. "Ha," he repeated, "Look here, Raoul, check this out. I'm famous, semi." He slapped the paper down and pointed to an item titled ONE ARREST IN FOOD STAMP RIOT. "Food stamp riot, my ass, do you believe it? God, that's rich! I wonder if Sval's seen this yet."

He jumped up and moved to the phone. After a few muffled words, Raoul heard him shout, "Amusing? I call it *out-fuckin'-rageous!* RIOT? I'm writing this up for the Ark—oh, you already did? Well, let's run both of 'em side by side, yours and mine. Or—ooh! Ooh! I've got it—yours, mine, and the Oregonian's—triple column! Put the facts out there, let the people decide."

At this moment a crash issued from the kitchen, followed by a ringing exclamation of "Shit! Shit! Shit!"

Raoul scuttled to the kitchen door with George at his heels. Martha stood there with tomato sauce splashed across her dress and broken dishes all around her.

"Kee-rist," George whistled. "What's all this?"

"You should know!" she cried. "I'm sick of living with pigs."

"You mean the kitchen?" Raoul ventured, only now noticing what a mess he'd made during the night.

"Hey, breaking all the dishes—that's RADICAL, Martha! Didn't know you had it in you!"

"That's right. Turn your back." Martha followed George out of the kitchen. "Make a big joke out of it. That's right."

"Laughter is sanity, Martha."

"To you! I'm too busy to laugh. I cleaned this whole kitchen yesterday!"

"You want a medal?"

"You could help me!" she squealed. "You could help!"

"You must be kidding," he said incredulously. "I've got a *story* to nail down."

"Well, I've got a *job* interview!" wailed Martha.

"Fine, you're excused too. Raoul, my boy—" George threw his arm around the little man. "Looks like you're elected to clean this shit up."

"I think whoever made the mess should clean it up." Martha took a step toward George, glowering accusation.

"Martha," Raoul began timidly, but Martha powered him aside to continue advancing on George. But she had to fire her curses at his back, because he was busy rooting in one of the storage bins now, for paper and pencils.

"Look on the bright side," he barked over his shoulder at the plump Martha. "You can't cook a genteel breakfast, this could be your chance to skip a meal. Might do you good. Think of all the starving people in Tierra Del Fuego." He slammed out of the house to chase down his story.

Only Raoul saw the stricken look on Martha's face. "Martha," he said timidly. "Can I drive you somewhere for breakfast? And then to your interview?"

"Oh, Raoul!" She turned and tearfully hugged him. "You're such an angel. That hateful George!"

The Airport

After delivering Martha, Raoul came back to clean the kitchen. What a wonderful surprise he would give his roommate. He began looking for a sponge. But wait, he couldn't use a sponge yet. He had to stack the dishes first. No, come to think of it, before he could stack the dishes, he had to clear the counters. No, wait, garbage out, that came first. No, no, first of all get organized. That was step one. But how could he do that when his whole life was so chaotic? That's when it struck him: the very first step in cleaning the kitchen was reforming his entire life!

Too long had excess been his strategy—the hope that pushing to the limit with weed, work, and wakefulness would break him through to the next level of reality. Now a thrilling vision of austerity swept him. He would clean his room. Yeah! He would stop eating meat. He would go to sleep early at night and get up at dawn each morning to run five miles in Washington Park. In fact, why stop at five? Why not ten miles?

Raoul's mind filled with romantic scenes from his new life— pictures of himself doing jumping jacks in a meadow at dawn. The images were so vivid, in fact, that they wearied him a bit. He felt ready for a break. Rome wasn't reformed in a day. He decided to smoke some dope and have breakfast at the airport.

He rolled two neat joints in the kindergarten and trimmed them to fit in a wooden matchbox. He wrapped the box in cloth and put it in the same pocket as the letter from Zara. He took a paper bag out of the refrigerator and stashed it in his glove compartment, then drove to the airport.

A pretty good crowd had turned out for a Wednesday. Plenty of cars in the short term parking lot. Raoul spotted one pretty girl immediately and another within a few minutes. He lit a joint. Then, from the paper bag in his glove compartment he took a bottle of wheat grass juice, a soy cake, and a vial of dried kelp. While consuming this breakfast, he opened the letter from Zara and skimmed the single handwritten page. Yes, it was short, but then she never wrote long letters. It opened in the usual way: "Dear Raoul, I haven't heard from you in a long time. What's happening? I haven't written to you either, I guess, but my letters are so boring anyway, unlike yours." And it went on in the usual way: she talked about her job and the color of her new room and the size of her closet and the new diet she was trying out. Yes, Raoul thought fondly, she did write extraordinarily boring letters. And then, right near the end, she slipped it in, so casually: "After all this time, guess what: I've fallen in love again." For a moment the page whited out before his eyes. Wordless thoughts whistled in his head. Raoul backed up to the beginning of the sentence and read slowly to the end:

"After all this time, guess what, I've fallen in love again. And this time I believe it's the real thing. But that's enough about me, how about you? How are you doing? *What* are you doing? Maybe I'll see you one of these days. I have to go to San Francisco for my grandmother's 70th birthday. Portland isn't *so* far out of the way. Anyway, do write to me, will ya'? Your letters are always so full of crazy ideas. Love, Zara."

Raoul lit his joint again and took several short, choppy puffs. "In love *again*," he muttered. His heart flopped inside his chest like a wild animal trapped in a house. "With who?" his thoughts screamed. He took another drag off the joint and his blood settled. Nearly a year he'd been hollering this question. But now a new interpretation struck him. In love *again*. "Again" could only mean "for a second time". The person she was in love with *now* was someone she had fallen in love with before. Well! She was talking about him, of course. She had fallen in love with Raoul for the second time. That could be what she meant. Had to be. Sure.

Looking out, he saw a luminous spot in the gray sky, where the sun was beginning to wear through the cloud cover. The heavens themselves had approved his interpretation. Raoul jumped out of the car and ran to the terminal. He examined the "arrivals" board to see what flights were coming in from the East. A plane from New York and one from Chicago were due within the hour. She could be on either of those. Raoul met them both and lingered for several minutes after the last passenger had disembarked from each one. Well, the signs didn't say she was coming in today, just that she was coming. Someday. Maybe soon. He retraced his steps through the terminal.

Something caught his eye—a window display of furs and jewelry. The complexity of the image riveted him—a reflection of himself overlaid on merchandise. He was wondering how he might render this in a painting. At that moment, she hurried past.

His camera eye caught only a quick snapshot in the glass: high cheekbones, long, full mouth. He gasped and whirled. The corridor was packed. Someone bumped into him. He caught his balance against the display window. The crowd parted for a second, affording him another glimpse of her just as she was disappearing around the corner.

Raoul rushed out of the corridor but she was gone. Where could she have gotten to in such a short time? He blustered into the souvenir store and explored it all the way to the back. Not there. Must be the coffee shop.

His eyes took a few seconds to gear down to the gloom in the restaurant. The first item to emerge for him was the gray coat. Then the face came into focus. There she was, at the end of the counter.

"One?" The hostess had appeared beside him."

"THE one," he told her and started toward the counter, toward the woman who looked so much like Zara. Slight motions of her head that brought different aspects of her face to view, that was Zara. The languor of hers that others mistook for boredom. That was her. But as he moved toward her the chestnut waves of hair dissolved into a beehive hairdo held in place by hair spray. Not even a Zara look-alike. She was a different person and yet there were traces of Zara in her. What did that mean? He made his way back into the crackle of the hall, where announcements boomed, of arrivals and departures.

The background thrum of desire was gone. Now it was dread that drove the blood through his body. Apparitions of Zara had appeared before, as faces in a distant crowd. This was the most jolting one yet. He had driven 20 blocks down Sandy Boulevard when he suddenly understood the meaning of the sign. The universe was trying to tell him Zara wasn't actually The One. Zara was only a precursor to the One, like John the Baptist had been for Jesus.

Then he pressed the gas pedal, gunning his car into traffic. If Zara wasn't The One, how would he recognize her when they met? She might not look like Zara but she'd have traces of Zara. That's what the Universe was saying. But lots of girls were like Zara in some ways. How could he know which were the important ways? For all he knew, The One was somebody he'd already met without knowing she was the One. Marica, for example. Or if she was a complete stranger, was he supposed to go out and look for her? Or just wait? It was all so difficult. Why weren't the mystic signals from the heart of the universe more clear?

Raoul went home and took out the box of Zara's letters. He put today's letter back into its original envelope and filed it in its correct chronological place: it had originally come a little over two years ago today.

Then he browsed through the rest of the letters until he found the one in which she had scolded him, "I wish you'd quit complaining that I don't care about you. I care about you at least as much as you care about me, but you must see, my dear, that my first commitment is to Travis. He needs me, Raoul, don't you see?" Oh, that was a painful one the first time around. But now it had acquired, as they all had done, a patina of melancholy sweetness.

Raoul took that letter out of its original envelope, trying to avoid seeing any more of it than he could help; that would make it more fresh when it came in the mail. He put it in a new envelope and forged his own address and Zara's return address on the envelope in Zara's handwriting; he had gotten pretty good at copying her hand in the time since he had been doing this, recycling her old letters to himself. He got a pleasant jolt of pain and love each time one of the letters arrived. He wasn't crazy. He knew he wasn't really getting any letters from Zara. He just knew how to give himself that jolt of pleasure and pain. Sending himself Zara's old letters was just a mechanism.

George Writes a Story

George heaved mountainous sighs of relief as soon as he hit the street. Thank God he was out of there. He didn't want to be around when Martha figured out who had made that big mess. She would probably eat poor little Raoul alive. Well, George's conscience was clear. He hadn't ratted.

Anyway, Raoul was on his own. George had a deadline to beat, the same one as always. If he didn't finish this piece within the hour, he would never finish it at all. The hellhound of futility was never more than a step behind him. Time was limited.

George parked his car on quiet elm-shaded Main Street and walked the pleasant block and a half to the stately old Multnomah County Library. It was a stone building trimmed in red brick. Inside, a warm bustle of humanity engulfed George, a swirl of families and teenagers, of clean-shaven old men and bearded young hippies, of scholarly-looking bums and girls with long pioneer-style dresses.

Along the wall to the right stretched corkboards bristling with cards and announcements. Someone was offering a class in techniques of dreaming. Someone was selling a 57 Chevy with all the trimmings. George was surprised and amused to notice a card by Raoul. On the card a cobweb of decorative letters spelling out the words "Home Blown Stones" framed a line drawing of a man with long hair. The man held something in his mouth. It might have been a cigarette, except for the flask ballooning out from the tip of it. Evidently, then, the man was blowing something out of glass. The graceful flask was filled with a dim suggestion of what seemed an impossibly detailed cityscape from afar but dissolved into scribbles and dots on close inspection.

"What the hell is this guy doing in Portland?" George wondered. One expected this kind of facile skill in New York or L.A., pulling down big bucks from an ad agency. George studied the card a little more closely. Evidently it was advertising some kind of product or service: below the logo and the picture were the words "MADE TO ORDER" and the Yamhill House telephone number, but there was no mention of what product was made to order. Well, perhaps Raoul did not belong on Madison Avenue after all.

George pulled away from the board with regret. The story. He still had some faint glimpse of how delightfully absurd it all was. But getting it down! Ouch! Well, he would have to grit his teeth and get to work.

He found a spot in the Literature Room and scribbled with manic intensity for 45 minutes, pausing now and then to grab his face and think. Then the pauses became longer and the fits of writing more brief. He began to wriggle as he wrote. Ever more frequently he adjusted his collar, twisted his neck about, and took deep breaths. He began to notice the close warmth of the library, the smell of the bum at the same table. Corrosive thoughts came through the cracks in his concentration. Why bust his balls over this trivial project? For what? For whom?

"Ha!" This time he uttered his sardonic laugh aloud and drew glances from two shabby scholars. For friends and family of the staff and their friends and families, or as Sval so pompously called it: The Community. Jesus! A herd of isolated souls moving temporarily in the same direction—that's all the fancy label meant. Community! "Ha!"

That did it. George was finished writing for the day—which, on this piece, meant forever. He gathered up his papers and paraphernalia and left the library. At two o'clock on a Monday afternoon, traffic on 10th street was sparse. He hurried across Main Street to Pepys Cafe for a hamburger and a cup of coffee.

George had a fondness for his natural urges. When a guy was good and hungry it was easy to have a purpose in life. He ate peacefully, staring out at the slick sidewalk and the beautiful sfumato of fog blending red bricks into the milk-grey stones of the venerable old library building.

Then, in walked trouble. Marica Margolis in an orange Day-Glo poncho came pushing through the double doors with a stack of books under her arm. She stood at the threshold for a moment, puffing and blowing into her hands for warmth.

George began at once to gather his belongings. He knew well enough that even though she didn't like him, Marica would come sit with him and play catty-polite, just because they knew each other and were, ahem, both part of the, hats-off-please, all-bow: Community. Easier all around if he left.

But they met at the door, and he had to say something.

"Hey, Marica," he mumbled, flinching inwardly in anticipation of a putdown.

"Hello, George." she said, looking at him benignly. Her lofty smile at once fixed and beatific, announced that she was above petty quarreling, civilized enough to be polite so long as he behaved himself. "What are you doing here?"

"Just using the library for an hour," he said, a trace too loudly. "Knocking out something for the Ark."

"Oh, just 'knocking it out,' huh? In the library? I thought 'photography' was more 'your bag.'" She mouthed each word separately as if it had a contagious disease and must be kept away from its neighbors.

"Yeah? That what you thought?" He grinned, but it was merely a show of teeth. "I don't have a bag. I'll take a shot at anything, hit or miss."

"Oh, a Renaissance man."

"But trapped in the 20th century. A dinosaur, you might say."

She jumped a little at the word. "Well, I suppose that's one way to look at it. What kind of 'something' are you 'knocking out' for the Ark?"

"Straight-ahead fact piece about this so-called Food Stamp Riot me and Sval were involved in."

"Yes, I heard all about that from Sval." She compressed her lips. "I heard you got arrested on purpose so you could get an exclusive interview with Guillermo Sanchez, is that true?" She was smiling archly at him.

His eyes flashed a fire that died out quickly. "Read all about it in the Ark," he said finally.

"If," she reminded him, "the collective approves." Still smiling.

"Yeah, sure. Nice talking to you."

"The pleasure was entirely mine."

As with Martha and Raoul, George sighed with relief when he got away from Marica. Thirty whole seconds with the Dragon Woman and he had come out relatively unscathed.

Unlike the encounter with Martha and Raoul, however, this one resonated in his mind. As he drove to Sval's house the memory of it continued to emanate a curious, steady, almost physically palpable hum.

Sval opened the door to let in a moist and miserable George. "Come in," he said. "Can I get you a beer?"

"Brrr. On a day like this? It's got to be cognac."

"I don't have any."

"Figures. I'll get some and park it here. So there'll be some every time I come. Here's the story."

Sval's nerves faltered at the sight of the thick, soggy sheaf of pages covered with George's hieroglyphics. "Great. Great," he said in a soft voice, privately framing diplomatic ways to couch his rejection of the manuscript. "I'll read this in the kitchen, if you don't mind, away from the watchful eye of the author."

George snorted and hurried into the living room to plop in the overstuffed mauve armchair. Springs sproinged when he landed. He laid his pipe and pipe tobacco on the broad threadbare arm of the chair and set to work searching his pockets for a pipe tool. "That thing's a mess, huh?" he called out.

From the kitchen came a grunt in reply.

George lit his pipe and sucked on it fiercely. "Just tell me if anything can be salvaged out of all that crap," he yelled suddenly.

A grunt came back in reply.

George puffed away for a few more seconds. Then he called out, "If you can't read my handwriting, speak up."

"Ssssh," Sval said. After a short silence a slight chuckle issued from the kitchen.

At that George bounded out of his chair like a human cannonball shouting, "What? Which part? What?"

"The title," Sval shouted back with some irritation.

"You've only gotten to the title all this time?"

"Will you relax and let me read? Let me read it, for God's sake, and then we'll discuss it."

"Okay, uh huh. Fair enough," George receded back into the armchair and into abstraction. Another chuckle got a slight start out of him, but he controlled himself. Then came another chuckle and another from the kitchen. George only sucked more fiercely on his pipe and let his gaze hop around the room, from the brass-banded tea chest to the stacks of magazines to the poster of a man in a trench coat flashing for a statue above the plea: "Expose yourself to art."

Sval glided back in. "Well," he declared coolly, "You've rendered my own shabby half-effort on this theme obsolete."

"What's that supposed to mean?"

"I mean that this account tells the story more than adequately. There's no point in my plowing the same ground for the sake of some slight variation in aesthetic approach."

"What are you saying? It's okay? It goes in the paper or what?"

"Oh, in my opinion, definitely, yes. It should, I'll back it. Of course it's a bit on the crude side—does need a little polishing."

"Yeah? Well, that's why I brought it to you, Flaubert—but not all the way polished up to your bread thing. My story doesn't go with that kind of polish."

"Oh, precisely. It's the wham-bam karate-chop style of your voice that I like in this piece. And of course, you've achieved just what I would have wanted to get across, that impression of two befuddled good guys stumbling into the surreal—but I'm just concerned that a lot of people may not stay with the piece long enough to appreciate that aspect of it...the way it stands, that is."

"What do you mean, the way it stands?"

"Well, it's like a garden gone to weed, so to speak. Someone needs to go through it with a rake."

"So it's more or less okay."

"Oh, a cut above mere okay. The flaws are nothing a little editing can't fix."

"What kind of flaws?" George asked somewhat suspiciously.

"Just a few burrs that need to be filed off here and there."

"I see...burrs, huh? Weeds, huh? Well, I figured it for salvage. Chop it up if you want and use the parts. Let's just get it written—not that it really matters, come to think of it."

"No, no, that's not what I'm saying. You've got a gem here—but a gem in the rough, so to speak. The ending, for example—"

"I didn't get to the ending! You were there. Graft one on, we'll run it as a collaboration. Will the collective go for it?"

"I think it will."

"Then what's the problem?"

"Problem?"

"Yeah. You keep acting like there's an umbrella up your ass and any moment now it might open. What's the problem?"

"Well, since you're exercising your mastery of the blunt phrase, let me respond in kind. I've got a little bit of rancor stored up against you from Monday."

"From Monday?" George was astonished. "Draw me a map, Pap. I don't get it. What did *I* do to *you*?"

"I'm stunned that you could even ask. You came charging into my life like a drunken bull and now you haven't a clue what's bothering me? You come blasting in like a hurricane, just about got me thrown into jail, made me miss the Ark meeting—possibly the most important meeting this paper will ever have—collecting your bail, and when it's over you don't have one word of apology. No sign that you even know you've broken all the furniture of my life. I hope you're following my metaphor."

"Fuck your metaphor. Let me get this straight. *I* came charging into *your* life? *You* called me, remember? To help you get your car off the road. A life-or-death situation, you said. Huh? That's number one. Number two, *I'm* the one that got thrown in jail. How come you're the one griping? Third, you collected my bail and hey, thanks—but I paid you back cash, soon as we got home—right?"

"Granted. But I spent an hour collecting that bail of yours. Getting that money back to all the people I borrowed from is going to be a chore on my schedule all next week!"

"All right, listen: I came out on the freeway and saved you from a life and death situation, right? Chalk up a couple of hours for me. You went around collecting bail. Chalk up a couple for you. Comes out about even, you ask me. Want to quibble about minutes? Maybe you came out short, I don't know. I'm not used to bookkeeping in a friendship. Who owes who. But maybe you don't look at this as a friendship. I don't know."

"Well no, I—I do actually. An incipient friendship at any rate. But the way to move a friendship forward is not to sweep things under the rug. I felt bullied and badgered by you Monday, so I'm bringing it up. Is that wrong? I don't think so, but I stand willing to be edified."

"Nah, not wrong. Spill your guts. What'd I do? Bottom line. I didn't show enough gratitude? I'm not the type to gush, you know, but if that's what you want, I'll go ahead and say it. You went to bat for me yesterday, goddamn it, I appreciate that, man. Really. I respect that." George, looking solemn, thrust his hand out for Sval to shake.

"All right, all right," Sval's face reddened. "I wasn't looking for a male bonding ritual." But with that ironic disclaimer he did take George's hand and the two men shook, then dropped their hands in embarrassment as soon as feasible.

Sval picked up George's manuscript again. "All resentment and weirdness aside, this is wonderful—unexpectedly, I might say. But I also say, without prejudice, it needs editing. Nine out of ten people aren't going to get this."

"And I say, edit it," George said. "I leave it entirely in your hands. In fact, you sell it to the collective. I couldn't sell cheese to a rat."

"It won't need any selling when I'm through with it," Sval promised loftily. "The collective is going to love it."

"Even when they know who wrote it?"

"What difference'll that make?"

"It'll make a difference to one person, I can tell you."

"Who?"

"The Dragon Lady."

"Who's the Dragon Lady?"

"Marica Margolis, of course—who else?"

"You think she—"

"I know she. I ran into her downtown and she put it on the table. Brr."

"Dragon Lady, huh? I never heard that one before."

"What would *you* call her?"

"Oh, I suppose she can be somewhat prickly at times, but—"

"To put it mildly! Ouch! First time I saw her she laid into me—remember? At that meeting? And she didn't even know me then. Insane!"

"But not inexplicable." Sval directed a professorial look at George over the rims of his wire spectacles.

"What do you mean? I remind her of her father or something? What're you getting at?"

"I mean," said Sval, "that you make a great show of not worshipping at the same church as the rest of us—the Church of the New Consciousness, so to speak."

"Church of the New Consciousness—yeah. I've noticed that church."

"So you must have noticed that Marica is something of a priestess in said church. Ergo there's hostility between the two of you. Make sense?"

"Not so fast there, padre. You're a deacon in that same church—how come I get along with you?"

"Well, in part because we're both men. She's a woman."

"Can't be denied." George placed his chin on his fist, "She's a woman."

"Further, the issue of sexism is the central pivot of the New Consciousness."

"Yeah, I'm starting to pick up on that." He scowled thoughtfully. "What is it with this country? I leave for a coupla' years and suddenly men and women aren't talking to each other."

"I wouldn't say that," Sval demurred. "I'd say men and women are talking to each other more than they ever have, but not in the old ways. No more proms, so to speak. The word 'date' is taboo and it's just as well, I say. The old conventions are dead, long may they stay dead. But that's not to say there are no rules. There are rules. Especially here in Portland—in the community, I mean. There's an unspoken code, and you, George, if you'll pardon me for saying so, trample on it right and left."

"Yeah? Like how?"

"Like, for example, bringing up baseball scores in the middle of a serious—"

"How could I do that? It's not even baseball season."

"Well, football then—"

"Basketball. In April there's nothing but basketball. The NBA playoffs, for God's sake—"

"All right, basketball, then. Whatever. The point is—macho, capitalistic, mainstream, competitive, Amerika-with-a-K sports—"

"Hold it, pal. You want to talk religion, let's get one thing straight. Sports are my religion. Have a little respect—"

"All right, but remember this is not my personal criticism of you. I'm just trying to acquaint you with the Code. If you want to live in Portland—in the community, I mean—you've got to know where the rocks are and which way the currents are flowing. It's just like fishing. And what I'm trying to tell you is that sports are in there with white sugar and wonder bread: uncool, definitely much to be downplayed or avoided. Unless of course you're talking about something like lacrosse or better still, bike riding. Would you like to hear more? I don't want to get personal but you know how it is nowadays, the political being personal and all."

"Go on, this is interesting. What else is wrong with me?"

"Another thing wrong with you is that you win a lot of arguments. And that's not done around here. It's impolite to win an argument or anything else, though somewhat less so if you're a woman—no, don't laugh. I'm serious. Winning in general is a stain on one's honor— winners create losers, you know. And then too, there's the way a person goes about winning an argument. All ways are dishonorable but some are worse than others. For example, people are not to interrupt each other. They are not to raise their voice in—"

"All right, all right," George interrupted, raising his voice to out-shout Sval. "I get the picture. Guilty, I admit it. But that's George Lubick the animal, he's built that way. It's bio-chemistry. Everyone's got their DNA, even Marica. People who rub each other the wrong way should stay out of each other's hair—that's my philosophy. Simple, huh? But no—I walk into a room, she comes right over to bristle at me close up."

"She does?"

"Hell, yes, I tell you, she's got it in for me personally. She's never going to let a story I write into the paper as long as she's got veto power."

Sval leaned back in his chair, resting his head in a web of his fingers. "Well," he said, "I'll shepherd it through the collective meeting. Don't you worry."

First Facilitator

Marica, the first to be elected "facilitator" under The Proposal, launched into her duties with zeal. What these duties were, no one knew, which only meant that Marica, as First Facilitator, would define the role for all the ages: heady stuff.

But Marica felt well up to the challenge. Ordinarily she worked two or three times a week as a substitute teacher, but she let the district know that this week she was not available. She let her roommates know they would have to get by without her company at dinner. She put Dare-to-Juggle on hold. As a teacher she knew the importance of dealing with bad energy early. Therefore, she intended to spend every possible moment at the Ark: if trouble arose, by God she would detect it early.

At the Monday Copy Meeting she announced her coup: she had finally talked Maureen Junechild into writing a long piece about Witchcraft, the modern-day feminist religion. At last, a page three feature by a woman! George presented a long piece about his arrest. She set aside her personal feelings and presided over the discussion of George's with sublime equanimity, knowing that as First Facilitator, she had to set an example for all facilitators to follow. Some people found George's piece hilarious, but since page three was taken, it was given page 7. On Monday, Tuesday, and Wednesday the collective—that is to say, whoever happened to be in the office—facilitated ably by Marica, solved a challenging series of small crises.

Then came production night and the office was packed. Martha was sitting at a table in the center of the room, pressing out headlines.

George was laying out his story on page 7. Marica was laying out the "Letters" page while keeping a motherly eye on the room as a whole.

A small group had gathered around page 7 to read George's story. Sporadically they burst into laughter, pointing out or loudly quoting phrases to one another. The laughter grated on Marica. All right, the story had a certain breezy wit—surprisingly literate from such a brute— but then, according to rumor, and she wouldn't be surprised, it was actually Sval who had written the story and let George have the byline. Some kind of male loyalty thing. Marica's lips compressed, and she let her gaze wander. Martha, doggedly pressing out headlines, looked up and frowned every time laughter exploded from the group at page 7. Marica understood her feelings perfectly—a George Lubick fan club was bound to gall.

Presently George sat down across the table from Martha to proof his corrections. As he sat down his knee knocked into the table leg. Martha tsssked and glared, but George didn't notice. He was leaning over his paper, biting his pencil, his eyebrows drawn together in a bushy V. In his absorption, he reminded Marica of Rodin's Thinker—a muscular brute massively engaged in simple thought.

Then, making some mark on the page, he bore down so hard that his pencil lead broke and flew away with a ping, drawing fresh hostility from Martha. George flung his pencil down and grabbed another from a group situated halfway between himself and Martha. The neat arrangement of those pencils—set along precise lines radiating from Martha—should have warned him they were not for general use.

Martha hrumphed, clapped her hand on her waist, and hit George with the strongest disapproval a mere look could fire, but this too bypassed George's notice.

Martha then swept all the remaining pencils and implements closer to herself and made a great show of arranging them in neat rows by her elbow.

Marica observed this little drama with growing discomfort. She considered stepping in, but while she hesitated, George finished his job at Martha's table and sprang to his feet. He elbowed between a couple of stragglers still reading his story, dropped the sheet of corrections on the table, slashed individual phrases out of the sheet with an Exacto knife, and positioned them quickly with his thumb. He could not possibly have gotten the words aligned with such rapid, careless motions, but he glanced at his handiwork and seemed satisfied. Then he stared around the room for a moment. Martha was watching him like an owl now, and Marica was watching them both. George caught sight of the plywood press type files in the corner—aha! Just what he was looking for. He moved to the cabinet like a runaway train.

One by one he started yanking folders of press type out of the shelves, riffling through them, and dropping them on the table. Martha watched in dour dismay, until at last she had seen enough. With a low slow rumble, she rose. Her chair scraped harshly against the tiles. She descended upon George. "Stop that. Just stop. You stop." The sounds sputtered from her like artillery bursts.

"Huh?" He frowned and turned.

Martha gulped. She looked scared now, to have taken on George, but she waded bravely on. "You're doing it all wrong. You don't have to take out every sheet. Can't you see the shelves are marked? Which one do you want? Helvetica? Times Roman?"

"Names don't mean shit to me. I gotta see 'em. Do you mind?"

"Yes, I do mind. I spent all weekend organizing those shelves and now—put that down, put it down! Get away! Move *away* from the press type." She snatched the sheets he was holding and started putting them back, one here, one there.

"What the hell do you think you're doing?"

"Cleaning up your mess," she barked.

"What mess? I'm not finished yet."

"Oh, you want to finish, do you? You tear up half the files in two minutes and you want me to leave you alone *so you can finish*? No way. Give me your headline. I'll do it."

George gawked at her speechlessly. He had picked up one more sheet of press type idly, but Martha snatched this away from him too and sat down at the table heavily, hunching over the press type like some animal protecting its young.

"Oh, all right," said George, disgusted. "If you're that eager to press out headlines, here. Two columns." He tossed her a scrap of paper with his headline written on it. "48-point type should do it."

She glanced and snorted. "Descent to Hog Heaven? What kind of headline is that?"

"Hey, if you've got a better one, spit it out."

"I'm too busy to think up headlines for you," she said sharply.

"That's the headline then. Do it."

"When I'm ready," she hissed.

"When you're ready? The hell if I'll take that shit! Do it now or get out of the way and let me do it."

"Oh? You'll do it?" She gave him a thin smile. "You're going to press out a headline? That I'd like to see. If only we had enough press type to waste. But we don't. And I sure don't have time to teach you."

George threw his head back and roared with laughter. "The fine old art of press type?" he shouted, awash with mirth. "You don't have time to teach me? Gimme' a break! It's kindergarten work, Martha! Look, I don't have the mindless stamina to hang around this place for six hours. See? So, one of us is going to do this headline now. Now! Get me?"

Martha's eyes went dead. She stepped away from George and shuffled to her chair, her face the color of plasterboard. Suddenly Marica felt very helpless. She had missed her moment. She knew what Martha was doing as she gathered her tools and papers into neat piles and trundled them with ant-like industry to their various drawers, shelves, and cubbyholes. Martha was going home.

Marica scuttled quickly to her friend and put her arm on Martha's shoulder, feeling taut muscles under the soft flesh. "Where are you going?" she asked.

"I can't work with that man George. I'm sorry. I have to leave. Don't worry, I'll be back Sunday to clean up the mess you-all leave behind."

"Martha, you can't leave. You're essential around here."

"Oh sure."

"I mean it. Who's going to do headlines? Linda's going home at eleven and no one else is coming in. We've got a ton of them left to do."

"Oh, anyone can do headlines," Martha said. "It's kindergarten work."

"Well, but most people don't. Martha, look. If it's him or you, I choose you. Why should you be the one that goes home just because the two of you can't work together?"

Martha gave Marica a long look: respectful, but loaded. "What difference does it make who *you* choose?"

Marica understood the reproach. "I'm—I'm the facilitator this week," she faltered.

"So? Can you make him go?"

Marica paused on that one. What could she do—walk up and tell the brute to get out? What if he refused?

It was a question Marica had faced often as a substitute teacher, especially with 13- or 14-year-old boys. You could never tell when a group of those would coalesce into a gang and discover their physical strength. Redefine-the-situation was the only wisdom she had ever found for dealing with male energy on the brink—turn it into a game, a learning experience. Define the male sexuality right out of it. And never give a direct order—because if you pushed them and couldn't budge them, you let them know their power—

"Just what I thought," said Martha. "Don't worry, I don't blame you. I'll just go."

"No, wait." Marica restrained her with a light touch. "Just give me a minute." She went over to George and murmured in a low voice—she didn't want to get the whole Ark involved in this after all—"Come over here to page 2, will you?"

She leaned over the boards with him as if to show him something on the page, and he, taking her gesture at face value, leaned and looked. Then, with their heads close together, their sides actually touching, both of them looking down at the page, she told him, exactly as if discussing a problem in design, "I think you should leave right now."

"Leave?" He jerked his head around to look at her.

"Ssh. Please—let's not drag the whole staff into this. Yes, leave."

"Leave," he said again in a stricken voice, not perceptibly lower than before.

"I don't mean permanently," she said quickly. "But if you've got any sense of decency, leave right now or else Martha's going, and there'll be no one to do headlines. You've got your piece in, the only helpful thing left for you to do is go home."

He stared at her, his eyes flashing with more hurt than anger. "Why me?"

"I told you. Martha—"

"I never touched Martha. She can do her thing, let me do mine. I'll leave her alone, she leaves me alone. Fair?"

"No, George. People can't work in a tense environment. I know this has to be worked out openly in the long run, but not tonight or the whole staff might get involved and this is production night, so we can't—"

"Having me in the room spoils the atmosphere? Is that what you're saying?"

"You're a disruptive force right now, yes."

"I'm crude."

"Crude. Okay. That's your word."

"Working class."

"I didn't say that."

"Why don't you like me?"

"I never said I don't like you." She colored. "Can we stick to the subject please?"

"I'm sticking to it like glue, lady. You think I should leave. Isn't that the subject? Why don't you like me? Give me a clue, Chri'sakes. Maybe I can change, huh? Not likely, I never have, but hey."

Marica almost let herself be drawn into his game: he wanted to know what was wrong with him? Oh, she could give him a list. But that's just what he would want: turn it into a battle and then he could win. She had to maintain control of definitions somehow. Something flashed in her soul; and though it vanished like a minnow she knew what it was and that it was good. It would be so daring; it took her breath away, but she knew she had to take the risk.

"Give me your hand," she said.

"Huh?"

"Your hand. Give me." She reached out.

"What? Huh?" George spluttered his befuddlement as she towed him toward Martha. Of the two, Martha actually put up the greater fight, pulling back with a sour, "Let me go," but Marica held on, and soon she had managed to tow her two problem cases out to the hall.

"Now," she said, striking just the right note between severity and sorrow, "You two are going to work on this. You have a history, I know, I can just tell. You have a lot of anger to let out, so why don't we make a circle, hold hands, and get centered, then talk."

George of course rolled his eyes at the suggestion, but he did as she said; he took Martha's hand, albeit with a great show of overburdened tolerance. Marica glowed from within. She felt almost holy; this was facilitating for the ages!

Scarcely had the three joined hands, however, when a clatter of footsteps sounded in the antechamber. A door jerked open and Ray Perkins burst upon them with a raucous: "Holy shit! What's this, a prayer meeting? People, it's Thursday night! Chop!"

"Oh, shoo, Ray! Go back to your own work," Marica barked at him.

"Well excuuuuse me! Is this the famous Proposal at work? We going to shave our heads and chant Hare Krishna, is that what comes next?"

"Don't be an ass, Ray," she began.

But then Sval poked his head around the left side of Ray. "What's the problem out here?" And soon a whole herd of murmuring curiosity seekers were pressing into the hall, and someone near the front was explaining to those further back, "The Martha-Marica clique is ganging up on George Lubick out there." Dizzily, Marica saw control of definitions slipping away from her. Already Sval stood there, listening earnestly to Martha's troubles, nodding and pursing his lips and considering, as if it was his job to consider things tonight, and he was keeping George's eruptions and interruptions at bay with a raised finger and an occasional cursory, "Excuse me? One moment?" Then he had finished with Martha and he turned to listen to George, keeping Martha at bay.

"So," he summed up finally, "The issue seems to be press type: who is going to do George's headline? It seems to me you have a significant area of agreement: you both want George to go home as soon as possible. What—"

"This is *not* about press type," Marica vehemently asserted. "Sval, it's deeper. It's about a relationship. There is a history here—"

But Martha cut her off with an outburst. "It's gotten to a point! I mean it's him or me. I can't go on like this night after night. The way he treats me, Sval—you should see: the kitchen at Yamhill House—five nights in a row I cleaned it up spotless and every time, by morning—by *morning*—"

"I did it!" Raoul suddenly shouted from the corner. "It was like a flood—there wasn't time! If only I could've gotten that picture of Mr. Natural up over the sink—but I had to get the ideas down. Honest! When you hit a gusher, you can't waste time washing dishes, you have to get the ideas down or your head will explode. And the woman you love—"

"Yamhill House," Marica cried out. "Of course! You two live in the same house! Go on, Martha—what about the kitchen? Now we're getting somewhere—"

But quick as a knife, Sval sliced his cool voice between hers and the rising din: "I beg to point out that most of us don't live at Yamhill House. Let's keep the discussion focused on the issue here and now—"

"The kitchen at Yamhill House is the issue. It's here and now in their hearts," Marica protested. "Don't you get it, Sval? Between these two human beings—"

"Booooo!" someone shouted. "Yamhill House off-limits!" The entire staff had gathered in the hall by now. Marica's intimate session with two confused human beings had turned into a full-fledged collective meeting tied in knots around "issues."

"Tell them, Martha," Marica implored. "Go on about the kitchen."

But Martha only shrugged unhappily. "All I know is I can't work at the Ark anymore if George is going to be here."

"And all I know is, I ain't leaving," George declared.

"Oh yeah?" Ellen, a sometime production volunteer from Athena Coffeehouse raised her voice. "How about if we throw you out?" She turned angrily to the bulk of the crowd. "What are we, a bunch of liberals? There's a woman in pain here, people! She needs our support! What's wrong with all of you? Is there anyone who thinks this man is *not* a pig? Why do we tolerate him? He's a disgrace, he offends me. I say, let's vote him out of the collective, right here, right now. All in favor, say aye." Some half a dozen voices raised a lusty chorus.

"Um— that's not procedurally legitimate under The Proposal," Sval demurred.

"In fact, it's a pile of shit," Bill the Typesetter barked. "Why the hell should anyone have to leave because he offends Ellen? *She* fuckin' offends *me*! If someone's got to go, I say dump Martha. And as long as we're dumping, dump Ellen too. Troublemaker."

"All right, motion on the floor," shouted Ray Perkins. "One of these two is out of the collective as of tonight. If Martha goes, so does Ellen. Do I hear a second? Let's get this thing done and get back to work. We've got a paper to put out."

"Excuse me." Sval cleared his throat and held up his hands in a plea for silence. He remained in that posture, frozen and polite, until the last rustle of sound had faded. "For God's sake," he said finally. "We're trampling on procedure here. Don't we usually have some discussion between motion and vote?"

"What's to discuss?" Ellen scoffed.

"It seems like we're doing verdict first, trial afterward. I think there should be some discussion. Maybe someone wants to comment on this motion. Maybe we should discuss what it means. Anyone?"

No one spoke. And no one spoke.

Finally, Marica picked herself up off the floor. "Okay," she said in a tight contralto. "I'll say something. I'll tell all of you. This motion gives me the creeps." She was gratified to see that she still had some moral authority left. The whole room fell silent at her words, and she saw plenty of faces that looked ashamed.

"The creeps," Sval urged her gently. "Would you care to elaborate?"

"Kicking out one of our own like this, even a creature like George Lubick. What does it solve? When emotions come to the surface it should be an opportunity. We should dialogue around it, shout and learn and laugh and cry, come out of it changed. Ray says we've got a paper to put out. Is that all we're doing here—putting out a paper? I don't think so! I know I'm here to build a better Marica. I know *we're* here to build a better world. We don't have to say George is George and Martha's Martha, nothing's ever going to change. Change is what we're all about. We can be better. Our relationships can be better. The way we do things—we can rise to higher ground, if we don't give up when a situation like this comes up! This motion—huh! We'll all go home feeling worse and in the morning, there'll just be more suspicion and then pretty soon there'll be another motion, someone else moving to vote someone else out of the collective." Marica liked her words as she heard them and she hoped the collective would be quiet for a moment and absorb what she had said.

But Sval did not allow the necessary beat of silence. "Well..." he jumped in, "it sounds like the vote on this motion should be tabled until we can have a real all plugs-pulled-out one-on-one between George and Martha. Is that the sentiment? Let the two of them confront each other, no holds barred? I mean, I'm with Marica. A session like that, maybe we can all come out feeling better. Then when it's over, if we still want to vote on this motion, okay. That'd be the time."

"That's not—" Marica began but Sval cut her off before anybody even heard her voice.

"My house would be available if we want to do it. How about a week from next Friday? I could see about getting a keg."

Perkins raised his head and looked interested. "A keg?"

Marica knew then that it was over. The few loose threads that remained, Sval tied up quickly. He arranged to press out George's headline, liberating George to leave at once. Martha, mollified by this outcome, settled down to do a solid evening's work. The rest of the collective drifted back to their occupations.

And Marica, left alone in the hall, muttered at the emptiness, "*I* was supposed to be the facilitator."

The Showdown

The next week Sval took over the facilitator's chair, and thanks to blind luck his tenure went smoothly. George was in a dormant phase and Ray Perkins behaved himself. Maureen, who had run into a writer's block and missed her deadline during Marica's week, finally brought in the story about witchcraft, the feminist religion. It went on page 3 and enhanced Sval's reputation as a feminist man, even though Marica had solicited the piece, and Sval had done nothing whatsoever to reel it in.

On Sunday, after the paper had come out, Sval went into the office around noon to sweep up. He found Marica there scraping slivers of waxed paper off the layout tables. She was alone.

Sval said hello and received a small, cool response. He fetched a broom and a dustpan from the closet for himself and an extra set for Marica in case she wanted to join in. After a few minutes of silent sweeping, he broke the silence. "Well, we got the paper out. The forces of reaction foiled for another week, eh?"

Marica tossed her head. "I'm furious with you, Sval Hofby."

"With me?" But he knew what she was talking about, and he dropped his gaze. "I don't see why. I didn't do anything wrong. I invoked the provisions under 'Marica's Proposal.' Is all I did."

She was sweeping now too, bumping against the motley tables that filled the room, pushing the chairs aside with her body to make room for the broad, black, bristle-studded broom to run over the checkerboard pattern of slate tiles.

"Just took over the meeting, that's all," she muttered.

"I see." He kicked the dustpan to the corner and began sweeping. "Is that what's bothering you? You feel that I... what? Usurped your position? Marica, the situation was out of control. Perhaps I over-asserted a little," he admitted, "but—"

"Oh, it's not that," she snapped petulantly. They were sweeping misshapen circles around each other now, pushing dust into each other's piles.

"Then what is it? Frankly, Marica, I thought a bad situation came out all right that night and if I had anything to do with that outcome, I'm not ashamed. Why should I be? You'll have to draw me a diagram. Maybe I'm just ethically obtuse."

"I wanted to try," she burst out. "I was trying out a different way of dealing with a problem. But no! You had to barge in and turn it into a discussion of 'issues!' Why are you so afraid of your feelings, Sval? Why do you have to put yourself at arm's length from everything, turn everything into an abstraction and then explain it away? Just like a man! Honestly, you can't just turn George and Martha into a problem in Western Civ. They're two human beings. I'm disappointed in you, Sval. Disappointed is all. I expected a more sensitive approach from you. I was wrong. You're just like all the rest."

Sval frowned. "Are you sure that's it? Are you sure it's not because things got out of hands when you were facilitating—I'm sorry, I have to voice the possibility. You were supposed to keep things under control and you couldn't, so you're blaming me."

"Under control! That's exactly what I'm talking about—exactly! Controlling things might be your idea of what a facilitator should do at the Ark. It's not mine. Control," she repeated contemptuously. "Really. You're supposed to be a conscious man, Sval! Honestly, sometimes I have to wonder about your politics. I really do."

With tight lips and a clenched smile, Sval pushed his broom in swooping circles, his eyes fixed on the floor ahead of him. "Well," he muttered finally, "process is vital, but everyone went away happy that night. That says something about the process we used."

"Everyone?" Marica stopped sweeping and leaned forward furiously on her stick. "Don't you have any awareness of that poor woman?"

"What poor woman? Martha?"

"Who else! Don't you have any idea what she was going through that night? Oh, but I suppose you don't really take the trouble to be aware of *her*, do you?"

"I—" A ball of dread formed in Sval's stomach. He felt busted. He tried to think back—what exactly had Martha been saying? His thoughts rushed in wild fragments. Was she in trouble of some kind, and he wouldn't let her bring it up? His thoughts were debris carried on floods of guilt. Oh God, what a boor he must have seemed to Marica. He thought about that New Years with the Hofby clan. Everybody drunkenly singing Auld Lang Syne. Him and his mother off to one side, like always, feeling awkward about joining in. "What was she going through?" He forced the words out, his voice lacking any combative edge. He dreaded learning what he'd done.

"Oh, Sval." With the change in his tone, Marica's tone changed too. It still carried reproof, but such reproof as a loving mother might lavish on an incorrigible son. "You really don't know anything about Martha, do you? And you two are supposed to be such old, good friends! Do I really have to tell you?"

Gravely, stiffly, Sval said, "I'm not sure I take your meaning."

"You've been all over the world, Sval. She's never been out of Oregon. Just think about that for a moment. I'm exotic to her because I once lived in Berkeley. Don't you know what working at the Ark means to her?"

"I know. But—"

"Don't you understand what it means to her to be surrounded by people like you, who have had so many advantages in life? And she's so humble! Take the trouble to talk to her on a human level, Sval—she worships you. Doesn't that mean a thing to you?"

"Her feelings are her own. They don't impose some responsibility on me."

"They don't? You shock me, Sval."

"I'm the one that's shocked. Human beings should not worship one another. I thought on that point at least we could agree. I never asked her to feel that way about me. If she has that ailment, she has to be cured of it. And I can't be the one to cure her. I can't help her—at least not in the way you mean."

"And what way do I mean, may I ask?"

"Oh, pray, no: you tell me."

"No, I want to hear your idea first. Just what do you think I'm asking you to do?"

Sval pondered for a minute. To say what he thought would be utterly impolitic. "All I know is this," he said finally. "When I came out to the hall last Thursday night there was a quarrel well in progress between George and Martha. I tried to approach the thing impartially— I think I succeeded—and the issue was resolved. Not because I forced a decision on anyone but because the whole collective behaved in a rational manner. What I'm hearing from you now is that I had an obligation to take Martha's part in the quarrel, that I should have exhibited prejudice in her favor. And why? Because, for reasons of her own, she puts me on a pedestal. I can't agree with your proposition."

Marica shook her head slowly, pityingly. "Impartial? Is that what you call it? You took George's side totally. I don't mean your words. They don't matter a drop. Her feelings were hurt and you only wanted to deal with practical details, you made it seem like her feelings didn't matter, the only thing that mattered was the job. You showed no compassion for Martha. You made a fool out of her in front of the whole collective."

"The facts made a fool of Martha. She was being unreasonable."

"Did you have to call press typing kindergarten work?"

"I never said that. George—"

"Oh, what's the difference—George—you...You're one lump of attitude, the two of you. It's hard to say where one of you ends and the other begins."

"That's not true!"

"Yes it is! You're the brains, he's the brawn, you work as a team. How do you think poor Martha could stand up to you and George together? How could she stand up to the both of you?"

"Well, I never looked at it like that, but—"

"And besides!" Marica saw that she had chased Sval across his border and she came after him now in hot pursuit. "It was never really about press type. They have an interpersonal process they have to go through. I suppose you don't know what happened at Yamhill House the other day. She complained about a mess he'd left in the kitchen, and you know what he said? He said why does a fat pig like you need breakfast!"

"What?" Sval gasped. "She's not fat! How do you know?"

"She told me his exact words! Don't you think Martha feels insecure enough without a jab like that? Just when she needed a confidence-boost! She was so upset she blew a job interview. Now she might have to quit the Ark, because she didn't get that job."

"She has to quit the Ark because she didn't get a job?"

"It was a part-time job. It would've left her time for the Ark. Martha could get another full-time shit-job any time she wants, but a part-time job—that's gold. Do you see? Do you understand now, Sval? And who took time to find out any of this? No one. George gets off scot free, Martha's the whining troublemaker. Press type! Honestly, I don't know what makes that man tick! Or you, for that matter."

"Marica," he remonstrated. "Please! Recognize some hair of difference between George and me."

"How can I," she sniffed, "when you're always taking his side?"

Sval saw where this was tending. She was trying to maneuver him into abandoning George and denouncing him at the Friday night meeting. A picture of Martha fawning with gratitude flared in his mind. He bit his lip. "I don't know what went on between George and Martha in the Yamhill House kitchen, because I wasn't there," he declared stiffly. "I'm not prepared to make judgments on hearsay."

"Hearsay! Well I happen to know what George Lubick is like—"

"No, I don't think you do, Marica. I don't think you've looked beneath the surface."

"Ha!"

"There's more to him than you think. If you just opened up to him a little—"

"Life is too short, Sval. I do not have time to waste 'opening up' to George Lubick."

"I think he might surprise you if you would."

"That'll be the day."

Sval entered the Grog House and looked around. The low ceiling with its huge bare beams of rough timber seemed to compress the hot air. From the jukebox boomed the Steppenwolf song "Born to Be Wild." The first twelve people Sval focused on had tattoos. Then he spotted George in the corner and hurried to his booth.

"You're late," George scowled.

"You're lucky I'm here at all. I had to hitch part of the way," Sval reported gloomily. "My car broke down again." He poured himself a glass of beer out of George's pitcher and lit a cigarette, then glanced around at the big, bearded men with greasy hair and metal-studded clothes milling around in the smoke-filled room. "Savory clientele."

"You got that right. Why are we meeting in this hole?"

"I didn't want to run into anyone from the Ark."

"That ain't too likely here," George admitted. "So, what do we need to talk about that's so urgent? And so secret?"

Sval set his cigarettes down on the table and leaned sideways to probe in his tight pockets for matches.

"The Friday night meeting, George. The showdown between you and Martha."

"Oh yeah, me and the Duchess of Press Type, one on one."

"You're going to get your ass kicked."

"By the Duchess? Ho. She tries to lay her shit on me, I'll give it to her both barrels. We're supposed to be brutally frank, right, that's the idea? That's where I got the advantage, pal. She's never seen brutally frank like she's going to see next Friday—"

"Which brings me to my point. What do you think is going to happen at that meeting?"

"She'll call me names, I'll call her names."

"And may the most corrosive win? Think about it, George, what are you charged with? Being aggressive, insensitive, insulting—" Sval counted off the charges on his fingers. "And you're planning to storm in there and out-aggress, and out-shout, and out-insult Martha? You think that'll prove you innocent of all charges? You think that's what winning looks like? Let me tell you something, George. She's not going to call you names, she'll come in and be pathetic—Martha Williams, the harmless victim, poor, put-upon, and jobless. That's her strategy. You'll come out of that meeting looking like cream of shit. After you stomp on her, don't hold your breath waiting for applause. Weakness is a powerful weapon, my friend. You have no shield against that one. None."

George gulped. "Jesus, I see what you mean." He leaned against a thick wooden post grooved by generations of knife blades. "So what do I do? Shit, I can't put together a sob story to whine to the collective, I'd feel like a jerk."

"Why not offer her your job?"

"Huh? Offer her my...whaddaya'—are you nuts?"

"Why not? You're sick of it. You say it's killing your back, you're always grumbling. It's too many hours. Isn't that your daily drone?"

"I need the bread."

"You said you could get by on $30 and the census. You've got the census."

"Yeah, but it's not enough. I still need the 30 bucks on top. The fuckin' bookstore's more work than I need, but if I give it away, I'd have the census plus zip. I can't live on the census plus zip, I need another 30 bucks a week."

"How about a minimal under-the-table gig that nets you $35 a week and takes four hours?"

"What gig is that, professor?"

"My Ark route."

George had picked up the pitcher, but he put it down without pouring. "And what do you do?"

Sval shrugged and a frown passed across his clean blond features. "I've got other sources I can plug into," he said vaguely. "With my dying car, this route is getting less viable all the time anyway."

George shook his head. "It won't wash. She's trying to kick my ass off the Ark, I'm supposed to give her my job? No way. Look, she needs a job? Is that what's making her crabby? All right, look. You and me trade jobs, then *you* give her the bookstore job if you want. I can't do it. Not me."

"No. It's got to come from you. In fact, you've got to give it to her without mentioning one word about getting my route in trade. Promise?"

"What kind of sneaky shit you trying to pull?" George demanded uneasily.

"It's the deal. Take it or leave it."

"Pass."

Sval let out an exasperated sigh. "Why are you so dead-set against committing an act of public generosity?"

"I'd feel like a jerk."

"You'd look like a saint."

"What difference does it make to you?"

"I have a personal interest in making you look like a saint. What's the difference why?"

George frowned, drank some beer, and scrutinized Sval closely. "What are you, my agent or something?"

"Worse. I appear to be your partner in the public mind. There's talk of a George-and-Sval clique. Just the other day I heard someone imputing a statement to me that actually came out of your mouth, and when someone corrected this person, she said, 'Oh what's the difference, Sval and George, they're just one lump of attitude.'"

"Who was 'this person'?" George demanded suspiciously.

"Someone at the Ark. It doesn't matter who. The point is, my reputation currently seems bound to yours. If you're a jerk, I'm a jerk.

This gives me two options. I could cut loose from you, make clear to one and all that Sval Hofby is by no means implicated in any 'lump of attitude' represented by George Lubick. The Friday night meeting would be a good opportunity to play that card. I could join forces with Martha and call for your ouster from the paper. But you know something George? I don't feel like doing that."

"You don't."

"No I don't. It would be disloyal. The demands of honor on this question are clear. Which leaves the other option. I can try to rehabilitate your image. Understand what I'm saying?"

"Hmmm." The darkness washed out of George's face. "I see. You're telling me, if I give my job to Martha and take yours, I'll be helping *you* out."

"Exactly. It would be the *loyal* thing for you to do—as a pal of mine."

"Main point here is not to help out Martha, even though it's going to look that way. It's to help you."

"Exactly. It's to help out me. Will you do it?"

"Jesus. What am I, some kind of asshole? Of course I'll come through, man. You popped me out of a jail cell, buddy. I owe ya'."

"But George—" Sval cautioned, "—verisimilitude is of the essence. We want you to come out of this looking like a caring, decent guy with a lot of unsuspected depth."

"Well, that's not *so* fuckin' off the beam!" George protested.

"No, no, of course not. *You* know that, *I* know that, but we've got to get that message across to the most hardened, the most intractably bigoted, the most...oh, let's see, who's the most outré example I can think of? Well, this Dragon Lady, for example."

"Marica Margolis?"

"The same. Can you convince her? That's the challenge. Get to her and you've saved my standing in the collective."

"Jesus. That'll be a tough one. I see what you mean, though. Change her attitude and you've really done something." George pondered the problem for a moment, then pursed his lips. "Got to hand it to you, if there's any way at all, you've come up with it. Hand my job over to Martha right in front of the whole meeting. But I can't come in there and grow a halo all of a sudden, I've got to do it sort of offhand, maybe even hit her with a couple of low-key insults while I'm at it."

"Good. Good." Sval vigorously nodded his approval. "But low key, George. Barely there."

"I might say, here, Duchess, take my job, and I hope you choke on it, pigface."

"Well..." Sval tilted his head and fluttered one hand in the air dubiously. "We might have to work on that approach. Refine it a bit. Downscale it. Go for a little more subtlety. We'll practice between now and the meeting, get it perfect. We do have all week."

The Ark came out on Friday morning with another George Lubick triumph on page 5: an interview with Duke Silver, president of the Hell's Outcasts Motorcycle Club. George had shared a jail cell with Duke Silver after the food stamp riot and made friends with him. By the time the collective met for the big George-versus-Martha showdown, everybody had read the interview. Time alone had eroded some people of the fervor to impeach George, and the Duke Silver interview killed what was left of it. Most members of the collective could not quite remember what all the fuss had been about on that long-ago Thursday night. In the pre-meeting chatter the term "Thursday Madness" came up frequently, always spoken ironically, as if the speaker had been a bemused spectator at the madness, not a participant.

Martha's moment had passed and she knew it, but doggedly read her entire prepared statement in a plodding voice like someone giving testimony to a senate subcommittee. She said nothing about ousting George, merely offered a plea on her own behalf. She listed her contributions to the paper and pointed out that, however pedestrian they might be, they had some value. Or at least she did no harm. She thanked those who had treated her with respect and helped her to believe in herself—Marica especially (and she fluttered a glance at Sval that only he noticed). She went on to explain how much the Ark meant to her.

"This is my social life," she said, her throat thickening around the words, and she gazed around at the group. "I feel like you've become my family." Palpable discomfiture hung in the air. "But if you want me to quit coming here," she went on, "I guess it doesn't matter, because I'd have to quit pretty soon anyway. I have to go look for a full-time job, 'cause I just can't find any part-time job. I thought I had a good one a while back, but I blew the interview. Something happened that morning—" Here she cast a long look of reproach at George which no one failed to notice—"and I went to the interview so upset that I screwed up and they turned me down. Now I need money. I guess I'll have to go back to the old nine-to-five. After next week I'll probably be gone from the Ark forever anyway, so I don't know if this meeting was even worth having. I'm sorry I wasted everybody's time."

Martha had spoken for half an hour. George's response took only a few minutes. "Martha, if the Ark has to choose between you and me, I vote for me because I like me better, you want the truth, but I don't see why it has to come down to a choice. All right, we don't have the makings of a beautiful friendship, but why can't we just ignore each other? You wouldn't believe the shit I have to ignore, just to get through life. I'm sure it's the same for you. How about if I just add you to my list, and you add me to yours? And then, this other thing: you can't keep working at the Ark unless you get a part-time job? Hell, why blame me, I'm not against you getting part-time work. Tell you what, just to show good faith, you can have my job over at Powell's Bookstore. No—" he insisted against the flurry of titters. "I'm serious. I've been itching to quit that piece-o-shit job anyhow—my back can't take it, all that leaning and bending, and he wants me to recommend someone else if I go. It's four bucks and some an hour, 11 to 3 on weekdays. You ought to like it, with your insane passion for order—getting 5,000 books each in its exact right place...that ought to appeal to you."

All around George a puzzled buzzing flared up. Marica stared at him, doubt struggled with astonishment in her features. Sval leaned back, his arms folded, stealing a look at Marica and beaming with pleasure at this happy outcome.

Giant's Playground

The meeting had been over for hours, but Marica was still wandering around her house, straightening up, carrying dirty cups to the kitchen, feeling restless. She glanced at the clock: 11:30. Too late to call Sval: the risk of misinterpretation was too great. She only wanted to talk.

She put on a jacket. Her notes of the meeting were at the Ark, and she ought to write them up while it was all still fresh in her mind. When she got to the church, the Magic Lantern Theater's production of *Indians* was just letting out and she had to wade against an audience stream to reach the stairwell. Above the first floor, the church was deserted and all the offices were locked. Marica had a key to the Ark, however. She let herself in and turned on a light. As she was rummaging for her notes, she heard footsteps coming up the stairs. Sweat beaded on her upper lip and she felt the weight of darkness outside the door and throughout the three floors of emptiness below. Those motorcycle gangsters were coming up, she thought—the Hell's Outcasts. They didn't like the way George Lubick had portrayed their leader Duke Silver. They were going to sack the church and rape any women they found. She glanced at the back door: she might have time...but the footsteps had already reached the fourth-floor landing. A second later George Lubick's face appeared in the doorway.

"George!" she exclaimed in relief. "I'm so glad it's you." Then, with a blush, she amended her statement. "I was afraid it was someone worse."

"There's worse?"

"I meant—"

"I get what you meant. What're you doing here?"

"I could ask the same of you."

"I saw the lights. Asked myself what kind of brain-fucked fanatic would be up here working at midnight on a Friday."

"I wasn't working. I just came by to get some notes. And," she confessed, "I was feeling restless in the house—claustrophobic. It must be the weather."

"Me too, but it's not the weather. I came by because I had a feeling you'd be prowling around here and I wanted to run into you."

"Me? How come?"

"I was hoping you'd ask me why I gave my job to Martha."

"Why?"

"I was hoping you'd want to hear what I'd say."

A smile struggled for possession of Marica's lips. "Okay," she said finally. "Tell me and get it over with. Why did you?"

"It's a long story. Let's get a drink somewhere. You wanna'?"

"I don't know."

"That's got to mean yes."

"Explain." Her voice had a sharpness.

"Because when Marica means no, she says so, loud and clear."

"Maybe I mean maybe."

"You don't sit on fences. With you it's yes or it's no."

"Should I be insulted? Or is that some kind of compliment?"

"Let's talk about it over a drink. Where do you drink in this burg? I don't mean this beer and wine jive. Real hooch and no goddamn live band. Where d'you go?"

She took him to good old Hung Far Low's. It was nearly one a.m. by the time they arrived. Hung's had accumulated its usual late-night quota of crawling night-creatures. The light was yellow and looked like old varnish coating the faded calendars, the plum blossom prints, the plastic replicas of jade temples. The bar had a low ceiling and a thick carpet, but George wanted to sit in the restaurant where the high wooden booths afforded privacy. Marica felt more comfortable in there too. The bar reminded her too much of middle-aged men, menopause, and goat sex; all cocktail lounges did.

George talked about bookstores. She thought he was working up to an explanation of his job offer to Martha, but he never got there. Instead he rambled on about all the different stores he had worked in—big ones, little ones, college, trade.

"The worst was this big, mechanized franchise in New York City," he confided. "New books would get two days on the shelf, tops. If sales didn't boom, bam! Outa' there. Books had to be like gags. These big book chains are in business to rape books, stomp out ideas. It's right livelihood to rip 'em off. That's why I hadda' grow magic fingers at the cash register there—"

"Magic—you dipped money out of the till?" she gasped.

"Dipped? Ha! Ladled," he shouted. "Ladled, more like! It was a political act."

"Oh, I'm *sure*—'liberating' the money, I suppose."

"They wouldn't hire Black people to run the cash register. What was I supposed to do? Hell yes, I liberated their money. I had to be a debit to my race. It was my duty as a white man."

"But how much—"

"—Never counted. Ten here, twenty there. All I know's I never rode the subway. New York's almost do-able if you can always take cabs. If only I'd had an apartment. Every morning, when I got to work, I had to get on the phone first thing and line up a place to crash that night. But the good part was, I could give books away. That's the benny, working a book mill. One time this girl was paging through *Canterbury Tales*, a $50 job with the Rockwell Kent woodcuts—you know the kind, made for some rich pig's coffee table—and she's yukking it up like it's dead-cat jokes. She deserved that book. Anyone who gets a belly laugh out of the *Canterbury Tales*, right? As opposed to these fools who come by looking for books by the yard to fill out a design concept. I went up to her and said, you like that book, take it. That's yours. Take it and get out of here. Yeah, you get some compensation at a bookstore like that. You get to strike mighty blows against management."

At last Hung's began to shut down, and George and Marica were asked to leave. Without much discussion, they decided to move to the old Hotcake House, a 24-hour greasy-spoon on Powell Street, sleazier than Hung's in a different direction. Instead of deep-sea somnambulance, the Hotcake House offered glaring neon brilliance. Every fly speck stood out. It was a hangout for tough, jittery white kids with bad skin, greasy pompadours, stiff pointed bras, and cars with rear ends jacked up so high that they were always rolling downhill, a piece of the fifties that had survived into the seventies intact.

"So, at Powell's bookstore—" Marica resumed as she and George settled into a corner booth with mugs of thin, scalding coffee. "Do you…the magic fingers—"

"Hell, no. Powell reveres books. Plus, he's selling used books. He's expanding into a warehouse on Burnside, and the books keep pouring in. But he's got this mania for order—that's where Martha's going to fit right in. It's an okay job, but hell on the back."

"You have a bad back?"

"Does a bear shit in the woods? All down one leg and through the middle, woof!"

"You should see a chiropractor."

"Bah! There's no cure for back pain. You hear theories but it's all bunkum. Believe me, I've looked into this. A bad back is forever."

"That's what I don't understand about you, George."

"What?"

"Your hopelessness. You never even *try* to try. You're always downgrading everything, nothing's ever going to work, nothing's any good, in your opinion. Well, it's tough to be a human being, but we've all got that burden, you know? Sure a person gets depressed, but when you do, why try to bring everyone else down?"

"I'm a nihilist," he admitted. I know. I'm a nihilist, it's true. You know my problem?" He sat up in his seat, even leaned forward to make this important point. "I can't hide what I am. Wish I could—I'd do it in a minute, believe me! You think I want to deal with all this grief? The reaction people have to me? I'd love to be all polite and nice, but I just can't."

"I never said hide what you are, George. I would never say a thing like that. Me, of all people. I only say it's partly up to you if life is ugly or beautiful. You do make choices. You can't help whether you're up or down, but you can choose what to do about it—either you try and change, or you just sink into a hole. You do have a choice to make, and you choose to wallow in despair, that's what you do. Well, you're free to wallow in anything you want, and I'm sure you will, but it's not fair to the rest of us."

"Listen, you've never seen me when I'm really wallowing. When I'm out here where people can see, this is as good as it gets. When it's bad, you don't want to see. Anyway, I don't want to change the way I feel. I want the things that make me feel this way to change. Understand what I'm saying?"

"All right, that I can respect. Do something about changing the world. All *you* ever do is talk about going fishing and what's the score for the Dodgers—"

"Please! The Yankees—"

"Will you cut that out?"

"See? There you go! I crack a joke, you jump down my throat."

"Well, I just didn't think it was funny," she defended.

"Is that a crime? I cracked a joke, it wasn't funny, hey! Is that a crime?"

"You still haven't answered my question."

"What's your question?"

"Why don't you get active politically, if you're committed to changing social conditions?"

"Whoa. I never said I was 'committed to changing social conditions.' Not that I'm against them changing, I'll go along, but let's face it: who's got the power to change anything? Not me. All I've got the power to do is break a few things and what good is that?" He clasped a powerful hand over a powerful arm. "An arm, a window, a head— what good does it do? Back in the sixties, believe me, I was the first one on the barricades yelling off-the-pig, smash-the-state. Where did it get us? Nah, I don't waste time with marches anymore."

"Okay, maybe I was thinking of marches, but that's not the only thing a person could do."

"What else could A Person do?"

"A Person could offer to help with child care at Athena Coffeehouse—"

"Ha! Are you serious? Can you imagine ME walking into the Athena Coffeehouse and saying, gimme' some children to take care of? What mother in her right mind would leave her children with me? Besides, children in any form are against my religion."

"You were a child once yourself. In fact—" She was going to point out that he was still a child in many ways, but he cut her off.

"My parents made a lot of mistakes. I was one of them. I don't want to repeat their blooper. People giving birth to more, for Chris'sake, people, of all things! That's what I call being insensitive to the needs of the earth. You asked about my politics, there's my plank: everyone should be committed to the dying out of the human race."

"Oh, my God! What a perfectly horrible thing to say!"

"Why? You've railed against children in your time. I've heard you."

"That's different. I'm talking about choice. No woman should be forced to have children—it's not required for the survival of the human race. God knows we're all-too-fertile as a species. But never would I ever say I wanted the extinction of our wonderful human race. We've done awful things, sure, but we've got the angel in us too. That's my opinion, so there."

"Uh huh. Basic difference. We'll never settle this one with talk. I'd wrassle you for it, if my back wasn't killing me."

"I could rub your back—would that help?"

George squinted at her. "What's that supposed to mean—you don't really want to get physical with Cro-Magnon man, so why say a thing like that? All right, you haven't pulled it much with me, but you've got that guy Sval shaking like a tin can on the end of a string. What for? Just to know you've got it? Woman, you have got it. You're a goddamn dream, there isn't one guy ever sets eyes on you doesn't fantasize about having you, and you know it. You can't possibly need to check on it. Jerking the string just 'cause you can, that's like some rich pig showing off his money. No difference."

"Well..." Her voice came out nasal because of her tension. Suddenly she saw herself as a certain housewife with a beehive, trying desperately to look young. "Well," she repeated in a thin, tight voice, "Are we doing metaphors now? You can't compete with Sval, you know, when it comes to dreaming up metaphors."

"Compete? How am I competing with Sval? Everything's competition with you. You talk about me knocking things down. You've got a knack for that yourself. What's the catty cynicism for? Why are you always shooting me that crummy attitude? It pisses me off."

Marica sat back abashed. She had just seen herself as ugly, and therefore his words struck home. For a moment she did not want to move or speak because she knew this was a moment of truth, and she wanted to hold still and learn from this moment of truth. "Yes," she said finally.

He waited for more. "Yes?" he demanded finally. "Yes what?"

"Yes, I get sharp sometimes. And yes, I'm..." She had trouble forcing out the words. "I'm vain. Okay? We all have our personality...flaws. You think I don't know that?"

"I'm just telling you what I see."

"I know I can be mean, sometimes. There are times when I don't like myself very much."

"Amen, sister. But there's also times when you ain't half bad."

"Oh, I ain't half bad. I like that. What a compliment!"

"From me, it is. I'm not going any further out on any limb. I've got my rep as a nihilist to protect and besides, you'll kick me in the balls if I let down my guard."

The words hit Marica like a bat across the belly and her breath stopped. "I'm sorry you feel that way," she whispered.

He reacted instantly, sitting forward, his face falling. "What—I've read you wrong? You wouldn't? All right, maybe not. Or what? I hit you where it hurts? What?" She was too upset to answer and only shook her head. He continued to hazard guesses. "Yes, I'm right and it bothers you? Or I'm wrong and *that* bothers you?"

Then he gave up and sat back. "Relax. You got your faults, like you say, but think how I feel, known far and wide as the king of assholes."

She forced a meager smile and nodded, admitting his point: whatever her flaws, his were much worse. She was still moved without knowing why, and she could not trust herself to speak. She fiddled with her drink. He pulled a flower out of the dead bouquet, broke it in half, and handed her the brown bloom saying, "Here," then began using the stem for a toothpick."

Suddenly he touched her on the arm. "Come on," he said, jerking his head toward the door. "I want to show you something."

"What?"

"A place in Portland. Let's go, it's four-thirty. It'll be first light soon."

She laughed. "You, who've been here all of what? Two months? *You're* going to show *me* Portland?"

"Just a piece of it. A piece you've never seen, trust me."

"Trust you? What piece?"

"You'll see."

They climbed into George's car. He took something flat, white, and elliptical from his wallet. "Here," he said. "Might as well blow some weed."

She held her hair back with one hand as he held a match to the tip of the joint for her. "Thank you," she said, and they sat quietly for some moments, passing the joint back and forth. Presently Marica began to hum a tune from the latest Dr. John album, the lyrics echoing faintly in her mind: "Sweet confusion... under the moonlight...such a night..." The moon was full, she noticed, and it looked awfully much like a big gold coin. George handed her the joint again. "It's so flat," she giggled. "It looks like a flounder."

"The flounder is not an especially quick fish," George observed.

"Sheesh! We must be stoned." Marica set down the roach. "Where are you taking me? Why aren't we there yet?"

"Because we haven't started moving yet. We're waiting for dawn. But it's close enough now." He turned the key.

Looking east, Marica saw that indeed the ebony had given way to the darkest possible shade of purple. They drove west, across the Ross Island Bridge and then up Jefferson Street, into the hills on winding roads crowded by trees until they reached Skyline Boulevard, which was like a country road, although it was within the city limits. After several miles, George parked and got out. A swooping hillside plunged down on the left to a valley far below. There, in the dissipating darkness, Marica could just make out block-like shapes of suburban houses, some kind of little village, a Portland suburb nestled in the valley among generous billows of vegetation. And to the right, the hillside went up just as steeply, and it was just as thickly wooded. The place where they had stopped was an intersection, with no evidence of human habitation except a store and a gas station on opposite corners.

Both buildings were dark, but the sun must have broken over the horizon on the far side of the hill, because the sky above was no longer a purple just one subtle shade removed from black but identifiably the darkest possible blue. And down on the ground, among the scattered trees, just enough light now shone for them to make their way.

George strode briskly ahead of Marica. She was just as long-legged as he, though perhaps five inches shorter overall, but his legs were beating so fast she had a hard time keeping up with him. A frown of concentration hugged his face. For a moment she almost thought he had forgotten she was along. He led the way past a lawn that apparently belonged with the store and on into the forest.

There he stopped. She caught up, holding her jacket shut at the throat. And a thrill ran through her and a fleeting thought: what if he'd brought her up here to rape her? The thought vanished before she could even clothe it in words. She felt the darkness surrounding her as an almost metaphysical presence. It was not the cold alone that made her shiver. She could feel something more in the undifferentiated darkness between the trees, where shrub was indistinguishable from empty space and all the tickling sharp-bladed grasses merged into one clump—a greater darkness, a cold breath from the heart of all things that made her cherish and pity her own humanity.

"What is this place?" she whispered.

"You don't have to whisper," he rasped. "There's no one close enough to hear us even if we shout. It's a gigantic playground. The guy that runs the store made it. Look."

He moved forward again and presently Marica, groping, found her way to an enormous swing. It was a stout plank at least four inches thick and some 20 feet long, suspended by two pairs of cables from some invisibly distant branch. The cables were so long they too vanished into the upper darkness. For all Marica could see, the plank might have been suspended from darkness itself.

"I can hardly even move it," she whispered, marveling at the size of the swing.

"Get up on that end," said George. A few feet of the plank extended past the cables on each side. She climbed up on one extension. He pushed until the plank was swinging a few inches from side to side, rather than forward and back like an ordinary swing. He jumped onto the other end. "Use your weight," he called out. "Keep it going."

Standing on the end of the plank and looking down, Marica saw the ground move a few inches forward, then a few inches back. As the swing reached its furthest point in her direction, she dropped to her knees, letting her weight bear down and dragging down on the cables at the same time. The effort seemed absurd. How could her miniscule weight affect the motion of this enormous plank? But when the swing reached its furthest extension in the other direction George did the same as she, dropping to his knees, pulling on the cables, bearing down with all his weight. After five or six oscillations Marica realized that merely by the well-timed application of their weights and efforts, she and George had actually gotten the swing to move further in each direction. Not a great deal further, true; but some few inches.

"Wow!" she exulted. In the enormous weight of the wood swinging back and forth, she could feel a medium of wordless communication between herself and George. She understood that George understood, and it stunned her. This was not the sort of thing she could explain or ask him about or discuss with him—or with anyone, for that matter: inherently. It was outside discussion, this mystical insight that she sometimes had, of a realm beyond words, even in a sense beyond feelings, a realm of pure... physical ... Being in the universe.

After about fifteen minutes, the swing was moving with dazzling speed and tremendous force. Each time it swung her way it lifted her up at least 30 feet. And yet, when it swung the other way, her end of the plank came so near the ground and paused so long, she could have stuck her foot out and scratched her initials in the dirt with her toe. And all the mighty motion had come from no force other than her own weight and George's, the motion of their two bodies in precise cooperation.

By the time they slowed down and then stopped, Marica felt utterly breathless just from stoned appreciation of all the beauty shining around her as the world grew bright. "That," she breathed, "was incredible, George. It was so deep. I felt in touch..."

"Save it." His scowl glowed with good humor. "There's more."

"More?"

"Come with me." He clambered up the hill. Marica saw a cable attached to two trees, one of them near her and George, the other about 100 feet further uphill. Stretched like a clothesline between these points, the cable ran roughly parallel to the steep slope. Balanced on the cable was a pulley wheel, and hanging from the wheel was a rope with a fat knot tied just below the middle of it.

George grabbed the rope and started up the hill. The wheel rolled along the top of the cable after him. In some places the cable was 15 feet or so above the ground and George had to stretch his arm high above his head to keep hold of the rope. He was panting by the time he got to the top of the hill, and so was Marica.

"Okay," she said. "Tell me. What are we doing up here?"

"It's like a slide," he panted. "You grab this rope. You lift your feet up and down you go. Stand on the knot." He pointed to the sizable clump in the rope. "Grab on tight near the top of the rope and really clamp your feet around that knot and down you go."

"Grab that rope?" she stammered. "Down I go?"

"Yeah. It's not really all that dangerous but it is pretty fuckin' scary. Gets your blood moving. You wanna' try?"

There was no pressure in his voice, but she felt the stakes: if she refused, he would chalk it up to her being a woman. "You mean just grab the rope?

"Uh huh. Grab and let go of the ground with your feet. Once you're going you're gone, *way* gone, so hang on tight. Tight! Because that wheel moves fast—"

"And what, I go crashing into a tree when I get to the bottom?"

"No, there's a clamp on the cable down there. When the pulley hits the clamp, it stops dead. You swing on forward till the rope snaps taut. That's what you have to watch out for—hold on tight—tight, or you'll get thrown and then you *will* hit the tree."

"You first."

"No, you've got to do it cold, or the mystery goes out of it. Just remember, you get jerked good at the other end, so hang on tight."

"Jerked..." Marica heard the slight challenge in his voice now. He must have done this alone the first time. Well, she thought, if he could do it, so could she. She took the rope out of his hand and stood for a moment, letting her courage accumulate. She thought she was ready once, but at the last moment she felt the rope slipping in her sweaty palm. She rubbed her hands dry against her pants. The physical danger, if any, was not what she feared. She was afraid she would make a fool of herself—get thrown and land like a sack of potatoes.

At least that was her main fear until the moment she leaped from her perch at the base of the tree. Her brain knew the wheel would start to move the instant she left the ground, but her body was somehow not ready for the rocket-rush of motion. And neither her brain nor her body was prepared for the visual horror—the sight of the ground dropping away beneath her feet and the tree that was 100 feet ahead one instant and then 50 feet away the next—or the sense of panic as her feet scrabbled at the rope, unable to find the knot, so that her whole weight was hanging from her finger-grips, while tree limbs, branches, leaves, the whole forest rushed toward her, past her in a blur, and the tree ahead came hurling toward her face. She forgot, then, about the danger of looking stupid and prayed that she wouldn't die.

In the next moment—it must have been the next moment, although time did something funny just then as her senses, sparked by danger, blazed into such life that even the blurred forest slowed down to a crawl—her feet gained purchase on the knot. She was standing on something then, and holding on with her hands for balance. Her consciousness caught up with her and slammed forward. Far away was the end of the cable and then, like some tricky zoom-shot in a student film, it was roaring up in her face. The pulley wheel hitting the brake clamp registered as some distant click. It sent her into free-fall except that gravity was sideways. Then the rope snapped taut and her insides slammed up toward her throat... the rope swung back all the way, then forward...and then back more gently, and then smoothly forward. Then, the world stopped rocking. She jumped down from the rope, exultant to be alive, first of all, but exultant also, a close second, at the memory of a motion that was more than flying.

She heard George come crashing down the hillside, yelling, "You did it! You fuckin'-fantastic woman, you! You are fuckin' fabulous, babe. How do you feel?"

"I cannot describe—oh, it was so great—I can't describe..." She flipped the rope at him. "Your turn," she panted. "Hot shot."

"Are you kidding? The shape my back's in? No way!"

"Well, how'd you do it before? Wasn't your back—"

"What 'before?' I never went down that thing. Just seen some kids do it."

"You bastard! You creep!"

He evaded the fistful of dirt she snatched up and flung at him. She ran after him, but her anger dissolved into physical exhilaration and they fell into a laughing game of dodge and chase that lasted until the sun broke over the hilltop. Sometime in there Marica realized she had connected to her inner-child. She never imagined George would be the first one ever who could make her feel that way.

Celebration

Sval was already a bit drunk by the time Zoe arrived. Zoe, in plain Levis and a man's shirt which she left untucked, looked much like her usual self—a welcome sight against the strange, disorienting canvas of the party so far. When Sval saw her slip quietly through the door not even the word "like" occurred to him, much less "love." He knew only a warm sensation of relief, as if half a load had been lifted from his shoulders. He took her hand and pressed it lightly. No one paid any particular attention to them. The hall was packed with babbling new-age community activists chugging from beer bottles. The crowd in the living room pulsed to a Motown beat, bulging rhythmically into the hall like some single protoplasmic creature panting.

"Hey," said Sval, feigning disapproval, "what's with the quotidian getup? This is a come-as-you're-not party. You're supposed to come as you're not."

"What am I not?" she mused. "I can't think of anything I've crossed off my list yet." She took a six-pack of beer out of her daypack and handed it to Sval.

"Well anyway, I'm glad you're here." He pressed her hand again. "Let's take the beer to the kitchen and I'll get you situated. Dancing's in the living room, booze and chit-chat in the dining room, dope and deep discussion upstairs, coats in the hall."

"I'll find my way," she assured him; for now that Sval and Zoe officially had an "open relationship," they routinely split up at parties and pursued separate adventures, crossing paths only at the beer keg or the refrigerator, like wild animals at a water hole.

As Zoe picked her way up the stairs where dope was being smoked, Sval drifted toward the dining room, dipping into random conversations along the way as a perfunctory hosting duty. He had to pull up short and suck in his stomach to make way for Zack, the Zen Buddhist from Yamhill House, who barged through the kitchen, knocking people around and causing a ruckus. Normally an austere ascetic, he had come tonight as a debauched medieval monk in a long robe, with a flask of wine hanging at his belt; and true to the come-as-you're-not mandate, he was playing his persona to the hilt, flinging his arm around every woman he approached. At least, he claimed it was a persona; but he played the part of lecherous monk suspiciously well. This hardly surprised Sval, for under cover of coming as they weren't, many people seemed to have come as they really were. Ken Singleton, for example, Marxist intellectual, with his tough greaser act—that was not entirely an act; his slapping and pushing sometimes went right to the border between fun and menace. And of course, Bob Brown and Lester Garibaldi, in their fashionable dresses, wigs, high heels, and padded bras—no pretenses there, or even the pretense of pretense. Sval watched the two men dancing together and felt a guilty discomfort. He wanted to be enlightened about the whole thing, but the sphincter-tightening anxiety remained: what if one of them asked him to dance?

Then there was dazzling Marica, who had come as a vamp. Was that a game or a secret revealed? She had dressed in a body-hugging velveteen dress with a floor-length skirt and cream-colored lace at the collar and sleeves, the soft, black fabric molding so closely to the contours of her flesh that it made the muscle tone of her flat belly apparent. In her hair, which was swept all to one side, she wore a red flower. She had curled her eyelashes and painted her lips and fingernails preternaturally red. She greeted Sval in a honeyed drawl, and Sval felt the sex-heat rolling from her in waves. A fantasy fell into his head and disappeared in smoke, something about making love on the dance floor. Marica gave him a merry, secretive look. "Tonight's the night," he thought, and a wisp of voodoo gris-gris wafted through his head. "Such a night..." Dr. John rasped. "Such a night..." Sweet confusion: he was sure she felt it too—so sure that he did not feel abandoned when she drifted away. She knew and he knew that all the other people were mere backdrop: they were the only two animals in the jungle tonight, and no matter where they were in the house, they were stalking each other. Tonight, he thought.

But then when he lost sight of her for a whole fifteen minutes, he panicked and thought she might have gone. He hurried through the hall and the kitchen looking for her. Then he entered the dining room, and stopped, and his heart thumped. There she was, sitting in the big easy chair, leaning back, her legs parted, her hands resting in the basket of velvet skirt-material stretched between her thighs. Several men at her feet—yes, actually at her feet, on folded legs, hands on knees, leaning on their struts of arms. They needed only to be panting to complete the tableaux. Marica chatted with them gaily and her body expressed a regal laziness as she lifted her hand to accept a joint. When she saw Sval, she beckoned to him coyly, and shoved the man sitting next to her out of his seat so that Sval might have it.

When Sval took that seat, he felt like a king sitting next to his queen. Now he too was looking down at the ring of men. Marica gave him a conspiratorial smile, and for a moment none of those men existed. "Quite a party you've thrown here, Mr. Hofby," she observed.

"It was your idea of course."

"All your best ideas are my ideas, darling," she whispered sweetly.

Darling! "And all *my* best ideas are really yours," he responded gallantly.

She puzzled over that one for a moment. "I need more wine," she exclaimed then. "Who will get it for me?"

"I will," beamed one of the drooling penitents. "What kind?"

"White," and she turned back to Sval. "Are you having fun at your own party, honey?" *Honey!* Her voice had such a languid sensuality about it that the marrow melted in Sval's bones and the bones themselves then melted. He wiped his brow. The temperature in this corner of the room seemed to be several hundred degrees and rising.

"Ever since I got to this spot, I would say yes."

"What is that supposed to mean?" Her voice was suddenly harsh.

He let a beat pass. Was he really supposed to explain his remark in front of this ring of drooling witnesses? Why did she pose such a question? But he swallowed his displeasure and took a new tack. "Good music, huh? Does it make you want to dance?"

"I know. Does it make you want to dance?"

"I'm bopping where I sit. Want to get out there?"

"Mmm—not really. I'm comfortable where I am. But why don't you go dance, if the music moves you so much? I'd love to watch. "

Again, Sval felt put out. How had he backed into a commitment to make a spectacle of himself, dancing alone. He stared at the dance floor, his lips compressed.

"What's the matter?" she asked solicitously. "Are you angry about something?"

He shook his head.

"You know, you're a wonderful host," Marica blurted out. "You're such a party animal, Sval Hofby."

"I am?" He colored, feeling pleased without knowing why. He crossed his long legs and fumbled in his pocket for a cigarette. "What makes you say that?"

"You're sociable. You put people at ease."

"I do?" Again, Sval felt himself jerked around a right-angled corner. "That's odd, I almost never *feel* at ease," he confessed.

"You must be joking." She leaned slightly out of her chair to look at him as if to ascertain that this astonishing confession had come from the bonafide Sval Hofby. "But Sval, you're always partying!" She put a warm hand on his knee and gazed into his face. "You're always going to places like...I don't know. The White Eagle. The Grog House..."

"The Grog House is a biker hangout. I was only there once with George Lubick."

"Oh—George Lubick. That reminds me—where is he tonight?"

"I haven't seen him, but he said he was coming. He's probably on his way. Now, Marica, admit it—George is not really so bad, is he?"

"Oh, he can be tolerable."

"He was wonderful at the meeting, don't you think?"

"He was all right there," she admitted.

Maureen Junechild came along and sat on the arm of Marica's chair. "Hello, Ms. Vampire—dazzling the boys?"

"I do seem to have collected a few," Marica allowed in liquid tones.

Maureen leaned over and whispered something in Marica's ear. Marica laughed. "Oh, Maureen, you're terrible. Yes of course I will, but not that!"

"Shall we dance then?" Maureen never glanced at Sval or the others; she just poured her gaze into Marica's eyes.

Marica shrugged. "I do get a little restless just sitting here."

She walked into the living room with Maureen. Sval spotted Zoe among that crowd, dancing by herself; but he made no move to join her. Marica and Maureen began to dance, not just near each other but with each other, watching and responding to each other's movements with such an obvious intimacy of wordless communication that Sval felt discomfited. Sweat sprang out on his forehead. Was Marica gay? Why had this never occurred to him? It seemed obvious, now that he thought about it—so obvious. And it would explain everything.

He stood up and moved to the living room door, but he couldn't contain himself there. The very floor felt hot. His clothes felt itchy and sticky. He ambled to the kitchen, but life felt intolerable there too. He couldn't stop drifting. He didn't want anyone to engage him in conversation. He didn't know what he wanted. He found himself at the living room door again, standing with his hands in his pockets, trying to spot Marica. A voice spoke near his ear. "Care to dance?"

He turned and flushed with embarrassment. Garibaldi in drag was stretching out his hand. "I'd like to—" Sval muttered. "But in fact—I have to run just now. The masses clamor for beer. I have to leave."

He hurried out. Once he was on the street he realized he was done with the party, even though it was his own party.

The Party's Over

Raoul left the party, feeling as lonely as a polar bear on a chunk of ice floating in the Arctic. Without Zara, the spectacle of other people having fun was hell frozen over. Raoul walked down toward the Genoa Restaurant and there, on a street as empty as any painting by Utrillo, he ran into Sval.

"Raoul, compeer!" the latter called out warmly. "What are you doing here?"

"Walking. Gee, Sval, everybody was looking for you back at the party."

"Were they? Yes, I imagine they were. Well, I failed as a host," Sval admitted. "I ran away. Too much craziness in there. Were you having a good time?"

"I wouldn't be out here if I were. I got to remembering Zara," Raoul told his friend. "Marica reminded me of her tonight. Golly, she looked beautiful, didn't she?"

Sval smiled and shrugged: apparently, he hadn't noticed one way or the other. "Zara's coming out one of these days, isn't she?" he said.

"Any day now," Raoul sighed. "I expect her any day." They had turned and were walking up the hill, and now Raoul stopped. "Here's Yamhill House," he said. "Hey, I have an idea! Want to come up and smoke a joint with me, Sval?"

"I would, in fact. Any excuse to stay away from my own house."

They climbed up to Raoul's room on the third floor. Raoul lit a strobe candle and handed Sval one joint from a pre-rolled pack he kept in a Marlboro box. Sval sat down cross-legged on Raoul's mattress, which was merely a thin cotton pad. As part of his new regimen of austerity, Raoul had gotten rid of his mattress.

"Yeah," said Raoul, "one of these days, she's coming." He began to talk about Zara. Sval nodded sympathetically and even in the darkness Raoul could see the interest in his blue eyes. Sval was such a big deal at the Ark, but he never acted like anything special, and Raoul was never afraid of him. Somehow that steady gaze drew the story out of him, and kept on drawing.

"But we never broke up," Raoul insisted, when he had finished telling about that tragic graduation day. "And afterwards, you know, the army came after me, and I did something stupid. That's how we got separated. If only she'd have come to Portland, we could have worked it out. And she will in the end. And we will."

"What did you do that was stupid?"

"Aw, I took acid when I went in for my physical. It was Zara's idea. She said fuck yourself up like Travis did, they'll think you're crazy—"

"Travis?"

"Her boyfriend before me. It worked for him. He got so weird at the physical they threw him out, and then he came down, and he could laugh about it. I must've taken too much, though. I don't know what went wrong. I used to have a cast iron head for acid, used to keep an extra tab in my wallet just in case I saw a sunset. But this time was different. I dropped the stuff, and nothing happened. Orange tab, you know. Angel of Death was the nickname. You know how every kind of acid has a nickname? Angel of Death. Nothing happened, and I thought wait a minute, what is this, dud tab, I've been tricked, now I won't get all fucked up and they'll draft me, that asshole dealer is going to get me killed. That's what I was thinking. Except that I was feeling a little weird, you know, a little weird. It was backing up, but I didn't know that. Some part of me must have felt how strong it was. Some part of me was trying to hold it back, so I was feeling nothing, but the pressure was building. It was getting ready to blow. And when the guy said bend over, and he shoved his finger up my ass, the whole 150 micrograms hit me and my brain exploded. I didn't used to be like this, you know: spaced out the way people think. Starting out, I was just another Bo Bolinsky— 'He's no big deal.' Then Zara came along, and made me a star. The Beatles had nothing on me then, Bob Dylan and the rest of them, nothing. Not when I was Zara's boyfriend. I was a star. Then suddenly school was over, Zara's drifting off with her other boyfriend, army's coming after me, and now this guy's finger—well, I lost all sense of time, I forgot what was happening, all I knew was the government had its finger up my ass and hour after hour was passing. I got paranoid—seemed like he was shoving his whole hand up inside me—that's when the acid cranked into second gear. Like a truck slamming into every brain cell. Everything vanished. I mean everything just went white—black—whatever. Then I must have screamed because I got back to reality for a second, but I was burning up electrically, my brain cells. I could feel them starting to fry from the overload and the world kept coming at me, all that pure sensation pouring into my every cell, harder, harder, harder—I tell you Sval, I could see every molecule in front of me—and all the time this guy's finger—and that's when it all turned into waves—the sound, the noise, the color—everything: and I saw right through all of it to what's really there. And you know what's really there?"

Sval shook his head. "What's really there?"

"Nothing. That's what's really out there, Sval. Nothing. The Void. Everybody knows it, I guess, don't they? It's the worst-guarded secret in the universe. Everybody suspects. But how many have looked The Void in the face? I never wanted to. But once it happened, it was too late. Once you know it's there, it's there forever."

Raoul lifted his hands to his chin. Oh, God, had he said too much? The Void was stirring. Even to speak of The Void woke it up. Once you had looked at it, face to face, you were a goner. The only hope was to look away. Now, Raoul tried furiously to look away. He tried every trick. He dug his fingernails into his face so as to feel sensation. He blinked and blinked to keep himself reminded of his eyes. But already the sucking wind had begun, the vacuum pulling him into the nothingness. Raoul felt his Real Self—the one who stood outside the world of sensation, the one who clung pathetically to sights and sounds—felt his

Real Self getting pried loose. He lifted his hands like an orator, intensely passionate to persuade, and just kept talking, though he had no idea what he was saying. The important thing was to do the pretending thing expertly. The illusion would come back, it always did, if he could just pretend the world existed. Look at ol' Sval over there across the room, leaning back against his own interlocked fingers, he looks so real, his lips pursed, his crinkled eyes looking wise and deep, like the eyes of some mythical bird-god from a civilization that was ancient when Egypt was a baby.

Raoul had to say these things to himself, even though he knew it was a trick. He knew that the room was actually a two-dimensional scene painted on the inside of a hollow egg, and that he was floating just outside the egg, looking in through two little holes: his eyes. And of course, that body lolling on the other side of the room, that long aquiline face, that tumult of blond hair, those crinkled eyes, wise and deep, they were all just part of the painting.

Yet suddenly, for just a moment, like a lantern passing in front of a window high up in a tower as glimpsed by a homeless man lost on a vast moor at night, Raoul spotted life. There it was in Sval's eyes. He was so startled, he physically jumped. Someone was there behind that painting of a face! And then it hit him. Just where that painting of a face happened to be were two other holes in the egg. Floating in the Void on the other side, huddled up against those holes, was—*another person.*

It was Sval. Sval was alive. Sval was real! SVAL EXISTED!

A spasm of intense longing swept through Raoul. If only he could move away from the egg, let go and float around it, meet Sval directly, soul to soul. Alas, only with Zara had that been possible.

Now, however, Raoul stumbled into an epiphany: communication *through* the egg was possible. The signals he was sending were being received. Sval, with his ancient bird-god eyes, was actually hearing and understanding what Raoul was saying. Indeed he was sending signals back. What were they? What was he trying to communicate? Raoul strained to ignore the word-noise and receive the hidden meaning. The straining turned his attention away from the Void and drew him into the illusion of Reality which was firming up now, gaining solidity. Sval was beaming him a message that...ah, yes: that he had heard all this before *in another life!* Holy cow, this was magnificent. Joyfully Raoul continued with the history of his deepest moments, his greatest love. The Void had receded to a breeze. The current of energy that ran between his own eyes and Sval's was stronger than The Void, strong enough to bind them to their two keyholes. They were saving each other's souls! Raoul kept talking, and every word left a tracer of pure flame on its way across the interior of the hollow egg, and every word ended in a brief bright explosion in those eyes, letting Raoul know: message received!

Sval had stretched out as Raoul got into the flow of his story and now, he was nodding and making sympathetic noises; but he was not really listening. He had stopped listening some time ago, and for a good reason. Lying on Raoul's pad, his head rested right next to the heating vent. And through that vent came a woman's voice, whispering, it seemed, right into his ear, in a breathless sobbing tone, "Oh—dear—you—oh! Oh! Please... mmmm—hold me! Oh! There...Yes, there...!"

It was Marica's voice.

He thought for a moment that he was hallucinating. The blood ran right out of his face. Someone in this house sounded a hell of a lot like Marica, was his first thought. And this Marica-clone was making love to some guy, somewhere in this very house, and the sound of it was coming through the heating vent, right to his ears. Who could this woman be? And this man? And where were they?

"... because I knew already it would never be the same with someone else," Raoul was saying, "We had soul-contact, Zara and me. That's beyond sex and conversation. It's the dream reality, pure and simple. Do you know what I mean?"

Sval nodded, pretending to follow what Raoul was saying: something about an acid trip, and the sixties, and beating the draft. But Sval could not tear his real attention away from that woman's voice. The acoustics of the situation were precise. If he moved his head a few inches either way he could no longer hear it, but he didn't move. All the words had dropped away now, replaced by moans, just moans, a woman's moans, and a man's loud breath; and in the background, Raoul droned on and on with glistening eyes. And then the sounds of sex reached a muffled crescendo. And then they stopped. And Raoul's voice emerged to fill the stillness.

"Because the moment you look, it starts to suck you in. It starts to suck you right out of this little room we're living in, the world. I've been trying to forget. Because the moment you let yourself remember—"

From the vent came the woman's voice again. "You got a cigarette?" Good God, there could be no doubt about it now: that was Marica's voice.

"You don't smoke." Unmistakably George's voice. Impossible. Incredible. But true.

From Marica a little giggle. "I know but I used to, and I still want one after I make love."

And from George, "Will a pipe do?"

And from Raoul, "That's the way it happened. I haven't ever told anyone about it, Sval. Not even Zara. Not even when she said, 'you'll find someone else,' and I said 'But I don't *want* someone *else*!' I still can't get over how they never came to see me in the hospital, not her, not Travis, never. Not once. As if I didn't even exist. And maybe I didn't. Maybe I never had."

"Depressing," Sval murmured. "A difficult situation all around."

Raoul's eyes were bright, his voice furry. "You're the first person who's heard the whole story."

"It's an amazing story, Raoul. Well, listen, I'd better be getting home." Sval stumbled blindly to his feet and mumbled goodbyes, only vaguely noticing Raoul's disappointment.

But he was in no shape to respond to Raoul's story just then, especially having missed the bulk of it. He walked out of Yamhill House into the drizzle and headed to Zoe's house, where he could be sure of receiving comfort.

He entered without knocking. As an honorary housemate, he never knocked at the front door, just as she never knocked to enter his place. He traveled on light steps downstairs to her bedroom door. It was closed, but he did not push it open. The privacy of the inner chamber was sacred. He gave a light tap with his knuckles.

Silence. Strange. He could have sworn he heard some rustling in there. He waited a moment, listening with vibrant attention to the creak of the house and the whisper of the rain outside. After a moment he heard another creak, this time not of old wood bending in the wind but of bedsprings, definitely, under the weight of a body shifting position. Zoe was in her room. Perhaps she had been asleep. He would not presume to violate her privacy; this was a point of honor. He tapped again, this time more forcefully. The creaking of the bedsprings stopped abruptly. There was no sound from within, no invitation for him to enter. The silence itself, the absolute held-breath silence, suddenly conveyed an unmistakable message.

And then he heard a whisper of voices. More than one voice. Fewer than three. Two voices in Zoe's room in the dark of night. The universe crumbled.

Sval turned and left the house in a hurry, his long hair streaming behind him. He arrived gasping at the offices of the Ark. He clambered up the stairs and let himself in with his key, turned on the desk lamp, pulled a typewriter close, and began to hammer out a piece for page three. For once the Ark would scoop the Oregonian. Fast-breaking news. He could see the headline now: 48-point type, two columns:

CONSCIOUS MAN COMMITS BLUNDER

Zoe did not come to see him until seven 'o clock the next evening. At that hour Sval, looking down from his bedroom window, saw a black Volkswagen pull up to the curb. Zoe clambered out; the driver stayed inside. Through the windshield, Sval could make out little more than a bearded face. He clambered down the stairs to meet Zoe at the front door. "Why didn't you invite your boyfriend in?"

"Excuse me?"

He swore to himself that if she dared attempt to hug him, he would shake off her hand. But she, perceiving his mood, attempted nothing of the kind.

"What's this?" said Sval. "Not even a little hug? Not even a peck on the cheeks? What have I done to make you angry?"

"I'm not angry. Sval, I—"

"Come on. What have I done?"

"Nothing."

Sval preceded Zoe into the living room and sat down defeated. "Who was the guy?"

"Someone I met at the party last night."

"Did you sleep with him?"

"Yes."

"So, that's how this goes? You meet some guy at a party and you jump into bed with him?"

Her face was pale, her mouth tense. She spoke in a low, slow voice "When you put it that way, yes, I guess those are the facts. I guess I wouldn't have put it that way."

"What way would you have put it? The facts remain the facts no matter how you put it, do they not?"

"You're mad. And I'm sorry. But we had an agreement."

"Well. We had an agreement, yes. But you might have warned me this was about to happen. Given me a chance to get ready—"

"I didn't know warning each other was part of the agreement."

"Ah. The contract needed codicils, you're saying. Perhaps we were careless. Perhaps we were. It's just—oh, Zoe, for Christ's sake, if it had been me, I think I would have given you a heads up."

"When? This happened last night. It wasn't planned, it just happened. When would I have given you a heads up?"

"I don't know. I don't know. I'm being unreasonable, I know. It's just—there are feelings involved here! When you said we trust each other, you were talking about feelings, weren't you? What does this do to the trust between us? Now, I have no reason to believe it hasn't happened before—every time I wasn't with you—even before the agreements—" He stopped to give her space for denial. When she said nothing the horror of it slapped him. "There've been others?"

"Yes."

"How many?"

"I don't see that the actual number—"

"That guy from Alaska with all his conspiracy theories?" Sval choked out in a stricken voice. "The night the proposal went through? Did you—?"

She nodded.

"But how? I was in your bed—"

"We did it on the couch...It wasn't planned—we were having a conversation, not starting a relationship. Neither of us thought. It was just what happened in the moment. Sometimes sexual tension builds up and it's distracting, because it's so irrelevant, and you just have to do the deed and get it out of the way so you can go on with the conversation. It wasn't important, what happened that night. It was just sex. He was going to Alaska the next morning. That was understood!"

Sval groaned and rested his aching face in his hands.

"Well, we had an agreement," Zoe said, letting a trace of challenge show.

"I know. I know. I know," he exclaimed irritably. "I'm not criticizing you."

"I'm sorry you feel this way. But you said yourself, you said jealousy—"

"I'm not jealous!" he yelped. "Me? I'm not jealous, for crying out loud. You think I think I own you? I know I don't. I'm just saying, I have to get out of town for a while. That's what I'm saying. Yes," he decided. "Portland is too small. I have to leave town."

"Sval, don't be like that."

"I'm broke," he cried out. "It's not about you! I gave my route to George. I can't pay my rent now. I've got to give up my room and take the job what's-his-face offered me, Redneck Bob. Putting up sheetrock on the goddamn coast. I've got to do it. I need the money."

"It's not that I—"

"It has nothing to do with you. This is an open relationship, we both agreed. I'm leaving town to earn some money, that's all."

"We still have a relationship?"

"Whatever we had, we still have. Nothing's changed, Zoe."

"Look, there were only—"

"Don't," he warned her. "I don't need numbers, I need to be in another town for a while."

He was packing his bag when George called. "Hey, pal, I hear you're splitting town?"

"Word travels fast."

"Well, what are you doing with your room?"

"Giving it up. Letting the roommates worry about it."

"Yeah? Hey, listen, I'm looking for a room—"

"Perfect!" Sval let out a wild high-pitched laugh. "Almighty God, it's perfect! Take my room, why not! Tell you what, I'll leave my typewriter—"

"Great, man! Great!" George boomed back heartily. "I could use a typewriter. Goddamn it, Sval, you're okay, man, you know that? You are a real pal!"

"Hey, my clothes—my bank account—take it all—"

"Naw, what, are you kidding? Your clothes wouldn't fit me. Just the room and the typewriter'll be great. You know something? Honest to God, you're a good man, Sval Hofby."

And those were the words echoing in Sval's mind the next morning as he drove between the West Hills at dawn, on Highway 26, headed for The Coast, headed for a summer of physical labor and hard brooding, a summer of struggle in the solitude of his own conscience with the Problem of Jealousy. He was a good man. Therein lay hope.

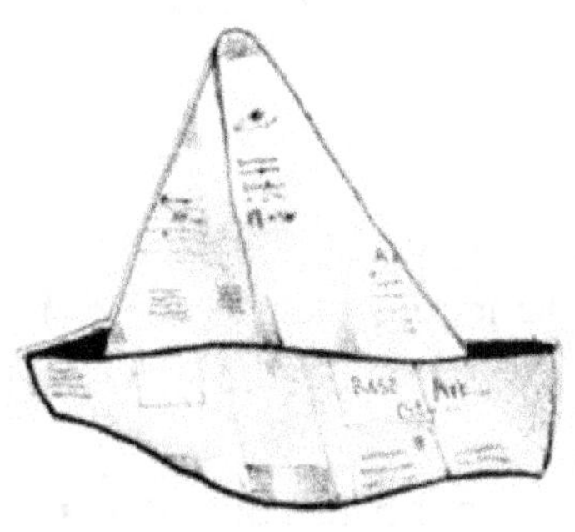

PART TWO
Saving the Ark

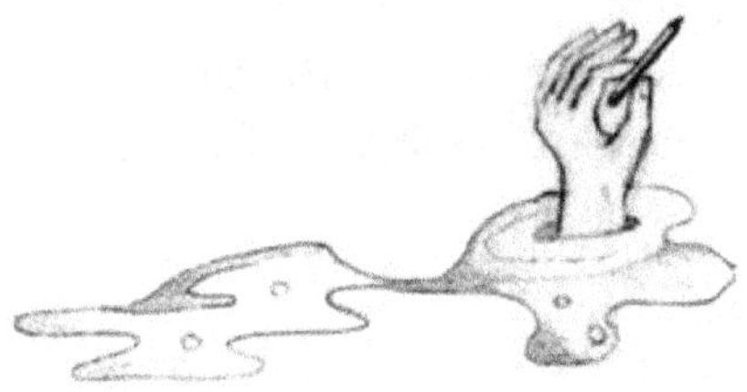

Sval Returns

Fat white clouds drifted across the sky. Shadows dappled the wooded hillsides of the Willamette Valley. Sval hummed tunelessly to himself and smiled as he drove through the soft late afternoon, back toward Portland.

He'd been gone since late spring and now it was mid-autumn, and he felt good. A summer of healthy labor on a hill overlooking the Pacific had tightened his muscles, but his Apollonian physique was the least of his transformations; for that summer, Sval had done what few men in history had achieved and he couldn't wait to tell Zoe: he had conquered jealousy.

Highway 26 came into town between solemn hills covered with dark stands of pine and fir. Sval bounced from Reubens Tavern to the People's Food Store, from Ken's Afterglow to the Athena Coffeehouse, garnering at each watering hole a half dozen offers of places to crash; but he made no definite arrangements. He was seeking Zoe. He found her finally, at Yamhill House, along with core members of his culture-tribe. They were all in the kindergarten, sitting around the big table, from which the usual arts-and-crafts apparatus had been cleared away. The table was covered with an old sheet now, and a forest of vintage wine bottles stood among chipped, cracked, and motley table settings. From the kitchen came the smell of roasting meats and dripping pies.

George jumped to his feet, knocking over a chair. He called Sval a dog. He slapped Sval's back and shouted bluff greetings. Zack the Zen Buddhist said "Namaste." Maureen Junechild gave him a wave. Marica leaped into his arms and hugged him with extravagant and confusing affection. Lined up next was humble Martha, awaiting her turn. And then Raoul, skulking close at hand, got swept into the general embrace and submitted to it with the bug-eyed helplessness of a kid submitting to the slobber of massive aunts.

And there was Zoe, sitting next to Stan the Man, rolling joints. She looked up and mouthed a soundless, "Hi." Sval understood and approved. At a public gathering, it was quite right for the least-connected to put on the most affectionate displays, while downright couples treated each other practically as strangers; that way no one would feel excluded from the group. Possible think piece for the Ark: *Counterculture Etiquette: the Unwritten Code*. Marica would insist on a snappier head, of course.

The hugging had subsided, meanwhile, and he stood alone. "I see changes," he said. "Martha, you've cut your hair." He scanned the group. "George, you've grown a beard." He turned in place, gazing fondly at his friends. "And what about you, Raoul? What's new with you?"

Raoul, who still seemed shaken from the hug, wriggled in the spotlight of Sval's attention. "Oh, well. Every day is new."

"Sval, buddy, this is a potluck," George bellowed. "You're not getting a plate 'less you brought some food!"

Sval dropped his backpack and drew out of it a ten-pound wheel of Tillamook cheese. "Let it never be said that Sval Hofby arrived at a potluck empty-handed."

"Hanging out at the White Eagle," Raoul cut in suddenly. "That's new."

Sval was impressed. The White Eagle was a bar in the warehouse district, a dank corridor with a 20-foot ceiling, famous for surly bouncers, kinetic live music, and the wall-to-wall flesh that pressed and ground together in that tight space. "You hang out at the Eagle now?"

"Every time the Sonny Black Blues Band is playing! You know what I like about electric guitar, Sval? Power! I wish I could be the lead guitarist for a jazz-blues rock'n'roll fusion band. Can you imagine the cosmic blast you'd feel in front of a jillion fans, cranking out decibels?"

"Power has its apologists," Sval agreed.

"I've signed up for guitar lessons," said Zoe.

George sloshed wine into glasses. "A toast to the good old days."

"And to the Ark!" Sval raised his glass and began to sip, then lowered his glass. No one had echoed his toast. Marica wiped her lips and set down her glass.

Martha said, "It's not really the Ark anymore."

Sval said, "You've changed the name? Oh my God. Why?"

"The name's the same. It's the paper that's different. Ever since the Whitaker gang took over."

"What the fuck? Who's the Whitaker gang!"

"Niles Whitaker. He's the managing editor now."

Sval raised an eyebrow. "Managing editor? What happened to Marica's proposal?"

"It's a long story," sighed Marica. "Honestly, Sval, before you start criticizing, you know what Mao said. No investigation, no right to speak."

Sval sat forward, his elbows at sharp angles. "Are you telling me someone swept in and took control of the Ark? How is that possible? We had the Proposal!"

George raised his right hand. "Bankers. I swear to God. Bankers joined the collective, and we never knew they were bankers. They look normal. They have long hair. Next thing you know, they're running things."

"I don't understand." Sval shook his head. "What's their power? Do they physically coerce? How many of them are there?"

George rolled his eyes. "How many's not the point, they move as a unit, see. There's no place to put a knife into a block of them and pry them apart. They're like Republicans."

"A block of men," Marica noted and her friend June contributed a clap of soft agreement.

"Well . . ." George waved away this observation. "They do have a couple of women in there."

"Who get their hair done in hair salons," Martha noted.

"Mostly though," George conceded, "they're men."

Sval took a gulp of wine.

When all the food had been eaten and all the dishes washed, Stan took off for the White Eagle with Raoul in tow. Zoe picked up her knapsack and shuffled in place for a moment. "Well," she said finally, "I'd better be shoving off."

Most of the group just murmured, but Sval raised his head. Of course, he wanted to go home with her—and she wanted him to. She just felt nervous about their first few minutes alone together. But that line had to be crossed sooner or later. "Coming with?" She lowered her voice to protect the group from their intimacy.

"To the door at least. Uh huh." He uncurled his limbs.

In the hall, where the velveteen curtain shielded them from public view, she took hold of his coat. "I've missed you. Where are you staying tonight?"

He smiled, his eyes slightly agleam. "Remains to be seen."

"Martha's moved out. Her room's empty upstairs."

He bit his lips. "I don't suppose there's a mattress up there. But I've got a sleeping bag. Beggars can't be choosers, I guess."

"Or," said Zoe, "You could stay with me tonight. Until you figure out what you're doing."

"Is that an option? Uh huh. That might be best. Might be best." She felt his muscles relax.

In her kitchen, she fixed hot milk for both of them. Sval opened a beer to drink with his.

"Tell me about your summer," she said. "Did you get my letters? I couldn't tell from your post cards. Why didn't you write? I thought about you a lot."

"You're tense," he replied.

She shrugged, gave him a tight smile. What women had he met on the coast, she wondered. What attachments had he brought back to Portland? "Well, you were pretty mad when you left."

"I know, but let me state right now. I understand your point. You were well within your rights."

"Oh, Sval. Rights," she sighed. "Who cares about rights? It's feelings we have to deal with. Let's not pretend we don't have feelings for each other. And this thing we're doing stirs them up, let's not pretend it doesn't."

"I know. That's what I've been doing all summer. Putting up sheetrock and thinking about my feelings."

"Good," she said. "Me too. And what were *your* thoughts. monsieur?"

"I thought about the way I reacted to your news and I realized something: this relationship can't last unless I learn to let go. If we want this incredible thing to last, we have to learn to let go."

"When you say 'this incredible thing'—"

"This relationship we have, the way we have it."

"So when you say letting go—"

"Of jealousy, Zoe. You're still my primary relationship. That's the rock. Ramble where you will, I'll be here when you get back. That's the bottom line. And I have to believe the same of you. I see that now."

Zoe absorbed his declaration. "I think I like the sound of this. Come downstairs." She led the way to her bedroom, chose Sval's favorite Santana album for background music, and turned the volume medium low so they could talk. They sat cross-legged on the bed facing each other. "Go on."

"Well," he said, "when we started this experiment, remember what we talked about: lots of hours in the day, we don't see each other, why should we care what the other person is doing in those hours? If we're not a couple what difference does it make whether the other person is off playing tennis or making love with someone else as long as our time together—"

"You're the one who talked about time. It's not just about time."

"Exactly! It's about the quality of our time together. That's the biggie. If I had a wonderful time with Marica, would it compromise my time with you. Yeah—it's Marica I was thinking of back then. It seems laughable now."

"Does George—"

"Never mind about George. My point is, look. You slept with all these other men and nothing changed for you-and-me. Our time together was pure sifted gold. What was my complaint? I didn't even know you were sleeping with random hitchhikers passing through—"

"Only one of those!" she protested.

"But who's counting? And why are they counting? That's my point! I had nothing to complain about! When you were present, you were totally present. What we said in the beginning was true. It didn't matter what you were doing with other guys when we were apart. It didn't affect our time together. Not at all." He paused. "Except? Once you told me? Oh wow. I had these intense feelings. But not because I was trying to own you. That wasn't it, I swear. What it was—somehow—knowing you were behind that closed door fucking some guy you'd picked up at the party—"

She winced at his choice of words.

"I guess I never pictured it that way. The dismay I felt, it had something to do with that fact that I care about you."

"I know." Zoe felt a lump in her throat. "I know you care about me, Sval. You care about a lot of people. You make people feel cherished. It's one of the things I cherish about you, I guess."

"But." He raised his hand to stop her from gushing. "I did wonder. How would you react if I suddenly started cruising bars at night, picking up loose women, having casual one-night stands…wouldn't you be asking yourself what's with Sval? Not because you want to own me! Because you care about me. That's the flip side of caring about another person. You have a responsibility to their moral health."

"You think casual sex damages the soul."

"Well, I don't really believe in a soul, but yes, past a certain point— what was it you said that night? *'You just do it to get it out of the way'.* Shouldn't sex have more meaning?"

Zoe studied her lap. "You thought I thought I was jumping into meaningless sex encounters. You were worried about me."

"Yes! You see your friend doing something self-destructive, do you support what she's doing? *Should* you? I merely pose the question. This is new territory for all of us. It's complicated. Granted."

Zoe nodded. "It would be different, you're saying, if it was someone I really cared about—if it was a *relationship* with meaning."

"Yes! Meaningful relationships, that's how a tribe is woven. We have to keep connecting. That's what we meant when we said 'open relationship.' We're building a new world here. We don't know what a given relationship should include. We have to be open to exploring alternative possibilities. I get that, I'm on board with it. You and me, though—we're in a whole other category with each other, aren't we? This is not just 'a relationship.'"

"I agree. This is a *primary* relationship."

"For me too. We have to think of this one differently."

"If it was a relationship, you're saying, with someone from the 'tribe', you're saying—"

"In a given moment, anything could happen," he allowed. "There's no prior way to know if it's right or wrong. The old rules are dead. We're building something new here so we have to try out stuff. But every time we make a right or wrong decision, we add a brick to this thing we're building. We have to be conscious of our deeper project in each given moment. You and me, though. We're not 'a moment', Zoe. We're a through-line."

"Oh Sval. You have such a wonderful way of seeing the bigger picture." She pulled him in for a soulful kiss. "You're one of a kind."

"Well. . ." he began modestly.

"Because I *have* met someone like that," she cut in, hurrying to finish, because this was the moment and she had to seize it. "Well, not met, it's someone we already know, it's the relationship is new. It's never going to be my primary relationship, but it's a *relationship* so, like you say, it has *value*."

A look like a guillotine blade dropped across his eyes. "George," he croaked.

"No! George? Please! I mean I like George, but not in that way."

"Then who?"

"Raoul."

"Raoul!" It started as a yelp but he gained control of himself. "Sorry. Didn't mean to sound like that. I'm just. It's so unexpected. Raoul?! When did this happen?"

"You're mad again," she accused him.

"Not mad. I'm—"

"Jealous."

He started to deny the accusation, but ended up hanging his head. "I do feel a certain indefinable dismay."

"Why can't you just say it's jealousy? We have to say what we're feeling, whatever it is."

"I wish I didn't feel this way," he said miserably.

"It's human, Sval. I'm not offended, I could take it as a compliment, you know. You value me."

"It's not for your sake I'm saying this. For my own sake it's not okay. I don't want to feel like this, Zoe. Jealousy or whatever, it feels lousy. It's not even a heroic hurt, it's more like a stomach ache or something. It feels shitty."

"I wish I could do something."

"No, no, this is mine to wrestle with. Don't say you're going to end it with Raoul, not for my sake. This is my problem, not yours, not his. I had this sucker beat! I'm going to get there. Just believe in me."

"It's okay. Let's not talk about it tonight. In the morning—"

"I should go. I have to work on me. I'm not my best self. I should go."

"Go where, Sval? It's the middle of the night."

"To Yamhill House. Martha's moved, you said. Her room—oh no. Wait."

She knew what stopped him. Raoul lived at Yamhill House.

"I'll go to—"

"Don't go anywhere, Sval. Stay with me, I've missed you so much. Stay with me tonight."

"But look at me, I'm all withdrawn now. I can't even get my feelings to my face. I'm better than this. Help me with this, Zoe. Let's do this work together. I need your help."

"You've got it, I'm your gal, lie down," she counseled him. He grumbled a bit, but obeyed and after a few minutes of rubbing naked bodies together, Zoe cooed, "How're we doing?"

"The pain has subsided a little," he admitted. "I'll stay."

She turned off the light.

Welcome to the Open Relationship

Sval knocked at the door of Yamhill House. He needed to welcome Raoul to the open relationship. After all, he and Raoul *were* related now, even if there was no name for this relationship. What did one call a friend who was sleeping with one's primary relationship? The community was going to need a whole new set of terms…

Raoul opened the door, beaming with delight. He led Sval to the kindergarten. From the next room came music Sval recognized as the second Weather Report album. He accepted a joint and said to Raoul, just by way of kicking off the conversation they would need to have, as two men sleeping with the same woman: "You and Zoe, how did that get started? If you're comfortable sharing. Not that you must. Zoe's got nothing to do with you'n'me when it's just you and me. We're friends, right? Just like we were before."

"Sure," said Raoul. "What kind of friends were we before?"

"The good kind," Sval asserted promptly. "We had conversations."

"What did we used to talk about?"

Sval couldn't remember. He passed the joint back to Raoul "We should do something together," he proposed. "What would be fun?"

"We could go fishing," Raoul suggested, "like that time with George. That was fun."

"Or I could help you paint a mural," Sval offered. "The People's Food Store wants one for the wall facing their parking lot."

"I know. They called me today, I said I'd get to it later."

"Why not now? We could go over there together," said Sval. "You paint, I'll keep you company. We could talk."

"You could help me paint," said Raoul

"Well, certainly, if my all-too-modest gifts in this area could add value."

The whole way to the Food Store, Sval's mind was buzzing with the question he decided he couldn't voice out loud. It wouldn't come out sounding right. He'd have to approach it from a less charged direction. "Raoul," he said, as the disheveled elf set out his paint pots, brushes, palette knives, and other less definable art apparatus. "What is your view of the future, what will your role be after the collapse of civilization?" Then Sval chuckled at himself. "What am I talking about? Role! Roles are what we're trying to get rid of, isn't it? I guess I'm asking, if you could be anything at all, what would you be?"

"If I could be anything I'd be an alien," Raoul responded promptly, "from a vastly superior civilization. A world where fish and people can live together, because they're not living in water or in air, they're living and swimming in something else."

"A worthy ambition, good sir." Sval said it with conviction. "A worthy ambition." He watched Raoul apply a splotch of forest green to the middle of the wall facing Powell Street. "You've painted a forest up there," he observed. "I could add a small man down here in the corner, walking toward your forest. What do you think, Raoul? Permitted?"

"Didn't you hear?" said Raoul. "God is dead, everything is permitted. Isn't this cool, you and me, painting a mural together? It's like having a conversation. You paint something, then I paint something, then you paint something—we can keep sparking off each other."

"Painting as a mode of conversation. Now, there's some food for thought." Sval felt his mind drifting. *How could you and Zoe*—no, that was the question he must not ask directly. He removed it from his thoughts.

The Ark drifted in to fill the vacancy. Niles Whitaker. He pictured a middle-aged chap in a blue striped suit.

Raoul was jabbering about some dream he'd had. "I'm in a gigantic stadium with thousands of people. It's so big, the people on the other side are just dots. Some of them aren't people though. Their eyes give them away. They're aliens."

Not without some effort, Sval reeled his attention back to this conversation. "A colorful dream, Raoul. My own dreams are more prosaic, I'm afraid. I dreamed I was a carrot the other night. I had these little arms, these little legs. I was dreaming that vegetables had taken control of the world and I was part of the new order. But there were procedures to be followed. Very strange. When I ask about dreams, though, I'm asking about real-life dreams, the kind we have when we're awake., the things we do in hopes of leaving a legacy. What would those be for you? I think we need to get to know each other better, now that we're—whatever you'd call this relationship we have with each other now. We've never really talked about stuff like this. I want to know."

"Well, actually, now that you bring it up, I do a lot of my dreaming when I'm awake, Sval. A lot! Working on my aquarium is like dreaming."

"The cardboard boxes. Yes, I've heard. Martha was telling me."

"Carboard boxes! Whatever you've heard is wrong. Cardboard boxes, everyone says. That's the trouble, Sval. They can't see that *it's an aquarium*! That's what I saw the moment it came into my head. It was so beautiful and strange, I wanted everyone to see it. That's why I started building it."

"I do understand," said Sval. "Our dreams must take concrete form, they're not real till other people can see them. I agree. The Proposal was like that for me. It was real. We set it up and it was working. We were a true collective, we met on Mondays—it was so concrete. No one told anyone else what to do, no one felt coerced, and yet on Friday, there it was, all over Portland, stacked up on bar counters. Everywhere you looked, people were reading the *Rose City Ark*. It was the Community in the form of words and paper. Now, it exists only in the memories of people who were part of it. I've been reading what they're publishing now, and man! Fashion essays? Hot new *businesses?* Profiles of city bureaucrats? What kind of crap is that? Nothing about the war. Nothing about the farm workers. Nothing about the outsider art emporium out on Sandy! It's like none of it is happening or ever happened. Ah, the Ark! It started out as a dream, it's gone back to being just a dream. There is no Ark anymore."

"*Just* a dream, you say? Like dreams are nothing? Sval! Dreams *are* what's real.   They're like windows, when you dream you're catching glimpses of what's really out there. And what really out there is always out there. You just can't see it most of the time. You pretty much have to enter dreamtime to even catch a glimpse of it."

"I beg to differ. I want my dreams to be real-world real right here in physical reality. I want the Proposal to be real again. I want the Ark to come back to life. And I feel like it's up to me, that's the hell of it, I wish I didn't feel like that, it isn't fun, but there's this voice that keeps hectoring me. Quit shirking, it says, quit shirking, something's wrong, do something, if you don't, no one will. There's no reason to think that's really true. It's just me bullying myself, but I can't help it. This is an illness that I have."

"I've got those voices too!" Raoul exclaimed. "Get that aquarium built is what mine say. Get it built! One of 'em's a guy coming after me with a whip, a big angry guy, naked to the waist, with these floppy trousers he wears—some kind of Turkish prison guard, I guess. That's what he feels like, giving me orders. No matter where I go, there he is, real as anyone I see in so-called Real Life." Raoul spat the words *real life* with contempt, waving his brush for punctuation—thereby splashing red paint right next to a gnome-like figure Sval had just colored in for him. "Nice!" he exclaimed, stepping back to admire the happy accident, and then went on. "He's not always a prison guard, though. Sometimes he looks like a boss I had one summer. 'Load 'em up faster son or I'll kick your butt right up into your shoulder.' Jeez, Dad! Now he's inside me, and the only way I can keep him quiet is to keep building."

"In sum, you feel driven." Sval's gaze was pinned to the work he was doing. "I understand 'driven'. Driven comes from way down deep.

It's not coming just out of your *own* life, it's coming out of all of human history, from way down deep in the life of everybody." He was painting a lawn for Raoul's scene, rapidly, rapidly putting in one blade of grass at a time. "That's why connecting is the thing. That's what we have to pursue."

"Another part of me," said Raoul, licking his lips, "can remember how it felt in the beginning, building the aquarium. It was like climbing a mountain at dawn and when you got to the top, there was the whole world spread out below! It wasn't work. But the realer it gets, the wronger it gets. That's what I don't like about Reality." Raoul put his head back and sniffed the moist air like a dog.

"Raoul," said Sval. "This is all very interesting. Reality versus dreaming, we could bat this one back and forth all day, but you and me…? We've got to talk."

"Isn't that just what we're doing?" Raoul didn't look at him. "We've been talking."

"I know, but there's a question I wanted to ask you. I hope it's okay."

Raoul looked a little alarmed now. "What?"

"Whose idea was it, yours or Zoe's? I'm just asking."

"You mean when we—"

"Yes. I don't mean to pry, I'm just wondering. Was it her idea? Because what we're saying about our relationship, Zoe and me, it's open. But we're still working out what that means. That's why I'm asking how it happened. I'm trying to figure out the rules."

"I don't know. It just happened. I don't know."

"Okay. But when did this happen? I'm trying to picture it. We're friends, right? We can talk about this. What was the situation? Were you partying?"

"Well. . ." Raoul thought about that one. "We'd just come back from Euphoria. We were both kind of drunk, I guess. We were having fun."

"Euphoria. An evening that wouldn't quit. I've been there, compeer. I can picture it. But Raoul." Sval dropped his voice and set his hand on Raoul's shoulder. "I bring this up only to reiterate what I said before. Let this not create any bad feelings between you and me."

"No, no," Raoul giggled. "Why should it?"

"Exactly. Nobody owns anybody. Rooting out the anachronisms, this is our work now. The world we used to know will soon be lying all around us in smoking ruins, Raoul. We'll have to be growing and changing constantly, endlessly, on a dime if need be. That's the skill we'll have to start cultivating right now—we're going to need it in times to come. Because it's we men who'll have to adapt, have to change. We're the dinosaurs."

"We're dinosaurs?" Raoul looked up, startled.

"Oh, absolutely," said Sval with a rueful smile. "We're dinosaurs."

"Cool!" said Raoul. "I love dinosaurs."

Late that night, while all of Yamhill house slept soundly above him, Raoul was in his laboratory, testing the seals and fittings of his aquarium. They still leaked a little, enough to make small puddles on the laboratory floor over the course of 24 hours. He'd have to tighten them up. He went to work but didn't notice his fingers working, lost as he was in solitary thoughts about the thorny problem of Sval and Zoe.

Whose idea was it? Raoul wished he could say. He couldn't remember himself ever making a decision. What he could remember was him and Zoe going for a walk in Washington Park that afternoon. They were part of a little herd at first, but the others dropped out or wandered away. He was telling her about Zara and she was listening with interest. Real interest! The park was especially beautiful because the rain had just stopped and every leaf was wet. He found he could talk about Zara without embarrassment because Zoe never seemed to doubt the premise of his story, that once upon a time, the most desirable woman on earth had fallen in love with a humble little turtle named Raoul.

Someplace along the walk, they picked up company and then they were a bunch of folks again, ambling down into the streets of Portland, looking for something to do. They'd migrated down to Euphoria, where Street Stomp was playing. Everyone danced with everyone, everyone got high, everyone lost themselves in music and motion, it was just another typical night. At one point, he and Zoe, tiring at the same moment, plopped into chairs across from each other, both of them panting, and Zoe touched Raoul's hand for a second, but just friendly-like. That wasn't "the moment". It was only the panting that made it feel flirtatious, that wasn't when they crossed the line. But then she said, "I hear you're making an aquarium. Do you ever show it to people?"

"It's not done yet."

And she said, "I know. But is it done enough for a person to imagine it?"

No one had ever asked him such a question before! "I could show it to you, but *seeing* it, that'll be up to you," he warned.

"Try me," she said. "I'm curious."

So they left Euphoria together and made their way to Yamhill House. They stumbled down the basement steps to his laboratory. Raoul went first to find the light switch, then called to Zoe, "Come on down." He had the basement to himself, now that George had moved in with Marica. His laboratory was enormous now.

He assembled the aquarium and stepped back. Zoe strolled among the tanks, touching the coils of plastic tubing that connected them "It's going to be like the bottled city of Kandor," she said.

"You know about the bottled city of Kandor?"

"It was my favorite thing in Superman. I always wanted a bottled city of my own."

"It wasn't just a city, though." Raoul knew why her voice had gone furry. He knew what she was feeling. She was remembering childhood. "It was a whole world."

"That's what I loved about it," said Zoe. "Kandor reminded you, there could be millions of whole-other-worlds. When I was a kid, that's how it was."

He picked up on that and took it further. "It made *me* realize I might be in somebody else's bottled city right now."

Zoe turned in place, absorbing the aquarium, there in the cluttered darkness of his basement laboratory.

"In dreams," he said to her, "you visit other places, and they're just as real as this place."

"Dr. Freud might argue with you about that," she said, "but I like your version better. Other worlds that are just as real."

She liked his version better! They were feeling comfortable together, down here in his laboratory, just the two of them cozily stoned in this warm, dark space.

"Wouldn't it be cool," she said, "if you could just stay in one of your good dreams."

"I even like the bad dreams." said Raoul. "Dreams are stories. You need bad things to happen in a story. That's what makes them exciting. Of course, this is just a story too, but this one's dull and stupid. *This* reality is the story I want to wake up *from*."

"Hmm," said Zoe. "But isn't this reality the one Zara's in?"

Wow. This Zoe! She really understood! "Yes, Zara's stuck in this reality too except, in this reality, she's on the east coast. See what I mean? Although…" A thought struck him. "In *this* reality, she might be thinking about moving to Portland at this very moment. She hasn't told anyone yet, so I don't know about it. That's what might be happening right now in this story. She might be *coming* to that decision. There's no way for me to know. I just have to wait and find out."

"But you're not just a character, Raoul, you're also the author of this story. You can make things happen. And you don't have to be such a loner while you're waiting." She tousled his hair. "If you can't be with the one you love, why don't you love the one you're with?"

He recognized the Steven Stills song. "I'll tell you why. Because The One might come along just then and think I'm taken. I can't risk it."

"The One." Zoe favored him with a skeptical half-smile. "I have trouble with that bullshit One-and-Only story we always hear. Snow White and Prince Charming. I have trouble with that one."

He could see something like a monkey sitting on her shoulder. She was frowning but her monkey was laughing. Raoul picked up a sketchpad. "All right, forget about Snow White. They say you split in two when you come down from the astral plane, and your other half is out there somewhere. I *believe* that. True love is what happens if you meet your other half. *If* you meet. There's a billion people out there and only one of 'em's your other half. So, what are the chances? A billion to one. So, you have to be careful not to blow it if you do cross paths. Because you might never get another chance."

"And yet you and Zara met. How do you explain that?"

"Once out of every billion times, a billion-to-one chance does come true. It's mathematics."

She smiled. "Touché. Score one for Raoul. But how about another explanation? Maybe there's lots of Zaras out there, and you just haven't learned to recognize most of them yet." She gave him a teasing nudge and then lost the smile. "I'll tell you one thing. There's no Other-Half of me out there. There's lots of other-halves of somebodies. Lots of possible combinations is what I think is true. I could still be anybody, is what I believe. That's the one belief I can't live without. I have choices, lots of choices. Nothing's off the table."

"Hmm." He set down his sketchpad and rolled a joint. "What does that feel like? Are you happy?"

"Happy enough most times. Is that me?" She picked up his sketchbook and smiled at the drawing of a monkey capering on a woman's shoulder. "I'm happy when I'm with Sval. I feel like we're important. We're changing the world. People will remember us. That's a good feeling. But I don't know, I keep thinking, there's other ways to be happy. Who knows which is best? I'm still looking. How about you?"

"As long as I'm working on the aquarium, I'm happy."

The unnoticed joint uncurled slowly into smoke between Zoe's fingers. She was in his armchair now, half-reclining, her free arm resting on her thigh, her legs slightly apart, her head tilted back, her lips slightly parted, her fiery hair spilling down to her shoulders on either side of her freckled dusted face. It struck Raoul that Zoe and Zara were both Z-names. Could that have cosmic significance?"

"I'm curious about this Zara," she said. "What makes you so sure she's your other half?"

"Because of what happened when we met."

"That's what I'm asking. What happened when you met?"

"We got together."

"Oh, no, you're not wiggling out of this so easy. Got together how?" Zoe leaned forward out of her chair to pose that question. "Tell me the story. I want the *story*."

"Okay." The request aroused him. He was sitting on a stool now, facing her, scrunched up pretty close, their knees almost touching. "For the longest time, I never spoke to her. We just saw each other around the studio—"

"Huh. She's an artist. Okay, that makes sense." Zoe was attentive and absorbed. Their knees were now touching.

"Oh, boy, is she ever. She invited me home to see her sculptures one afternoon."

"Come-and-look-at-my-etchings." Amusement showed in Zoe's eyes.

"They weren't etchings" He wanted her to appreciate this fully. "She'd made a whole world out of cloth. Plants, rocks, animals, everything: a whole world made of cloth and stuffed with cotton. That's when I saw the aquarium for the first time. I glimpsed it in my mind. All the cotton was water. All the cloth was glass."

"And then?"

"And then it happened."

"There you go again. What happened? You're skipping over the story." Zoe set a hand on his knee to prop herself as she leaned forward further. Her free hand moved up to his shoulder, her warm fingers circled Raoul's neck and stroked up into his curly hair. "One moment, you're appreciating each other as artists. The next moment, you're lovers. How does that line get crossed? That's the mystery. From stranger to friend, that I get. That's not so strange. From friend to lover? How does *that* line get crossed? Did one of you say something?"

Raoul savored the wakefulness of all his cells. "Well… I might have said something like: 'you're so beautiful you make my eyes feel hot.' I meant to say 'your art is so beautiful," but instead I said 'you'. It was an accident. It just happened."

He and Zoe were both on the floor now, piled together as two bodies, chuckling about what had happened with Zara. It was warm in the laboratory and dark and nice. She said, "I see where a line like that might get a girl going. 'You make my eyes feel hot.'" Her arm encircled his waist. "Don't worry, you don't have to tell me I make your eyes feel hot. I'm not Zara. I know that. But I *might* be. You know? How can you tell unless you try? You want to cross that line with me just once? We don't have to, but I think we both want to. Don't we?"

Raoul felt young. The air crackled with reckless excitement. He was wallowing in the warmth of his aquarium's shadow. He was wondering about Sval but Zoe didn't seem to be. She knew more about these things than he, so this must be okay. She was being careless with her body, letting it loll against him, like they were such good friends now, it didn't really matter where they bumped or touched. But only because they'd gotten so comfortable with each other. This wasn't when it happened. "Sval would be okay with this," she said, "if you're wondering. We have an open relationship."

Raoul knew that term. He just never knew it might have anything to do with him.

"He'd be pleased for us," said Zoe, "in case that's important to you. Sval says people should explore all the ways people can be good together with each other. I think I could like this way, for you and me. What do you think?"

"I like it," he admitted. "For now.

"How long is 'now'? You don't want me to leave, do you?"

"No." He nuzzled her with his lips. "Let's stay right here." She nuzzled back. His mind was a soap bubble swelling with wonder. How could this be happening? "Are we crossing that line?"

"It's not official," she said, "till we kiss."

And so they kissed; but that wasn't really when it happened. By then it was already happening, had been happening for a while. By that point, in fact, it felt like it had started happening so long ago, its origins were shrouded in mist.

The Leak

On an overcast Sunday, Sval went to see Martha. She had moved to an isolated residential neighborhood separated from North Portland by railroad tracks and industrial workshops. Sval pulled up behind a half-ton '54 Chevy pickup on cinderblocks. A cat with ragged fur slunk away. He climbed rotting steps to a rotting porch. An overgrown holly bush bulged halfway to the door. He tried the door. It was unlocked. He pushed it open, stepped into a dusty foyer. The building had two flats and the one on the first floor was vacant. Martha must live upstairs. Sval took the steps in gliding bounds. "Martha?"

The door opened. Martha peered out. "Sval." A smile creased her cheeks. "You came."

"I should've called. Is this a bad time?"

"Not at all. Step in. You're letting in the cold."

"It's a nacreous day." He stepped across her threshold, slapping his sides

"Nacreous?"

"Pearl-like. To wit: gray. I meant to drop by sooner, Martha. Honestly, I've had just such a hell of a lot of settling-back-into-Portland stuff to do." He set forth anecdotes to verify his claim: red tape at the unemployment office… meetings at the People's Food Store …

"You're such a man-about-town," Martha beamed. "Always on your way to meetings."

"I'm addicted," he confessed. "I haven't tested the waters at Ark yet though. So this is your place, eh? I must say: wow. You have it all to yourself?"

"Three whole rooms. It's like heaven! I just couldn't take any more of that *Yamhill* House!"

"I bet it got noisy there, didn't it? Tell me: what's the best thing about living alone? I'm thinking of writing a think-piece for the Ark: living alone versus living with roommates. Your thoughts, ma'am?"

"The best thing about it?" Her eyes twinkled. "Cleaning house. No, really. You leave for ten hours, and when you get back the dishes are still washed. So how do you like it?" She turned in place, presenting her home.

Sval let his gaze roam. Martha's Indian print dress, all earth-tone colors, blended with the room's décor. "Astounding, what you've done with it." The living room was small, and it wasn't warm, but the furnishings made it look warm: strips of fabric hung on several of the walls, giving rust and ochre and autumnal forest hues to the room. Here and there a dramatic streak of red caught his eye. Interspersed among them were several matted photographs. He noticed one piece by George. So, these two were friends now! Good. The community interweaving, growing. Martha had given the woodwork a fresh coat of white paint, and the floors looked newly sanded, oiled, and polished. Two windows let in light through complementary lace curtains.

"And then through here..." She led the way into a tidy little kitchenette with a window that looked out upon a luxuriantly unkempt yard. A branch of a neighbor's fig tree brushed against the windowpane. The branch was stripped of figs for a distance of an arm's length from Martha's window.

"This *is* nice," he declared. "How much did you say you're paying?"

"Fifty dollars a month."

"Unbelievable. You'd never guess what you've got inside here from what's outside. Where'd you get all this furniture?"

"Goodwill, mostly," Martha told him. "A few from St. Vincent de Paul. I know how to spot a bargain."

"Your bargain-spotting powers are indeed the stuff of legends. Marica calls you the Einstein of the twenty-nine cent bins."

"I do like to root around in those. But it's 29 cents a *pound*, Sval. See that thing?" She pointed to a tapestry hanging on the wall: a troubadour with a lute. "That weighs three and a half pounds, so it came out to a dollar plus change. I was about to make some tea. You want some? Or a cold beer? Or a piece of homemade cherry pie?"

"The latter two." Sval trailed her into the kitchen and watched her gather up drinks and food from around the small room. He followed her back out into the living rom. He settled into her beanbag chair.

She set the tray down on a board stretched between two orange crates. "So you're going to write something about living alone. That's exciting."

"Well, it's a thought. I haven't been to Monday meeting yet. I want to have a story idea to propose when I go. I'm not sure if the living-alone piece is going to work, though."

"There wouldn't be much to say," she agreed.

"Oh, that's not the trouble. There's much to say, but it would be a quiet philosophical piece. I'm thinking I need to go in with something more provocative. Given what I hear about this Niles Whitaker—guns blazing. What's the procedure these days? Is it still, go to Monday Meeting, tell everybody what you want to write, and people say yes or no?"

"Well, sort of. But Niles runs Monday meeting now, I mean really *runs* it. It has to be something he likes, or you won't get a chance to talk about it."

"So I've been hearing, but I'm truly baffled. This chap comes in and suddenly he's the boss? How does that happen? The proposal was supposed to stop that kind of thing."

"He's not the boss. He's just the facilitator, like you were, only he does it every week now. It's only for Monday Meeting, though."

"As opposed to what?"

"Well, now there's Saturday meeting too. He doesn't run that one or even come to it. That's where we discuss important stuff. Monday meeting's just for nuts-and-bolts stuff."

"As in?"

"Like, 'do we need more wax' and 'how many boxes should we order'. Stuff like that."

"And copy for the next issue?"

"Yeah. That too. People vote."

"That's not important stuff? Copy for the next issue? What's the 'important stuff'?"

"Oh, you know. Like, who do we root for in—I forget which country. Angola? Anyway, someplace in Africa. There's all different groups of armies fighting there."

"I know. Independence movements. Sure. MPLA. FNLA. UNIDA—"

"Anyway, some people thought the Ark should take a stand about that. Some people said no. Some people said this group, some people said that group. We spent one whole day arguing about who the Ark should root for in Angola. Honestly, that's when we decided we should have a separate meeting for all that policy stuff. We said, on Mondays, let's just focus on nuts-and-bolts."

"And Niles runs Monday meeting?"

"He doesn't tell anyone what to do. He just kind of decides what gets talked about. Sort of like you or Marica used to do. If there's something people want to argue about, he says take it to Saturday Meeting."

"And what happens to it at Saturday Meeting?"

"You know. People talk about it. Over dinner or whatever. It's a potluck, most times. Saturday Meeting's sort of merged with Acme Music Club."

"I see." Sval sank into rumination. What sort of story would please this Niles? He'd have to meet the man. Figure out what would please him. Although, come to think of it, why should he have to please Niles?

The collective had final say. He just had to offer something the *collective* would approve. Who was the collective now?

Rain rustling on the roof sounded like rice rolling on paper. "First rain of the season," Sval commented, just to break the silence.

"It's depressing," said Martha.

"And yet somehow, every year, we get used to it. How's your heating system?"

She made her mouth smile. "It's in my prayers. Ha ha."

Sval noticed a bead of water forming along a crack in the plaster. It swelled until it was heavy enough to detach. Then it dropped into an aluminum pan that already had some water.

"Martha, you've got a leak."

"I know. Six or seven of them. What can you expect? I'm getting three rooms and a yard for $50 a month. Rent like that, you can't expect perfect."

"Perfect? Martha! In Portland, for Christ's sake? It's going to rain every day for the next seven months. It'll be like you're living outdoors. This goes way beyond 'imperfect'. Does your landlord know about these leaks? You better talk to him."

"Ha ha. And he'll say what? 'Fine, I'll fix your roof? Let me get out my checkbook?' " Martha released a sigh. "I'm pretty sure I know what he'd say. He'd pull out the contract and say look what you signed here. He told me out-and-out, I'd have to take it as is. I said okay and I signed. I was desperate."

"Well, even so, talk to him. What's the worst he can do? If he says no, you'll just be where you are now."

"The worst he can do is evict me."

"If he does, you can crash at my house," Sval vowed. "We've got a couch. At least you'll have a story to tell your grandchildren: how it was back when civilization was collapsing."

"For my grandchildren! Why don't *you* write a story about it right now, for the *Ark*?" Then she laughed at her own audacity. "As if anyone'd be interested."

"Why wouldn't they?" A light had gone on in Sval's eyes. He leaned out of his beanbag chair, energized. "You're not the only one with a bad landlord."

"Extra! Extra!" Martha scoffed. "Read all about it! Martha's Roof Is Leaking!"

"I'm serious. This could be a great one for the Ark: a human interest story about a tenant having problems. Most of us who read the Ark are tenants. This wouldn't just be *your* story, it would be *our* story. This is what we need to do, as a newspaper. Tell the community its own stories."

Martha's eyes sparkled at the thought. "You could write it like the one about the dog that wouldn't stop barking. I liked that one!"

"Indeed. A trace of irony might add salt. I'm thinking of something more hard-edged, though. *Tribulations of a Tenant.* Eh? A story with political implications. We might have a sidebar with tips for readers. If you find yourself in a situation like this, here are ten things you can do. I'll drop in on Monday Meeting, see what they think."

"Just watch out for Niles. If he decides he doesn't like it, you won't really get a chance to convince anyone. Niles has his people around him. If you go against anything he says, he makes you look like a fool."

"I'll step carefully." Martha's warning sent a slight shiver through Sval. He'd be stepping into the Lion's Den, it seemed, if he dropped in on Monday Meeting with a proposal for a story. This Niles Whitaker? He had some strange power, apparently.

Letter from Prison

Zoe felt bored. Once again, a day of unrestricted freedom yawned in front of her. Today, she could do anything she wanted. Yesterday had been the same. Start her long-postponed study of Turkish . . . Try peyote. . . Sign up for zither lessons. Life was like Baskin-Robbins: full of options. Why did she feel like there was nothing to do? For lack of better, she tagged along with Sval to George's house. Maybe she'd find something there. George was just getting set to leave for Salem. "Hot story," he explained. He was going to interview some prisoners at the Oregon State Penitentiary. "Duke Silver set it up. Remember him? Guy I shared a cell with after the food stamp riot."

"How could I forget," said Sval. "The biker who was going to kill you."

"He teaches some kinda' class down there. Motorcycle repair. You wanna' come along, Sval? Should make a decent piece for the Ark."

"You've cleared this with what's-his-name? This Niles Whitaker fellow?"

"Whitaker!" George flung his hand up in exasperation. In the process he lost hold of his backpack, which knocked over a floor lamp, which crashed against the wall and brought down a picture hanging there. "Why do I need to clear it with that motherfucker?"

"Well, if he and his people control the Ark now—"

"Yeah, yeah, I know." George stuffed a tape recorder into his backpack. "Doesn't fit the concept of the Hot New Ark. We'll have to put some puff-piece angle on it: Ten Best Prison Cafeterias

of the West. How 'bout that? Or we can go the Leninist route—
take control of the means of production. Use a baseball bat to get it
into the paper."

"That," said Sval, "sounds ill-advised. Perhaps at the next
Monday Meeting we could—"

"Tell you what," George interrupted. "*You* take charge of
getting it into the paper. You're better at twisting people around—"

"I don't twist—"

"All right, manipulate, or whatever's the polite word. You
know what I mean. Negotiate. That's it. You negotiate with the
Whitaker gang. I'll get the interview."

Sval disapproved. "If you're doing the interview, *you* should
present it to the collective."

"Let's both do the interview," George belched. "What else
am I telling you? Hop aboard. Train's leaving in two minutes."

But Sval had gone quiet now. He cracked his knuckles. He
fumbled for cigarettes. He checked his watch. "What is it now?
Noon-ish? I can't. I'm scheduled to meet Raoul in a couple of
hours." He glanced at Zoe. "We're painting a mural together."

"What do you know about painting murals?" George
scoffed.

Zoe stepped forward.   "Sval is right. Him and Raoul need
to spend more time together. I'll go. I've always wanted to see the
inside of a prison."

Sval looked startled, but he nodded. "I have commitments," he
declared solemnly.

On the way to Salem, Zoe took off her shoes and propped
her feet up against the dashboard. "Got a cigarette?"

"Just see-gars."

"All right. Let me bum one of those."

"In the glove compartment."

She found a stogie wrapped in cellophane, stripped it, lit it,
took a couple of inexpert puffs, and spewed a cough. "Gaaaah!
Disgusting!"

George chuckled, pleased. Women and cigars. He knew this would happen. She let the stogie burn down between her fingers.

"How long have you 'always' been interested in prisons," George demanded.

"Ever since I 'didn't' get arrested in the sixties." She let her voice add the air-quotes, just as his had done.

"Arrested in the sixties." The phrase put George in a nostalgic mood. But he shook off the mood. "That was jail for a couple of days. This is prison we're going to now. Real criminals—cutthroats. Rapists. Much heavier."

"Didn't draft resisters go to prison too?"

"Not ones like us to places like this. Boojhie kids like me and Sval, we got sent to playpens, not state pens."

"How do you know those ones were playpens? Were you in one?"

"Not me."

"You weren't a draft resister?"

"No."

"How'd you get out of the draft then?"

"I stuffed peanut butter in my ass."

"No, really."

"You think I'd make up something like that? Yes, really. Just before my physical, I stuffed my ass full of peanut butter. When the guy checked for piles he freaked out and started screaming, what's this, what's this? I reached back and scooped some out and took a lick, I said, 'I dunno' but it tastes pretty good.' That did it."

Zoe made a face. "Four-F?"

"One-Y. Good enough. I had a whole bag of scams to try, but I gave this peanut butter thing first shot because it was the least hassle."

"Gross! That would've been my last."

"Because?"

"Because! Eating shit was never my idea of a good time."

"Who's talking about a good time? People were shooting their toes off to stay out of 'Nam. Eating shit was baby food. Besides, I told you, it was peanut butter."

Zoe shook her head in philosophical dismay. "Some people have it easy. You know what Raoul did?"

"I know, he dropped acid and freaked out for real at his physical. That's berserk. But then let's face it, Raoul is 60 percent cracked."

"I don't know about that," Zoe bristled.

George glanced at her appraisingly, then let up on the gas and pumped the brakes. "Here's Salem. Listen, we're picking Silver up, giving him a ride today. Don't ask him how he got out of the draft—"

"I know, because he didn't. He went to Vietnam and he's touchy about it."

"How'd you know that?"

"I read your interview with him. I read everything you write."

"Huh."

Duke Silver was waiting for them in front of a bar. He jerked his head at Zoe as he slid into the car. "Who's she?"

Zoe gave the answer herself and, as she spoke her name, thrust her hand out for a shake. Silver psychically withdrew from this mannish assertion but shook her hand with dry courtesy, then turned to George again. "Who's Zoe Madigan?" he asked as if she was not present.

"Friend of Sval's," she again answered for herself. "Sval couldn't make it, so I came in his place. I'm with the Ark too."

Duke gave a noncommittal grunt and gave George directions to the prison. On the way, he sat up straight in his place as if planted on a steel rod. Zoe pictured sleeping with this guy and decided no thanks. He would be like a dead tree in bed.

They drove through a neighborhood of small, flat, glum-looking houses. The closely cropped lawns and the pastel sidings had a dull color, as if the whole scene had been stored in an attic for several years gathering dust. Then suddenly there was the prison, looming up over the grey-shingled roofs. It looked like it had been poured out of concrete in one solid hunk.

"Pull over for a minute," Zoe gulped, pointing toward a Plaid Pantry on the corner. She ran in and bought herself a pack of

Camels and then didn't know why. Cigarettes never helped her feel at ease.

They parked at the base of the prison. The walls rose some 30 feet above them, it seemed, four stories worth, unrelieved by windows, ornaments, or seams. The building seemed to have been poured out of concrete in one solid hunk. The Foursquare Church of Portland, always previously Zoe's nominee for the most dismal structure on earth, now slipped into second place.

Duke stepped ahead of them and spoke to the guard at the receiving desk. The guard pulled several cards out of a file and studied them, then lifted his head.

"George Lubick?"

George nodded.

"And. . .?" His head rotated like a gun turret until his eyes were pointed at Zoe.

"Zoe Madigan," she said.

The guard consulted his card again, obstinacy slowly hardening behind his features. "It says here, Sval Hofby," he accused.

"I'm here in place of Sval."

"I'm not authorized to let in anyone except who's on the list."

Duke interceded. "It was supposed to be two from the Ark. Check it out, man. This is two from the Ark right here. The warden wants this to happen."

The guard pondered this for a minute, then shrugged. "Warden can decide. He wants to see you anyway." He motioned to another guard hovering nearby. "Take these two to the warden."

The guard ushered them into a room that might have been any office in any government building. The warden wasn't a huge bald man with a whip. He was a civil servant in a brown suit, a white shirt, and a dark, striped tie. His hairline had receded an inch or two. Several copies of the Ark sat on his desk. One featured craft breweries of the northwest, the other was the Halloween issue, with special pages for kids. George and Zoe didn't seem to be quite what he had expected to see, but he maintained his composure.

"I want to welcome you gentlemen of the press," he said, "and you, miss. We invited you in because we want the people to know about some of these programs we've started. Other than yourselves from—what is it now?" He glanced through the newspapers on his desk. "The *Rose City Ark*? The media's been ignoring our press releases. All you ever hear in the news is Attica, Attica, Attica! But what about the positive prison stories?"

George maintained a solemn face. Zoe suppressed the laugh she felt rising.

"We invited you in," said the warden, "to get a feel for what we call progressive penology. Beefing up the vocational training. Library privileges. Plus we've got vocational classes like the one Mr. Silver's running—motorcycle repair? It all adds up to one word. *Rehabilitate.* That's the key. Rehabilitate that prisoner."

"Interesting," Zoe allowed.

The warden locked his hands in front of him on his desk. "What you've got to have is money, though. This is where the legislature doesn't get it. Schools, schools, schools, it's all they talk about. And I get it. Parents are voters. But what about prisons? This is where *you* can make a difference, George—" He glanced at his scribbled notes— "and Miss Madigan. You could make a difference. Tell your readers! When you've got prisons strapped for funding, three or four men crammed to a cell, *this* is where you get your Atticas, Mr. and Mrs. Average Citizen, you *do* need to be concerned! Someday, most of these men are coming out, and when they do, you'd better hope they're *rehabilitated!* Let your readers know we need more money for prisons."

"Any limits on what we ask?" Zoe inquired.

The warden raised his hands to forestall misunderstanding. "Just stay inside of common sense guidelines. Steer clear of any talk about their trial, they'll all tell you they were framed. If you take a pencil in, bring that pencil out. Common sense. Some of these men can make a weapon out of anything. That tape recorder? It's got a strap. You leave that with the guard."

By the time they rejoined Silver, a small crowd of visitors had gathered in the antechamber. A pair of guards led them through a metal gate and into the prison. The walls were painted with glossy enamel. The floors were tiled in green, shiny slate. Nothing to be seen looked soft. The lights bounced and gleamed off metallic surfaces and so did sounds. The clang of the metal gate behind them ricocheted against walls and floors.

A second chamber was unlocked for them. Here, George's tape recorder was taken, tagged, and put away. They were frisked. Zoe gritted her teeth. Outside, she would never have let any man touch her this way, but in here, all she wanted was to make no trouble. So this was prison. Interesting.

They passed an open doorway through which Zoe glimpsed a stadium-sized room filled with—o-good-god, were those rows of cages with men inside them? Silver peeled away, following one of the guards down another corridor, to some other part of the prison, where he ran his motorcycle repair class. The remaining visitors followed the first guard through a steel door, which clanged shut behind them as they walked deeper into the concrete monolith. Zoe remembered the dread she had of small spaces. She paced herself by taking long, deep breaths.

They entered the visiting room. The guard motioned the visitors briskly to their stations. Plastic tables were bolted to the floor, flanked by plastic seats bolted to the table. At each table, prisoners sat on one side, free-world folks on the other; no bars, no mesh, no glass between them. A sign on the wall warned: "NO TOUCHING." Guards patrolled casually back and forth behind the prisoners.

Four men awaited them. All four were Black. Zoe felt their tension bristling as she approached. She took her seat at the table next to George. The men looked guarded

"Lubick," George thrust out his hand, then withdrew it: no touching, he remembered. "George Lubick from the Rose City Ark. It's a newspaper in Portland. This here's Zoe Madigan. We're working on a story about prisons."

"They told us. I'm Malik Carter." The prisoner at the end of the row nodded. He was a compact man with neck muscles like ropes. He tilted his head toward his fellow prisoners. "This here is Wallace. Next to him, that's Duane, some people call him Hippo. And down at the end is my boy JJ."

Wallace looked soft and had moist eyes. Duane was short and heavy. JJ looked too young to be in a place like this: he was a hangdog, overgrown kid among men.

"How's this work?" said Carter. "This here's a first for us, we never done nothing like this before. You want something for your paper, the man says?"

"Yes," said George. "How we'll do this—just start talking, I guess. We've got an hour, anything you want to tell us, let's just see where it goes. What your life's about, what it's like in here—whatever you want to tell us. Zoe will take notes."

"George'll take notes," said Zoe. "I might ask some questions, but mostly, fellows, we're here to listen."

"Notes?" Duane sat up straight. "Notes for what? Notes for who?"

"No no, it's not what you're thinking," George assured him. "Notes so we can write our story. They took our tape recorder. We just want to make sure we get it right."

"Hold on there, chief." Carter demurred. "Your story? This is going to be *your* story? 'How I Met Some Prisoners'? This is going to be about *you?*"

"Of course not, no." George backtracked. "It's your story, we'll just be the ones writing it up."

"Hmm." Wallace moistened his lips. "That's not the way we heard it. The way we heard, *we'd* be writing something and you'd be putting it in your paper. That's why we volunteered. Yeah—us four here, we all volunteers. JJ's a little behind but he's got gifts and the rest of us, we-all can write. We volunteered for this because we thought we'd be getting a chance to tell our own story our own way and someone'd be listening for a change."

"*You'd* be writing something," said Zoe. "Interesting."

"And we'd put it in the paper?" said George. "The trouble with that you see—" George pursed his lips. "We don't get to decide what goes in the paper. All we can do is write something and pitch it and the collective decides. They might say yes, they might say no."

Carter frowned. "You got bosses. I get it. Shit. Everybody answers to The Man."

"It's not the Man exactly," George demurred. "It's 20 or 30 people who get together every Monday for a big-assed meeting to decide what's going in the paper next week. Believe me, it's a pain in the butt, but that's how anything gets into the Ark. There's this whole group decides."

"Why should that be a problem, George? Why wouldn't the whole group go for this?" Zoe demanded. "This sounds like a winner to me." She addressed the men across the table. "If you write something, what would you be writing?"

"Each of us got our own thing to say," said Carter. "We're four different people, yo."

"Me, I'd be writing just about my day-to-day for starters," Wallace mused. "Every morning, you wake up, it's the same fuckin' block of stone you locked up inside of last night, and here you are, still today, tomorrow, every day—you looking at twenty more years. You know how that feels? Every day, you step into the mess hall, first thing you do, you coil up'n'get ready. You know how that feels? No way. That's why I got to write this. I know how this shit *feel*."

"Not just that. Not for me." Duane shook his head. "This ain't where it started." Behind his hooded eyes, something flashed. "They been fixing to send me here from the git-go. It took 'em a while to get me in here, but that's what you all don't get. Lockup ain't just in here, it's out there too. It's everywhere I could ever be. Never had a chance."

George's eyes were gleaming. "Holy crap. Voices from Prison. Zoe, you're right, the Ark should be carrying more of this, lots like this. The trouble is there's four of you. No way we're selling the collective on four whole pieces next issue. We could *try* to ram it through, but here's another idea. How about each of you writes something and we've got this man Sval, hell of an editor, he'll sew 'em into one piece so good you'll never know they started out as four. And all four of you get the byline. Voices from Prison. That'd work. Sure." George dropped his pencil and leaned back, pleased with his solution.

"Editor? See, there you go again," Carter snorted. "Editor. We want what *we* write to go into the paper word for word or not at all."

"Word for word! Well, look—"

"No," Duane interrupted. "You look. A man has got to *represent* himself. You said you be giving us a platform. Now, you're talking about taking *our* words and giving them to some honkey motherfucker—"

"Here's the point." Wallace was sitting forward, the moisture gone from his eyes. "The man behind bars never gets a chance to tell his own story to *anyone*. Ever letter come out of this place, the Man reads it first 'n if he don't like it, he scratches out words. You can shout all you want in here, the sound don't never leave the room. In here, you get to where you're working out what to write so's the Man don't scratch it out and you know what that means? Means you're still letting the Man pick out your words. Ends up, you don't even know what your own self be thinking."

"You don't even have a your-own-self anymore," Carter snorted. "You've let the Man inside your head, all you got's the game you're playing with him. He's trying to git you and you're trying not to git got. You-all out there, you flat don't know. That's why you can't be 'editing' what we write. You can't be scratching out our words and putting in yours. That won't cut it. No, no."

"It's about censorship," George protested. "That's not what it is. Everyone gets edited. Sval doesn't change what you're saying, he just makes it *sound* better."

Wallace favored this with a humorless smile. "How can he make it sound better if he don't know how it's *supposed* to sound? All we're askin' you is just let us write our own damn stories. We're trying to *educate* you, blood. You're telling me your man Sval can teach *us* how to educate *you* better?"

Zoe cut in. "Tell them the whole process, George. From the editor, it comes back to you men—isn't that right, George? You read what the editor's done and change it any way you want, you put it back the way it was if you want—yeah: you get full and final say. The editor is just someone to talk to, someone standing in for your readers out there. He listens and tells you what he heard, and that way you can tell if you're getting through. I tell you what. Forget about Sval. *I'll* be your editor. Tell me your story and I'll give you my feedback. This could be good. Your warden's big on classes, I could come down once a week, we could call it a writing class. When you get it to sound exactly like you want it to, that's what we put in the paper. Right, George? Isn't that how it works?"

"It could," George agreed, "but we've still got the space problem: getting the collective to give us four whole pages, that's a big ask."

"Maybe it's not one issue," said Zoe. "Maybe it's a series stretched across a month. Or a column, what about that?"

"A column," mused George, his brows knitting in thought. "*Letter from Prison.* Every week or every few weeks, or whatever, one of you writes something. You take turns."

"Maybe it's a book," said Zoe.

The men considered in silence for a moment. "I'm in," said Wallace. "We get a copy of the paper?"

"Sure," said Zoe. "Right, George? We could get them a subscription."

"Absolutely," George declared. "Of course. No doubt. We'll send it to you every week. By God, this could be real good. You write it, we'll run it, that's a promise. I give you my word."

When Zoe left the prison she didn't *want* to come back to this place, but if they got clearance to come back, she knew she would. What she'd felt today from start to finish was concentration. In her mind, what she saw as they drove away that day was JJ: that warm, hangdog, hurt, angry boy brimming with longing. At his age, what could he have done to end up in the state penitentiary? She wanted JJ's whole story. If she kept coming, she knew she'd get it too, because men told her things. *The Life and Times of Prisoner Jones* as told to Zoe Madigan. Maybe she had found her calling. Maybe, what she was deep down, was a ghostwriter.

Blocked

The first thing that struck Sval about Niles Whitaker was the way the room looked before he arrived. In the old days the chairs had always been set up in a circle for meetings, or if necessary, in concentric rings. Now they were arranged in slightly curving rows facing a podium, three chairs, and a stand-alone blackboard at the focal point.

Himself walked in, flanked by two lieutenants, and he looked to Sval exactly like his name—tall, slender, and dressed in faded jeans and a form-fitting blue T-shirt that hadn't come from any thrift store. He carried a briefcase that matched the tone of his healthy tan. His hair was rather long but groomed. The moment he appeared the noise died and everybody sat down facing the front, like well-disciplined school kids.

Sval saw George in the last row and sat down next to him. "I thought you didn't do Monday Meetings anymore."

"First one in a while," said George. "I need to get this letter-from-prison thing into the chute. There might be some resistance, Sval, I need you to back me on this one."

"Count on it," Sval whispered back. "I have a story to pitch too."

Niles took a stack of Xeroxed papers from his briefcase and had one of his lieutenants distribute the sheets around the room. They turned out to be the agenda. Crisply he began reading off items, explaining what various committees had worked out and calling for a vote. There was no discussion or dissent. The voting was run efficiently, and it always approved whatever the committees had decided.

After each vote, George raised his hand, but Niles ignored him. George gave forth loud sighs, crossed his arms, leaned back in his chair, the picture of jittery discontent. Niles went on. George let out a brazen guffaw and slapped his palm over his mouth in a mocking show of shutting himself up.

Niles put down his clipboard. "Would you like to share the joke, George?"

The tittering stopped and the titterers looked cowed. George sat beached in a glare of public disapproval.

"This bullshit committee stuff you're serving up. What the committees decided. How about *us* deciding something *here*? We're all here. Isn't this what Monday meeting's for? Deciding what's going to be in the next issue? Because I've got a story coming in and it's a doozy, this one. It's from prisoners down in Salem, in the state pen. Letter from Prison—"

"I'll add it to the list." Niles scratched a note on his ledger.

"What list?"

"The waiting list. We have more than enough stories for next issue. I'll put yours on the list, but I have to tell you, George—offhand? Letter from Prison? This one might have to go to Saturday meeting for discussion. Is letters-from-prisoners the direction we want to go? It's a policy issue, we discuss policy questions at Saturday meeting. This meeting's just for nuts-n-bolts. Here we just get through the business at hand for the next issue."

George gaped at Niles. "The direction 'we' want to go? So Monday Meeting's just window-dressing now! Bullshit! When the hell was this all decided?"

"Over the weeks, George. We talked about it and we voted."

"I wasn't there!"

"Exactly. You weren't there. The people who *were* there voted, and this is the way we decided to run things. All the prep work gets done in committees now—editorial committee, production committee, finance committee—it's just so much more efficient. And we need to be efficient. I know the paper used to have a first-come, first-serve policy, but the Ark has quality control now, and quality takes time."

Sval forgot his private vow to remain a neutral observer on his first day back. He cleared his throat for attention. Whitaker gave him a polite nod. "A newcomer. Are you here to volunteer? Don't worry, we're not usually this disorganized."

"I'm an old-timer actually. Sval Hofby. You're Niles Whitaker, I presume?"

"Ah… Hofby. I've heard the name. Welcome back, old-timer."

Sval recognized the wedge Niles was trying to drive between him and George. "Thank you," he said. "I've been away, it's true, but I'm planning to devote a lot of energy to the paper now that I'm back."

"Ah, good. Good," said Niles. "Let's talk after the show. If all of you would settle down now—"

"Quick question?" Sval raised his hand.

"Make it quick."

"You mentioned these committee. Who's on them? What's the procedure for joining?"

"Rules and procedures are all in the minutes now. Check with Martha, she's got copies."

"Could the members of the committee stand up, though? Just for a second?"

Niles calculated. "All right, quickly then, editorial committee, stand up, please."

Four men stood up briefly and started to take their seats again.

"Production committee?" said Sval.

"We've wasted enough time," Niles barked, but by then the same four men had stood up again.

"Wait." Sval held up a hand. "The same four people on both committees? Who's on the finance committee?"

The four men remained standing. A moment of uncomfortable silence ensued. "Niles," said Sval. "Are you on any of these committees?"

"I coordinate them." Niles said. He gestured at his lieutenants. "Take your seats, we've got a lot to get through. The question has come up about our cover price. Let's hear from the finance committee."

Sval raised his hand. "We're not done with editorial. I have a story to propose. If there's a queue like you said, I want to get on the list."

"You've got a story idea. Ah," said Niles. "You did a lot of writing for the Old Ark I've heard. We could use some good reporting. What'd you have in mind?"

"Well, the story is still unfolding, but it's a tenant-landlord saga. The gist of it is this." Sval told the assembly about Martha's problems with her landlord and felt a chill developing.

When he was done, Niles nodded, "Why don't I put it down as a possibility. The waiting list is long, though, as I said. I wouldn't start writing till we see what else comes in."

"What else comes in? I respect your opinion, but," Sval turned in his seat, "what do the rest of you think? I bow to the judgment of the collective."

"It's not a judgment call," Niles informed him. "What you've got isn't really a story. What's the hook? Someone's roof is leaking? That's not news. She wants her landlord to repair it, but he's dragging his heels? Dog-bites-man. If it's normal, it isn't news."

Sval rubbed his hands uneasily. "This one's a story *because* it's normal. This is happening to lots of people, it could happen to any of us tomorrow."

Niles rolled his eye. "All right, give me 50 words. I'll see if I can fit it into Community Briefs next week."

"Hold on, hold on, excuse me. I know you don't mean to sound this way, Niles, but you are speaking as if this were your decision alone. It's a decision for the collective."

"Everyone has a voice, but in the end, someone has to decide. I take responsibility for what goes on the stands every Friday, so yes, in the end that someone has to be me. Circulation has gone up by 2,000 paid copies since I took over, and numbers don't lie. If I say it's not a story, believe me, it's not a story."

"Since you took over."

"You know what I mean. Since we started doing things my way around here."

"But this paper doesn't belong to you! It belongs to the community of people who read it. Our print run used to be 10,000 but we figured out that at least five people read each copy, that's at least 50,000 people who were looking to this paper to stay in touch with their community. They looked to this paper because they wanted to read about things that mattered to them. And now, the story of Martha's roof, here's something that's happening to someone in our community. You think Ark readers wouldn't be interested? The Ark is here to give people like her a voice. That's the whole reason we exist: to tell stories like hers."

"I never denied that, I said I'd put your story on the list, that's all I can do. The editorial team will take a look at it and decide. That's all I can promise you, Sval."

"And when does the editorial team meet?"

"If you haven't been elected to the group, you can't participate in its decisions."

"When was the election?"

"It's in the minutes. Look it up."

"When does it meet? I just want to observe."

"You can watch the editorial committee in action by coming to the Ark and putting in the time. We pay for proofreading now. You can start there."

Confronting Bart Sloan

"How'd it go?" said Zoe.

"I got stomped." Sval slunk to the couch.

Zoe raised a skeptical eyebrow. "No, really."

"Really. I came, I saw, I got stomped. And then got eviscerated and then my body parts got scattered in nameless fields, there to rot and be forgotten."

Zoe listened to his story and rewarded him with laughs. She also let hm know his glum dejection was her own. "What about George's prison thing? That went through, I hope!"

"It didn't even come up. Whitaker wouldn't let it."

Zoe gasped. "He stopped George from roaring? How?"

"Oh, George roared, but I tell you: Whitaker made it sound like squeaking. I was no help. I said I'd have his back and I just sat there like a stump. I was worthless."

"Don't let Whitaker do this to you, Sval. Don't blame yourself, blame him. He can't make himself lord and master of Monday Meeting. Take him down, Sval. Today was just one battle. This is a war."

"Huzzah. For a war, one needeth allies. Come to Monday meeting with me, Zoe. Join the Ark, wouldja'? Help me win the war. You say you're looking for something to do. This could be that something."

"Something-to-do isn't what I'm looking for." Zoe's tone cooled. "I'm looking for a passion. Something meaningful, not just a way to pass the time. The Ark is yours. I want one of my own."

"I'm just saying. When I picture you and me at the Ark, shoulder to shoulder, it makes me yearn. That's all I'm saying."

"We'd be together too much if I started coming to Monday Meeting," she reminded him. "We'd become a couple. You don't want *that*, do you?"

"No," he agreed, "neither of us wants that, but must we on that account scrupulously avoid sharing each other's interests? You sit around with Raoul all the time, smoking dope, doodling and drawing, those are *his* passions. Aren't you afraid you and him'll become a couple?"

"That's different."

"Why?"

"Because he's not my primary relationship."

"Oh." With shy restraint, Sval inquired, "And I…?"

"Don't make me spell it out," she warned.

"Consider it unasked!"

Zoe released clenched breath. Another crisis averted. And now, since he wasn't pushing, she went ahead and said, "Sval, you *are* my primary relationship, how could you doubt it? I'm always here for you when it matters, how can you say I'm not. But I need time for myself too!"

"I get it," he said. "The Ark can't be your *main* passion. I'm just saying, join up till we get through this crisis. I need allies!"

"Okay, if it matters so much, I will for a while. But you don't need allies, what you need is to fight for your story. He says your story doesn't belong in the Ark, you know it does. Write something so good he can't keep it out—that's how you fight now. Find that story and write it."

Sval grew pensive. "The trouble is, all I've got is Martha's roof, and Niles is right to some extent. That isn't a story till something happens, and only Martha can make something happen. But she's dragging her heels."

"Give the poor woman a break. Confronting a landlord takes nerve," said Zoe. "Martha doesn't have much confidence, what she needs is your support."

Sval hung his head. "You're right. What was I thinking? Badgering poor Martha. I should have offered to help."

Zoe pointed to the phone. "It's not too late."

Martha was sitting in her beanbag chair, legs akimbo, staring at the rental agreement on her lap. There they were, the dreaded words: *AS IS*. And the worst of it was, she should have known. The man had spoken plainly enough. "If you'll take it as is, I can let you have it for fifty bucks. Can you manage fifty a month, dear?"

His name was Bart Sloan. On a warm day she went to see him at his shack of an office near the Whizburger on Sandy Blvd: Sloan Construction Company, sharing a building with a pest exterminator. His moustache and broad shoulders reminded Martha of boys she had grown up with in Estacada: a little more at ease with horses than with people. The kinds of boys she would have liked to date, except that boys like that never called girls like her. So it gave her pleasure when he said, "Place could use some polish but a gal like you, I bet you could fix it up real nice, you've got the knack, doncha'?"

A gal like you! Well, he was right, she did have a knack for fixing up a place. And she did like what she saw in his eyes: the feeling that he was looking at her as a woman and enjoying what he saw. And then he said rent would be $50 a month and nothing he said after that really mattered. He droned on about letting her paint the house any color she wanted, have parties … Martha was only half-listening. "I believe in freedom," he was beaming, as he pushed the rental agreement toward her. "Just don't call me when you need a light bulb changed." She chuckled as she signed the document. Call him to change a light bulb. As if!

Looking back, she could see she had only herself to blame. What she'd felt from him wasn't really attraction, it was a beam he could turn on and off for sales purposes. Now, with the storm pounding on her roof and raindrops plinking all around her, she wondered what else might be wrong with the house. She'd been in such a hurry to sign, and after she'd moved in, too busy making the place "real cozy" for some hypothetical man who looked like Bart Sloan. Did she even have heat? Pessimism was among Martha's basic life strategies: expect the worst and you'll give yourself a chance to be pleasantly surprised—so she spent a few minutes imagining the worst about the heat—that there *wasn't* any. Then she turned up the thermostat and sat by a floor vent to wait for the pleasant surprise. But the heat never came.

Then, the phone rang and it was Sval. "Hi, Martha. Listen, I pitched your story to Monday Meeting, and you were right. Niles Whitaker doesn't want it in the Ark, but I've decided to fight for your story. What I need, though, is a story to fight for and it isn't a story until something happens. So how's about you and me making something happen?"

"Something happen? Like what?"

"Like, you and me pay a visit to your landlord and demand that he fix your roof. We'll go together and I'll do the talking, if you want. Or I'll just take notes, if you'd rather, while you appeal to the better angels of his nature. Then, when he reveals that he has no better angels, the gloves come off."

"What are the gloves?" said Martha. "What happens when they come off?"

Sval was silent for a beat. "We'll cross that bridge when we come to it. The point is, whatever happens, it'll be a story. You in? No pressure."

"I'm in."

Entering Bart Sloan's office, Sval was struck by the huge map of Portland with brightly colored pins stuck on it here and there. Nothing else decorated the light green walls except that map. Two desks occupied the back of the room, but only one was occupied.

That one occupant took in Sval and Martha with a diffident glance. His fingers were a blur, moving over a tiny calculator no bigger than a paperback book. He himself was wearing a stitched linen suit. His face was smooth and bland around the eyes and cheeks. A ragged moustache clung to his upper lip. His tie was pulled out loose, and his top shirt button was unbuttoned. "Help you?"

"You rented a place to my friend here, and the roof is leaking—drastically in fact."

"What's her name?" He turned his gaze. "What's your name, sweetheart?"

"Martha Williams is her name. I doubt you two are on sweetheart terms."

"She looks familiar. You look familiar, honey. Let me check."

Sloan swiveled his chair around, rummaged in a file drawer, then turned back. "I remember you now. You rented the place *as is*. You got *real* low rent. The deal was, no repairs. As is. Here's your signature."

"Yes, Mr. Sloan, she signed a piece of paper, but you led her to believe you were talking about minor repairs." Sval leaned toward the man. "You mentioned that you wouldn't change light bulbs. This is not a lightbulb, sir, it's a *roof*. In Portland, it's like you're condemning her to living outdoors. Listen to it now, how it's coming down. How is she supposed to make a home in a place like that?"

"Not my problem. I'm renting *space*. What you do with it is your business, sweetheart. I won't butt in."

"Oh, I forgot," Martha bristled. "You believe in *freedom*."

"You should be aware, sir," Sval warned, "I write about tenant-landlord issues for the Ark. Do you really want the kind of publicity you're piling up right now?"

"I never heard of the Ark. What is the Ark?"

Sval glanced at Martha and her eyes confirmed his instinct. Explaining the Ark to this waste-of-space would be a waste-of-time. "You're missing the big picture here, Mr. Sloan. You're in violation of certain city building codes with this roof situation. If push comes to shove, we do have friends in city hall."

"You?" Sloan could not hide his amusement. "*You* have friends in City Hall? What do your friends do at city hall, clean toilets?" He clapped his arms around his chest to keep his hilarity under control.

While he was throttling his laugh, Sval found one last shot to fire. "If we don't get some movement here, we'll have to take legal action."

"Ah! Abbot and Costello go to court!" Sloan allowed himself a roar of a laugh. "I'm *so* scared." Then he jumped to his feet and came around his desk, his dense build carrying enough momentum to sweep them into the hall. "Come on, kids, out of here now. I've got work to do."

Sval glared at the door, his gut clenched like a fist.

Martha offered what comfort she could. "If you want to kill him, Sval, I'll help you?"

"Thanks, podner, let's do it right quick and then get a beer. I owe you an apology, Martha. Talking you into that humiliation. I thought he'd cave. He's so totally in the wrong."

"You have friends at City Hall.'" She muffled a giggle with her palm. "That was funny."

"Well, I do. I know a bartender at Frankenstein's. His girlfriend used to room in a house with an ex-boyfriend of an ex-girlfriend of mine. He ran a pinball concession in the student center at Reed. After he graduated, he became something at City Hall, I don't remember what. Come to think of it, you might be right. Us and City Hall: what a larff."

"I'd like to see someone step on that Bart Sloan," Martha announced. "Someone with a really big foot. He's a worm."

"You and me," said Sval, "we are comrades in our thirst for vengeance."

"Step on him and squish him like a bug is what I'd like to see."

"We are siblings in sentiment," Sval scowled. "I relish the image of saying noooooo to that clinchpoop. I picture him on his knees, begging for mercy, and I'm saying nooooooo." They ambled along, feeling companionship in the hatred they shared.

"I wish someone could make him feel like you do right this minute, Sval."

"Is that so much to ask?" Sval lamented. "Where is God when you need him?"

"What about legal action," she said. "You were threatening him."

"Pure bluff and blarny, I fear. Lawyers cost money."

"A lawyer came to the Ark one time to give Walter some advice. He said he wasn't charging anything because we're a community service, like the Senior Citizens' Assistance League. The church gives us free rent, and this man came to give us some free lawyering. He called it pro bono work. I could look him up in the phone book. He might help us."

Sval stroked his long chin. "How soon could we do this?"

Test Case

While Martha was trying to make contact with the lawyer, Sval faithfully attended Monday Meetings and waited tables at La Bonne Crepe for money. He worked the lucrative brunch shift, which took eight hours out of each weekend day but left his evenings free. If he wanted to be part of the struggle for the Ark, he had to attend Saturday meetings too, rain or shine. Saturday Meetings tended to spawn subcommittees, and Sval had to attend those as well, for small decisions could have big downstream consequences. It took persistence to wean the people of the Ark away from Acme Music Club without hurting anybody's feelings. It took energy to turn Saturday Meeting into a focused force that could contend with the Whitaker machine, and Sval couldn't shirk these duties.

At the same time, he needed to build a presence at Monday meetings. Ultimately, it was Monday Meeting that mattered, for that was the furnace in which each week's issue was actually forged. Sval attended quietly, made no trouble. Zoe started coming with him, and she never made trouble either. Marica became another increasingly dependable presence, and even George overcame his disgust and began attending. At Monday Meeting, none of the old-timers made any mention of the Saturday group. The Whitaker people thought that group had dissolved into potlucks and drumming circles. They didn't know that Saturday Meeting never went extinct, quite. Sval said nothing to alert them. Best to stay quiet until the Saturday group was ready to make a move.

Martha had her money-job at Powell's Bookstore. She joined an exercise class to get tuned up for the struggle. Her days ran from dawn to midnight. She had all her responsibilities at the Ark: keeping the press type files in order, making sure supplies never ran out, sorting the bills, signing the checks, stamping the envelopes. It was scut work but someone had to do it, and as long as it got done, no one paid particular attention to who was doing it.

Getting an appointment with the lawyer was no cakewalk. There were phone calls and return calls, tentative dates, and postponements due to crises in the lawyer's money-making work, but Martha finally found a date and time when all their schedules coincided.

Arthur Oliver's office was on the fifth floor of a building on Water Street. It commanded a fine view across the river of a new downtown construction project, a bank annex going up where a rickety transient hotel had only recently teetered. With his feet on his desk, his back to the view, and his hands behind his head, he listened to Sval and Martha, a smile lingering on his lips until Martha had finished. Then he stroked his suspenders

"You write a letter about these repairs?"

"Yes."

"Kept a copy?"

"No," Martha admitted.

"Okay. That's okay, it's not hopeless. You'll write him another letter, and this time you'll keep a copy. Tell him you're following up on your letter of such and such a date. Do you know when you sent the first letter?"

"I do," said Martha.

"Good. If he acknowledges the first letter, he's on record. If he doesn't, you've got a copy of the second letter. If he calls or comes over to talk, tell him to put it in writing. Build a file. We'll get the man to hang himself."

Sval lit a cigarette. "So, you think Martha's got a case?"

Oliver pressed his fingertips together, making five arches. "If we bring a case, we'll find out."

"But you're optimistic?"

"I would say, I'm interested. They just passed some new tenant-landlord legislation down in Salem. It says landlords have an obligation to make their rentals 'habitable', and landlords can't evict tenants for demanding legal repairs. What's habitable mean? What's a legal repair? No one knows. No one *will* know until someone brings a case. Yours could be that case."

"You're going to file a suit then," Sval said. "Is that what I'm hearing? If you win, she gets her roof?"

"The suit comes later. There is no suit until there is harm. We get him to evict her, then we have a suit. Before that, though, we'll need to set him up. Step one, demand a costly repair, something he wouldn't dream of spending money on, something he's obligated to fix, get him on record refusing to fix it. If we're lucky, he'll evict you the day you make that demand, ideally *that* very day, and *then* we can go to court because then we can get him on retaliation. He'll never know what hit him."

"But I have to get evicted first?"

"Well, yes, but it has to be in retaliation for demanding legal repairs. If he evicts you for no reason, that's still legal. But if you've just demanded a repair and he evicts you, that's illegal. Are the leaks enough? It depends how bad they are. Instead of fixing them, he might fix them on the cheap, and wait a couple of weeks, and then evict you, and we wouldn't have a case. So right now, hold off, let me do some research. I'll talk to a contractor. How's your plumbing?"

"The water comes out rusty."

"That's not enough. Any sewage backup?"

"Not that I know about."

"Too bad. Well, we'll find something. Dry rot might do it, if it's in the rafters. Then we could argue the leaks risk bringing the whole house down. I'll check with a contractor, hopefully he'll confirm it. Sit tight till I do some research. One way or another, we'll get you evicted."

"Isn't there some way to do this *without* me getting evicted?!" Martha said.

"Relax." Art Oliver grinned. "We're planning on winning this case. The moment you demand legal repairs, you're protected—that's how I read the law. Let's just see if I'm right. Now, let's discuss payment. You're indigent, I presume?"

On the way home, Martha broke the moody silence. "My case could set a precedent. I guess that's exciting, huh, Sval? I just hope I don't end up on the street."

"Your wish is my wish, and incidentally my house is your house. If you need a couch to crash on, you've got one with us. How are you feeling about this, do you want to keep pushing? You're the one taking a risk, this is your decision. Do not hesitate to bow out. I'll find another angle for the story. Or another story, if I have to."

"No. I've got to stand up for myself. He made you'n'me feel like worms, Sval, and I don't like that. I don't like that anyone can just do that to you'n'me."

"Well, a legal case does give the story some gravitas. Martha Williams sues her landlord and makes legal history. Mr. Whitaker: your response?"

"You could write it like a crime story. You're good at that, Sval. You could make Mr. Oliver, like, a character. Mr. Sloan, he'd be a perfect bad guy if this were a movie."

"A vivid gallery of portraits," Sval mused. "Portland, circa 1974. Many years later, these pieces gathered into one slim volume give a vivid picture…" He stopped talking for a moment. Wheels were churning in his head. "This could be a series, Martha. Every Friday, another chapter in the unfolding saga of The People vs. Bart Sloan. And while we're laying out this epic legal tale, we're providing a primer on tenant-landlord law. Vital information for renters: how to protect yourself from eviction, how to negotiate with a landlord—news you can use! Oh my God, this could be good, Citizen Martha. Really good. But I can't start writing yet. We have to see where the lawsuit goes."

Martha waited to hear from the lawyer. One week went by. Two weeks went by. Finally, she called Art Oliver's office and asked his secretary what was going on. The secretary informed her that Mr. Oliver was very busy but hadn't forgotten her case. Right now, he was looking for other cases to bundle with hers. This was looking like a class action suit. He had a strategy. Martha should be patient.

Sval dropped by from time to time for updates, and they talked about the story. He commiserated with her about the lawsuit and told her about *Bleak House*, a novel about a lawsuit that wouldn't end. Martha told him about a song that kept running through her head: *Raindrops Keep Falling on My Head*. Sval assured her he would write *something* about her situation, even if the legal angle petered out. Something heart-wrenching, he promised. The melancholy in her eyes touched him.

Sval was at Martha's the day she finally got a letter from Art Oliver. She had expected a phone call, but oh well. The letter told her that Mr. Oliver had not forgotten her. He had a strategy. She should be patient. And then there were a few sentences about a class-action suit. The language was so similar to the secretary's that Martha suspected it was coming from a template. There was, however, one additional admonition. Mr. Oliver asked her to draw up a list of repairs the house might need. Nothing in the laws specified exactly what repairs were obligatory, so he wanted her to give him a list of possibilities to choose from, major things wrong with the house, the worse the better. She should look for electricity problems. Electrical repairs could be hugely expensive, and they were a fire hazard too. He'd start drafting a demand letter as soon as she had given him that list.

"A class action suit!" Sval marveled. "The gravitas groweth."

"I don't know what to find for him. Something worse than leaks? What's worse than a roof that's leaking in seventeen places? The plaster's coming off the walls, is that worse? I don't think so. The windows are all drafty. One burner doesn't work on the stove. I don't know. Shouldn't that be enough? I saw a cockroach one day."

"Where there's one, there're thousands," he assured her. "How much would it cost to get an extermination done?"

"Not enough, probably. He'd pay for it and then like Mr. Oliver said, wait a couple of weeks and evict me. I have to find The Big One."

Sval drove off in his dusty Rambler. Martha stood for a moment listening to the echo of his clanking tailpipe fade away. Then she went upstairs and shivered for a while in her cold flat, wondering what to do. She really didn't want to get evicted. She really didn't want to hit the streets in this rainy season, looking for a new roommate situation—even if it *would* turn her life into a test case, even if Sval's household would let her sleep on their couch. And then it hit her. The heat. Why didn't the heat work? How expensive was a furnace?

If the furnace was broken that might be the good news Mr. Oliver was looking for. Even better would be no furnace at all! She went down to the basement to see if the news was good or bad, not really knowing which outcome would be which. Dust fell as she pushed open the creaking door and descended. Well, there *was* a furnace down there all right, chained to the floor with cobwebs. Was it broken? Something skittered away from her in the dark, rustling and squeaking. She shone her light over the furnace. Oh lord. Was there some switch to flip? What would it look like? What on earth should she be looking for?

She went to her neighbor's house and knocked on the door. The neighbor might know. Her neighbor was a bent-over little Black woman with a shriveled prune of a face and bright pinpoint eyes. Her white hair was gathered in a neat bun. "Yes?"

"I'm Martha? I live over there?" Martha pointed to her building.

"Oh, saints in heaven, I didn't know anyone was camping there. My goodness, child. I'm Mrs. Harney. What can I do for you, miss?"

"My furnace doesn't work. I thought you might know how to turn it on. Is there a trick?"

"Honey, my furnace hasn't worked in years. Furnaces cost money!"

"I know," Martha exclaimed. An interesting thought struck her. "Who's your landlord? Have you asked him to fix it? Has he refused?"

"Landlord?" Mrs. Harney blinked through her glasses.

"Is it a construction company over near Sandy Boulevard?"

Mrs. Harney blinked again. "I don't have a landlord, child. Mr. Harney and me bought this house thirty years ago. He passed on before he could pay it off. Furnace! I got my hands full meeting the mortgage every month. Ever since Mr. Harney passed, I've been down to half his social. Furnace. Ha."

Sympathy made Martha forget her own troubles. "What happens if you can't meet the mortgage one month? Would you have to move?"

"Move? Honey, this house is *mine*. I'm not moving." Mrs. Harney spoke the words fiercely. "Anyway, how could I move? What could I get, I sell this house? Who'd buy it? Roof leaks. Furnace don't work."

"I see. I'm so sorry to hear all that. I didn't mean to trouble you."

"It's me that shouldn't be troubling *you*, child. Pay me no mind. An old woman like me, if I had to move, the only place would be the street. It's better here. I can put up with a little weather till it's time to join Mr. Harney." She grinned apologetically at Martha, excused herself, and closed the door.

Martha stood gathering her thoughts. Across the street was a single-family dwelling. A number of Black men lived there, she didn't know how many. They wore do-rags and football team sweatshirts. They hung out on the sidewalk on warm nights and their laughter was loud. One had a motorcycle he was always fixing on the lawn. Men knew about things like furnaces. These men looked a little scary, but you couldn't judge a book by its cover. Martha didn't want to be judged by her cover. She started across the street.

Hoist by His Own Petard

One blustery Monday, two days before Halloween, people were standing around in little clumps at the Ark, waiting for the meeting to start, and passing time with mechanical chatter about the latest Watergate news. Doofus Gerald Ford had just pardoned the master criminal of San Clemente. Could you believe it? He'd done it to save the nation, he said. Yeah sure, save the nation. And the prosecution of Nixon's aides on cover-up charges was still on. Interest in Watergate was a dead horse but new developments never failed to galvanize a twitch or two in the corpse. Besides, Watergate was one topic both old- and new-timers could discuss without discomfort: everyone at the Ark had the same opinions about the gangs of DC.

Today the chatter had a jittery, titillated edge. Something was afoot. The office was never this crowded for Monday Meeting. Only those who went to Saturday Meeting knew what the turnout meant. Niles and his people didn't ask any questions. They didn't want to look clueless.

Marica strolled through the room, greeting friends. She caught snatches of babble about things in the news. The river that had caught on fire in Ohio. The nuclear plant they were building on a fault line in California. A cluster of men were chattering about the upcoming Rumble in the Jungle. Someone was explaining to someone why reggae was better than metal. A couple who had just come in from a collective farm out by Estacada had brought news of flooding. Members of the Saturday group drifted in until they outnumbered Whitaker's supporters. As their numbers swelled, they relaxed and turned genial. Niles tapped his ruler to start the meeting, but the Saturday people were slow settling down.

Seated in the front row, Sval had his long arms draped across the backs of both neighboring chairs. George and Marica, along with Zack the Zen Buddhist from Yamhill House, had staked out the third row. Zoe, Bill-the-Typesetter, and Maureen Junechild had established Saturday Meeting dominance in the fourth row. Sval noticed the beatific presence of Bubba Sadhu, proprietor of the Truth and Light Vegetarian Pizza Retreat. And there was Jimmy H., one of the founders of the sassily named Flaming Liberation and Unity Now and Tomorrow (FLAUNT), the support group for gay men. Whitaker's people had been crowded mostly to the edges.

Ken Singleton of the Solidarity Study Group had made it too—a good man to have at the meeting; he might be a little cracked about Rockefeller, but he did project a certain charismatic air of authority. He had been on trial, once, for conspiracy to bomb the Army Recruiting Headquarters in Seattle—plus, the man really knew his world politics. No one felt easy disputing his opinions about the war in Angola because no one had as many hard statistics at their fingertips. Ken was a good man to have at the meeting. So were they all, Sval reflected. The crew was motley, but somehow they had become a team.

Niles rapped a ruler against his desk. When the room quieted down, he said, "I see we have some observers today."

"Not observers," Sval told him. "Members of the collective."

"Oh? You, I know, but some of these others, I've never seen."

"That's because you don't come to Saturday Meeting much. When was the last time?"

"Saturday meeting?"

"The policy-making arm of the Ark. Look it up in the minutes." Sval raised a sheaf of papers. "Anything that slows down Monday Meeting gets referred to Saturday meeting, that's what the minutes say. Anything Monday Meeting decides, Saturday Meeting can over-rule. Was that ever rescinded? I don't find it in the minutes."

Niles opened his mouth and closed it again "Well," he said after a beat. "Be that as it may. Let's get down to business." His gestures turned crisp. "Stories for the next issue: people, we've got a terrific lineup this week. Page three, the lead: we have an excellent profile of Tom Leonard, a Village Voice style piece but. . . more upscale. I'm very excited about this one. Tom's going to be one of the movers and shakers in this town and we're the first to notice it. What we bring out is the community-spirited side of Portland's new breed of entrepreneurs. Tom has had a big hand in creating Old Town. I'm sure you all know the delicatessen he created—yes, right here in Portland, a deli that leaves Elaine's in the dust. Leonard turns the concept of deli upside down. It's revolutionary."

Marica caught Sval's eye. Here it was already, a story that didn't belong in the Ark. Someone should object. Wordlessly, Marica and Sval deferred to each other. The result was silence. Ken Singleton let his heavy eyelids droop but didn't speak. When the outburst came at last, it came from George, a spontaneous outburst. "Wait a minute!" He sat bolt upright. "There's no room for my prison piece because some kiss-ass fawning profile of a fucking capitalist is taking up all the space? Is that what you're telling me?"

"Capitalist is a buzz word," Niles reproved him, but George had broken a dam. Through the breach poured alarums of derision.

Sval raised his hand. "Point of order."

The noise stopped dead, exactly according to plan. Niles could hardly deny Sval the floor. "Yes, Sval. Go ahead." His crisp tone let it be known, he was still in charge, this was him magnanimously granting Sval permission to speak.

"Tell us a little about this Tom Leonard?" said Sval. "Who is he? How is he part of this community?"

"As I said—he created Yer Mama down in Old Town—"

But again the flood hit.

"Old Town! Don't you mean *Gold* Town?"

"The neighborhood that money built!"

"Old! Town!" Niles swept the room with a fierce gaze. "Innovative community action at its best! These people have taken a blighted patch of urban decay and turned it into a vibrant center of culture and entertainment. What's wrong with that? You want to see Skid Row spread till it gobbles up all of Portland?"

"I would rather see the naked fed and the hungry clothed, my brother," Bubba Sadhu declared.

"Old Town *does* that! It has clothing stores, it has restaurants." Niles spoke with vehemence. "Which brings us back to Yer Mama. Making money on a creative concept for feeding the hungry—what's wrong with that? Yer Mama does a roaring business and that means the People want this place! They're voting YES with their dollars. And if The People like it, who are we to run it down? Ever been there? Sval?"

"It's out of my price range," said Sval.

"Try the place before condemning it," Niles scolded him.

"I've been there," Marica said. "Something awful happened."

"We don't have time for anecdotes." Niles sensed trouble. "There's business on the table—"

"—which brings us to Yer Mama," Sval cut in. "That's the business on the table, that's what Marica wants to address. Right, Marica? Something happened, you say? This bears on the story. She should be allowed to speak. Should we put it to a vote? All in favor—"

"All right, all right," Niles chuffed. "Tell us what you saw, Marica. Briefly."

"Thank you, Niles." Marica took square hold of her space in the conversation. "I was there with Martha and Zoe sitting by a window when this homeless guy came shuffling down the sidewalk. He stopped and gazed through a window at people's food. Someone complained, I guess. And someone rushed out, I guess he was the manager, and he grabbed that old man by the coat and flung him onto the sidewalk, and shouted something at him and then kicked him—yes! Actually kicked him! It was horrifying. And then came back and went to work like nothing had happened. A hungry man got beaten and kicked for looking at some rich man's food and everyone just went back to business as usual."

"THAT," scowled George, "better go into any story we run on Tom Leonard and his revolutionary fuckin' deli."

"No!" Niles voice had a nasty edge to it now. "Old Town's going up where Skid Row used to be. No one's denying the problem. But that's another story for another time."

"Coverup!" someone shouted. "Tom Leonard-gate"

"No! We have in hand, right now, this excellent, *edited* profile—"

"Worse than the crime!"

"Stop it," Niles barked. "*Someday,* yes, merchants' problems with Skid Row elements, we'll cover that. But right now, we have this upbeat profile of a far-sighted individual—"

"Merchants Versus Skid Row Elements," mused Sval. "That could be the headline."

"How about Money versus Human Beings," someone said.

Sval raised his hand. "Let's not get ahead of ourselves. Is this piece going in? A piece like this, we can't just hear what the committees have decided. We have to talk about it here at Monday Meeting. Did Tom Leonard buy an ad for this issue? I apologize for asking, but if he did, we can't run a glowing profile of him next to that ad or even in the same issue. Can we? That would raise policy issues."

Niles's face made a pucker of distaste. "There's no quid pro quo, if that's what you're implying. Editorial and advertising are separate departments here. I resent—"

"Hank. You're the ad manager." George turned his scowl on the neatly-groomed man sitting next to Niles. "Did you sell an ad to Yer Mama this week?"

"Uh yeah. That's what I do. Duh. Yes, I sold a full-pager to Yer Mama for this week. You got a problem with that?"

"Not at all," Sval reassured him. "A full-page ad, good for you! That can run. It's the profile we're discussing. The profile, I think, has to go on hold."

"What are you talking about?" said Niles. "The profile *has* to run this week. The ad—" Then he stopped short.

"Is contingent on the profile?" Sval cocked his head. "I'm just asking. See, that's where we get into a policy issue. Saturday Meeting really needs to discuss this piece."

"Let Saturday Meeting bluster about it. That's fine. Hash out a policy going forward. In the meanwhile, we'll run this piece and plan to write another story—"

" 'In the meanwhile' nothing. If this story violates Ark policy, it can't run. And we can't know if it violates Rose City Ark policy until Saturday Meeting has looked at it."

"You see what he's trying to do?" Ray Perkins glared around the room. "He's taking money out of our pockets. We can't run this paper on fumes, people."

"Thank you, Ray. Your point is well-taken," said Niles. "Sval, I appreciate your input but this story does not raise policy issues. We'll go with it on page three—"

"Excuse me." Sval cleared his throat. "You're not authorized to make that decision. It hasn't been discussed yet, not even by *this* group. If we're not going to send it to Saturday Meeting, we have to vote it up or down right now. I move we make that the next item on our agenda."

"I second the motion!" George clapped exuberantly.

"I third it." Phlegmatic Ken, inscrutable behind dark glasses, raised his hand.

"I fourth it," from Bubba Saddhu.

"The motion is on the floor," said Sval. "Mr. Chairman: call for discussion."

"I'll do no such thing."

"You oppose discussing it? Why?"

Niles blew out a sigh. "Because it's not open for discussion, that's why." A titter sounded from his troops, but it faded quickly in the thick atmosphere of disapproval.

"Well, if it's not open for discussion," said Sval, "let's take a vote. All in favor of this piece—"

"That's enough," Niles barked. "No discussion, no vote, the matter's closed. Let's move—"

"I beg to differ, Mr. Chairman," Sval insisted. "A motion is on the floor. Call for a discussion or bring it to a vote. Majority rules. That's parliamentary procedure. And it's *our* procedure. It says so in the minutes. We either vote on it or we send it to Saturday Meeting."

Niles fingered his moustache, as if giving consideration to this point, but actually, surreptitiously, counting heads. "All right," he said, "If you insist, we'll refer the Tom Leonard profile to Saturday Meeting. For now. That leaves a big hole on page three. Brings your story one step closer to getting in. Eh, Sval?" He laughed as if pleasantly, but few laughs ever sounded nastier. "Well, we've wasted enough time."

But the next story was challenged too, and the next one after that. By late afternoon only half the content for the week's issue had been ratified. The exhausted collective poured out of the room with its business unfinished. Monday had dissolved into dusk and drizzle.

Sval kept a cap on his feelings as Niles came striding alongside him.

"What do you hope to achieve with this, Hofby?"

Sval kept walking in uncomfortable silence.

"You want the old chaos back? That sloppy rag you buffoons used to put out? How long do you think you can hold that crew together? Two weeks? Three tops?"

Sval shrugged. "It remains to be seen."

"Don't be stupid. You had a majority today, but my people are adults. Their attention span lasts longer than a week. You're going to find out what a difference that makes."

"Let me guess," said Sval. "The day you've got a majority, you'll propose some new rules about who can vote."

"What's wrong with that?" Niles scowled. "You want a vote at the Ark, you damn well better meet some standards."

"Agreed. The question is, what standards and who sets them? If you ask me, voting *should* be restricted. We can't have different factions packing the meetings, pulling the papers right or left depending on who's got the majority on a given day. We have to establish some criteria for voting membership."

"You're with me on that?" Niles looked skeptical.

"I'm ahead of you, actually. I say it takes time to get a sense of this paper. It takes time to get a feel for the culture of the community we're serving. That's something you can only get by osmosis, there is no shortcut. That's what I'm going to propose next Saturday. Let's limit voting to people who joined the paper, let's say, oh…more than nine months ago. If Saturday Meeting agrees, that's how we operate from now on. You'll still have input. You won't be able to vote at first, but you'll still have a voice, you'll be part of the conversation. If you want to help us set a direction for the paper, you'll have to do it with your voice, not your hammer. And when you get a vote—which you will if you hang in there long enough—you won't be the decision maker, you'll be part of a decision-making process."

"Saturday Meeting will never consent to that."

"You might be misjudging the mood over there."

"No," said Niles. "I'm telling you right now, you'll never get Saturday meeting to vote yes to that proposal because don't forget, over there you're going to need consensus to get anything passed, and it only takes one vote to block consensus I'll be that one vote. In fact, I'll be there with my whole crew. You'll never get consensus with us there." He veered away into the rain.

Zoe and Marica hurried up on either side of Sval. "What was that about?"

"He's coming to Saturday Meetings from now on. He'll use consensus to block anything we propose."

"Fuck! You think he will?"

"I hope so. If him and his crew start coming to Saturday meeting, we've got 'em. We win. We'll tie them up in so many meetings, they won't know what hit them. They don't have our meeting-stamina, these guys. They can't take seven-hour sessions of philosophical hair-splitting and emotional breakdowns and interpersonal explosions day after day. We on the other hand thrive on such. One month. Mark my words. One month and they'll be begging for mercy."

It took less than a month, Niles swept into the office one Monday morning with his usual whiff of pomp but this time a whiff of portent too. His lieutenants deployed to the sides of the room. Niles sat down, spread a sheet of paper on his podium, and began to speak.

"When I took over the Ark," he said in measured tones, "this paper was no better than a rag assembled on somebody's kitchen table. Now it invites comparison with any newspaper of its kind in the country. My leadership turned this ship around. My crew of dedicated workers, men who care about quality. Under my leadership… " And he began to list his achievements, but he was speaking to a room packed mostly with Saturday Meeting people, and in this milieu his words of self-congratulation turned into dead tennis balls hitting a wall and failing to bounce.

Finally, his tone changed. "Sadly, the Ark is no longer a newspaper. Because of a few rotten apples—and I won't name names. You know who you are. Because of you, the Ark will never amount to anything. Under my direction, it could have hit half a million in revenues within two years. But that'll never happen now. The Rose City Ark will be the weekly newspaper Portland deserves. You win, I quit. Any of you who care about quality, follow me to higher ground."

Niles Whitaker rose from the table and walked out.

Seven people including all four of the committee chairmen Whitaker had appointed rose from various locations and trooped out as well. They said nothing about quitting, but their mass departure had an air of finality.

"Satisfied?" Ray turned on the others in the room. "You think I'm going to stick around? Think I'm going to bail you out? Think again, Hofby. This is on your head. You broke it, you fix it." He followed Whitaker's troops out of the room.

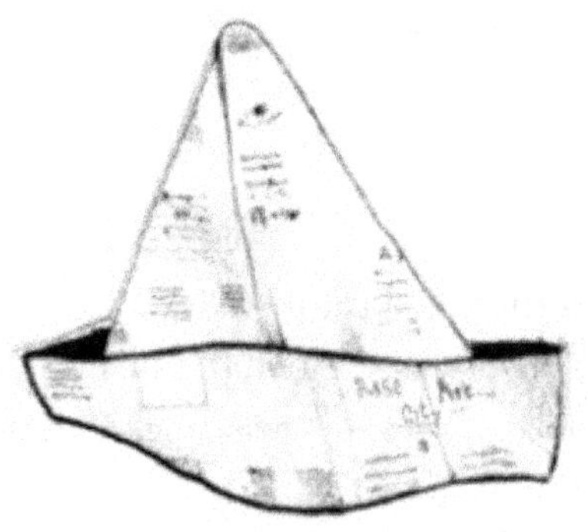

PART THREE

Cracks in the Egg

A Vision

"Bullshit!" Ken hurled the word out.

Not even two months had passed since the ouster of the Whitaker crew, and once again, Monday Meeting was packed. Packed because, once again, there was tension at the Ark.

"A lot of comrades contributed to this! It goes on page three! Page *three!*" Ken shouted. He thumped a sheaf of papers and sat back, bristling.

The rest of the room wriggled in discomfort.

"But what the hell is it?" someone bleated finally. "I couldn't get through page one."

"It's a rev'lutionary analysis of Our Present Moment," Ken glowered. "Are you people blind? Rockefeller just moved himself up to VP! Can't you see what's coming? We got to wake the people *up*. I've been writing this manifesto for months. It's got to run *now!*"

Sval studied his copy of Ken Singleton's treatise. "Something about the title bothers me. *Workers of America Unite!!!* It lacks … I don't know. Originality? And another problem, Ken. This oeuvre's only slightly shorter than *Das Kapital*. How do you propose to fit it all on page 3?"

"It's 8,000 words, we run it in six installments," Ken growled.

Uproar erupted. "—six!" "— page 3!" "What the fuck—?!"

Marica watched silently. Niles Whitaker was gone but the Ark felt more alien than ever. Men and their endless macho games! Banging and crashing like monster trucks at a demolition derby.

"All in favor, say aye." The voice broke into Marica's meditations. She had no idea what they were voting about, but Sval and George and

Martha had all raised their hands, so she did too. Afterward she asked Martha, "What did we say aye to? I was pulling a Raoul."

"Sval worked out a compromise on Ken's piece. He'll cut it down to 2,000 words and we'll run it in four installments, all on page five."

"Wow! He sure came down some!"

"Well, Sval. You know. Ken came down, the rest of us agreed to hold a special meeting for Ken to explain something to us about neo-something-or-other. Colonialism, I think. Or capitalism? No, neo-colonialism, I think. Anyway."

Marica groaned.

Sval, strolling past just then, cackled: "Before the revolution, a plague of taxes. After the revolution, a plague of committee meetings."

Marica stared at his departing form.

"Are you mad at him?" Martha fixed a searching gaze on her friend.

"No, just weary. He puts out such a lot of struggle-karma, our Sval."

Martha frowned. "Want to talk about it? I'm hemming drapes tonight. I've got some weed. We could cook something."

That afternoon, Marica ran into Maureen Junechild at the Athena Coffeehouse. They hugged and settled into big cushions piled around a laminated cable-spool in a corner shielded from public view, to discuss that day's Monday Meeting.

Maureen sipped an espresso and let Marica vent. "I never say anything at meetings! Sval spouts theories and I just sit there," she fulminated. "All I am at the Ark anymore is a body and a vote."

Maureen sighed. "It always comes down to that, doesn't it? All you are to them is a body."

"And a vote."

"And a vote," Maureen conceded. "But the Ark—And I've always said this, Marica. You know I have. The Ark is corrupted with male energy. It's never really going to serve the needs of the community. You're always going to have to grit your teeth and get ready for some outrage when you walk into the office. You'll always have to close your eyes when you open a new issue and pray that you won't find something that makes you cringe on page three."

"Someone has to educate these men!" Marica fumed. "But why does it have to be me? I'm not good with words. *Why* does it always have to be me?!"

"Don't sell yourself short. You've done all you could," Maureen assured her "Some of these men, honey, they can't be educated. What the community needs is a paper run by women. Read by everyone, but run entirely by women. Written by women, all the production done by women, all the decisions, women, you walk into the office, all the people you see are women—well, why not!" She shot a shrewd look at Marica. "We already do three-quarters of the work, we get one quarter of the credit."

"If that!" Marica laughed. "But a women's paper... I don't know. *You* should start one, Maureen. I'd help, but my problem, see. I'm wondering. Is a newspaper really me? Am I really a 'newspaperwoman'?"

"Is this about Dare-to-Juggle? Are you wanting to shift your energies back to theater?"

"I don't know. Dare-to-Juggle doesn't really cut it either. It's just juggling. How much can a person *say* with just-juggling?"

The sun had set. Marica crossed Colonel Summers Park and hurried past the wooden frame church, on her way to Martha's house. If she quit the Ark, who would she be? At the Ark at least she had an identity. Oddly enough for a Monday evening, the church was just letting out. Christians flooded the sidewalk. Marica thrust her hands into her pockets for warmth and threaded her way among the neatly dressed women. She found herself surrounded briefly by chatter about mayonnaise and potato salad. She reminded herself not to judge. They at least knew who they were.

The church sounds faded away behind her, muffled by the steady hiss of Portland rain. She wasn't wishing she had an umbrella right now. Why wasn't she? Because the rain sounded like children whispering poetry. *Lyrical.* The word formed visually in her mind. It stirred emotions she couldn't name. Lyrics. Words for song. Words and music. Music and dance together. Dance theater. She passed two girls, bobbing against each other as they chattered and giggled: middle-schoolers, they looked to be. So young! Such a lot of future to fly into, so little past dragging them down.

She turned the corner onto Hawthorne Street and lost her breath to some feeling rising inside her, that she dared not grasp at, lest it vanish. She emptied her mind to give the image room to rise into the light. But the image sank instead, back into the darkness of all her forgotten memories.

Marica stood gulping air. What had just happened? She'd seen something. What had she seen? Up ahead was the Hawthorne St. Theater. The movie *Walking Tall* had been playing there for a year. The letters of the title loomed huge above smaller letters spelling out in moving lights the words, "Audiences stand up and cheer."

She hadn't seen it, but she knew about this movie. A macho rant about a man with a big club who beat up bad guys. A distilled expression of man-life. Stand up, it said. Cheer, it said. Audiences. Marica glared, and the words on the marquee began to come apart, the letters drifted into a new arrangement... There on that large marquee, in her imagination, she saw waves of moving lights form the words WOMANSLIFE. Audiences stand up and cheer.

Images fluttered through her mind like a deck of flung cards. Snapshots of her parents in their dating days. A vivacious couple so in love, so charmingly Bohemian, so *smart*. To this day, newspapers asked her father for his thoughts, magazines called him a public intellectual, his students adored him. In Marica's earliest memories, he was already just a glamorous visitor to the house, coming home late in the evenings, going off to conferences on many weekends ... Having no doubt a string of affairs ...

Her mother, in Marica's earliest memories, was already an overdressed woman with nowhere to go, all her young-woman promise blown away, nursing a tulip-shaped glass with a finger of whiskey at the bottom, her social life reduced to a few neighbors, a coterie at the club, her hairdresser ... Nobody asking her for her thoughts.

WOMANSLIFE. Marica strode along. *All you are to them is a body.* And what was a body? Meat and fat, gristle and bones. Lost in thought, Marica quickened her pace, barely noticing the cluster of men whistling at her from the doorway of the Gofer Hole Tavern.

Zoe didn't seem like the curtain-hemming type, but there she was at Martha's that evening when Marica arrived with a bottle of wine. She and Martha were both busy with needles, hemming away. On the table between them sat an ashtray with a half-smoked joint, which Marica lit and sampled. From the kitchen came the aroma of meat-and-potato stew. Marica opened the wine.

"Hit me." Zoe proffered an empty jam jar.

Marica poured her some wine and sat down. She didn't have a curtain to work on and didn't feel like asking for one. She didn't feel ready to tell her friends she was thinking of quitting the Ark. But she did share with them the fear she felt constantly these days, like smoke thickening in the corners of her life.

"Fear of what?" Martha asked as she stitched away on her curtain.

"Oh, just, I guess, a fear that my life will somehow end up, I don't know, just … average?"

"Oh, good heavens! You're definitely above average!" loyal Martha beamed.

"Above average." Marica permitted herself a rueful smile. "What a thing to strive for."

"Don't knock it," Martha scolded. "Not everyone's above-average."

"By definition," Zoe twinkled.

"Me, for example, I'm just average," said Martha. "I'm not complaining, but I wouldn't mind being a little above-average, like you. Above-average isn't something to look down on, Marica."

"I'm not looking down, I'm just saying: we could *all* be so much more. We get so beaten down as women, it isn't fair. We have voices, we should be singing!"

"It's hard to sing when no one's listening," Martha hrumphed. "You don't know what that's like, 'cuz everybody listens to you."

"I live with George," Marica snorted. "I've got someone not-listening-to-me 24 hours a day. Believe me, I know how it feels."

"To be fair, the hours when he's sleeping shouldn't count," Zoe objected. "It's only maybe sixteen hours a day or so, tops, he's not-listening-to-you."

"I'm above-average with numbers," Martha boasted. "I bet I could be a pretty good bookkeeper."

"You are already," Zoe pointed out. "Don't you keep the books for the Ark? You're practically one of those uber-bookkeepers."

"A CPA?"

"One of those!"

"Ha ha, as if." Martha folded her curtain and set it on a chair. "I didn't even finish two years of college."

"I bet all my bits of college don't add up to much more," Zoe said. "What happened to that joint, Marica?"

"I finished it. There's still some wine, though."

"I'd better check the soup." Martha left the room, and clattering sounds soon issued from the kitchen.

"I'm jealous of her," Marica said. "Good with numbers is something to be. It is. Numbers are so concrete. I don't know what I'm actually good at. I'm an artist is all I can say. What does that even mean? What's an artist add to the pot? She expresses her feelings, yippee. So what? Everybody has feelings. Why should anybody care what *mine* are?"

Zoe shrugged. "Sval would say, they're not just yours. He'd say you express feelings everybody has but most people don't know how to express. So yeah. Artists add value. Sval would argue."

"Is that what I'm saying? My feelings are everybody's? Who dares even *say* such a thing as that?"

"Anyone who gets up on stage week after week in front of a bunch of strangers and performs like you do with Dare-to-Juggle. I'm the jealous one." Zoe sighed. "You do the same thing again and again and for you, it's always new. I do the same thing twice and the second time it's already kinda' ho-hum, been there/done that, what-else-you-got."

She started rolling a new joint. "Unless maybe this thing George has gotten me into. Talking to these prisoners down in Salem … I've been five times and it still feels—I don't know. I could still go back for more."

Martha returned from the kitchen with a tray. "There's more stew in the pot if you're still hungry. I don't have any bread, but there's crackers." She poured more wine for herself, a cautious half inch. Outside the rain was picking up. In the corner of the room the plinking began: drops of water leaking from the ceiling. Fortunately, Martha had two electric space heaters parked strategically to make their corner feel warm enough. She ladled herself a bowlful of steaming soup. "Help yourself, girls. No one's being served here."

"Marica's been telling me she's an artist." Zoe blew on a spoonful of soup. "I was telling her, I don't know how she does it, week after week, expressing her feelings to a crowd of people. Feelings are like shadows to me, flitting around so quick you can't even tell what they are. By the time you get a fix on them they're not even your feelings, it turns out, they're somebody else's."

"Well, maybe that's where an artist comes in," said Marica. "She turns the flitting shadows into something you can be with, something real."

"That's the way Raoul talks about his aquarium," Zoe mused. "He's at it night and day, and it's always made of glass to him. The rest of us just see cardboard, but he never stops believing. That's what I have trouble with. I don't know how to keep believing. I remember, once, I got to thinking I'd be an architect. I was making a replica of the Notre Dame with toothpicks and damn! It was actually pretty good! The next day I look at it and I'm like 'really, Zoe? Toothpicks?' Everything's like that. You look again and it's just toothpicks." Zoe chuckled. "Sval gets mad at me for talking like that. The Ark, he says. The Ark isn't just toothpicks."

"Well, he's right," Martha protested. "The Ark isn't just toothpicks."

Zoe smiled. "You and Sval should get together. He keeps telling me the Ark is important! 'Get involved!' he keeps saying. 'It's important!' I mean it's an okay way to pass the time, I guess, but how is it important? Don't tell him I said that. It would break his heart."

Marica pulled back from Zoe's blasphemy. "The Ark is not 'just a way to pass the time.' Sval is right. The Community needs a newspaper."

"What is The Community? Who is this Community? Who's in it," Zoe demanded. "Who's part of it? How can you tell?"

"Well, that's the question, isn't it? Who *is* the Community? You can't go looking for it. it's not something you find, it's something you create. *That's* what an artist does, actually. She creates the Us. She gives birth to the Community, if she's any good. She takes it out of imagination and puts it in the real world where everybody can see it. If she's any good."

"That's kind of what Sval says about the Ark," Martha jumped in. "He says he's trying to make the Community be something that really exists."

"The Ark is *his* way of doing that," Marica agreed. "I'm just saying, it's not the only way. He's noble though, our Sval, I give him that. You have a good man there, Zoe."

"I'll try to hang onto him," Zoe deadpanned.

"It's just, his way isn't my way. He takes joy in battle. I don't. George is even worse. They love spending the whole day tangling with Singleton-types. It's like they have this hunger that winning feeds. They love winning. I'm not like that."

"They are very mannish manimals, those two," Zoe agreed. "That's why I like hanging out with Raoul. He's not so mannish. He's not womanish either, he's some third thing. That's what's interesting about Raoul."

"Hmm." Marica was not interested in what was interesting about Raoul. "My way is not the Ark. My way might be more…" She groped for the word but couldn't find it.

"Art," Zoe prompted. "Like you said. You're an artist."

"That's the word! I had this idea today, see—it came to me on Hawthorne Street. For a piece. . ."

" 'It came to me on Hawthorne Street…" Zoe repeated the words like a Dr. Seuss line.

"A piece of what?" Martha said, scrunching up her face in puzzlement.

"A piece of art … involving, you know … movement …"

"So. A dance?" Zoe guessed. "You're a dancer too? I was not aware."

"I dance. I juggle. I do lots of things, Zoe. I can sing."

"Hmm."

"Not like Janis or anything, I'm not a virtuoso, but like John Lennon said 'Give me a tuba and I'll give you something.' He was on Dick Cavett."

"You could be the female John Lennon of tuba players," Zoe declared.

"You laugh, but seriously. I was walking across Colonel Summers today and I had this image of a way to weave different arts together … to make something that lets people *experience* … how it's different to be a woman or a man … Sval can have the Ark. I want to create—not a theater piece exactly. Not a dance exactly. But a performance of some kind—a performance piece … "

Martha stopped spooning up the last of her stew. "What do you mean, Sval can have the Ark?"

"Well…" Marica took a sip of a breath. "If I do this, I'll really have to commit to it. I won't have much time left over for the Ark."

Martha looked stricken. "You're quitting the Ark? Have you told Sval?"

"Why should I tell Sval? I don't need his permission. Anyway, he'll hardly notice I'm gone. I'm pretty quiet at the paper these days … I'm not a voice there anymore, just a body and a vote—"

"That's where you're wrong," Martha declared. "He was telling me just yesterday, Marica's 'the guiding light' of the paper. She's the moral voice, is how he put it. She's the critic we all need. That's what Sval was saying yesterday."

"Oh God. So nice of him but he has *no idea* how exhausting it is to be a moral voice and a critic all the time. You end up feeling shrill. But I'll talk to him. You're right. I owe him that."

Second Full-Time Job

Raoul was alone in the kindergarten, furiously scribbling a design, his eyes half shut, his lips half moving. Footsteps clattered on the porch and the front door swung open.

"Look what I made, Raoul!" Zoe came around the velveteen curtain, lugging a very large bottle. "A bottled city of Kandor. All it needs now is a city. Want to help me put one in?" She set the bottle down in front of him. It had a landscape inside: hillsides, rocks, moss, a pool of real water, little shrubs that looked like trees. Then her face fell. "What's the matter? You don't like my bottle?"

"I do. But there's something we'd better talk about."

"Hit me. What're we gonna' discuss? How much the soul weighs? How far light penetrates skin? I'm game. Whatever you want to talk about, let's dive in." She pantomimed sitting at the feet of a guru, waiting for enlightenment, except that she was panting: she was not just a student but a puppy.

"Zoe, I'm serious."

She put on her serious face and waited for him to speak. But he couldn't get the words flowing. He turned his attention to Zoe's bottled landscape. "How do you water it?"

"I have a funnel," she said. "It takes time."

"Seal the top with saran wrap. It'll make its own weather."

"Would that work? There's insects living in there. I don't want them to run out of oxygen."

"They won't. They're in there with plants. Plants *make* oxygen. Animals make carbon dioxide. They balance each other out."

"I guess I knew that. Wow. Life is a circle. Is that what you wanted to tell me? I agree, of course. It's all about balance."

"That wasn't it." He fixed his gaze on the bottled landscape. It was turning into Conan the Barbarian's world right before his eyes. He could picture a pool in that hollow space and a magician's ghostly fingers stretching out to the rippling surface, where a picture of Zara was slowly forming. "I think we should stop sleeping together."

Zoe stared at him. "You want to break up with me? Ouch. This is sudden. Why?"

He clasped his hands together. "It's complicated."

"Of course, it's complicated. Life is complicated. Is it because of Sval? Did he say something? He's struggling with this, but he really believes in it, you know. He's struggling with it, but he wants it to work. If we all learn to let go, we'll all become better people. He really believes that. It's like a religious thing for him."

"It has nothing to do with Sval."

"I see." Zoe's shoulders slumped a little. "So it's just me. I really didn't see this coming. I still like *you*, Raoul. Just for the record, okay? I shouldn't even tell you, but I love hanging out with you. I love having you inside me when we fuck. Do you not even want to be friends? You mean we can't get stoned and make a bottled city together tonight? How come you don't like me anymore? What did I do?"

"I do like you. But there's someone else."

"Huh. Really! Who?" Then, she understood. "Oh, Raoul. Zara? You poor boy. Zara still? Come on, Raoul! You really think she's moving to Portland and you'll be together again? Really?"

"No! You think I'm crazy? Jees! I know that's never going to happen." He paused to gather his thoughts. "But that's because Zara was never the One. I realize that now. She was only a harbinger of someone yet to come. The One is still out there somewhere. I haven't met her yet, but she's out there. I have to be ready for the day when our paths finally cross. Because they will. I can feel it. I like hanging out with you, Zoe, but you're not her. I can't be involved with somebody when she gets here."

"Raoul, you goddamned romantic idiot. I worry about you sometimes. Ideas like that."

"I can't explain the feeling," he groaned. "But it's real, I know it is. You don't have to believe me, but it's true. Last week, Stan wanted me go out to the country with him one day, and I said no. You know why? Because suddenly—suddenly!—there was this voice inside me saying, not today. Not today, it said, she's going to be in Portland today. You have to *listen* to those voices. You know?"

"So you didn't go to the country that day," said Zoe. "You stayed in town?"

"Yes—"

"And did she come?"

"Um—"

"No. Or she'd be here now. So your 'voices' were wrong that day. Why would you listen to 'voices' like that? Haven't they been saying the same thing, over and over and over? She's coming, she's coming? Haven't they *always* been wrong?"

"Well—so far—"

"I mean! Maybe there *is* someone special just for you out there. Maybe it's all true, destiny and fate and all that crap. Who am I to say? All I know—and you know it too! *She's not here now!* What the hell, we're not even a couple, Raoul, we're just friends who mess around if they feel like it. As soon as the One arrives, I'll make myself scarce, okay? And listen—promise me—if my 'The One' arrives—ha ha, which I seriously doubt—you do the same. Deal?" She offered her hand for him to shake.

Raoul didn't smile. This was too serious. "You mean we're friends who mess around, but when The One shows up—"

"—I respect your monogamy."

"What do you get out of that?"

"I get the Two. You and Sval. I don't see why I should have to give up one of you. The two, that's what I get—for now."

"Oho! But later?"

"What's 'later'? What does later mean? Someone pushes a button, we're all dead before the hour is out. Why don't we just focus on now."

"Well, when you put it that way … But I just think I'd better be free in case—"

"Free? In case? How could you be more free than you are with me? Come on, Raoul! You think *I'm* going to get possessive? Don't you know that's my problem, I *can't* get possessive! I don't know how!"

"I guess you're right."

"Drink your beer, funny fellow. You're such a character. And give me a cigarette." Zoe sat in his lap. "I'm supposed to meet up with Sval later, but he's at a meeting., and you know how his meetings drag on these days. Wanna' get naked and cuddle? We can do the bottled city of Kandor later. We've got all night."

The next evening, when Zoe went home, she saw her primary relationship standing at the top of the steps to her house.

"Zoe," he scowled, "where have you been! I thought we had a plan last night. Dinner at El Rio? Six o'clock?"

"Was that a plan?" Zoe swallowed. "I thought it was just an idea."

"To meet for dinner at a specified time and place? Upon which we had both explicitly agreed? I'd call that a 'plan'."

"But you said you had a policy meeting. Those go all night sometimes. Would you have called to let me know, if it went over? Or just left me hanging?"

He conceded this point. "Damned policy meetings! I can be forgetful. I know, I know. I get so wound up. But that's why I wanted to see you last night. I wanted to unload." Then he laughed at himself. "Can't be much fun for you, though, huh, listening to Sval unload."

"Don't be like that, Sval. We help each other. That's a given. If you want to unload, here I am now. What's going on? Tell me."

"Oh." He waved his hand. He wasn't going to trouble her. But then he went ahead and blurted out, "It's that blockhead Singleton and his Marxist pals. The Solidarity Quintet, George calls them. They've got this piece they call *Open Letter to Comrade Brezhnev.* They're after page 3. What does this have to do with serving the community *here?* We'll never get an editorial policy hammered out as long as they're part of the discussion. And on top of that! Marica quitting the Ark. She wants to work on a performance piece, whatever that is. Subtract Marica from production night and who takes up the slack? Me? For Christ's sake, the Ark is already like a second full-time job except it doesn't pay—but don't let me burden you. In fact, help me forget the Ark for a night. Help me with that, Zoe. Help me forget! What are your plans tonight?"

"I don't know. What are yours?"

"I thought I'd wait and see what you're doing."

Drops of rain falling on the sidewalk pocked the silence. "But I don't want to impinge," he offered, "on your plans if they don't include me. I'll hunt up George. What's on your agenda, though? Just curious."

"I feel flakey," said Zoe. She wanted to tell him honestly what she was feeling but honestly, she couldn't tell *what* she was feeling. "I guess I'm torn."

"Between what and what?" He spoke as if he were merely her advisor now, helping her make a decision by listening.

"Well, one plan would be to have dinner with you and then later go over to Yamhill House and smoke some dope with Raoul."

"Uh huh. Certainly. And what would be another plan? It sounds like you have more than one idea."

"Well, the other plan would be to stay with you. Not go to Yamhill House. I know you feel like talking."

"That's a feeling I shouldn't give in to. I'm sick of hearing my own voice," said Sval. "You'd probably be doing me a favor, leaving me to my own devices. If I'm not with you, I won't feel like talking. Pascal said 'All of humanity's problems come from man's inability to sit quietly in a room alone.' "

She stepped closer to him and linked arms. "How about all three of us going out together? You and me and Raoul. Go out and have some frivolous fun."

He laughed uneasily. "You talk like that's some departure. We go out together all the time. What about Villanova Pizza last Friday?"

"That was a whole gang of us. I'm not talking about a whole gang of us. Just the three of us, let's go out eating and drinking and dancing. Like I do with either of you only this time with both of you."

He glanced to the left, glanced to the right, looked at the sky, looked at Zoe. "Sure. Raoul's a hoot. Why not?"

She flung her muffler over her shoulder and did a couple of stretches. His wry smile reminded her of Errol Flynn. He had such a yearning to be good. She loved the innocence of his yearning, the purity: she could never be completely cynical when she was with Sval.

Zoe made the call and Raoul said yes. After corned beef sandwiches and beer at Produce Row, they drove into the northwest part of the city. Zoe was intensely aware of the two male bodies vibrating with pent-up emotion, one behind her, one beside her. She was the lightning rod, grounding out their energy.

"Hey, the car runs nice and quiet," she told Sval. And to Raoul, she explained, "Sval just replaced the carburetor and he figured out how to do it all by himself."

"Wonderful." Raoul rubbed his hands together. "Down here, machines are hard to fix. Up in the astral plane, they look like luminous eggs. You can fix them by stroking them."

"Where are we going, incidentally?" Sval broke in. "If we're going to discuss luminous eggs, I'd like to have a beer in hand—no offense, Raoul."

"None taken," Zoe said. "Any good taverns up this way, Raoul?"

"Well," said the brooding artist, "there's the Purple Earth."

"God, Raoul. You have become quite the sophisticated Club Man," Sval observed.

The Purple Earth was a vast, meandering tavern with a low ceiling. The wall facing the front door featured a surrealistic mural defaced by graffiti. Further in, two dim floodlights hung over a pair of pitted pool tables. Across from the bar was empty floor space for stand-up drinkers. Further inside, beyond a smattering of little round nightclub tables, was a sawdust-sprinkled dance floor. Deepest in the cave, finally, was the bandstand, where tonight a country-rock band was stomping out shit-kicking dance music loaded with thunderous lead guitar and wailing electric fiddle.

Zoe apportioned her dancing time carefully between her two men, keeping to a 60/40 ratio, for if Sval got less than 60 he would tense up, and if Raoul got less than 40, he would drift into some private world of his.

Her calculations managed to keep both men fairly cheerful and enjoyably engaged, with her and with each other. Whether she herself had any fun, or how much, she could not have said. She had only so much attention to give, and after she had given the men what they needed, she didn't have much left over for herself. Whatever "her own self" was. The only real oddness came at the end, when they drove home. Since Sval was driving, he drove to Raoul's house first. There, however, instead of parking, he pulled up in front of a fire hydrant, put the car in neutral, and left the motor running. They had come to a fork in the path. Here, it seemed, each man would go his own way and she would have to choose which of them to go with. She couldn't be with both.

Raoul got out and said, "Well." He looked in at her and at Sval, searching for a way to say good-bye. But who was Raoul saying goodbye to: her or Sval? The decision was hers. She looked for her feelings but couldn't make out what they were, amidst the welter of considerations swirling inside her. She didn't know what she wanted.

Then she did. What she wanted, really, was to sleep alone.

But that wasn't possible. If she didn't get out with Raoul, Sval would expect she was going home with him. If she stayed in the car, she'd have to explain to Sval that she wanted to sleep alone. This would lead to a discussion, and she didn't feel up to that discussion. She was too tired. If she stayed in the car, she would end up going home with Sval.

Sval was still idling the motor, like a good fellow, leaving the decision to her. His lack of pressure was pressure. Being with either man was fine. Being with both was impossible. It required her to be two different people at the same time. It was like a second full time job.

"Well," she broke out a bit too brightly, "I'm ready for a little more. How about you, Sval?"

He gave her an upside-down smile. "Early to bed, surly to rise—that's my motto. I'm looking at a hangover as it is. Raoul, man, see you soon."

"So, you're not coming in?" Zoe slid across the seat toward the door. In the darkness she couldn't see his expression.

"No," said Sval, "I'd better get some sleep. I have to work on the Policy Statement tomorrow. You kids have fun."

The Ark at 3 A.M.

Sval drove aimlessly south and east, restless and disconsolate. The thought of returning to his empty bed to read another chapter of Husserl felt too bleak to bear. Whenever he was between committee meetings and not with Zoe, this was his reality. He drove randomly through the blank universe of southeast Portland, trying to out-meander the blues. If only he'd sprung for that 8-track player, he was thinking. He started thinking about his father as he often did when he was feeling lonely. He was that man's replacement in the cosmos and how was he doing, he wondered. He could never really know. Everything Sval knew about the man came from his mother, and it didn't add up to much. She'd only know him for a year; and Sval was still in her belly when she got the call from Svalbard—the northernmost inhabited island on earth. *Hello, Mrs. Hofby? Your husband just died up here: industrial accident. Civil engineering can be dangerous work.* In Sval's earliest memories, he and his mother were always a world unto themselves, although always within shouting distance of his father's great, gracious, rowdy, rambunctious Hofby clan, always included in Hofby holidays.

Sval found himself driving past the First Unitarian Church where the Ark was housed. Home was wherever the current took you when you weren't paying attention. He saw lights in the fourth-floor windows. Someone else was up there at this ungodly hour.

The door was locked, but Sval had a key: Pastor Williamson had sympathized with his need to sometimes work late in this tense period of transition for the Ark. Sval had a key to the Ark office as well, but he didn't use it. Light meant someone was in there. Courtesy demanded that he knock. So, he knocked and it was Martha who opened the door. She was wearing a short-sleeved black blouse and a long crimson skirt. Her eyes looked solemnly deep "Sorry. I was a little nervous," she said, "up here all alone at this hour."

Sval stepped inside. "What are you doing here?"

"What are *you* doing here?" she countered.

"It's usually deserted this time of night. I thought I could get some thinking done up here."

"You can think with me here. I'm just sorting press type. What were you going to think about? Think out loud if you want."

"The editorial policy statement." He noticed the filigree of red earring dangling from each of her earlobes. "I've been noodling with it, and I'm stuck." He slung his raincoat over a chair.

"Stuck on what part?"

"Well. We need a policy that stops guys like Ken Singleton from overrunning the paper, right? But it can't violate our core principle— which is open access. Right? This paper belongs to the community, open access is the prime directive. So how do we keep some people out without violating our core principle?"

"Oh pish. Principle!" Martha dismissed his dilemma. "Singleton's a bully! Always trying to take page 3 for his stupid manifestoes. If anyone can figure out a way to shut him down, good." She gave her hair a toss.

"Still. It has to be based on principles. 'We hold these truths to be self-evident…' That's what I've been trying to suss out. The Ark has to stand for something. What is our mission? Wanna' bat some ideas back and forth? As long as we're both here?"

Sval did most of the writing and thinking, but he thought out loud, and Martha reacted to his thoughts, and they made good progress. Two hours later, when they broke for tea, Sval had several pages covered with scribbled notes. He'd make sense of them later.

"Incidentally," said Martha as she brought him a steaming cup. "Walter called me the other day. He wants us to do something about the corporation."

"What corporation?"

"You know. The Ark corporation."

"The Ark is a corporation?" Sval looked bemused. "That has an unsavory ring to it. A non-profit, I hope?"

"Yes, of course nonprofit. Walter set it up five years ago, but now he wants his name off the paperwork. He asked me to find some new people to be on the board."

"The board of directors." Sval snorted. "Does it really matter who's on the board of directors?"

"Not really, it's just a formality, but right now, Walter's listed as the president, Grace is vice-president and there's four or five other people we've never heard of. They're all from long ago. Walter says he doesn't want to be responsible anymore, if something happens."

"What could happen? What's he talking about?"

"Well, suppose someone sues the Ark. Or one of us gets arrested. Walter doesn't want to be the one who takes the phone call from the police in the middle of the night."

"I don't blame him! I wouldn't either. Huh. He wants out from under, doesn't he? Well, I guess we owe him, he's the founder. Is there a lot of work involved?"

"It's not like a job or anything," Martha assured him. "You just put your name on some documents. Walter sent me the forms." She rummaged in her bag, pulled out a file folder, and handed Sval a document on onion skin paper. It was labeled "Minutes of the Meeting of January 1st, 1975." It purported to record a meeting of the Board of Directors of the Ark. This was couched in long-winded legal language. Members present were listed. There was no old business and only one piece of new business. Every member of the board of directors had resigned and new ones had taken their place. Beneath this declaration were the signatures of the people who had resigned. Below those were blanks where the names of the new people were supposed to go.

Sval scrutinized the form. "Just plug new names into these spaces? Is that what he's saying?"

"People who are willing, yes. And get their signatures and contact information, like phone numbers, address, all that. You could be president," she said. "I could be secretary. That'd be two."

"I wouldn't think of it," he demurred. "*You* be president, I'll be secretary."

"I don't think so, Sval. I already am secretary, kind of. You be president."

"Well, all right, if it's just a formality, who cares which is who. What about George for vice-president? He'll die laughing but I'll put it to him."

"And Zoe for treasurer?"

"Would that be kosher? She hardly ever comes to Monday Meeting."

"When's the last time you saw…" Martha squinted at the document in front of her. "Bob Kuhlmeier at Monday Meeting? He was the treasurer before."

"Point taken. Well, I'll ask. She'll probably say yes. If there's no work involved, I don't see why Zoe should balk."

"Okay, but the old board had six." Martha signed her name in the relevant space and pushed the paper toward Sval. "Maybe it doesn't look right if everyone is a chief. We should get a couple of people to be Indians. Marica and Raoul, maybe? That would get us to six."

"It would indeed. Although this metaphor about chiefs and Indians might be offensive to a Native American," he counseled her.

"Shoot, I didn't think about that, I'm sorry. I'll get Raoul to sign, you get Zoe." She gathered the documents together, stacked them and squared them. "And I'm having dinner with Marica tomorrow…" She let the sentence trail out. Her mind had moved on.

"What?" he said.

"Oh, it's nothing. I was just wondering about your story." She cast him a glance. "About my roof?" she nudged.

"I know which story." He suppressed a flicker of guilt. "Rest assured. I've been mulching it mentally."

"You haven't written anything yet?"

"I've been waiting on the lawyer. Whom I don't totally trust, by the way. I can't really start writing until something happens. I've been worrying a little, I'll confess."

"Worrying! About what?"

"Well, suppose the lawsuit doesn't happen? What's my story *then*?"

"What about all the things you said? We're all renters, there's other people having this kind of trouble with landlords, this would be the story of our community, all that stuff?"

"I stand by it all. What's happening to you matters, to you and to me and to people we know especially. It's just, lots of people read the Ark, tens of thousands, and most of them are strangers. I ask myself, what would make a stranger stop and pick up the paper and say, this I got to read. You know? William Randolph Hearst once said he wanted every story in his papers to make people look up and say Good God. What's the Good-God element here? That's what I keep wondering."

"Well, I don't know, but it's not just about somebody's roof leaking. There's something strange going on with this building."

"Something strange." Sval favored this information with a nod of cautious interest. "What sort of strange?"

"I don't know, but I was talking to the people across the street and it turns out their landlord is Mr. Sloan too."

"And?"

"And they think his name is Robert Brody."

"Who's Robert Brody?"

"Exactly. Who's Robert Brody? I asked them to describe the office they went to and it was definitely *that* place. I asked them to describe the man they talked to, and it was definitely *our* Mr. Sloan. But when they write their rent check, they make it out to Robert Brody."

Sval scratched his chin. "You're saying Sloan owns both houses, but he's renting them under different names?"

"Yes. Isn't that suspicious?"

Sval shrugged. "Or: he owns one house, and he's renting the other for his good friend Robert Brody."

"When my neighbors talked to him, he said it was his house. When I talked to him, he kept saying 'my house', 'my house'. He's not a rental agent, Sval. He owns both houses. I'd bet money on it. But he rents them as two different people. Why would he do that?"

Sval shifted position. "There's probably some simple, boring explanation. It might be an informal arrangement between friends. But just for the sake of argument, let us provisionally grant suspicious." He opened his notebook. "If there's a story hidden in here, how do we dig it out? I suppose we start by looking to see what else this man owns— whatever his name might be. And talk to his other tenants, see if they have any light to shed. We'll be flailing though. I have no idea what we would be looking for." Sval's eyes were bright, his pencil poised.

Martha rubbed her smooth pink cheek. "Check under both names, why don't we. Brody and Sloan both. Check other houses on the block, too, see who owns *them.*"

"Good. Approach the middle from both ends. Good. In fact, good God, what if we turn up a crime, Martha?" It was improbable, of course, but Sval was enjoying himself.

"That would be a hook," Martha agreed. "That's what strangers like to read about, don't they? Crimes. Strangers love to read about crimes."

"Indeed they do." Sval chuckled. "Yes. Uncovering a crime would indeed meet the hook requirement if well employed. Especially if—" He savored saying it. "Someone goes to jail."

"This is starting to sound like a detective story," Martha said. "You could write it like that."

"Ah yes. Phillip Marlowe style. 'I woke up feeling like a short piece of chewed string.'" Sval delivered this line in his best Humphrey Bogart voice. " 'His face was white as cold mutton fat.' Just kidding." But he was warming to the plan. "An episode a week, the plot constantly thickening? Is that what you're saying? Readers coming back like hungry addicts, ravenous to see what happens next! Non-fiction, but with all the pile-driving momentum of good fiction. It could be done. Very feasible. Could be done. I'd just have to find the story. But of course," Sval added, worried suddenly, "there has to be an actual crime at the end of the series. I can't just pose questions for a few weeks and then fold my tents and silently steal away."

Martha was still wallowing in the story's glorious prospects. "Sval Hofby puts a bunch of crooks in jail." She arranged her pencils, warm with pleasure, like a cat. "I'd like to see Niles' face when *that* headline hits his eyeballs."

"Except," Sval smiled, "*that* won't be the headline; but otherwise, my dear, yes indeed: I am totally with you."

Boxing with Singleton

Ken Singleton cornered George by the mailboxes one day when few were in the office to bear witness and rasped to him in quiet, confidential tones: "You're working with prisoners, man?"

"Yes—"

"State pen, I hear?"

"Well—yes."

"What's going on in there? You're bringing out a story?" He was smiling, but the smile was only something he was gripping with his teeth.

George shook his fingers and moved his weight from left foot to right and back. He didn't like standing in the wedge between the mailboxes and the wall, with Singleton blocking his way out. "I get down to Salem every few weeks with Zoe Madigan," he said. "What about it?"

"What are you getting down there? Interviews?"

"What the fuck, Ken. This was all discussed at Monday Meeting. The prisoners are writing something up themselves. They're going to tell their story, talk about themselves, what life is like for them. It might turn into a column. Zoe's thinking about a book. Right now, it's a workshop. We go down there and help them write. There's six of them for starters, more might join. It helps them deal. We're helping them feel there's still a world out here, and they're still part of it. That's what we're doing."

Ken's brow furled. "How is their political consciousness?"

"Chri'sakes!" George blew out a gusty laugh. "How's *their* political consciousness? Just fine, thank you. How's *yours*?" He slapped Ken on the back, trying to lighten him up.

But the slap only stiffened Ken. "Prisoners…" Ken dropped his voice. He glanced around to make sure Rockefeller wasn't listening. "In the present political climate, they're the key to the armed struggle. The message coming out of the prisons has to support the correct line."

"Correct line?" George's nose flattened against his face. "You want to rewrite these guys? I really wouldn't."

"That's irresponsible, Lubick. You can't just go down there and get a story. This is much bigger than a story. You've got to *work* with these prisoners—educate them to the political realities of their situation—"

"Listen up, these guys are plenty hip to the political realities of their situation. Racism and what have you? Capitalism? Anything *you* could tell them? Imperialism and whatnot? They get it."

"Imperialism and whatnot?" Ken radiated his disapproval. "It's just entertainment to you, isn't it? 'Whatnot!' Just standup comedy!"

George laughed. "What mountaintop you talking from, Moses?"

"I've taken direct action," Ken boasted.

"Yeah, yeah, I know, you blew something up. I respect that. But you don't understand." George clapped Ken on the shoulder again, but this time forcefully enough to shoulder him out of the way so he could step past into the larger space. "These guys in the pen don't want to be lectured at. Get me? They want to be the ones doing the lecturing. And we're telling them, fair enough, lecture away, we'll hold the bullhorn for you. That's what we're doing."

"Lumpen proletariats, Lubick—at the very crossroads between brigandage and revolutionary commitment—which way will they jump? A class-based analysis could make all the difference. Marx said about the lumpen proletariat—"

"I know," George cut in impatiently. "'Capable of the most exalted sacrifices and the most heroic deeds as of the basest banditry and the dirtiest corruption.' God Almighty, you think I never read *The Class Struggle in France?*" George had inhaled Marx in college, but most of it had slipped like plankton through his memory's nets. Why this one fragment had caught, he couldn't have said, but the fact that it had made him want to laugh.

Ken didn't hear a joke in George's quote. To him, George had demonstrated impressive mastery of chapter and verse. With increased respect, he said, "All's I'm saying, man: we revolutionary intellectuals have a duty to get involved. I want to meet with these men, get involved in this."

George studied him. "Duke Silver has the connections. Talk to him, if he puts you on the list, we'll take you along, but you have to be on the list, and Silver controls that gate."

Zoe had laundry to do, so she told George she'd drive herself to Salem and meet him at the penitentiary. When she arrived, she saw George and Ken Singleton standing on the other side of the security gate. She knew Singleton was supposed to be joining them today, she assumed they were waiting for her before they went inside. Zoe stepped up to the guard and said her name. It should not have been necessary, the guard knew her. She'd been here with George three times already, and three times now on her own. "Zoe Madigan," she said. "From the Rose City Ark."

The guard glanced at her as if he'd never seen her before. He scanned his clipboard and scanned it some more. "You're not on the list."

"Of course I'm on the list. I'm with the Ark. I'm here practically every week. The Ark is on your list, isn't it? Check again."

"Ark's on the list but it says here, let in two. We already let in two."

"What?"

The guard pointed past the security glass. There stood George, inside already, calling out to her. "Zoe! I swear to God, I didn't know. They replaced you with him."

Zoe stood for a moment, feeling her stomach muscles tighten. She knew at once what had happened. Two from the Ark was the deal, and Duke Silver had the authority to choose which two. He'd chosen Ken Singleton over Zoe and had not even bothered to tell her because that's the kind of asshole he was. Him and Singleton were two of a kind, she'd sensed it from the start. But not George. "I'll wait for you outside," she called to George. "I'll wait in the car." George had his faults, but he'd never have done something like this. It wasn't his kind of misbehavior. It would violate that "honor" thing he had, burning in his gut.

She walked across the parking lot, sweating and smoking. This morning she'd been considering abandoning this prison project. Now, she felt she couldn't let it go. She thought about JJ's face, the last time she visited him alone. The way he looked when she handed him a whole pack of cigarettes instead of just one. He was on the verge of opening up finally, about to start telling his real story; and she'd been primed and ready to receive it. Now, that was the one and only thing she wanted to do: listen to his story, record it, and pass it on. But maybe she only wanted it so much now because now she couldn't have it.

She watched the men come out of the prison an hour later, saw them conferring outside the gate. She couldn't hear them but she could see the tension. George gave Ken a push in the chest and she thought she was watching a fight about to start, but George turned on his heels and walked away before Ken could react.

He needed a ride, it looked like. He must have hitched down here with Ken. He plopped into the bucket of the passenger seat and slammed the door. "I did not know." His eyes were grim. "Singleton got friendly with Duke, did an end-run on us. Motherfucker. He's already been here five times without us, the men think *he's* their connection to the Ark now. He's told them he's going to get them page three. That's the one thing we wouldn't promise, remember. And you know what they'll be writing for Ken. Open Letter to Comrade Brezhnev by another name, I swear to God."

Zoe had pulled onto Highway Five now and was headed for Portland at eighty miles an hour. "I am pissed as hell," she told him. She glanced his way. "But not at you."

After Zoe dropped him off, George decided he didn't want to run into Marica right now. She'd show serious concern, and right now he couldn't handle her version of serious concern. He had to cling to the only strategy that worked: laughing about all this with someone who appreciated life's comic absurdity.

He found Sval sprawled on a couch, reading paperback westerns. "Mr. Lubick," said Sval. "You look jangled, comrade. History been roughing you up?"

"Get this." George swept around the coffee table to the armchair. The draft raised by his body swirled several sheets of paper to the floor. "The prison thing's going off the rails. Singleton has pushed his way in, he got the prison honchos to cut Zoe off the list and put him on instead. So it's me and Singleton going down there now—for as long as *that* lasts. They don't even want to show me what they're writing. Singleton's their buddy now. Comrades in the revolution. And I'm telling you, Sval— whatever they turn in, we'll have to print it verbatim. *Verbatim*, see? Because that's what I promised them. George Lubick does not break a promise. Back me up on this Sval. This is—fuck! This is important."

"Don't worry," said Sval. "Loyalty is one of my key ideals."

Solidarity Makes Its Move

Singleton did not bring in a letter from prison that week or the next. But he said the men were working on it. Under his tutelage, he assured Monday Meeting, they would deliver something that would rip The Man a new asshole, maybe even kick off the revolution. In the meantime, he demanded that *Open Letter to Comrade Brezhnev* occupy the space being saved for the prisoners. The collective considered his proposal and rejected it. Two days later, when Raoul stopped at the Ark to deliver some cartoons, he found the door locked. He knocked, it opened just a crack, and a fierce face peered out. Then the door slammed shut again. "It's the bourgeois cartoonist," he heard someone say. "Should I let him in?"

"Tell him to slide his 'cartoons' under the door." That low growl belonged unmistakably to Ken Singleton.

Raoul fled. From home, he called Sval. George and Sval went to the Ark to see for themselves. When Sval knocked, the door opened only as far as a chain would let it. This time, it was Singleton himself looked out.

"What the hell's going on in there?" George snarled.

Singleton met him scowl for scowl. "The Open Letter to Comrade Brezhnev will be published. Let the masses judge. We recognize no other authority."

Within the hour (such was the efficiency of rumor) the whole community knew about the takeover. Various combinations of staff people went to the door and pleaded to be let in, but to no avail. No one knew how many people were in there, but Martha heard the patter of the IBM composer, so at least they were putting together an issue. She thanked heaven for small blessings. Any paper on the stands come Friday would be better than no paper at all.

That night scores of small groups huddled in taverns and living rooms across the city and argued about proper responses to the crisis. At Sval's house, a group of six collected. George was there, and Raoul, and Zoe. Bill the typesetter sat in, and so did Zack the Zen Buddhist, who had taken over bookkeeping duties from Martha. Sval chaired, George proposed a course of action. "Sooner or later, they go home to catch some shut-eye. Right? After they're gone, we grab the paper back and lock the door, and tomorrow we let in anyone *except* the Solidarity Quintet."

No one opposed this plan. Wordlessly agreement jelled. The next morning, shortly before dawn, the six met at the Hotcake House for breakfast and then proceeded in two cars to the Ark.

Raoul rode with George. The morning air was cool. Not even the faintest light had crept into the sky yet. Somewhere frogs were croaking. Neither man spoke. George was remembering a morning long ago when he and Marica had gone at just about this hour to the swings hidden in the southwest hills. Raoul was noticing that the air was so moist it was visible in the beams of the street lights. He could feel the Void bulging against the thin fabric of the visible universe and evil lurking in the streets.

They arrived at the church without incident. Sval parked directly in front of the building; George pulled up behind him and everybody got out. The front door was locked, but Martha had a key. Raoul was the last to enter, he pulled the door shut behind him. They were in the windowless central hall. Sval whispered, "Ssssshhhh." George groped his way toward the steps. The others followed him, arms outstretched, feeling their way forward like blind people. A tap sounded. Everybody froze.

After a long moment, Zoe whispered, "Just the pipes, I think."

"Why are we whispering?" Sval said suddenly. His voice echoed against the hard shell of that church interior. "There's no one else in the building. Isn't that why we came at this hour?"

He turned on his flashlight. The brightness made Raoul wince.

George was on the steps already, and Sval followed him closely, his bootheels making their familiar click-clack.

"Come on," Zoe urged the other three.

They climbed the three flights of stairs to the door of the Ark office. It was Sval who had this key, and he tried it in the lock.

But it wouldn't fit.

"Holy shit." Raoul trained his flashlight on the door handle. "They've changed the lock."

George said, "Gimme' some room."

"George—!"

But the cry came too late. George had launched himself forward, his right foot extended like a battering ram. The door shivered under the impact of his kick. In a fluid continuation of the motion, George rammed his bunched shoulder into the door. The jamb splintered and the door burst open.

And George had to fling up his arms to shield his eyes from a light blazing out of the darkness.

"Hold it right there, motherfucker!"

Sval saw a shape moving behind the light."

"My God," he muttered, "they've posted guards."

His eyes were adjusting. He recognized Tony Restucci of the Solidarity Quintet. Restucci was holding a gun: some kind of rifle.

"Back off," said Tony.

"Tony, man. Really. . ."

"Back the fuck up. This area's off-limits to all of you till Friday morning."

"You telling me that fucker's loaded?" George snarled. "You got the balls? You got the balls, tough guy? Fire away!" He tore his shirt open and exposed his chest. Buttons popped and flew. "Right here!"

Sval grabbed his arm. "George. I'm not sure this guy's kidding—"

"You bet your ass I'm not kidding. Back off and spread the word. The Ark has been reclaimed by the People."

"What do we do now?" Driven from the Ark, the group had reconvened at Martha's house where they sat hunched over coffee, circling back again and again to the same question. "What do we do now?"

Zack the Zen Buddhist suggested doing nothing: passivity, he preached, was mightier than activity. His proposal was dismissed with tired smiles. George's ideas ranged from baseball bats to tear gas. They provoked only impatience. Sval gave a short speech about broken trust. "The principle of consensus has been damaged. We cannot in conscience ignore this—"

"Enough," Zoe interrupted. "What should we actually do?"

"We have to rally the community." Sval had spoken the words before, but this time they sounded flat.

"I'm tired of rallying the community," Bill declared.

"And I bet the community's goddamn tired of being rallied." George let out a cynical chuckle.

Martha cleared her throat. "I think we should call Pastor Richardson. We should ask him to get a court order."

Sval wasn't sure he had heard right. He cocked his head at Martha.

"Get a court order," she insisted, "banning Mr. Singleton and his gang from ever setting foot in the Ark anymore. We can say we kicked them out of the collective, but they won't leave. And then, let the court enforce it."

"Is that a precedent we want to set," said Sval. "Suppose someone uses it to ban *us* from the Ark. They go to Pastor Richardson and say, hey, we fired those guys but they won't leave."

"That can't happen, Sval. Because—technically—we're the officers of the corporation," Martha declared. "You, me, Zoe, Raoul, George and Marica. Remember? We signed that document. We're the board of directors."

"Oh, that." Sval glanced at the others, "The Rose City Six. That was just a piece of paper. It doesn't give us any special authority. It's not how we do things in here. We can't exploit that document to violate our own rules, just because it seems convenient right now."

"What document?" Bill looked puzzled.

"Tell them, Martha."

She complied in a few swift sentences. The silence that followed was difficult to gauge.

"Let me just emphasize," said Sval, "I do not regard that document as conferring any special authority on me or any of us. In fact, let's make it official. We can draw up a statement and make it explicit: authority belongs to the collective. Anything we six decide, the collective can override. And we'll all six sign it. That way, if we *have* to use this piece of paperwork as a weapon, we can do it without appropriating any special powers."

The others looked embarrassed. Zack cleared his throat. "If that document does what Martha says, I say fuck it. Let's use it."

"With full collective approval, of course," Sval added.

"Fuck that," barked Bill the Typesetter. "There's no time for collective approval. What are we going to do, send it to Saturday Meeting? These people brought guns to the office. They don't belong in here with us. I say feed them to the system."

"Are you people out of your minds?" George cried out. "Even if the full collective approves, we'd be calling in the pigs. Dress it up any way you want it, that's what we'd be doing. You want to set a precedent like *that*? Singleton's a renegade jackal but he's *our* renegade jackal, and we've got to take him out ourselves. If we call in the pigs who's ever going to trust us again?"

"I'm with Bill." said Sval. "The moment he pointed that gun into my face, he crossed a line. I have a duty to the community, yes, but those men aren't part of any community I acknowledge."

"Hear, hear," Bill said. "I'm not taking a bullet in the head over who gets page three. Talk to the Pastor, Martha. See if he'll get that court order."

"I bet he will. He's responsible for the whole church. He doesn't want things like this happening in the church. Our problem is also his problem."

'I just hope he won't decide the Ark is the problem," said Sval. "I don't know what we'd do if we have to move out of the church."

On Friday morning, as Julio Martinez of the Chicano Research Center was entering his office on the second floor of the church, he saw six red-eyed figures coming down the stairs from the Ark office with a look of tattered triumph.

Mrs. Olson, who worked with the Senior Citizen's Assistance League on the first floor, reported that they were carrying a large, flat package wrapped in newspaper and tied with string.

Martha had been coordinating distribution and subscriptions lately, so she went to the printers at the usual time and sure enough: there was this week's Ark, stacked up in the usual bundles of fifty. As if this were just another normal issue.

She cut the twine on one bundle and looked at the paper. On the cover was a drawing of some half dozen people rushing forward with their fists raised, looking angry. They were Black, Latino, Native American, Asian, and White. Their fists dominated the layout above the fold. Across those fists, emblazoned in scrawling red letters was the word REVOLUTION! And across the top, where the title of two or three stories usually appeared, was the declaration, "The People Take Charge."

Inside, Ken's "Open Letter" filled up most of the front half. In the second half, Martha found reviews of obscure political films that had played at the Socialist Bookstore in San Francisco several months back. There was a full page of news briefs about demonstrations and militant actions around the world. There was a special section on strikes in the United States: the workers' demands in each strike were called out in boldface type and set off with bullets. Interviews with militant workers were presented in sidebars and boxes. The whole back page was an ad calling for the destruction of the U.S. Government, placed by the

Revolutionary Alliance for Social Progress (RASP)—which, as everybody at the Ark knew, consisted of three people (two of them members of the Solidarity Quintet). And of course, this week's feature essay, filling up all of pages three to six: *An Open Letter to Comrade Brezhnev,* by Ken Singleton.

Everything else—classifieds, guides, ads—were simply reprinted without change from the previous week's issue. All the information these sections delivered about dates, times, and venues was wrong.

The Solidarity gang swaggered into the copy meeting that Monday full of bluster and triumph. They took the best seats, slumped down in lordly fashion, and let their berets rest low on their foreheads, bristling with the pride of heroes who had served the cause without apology or compromise. Apparently, they thought their issue of the paper had scored a triumph. The sullen reticence of the others, they misread as new respect.

Ken stood up to deliver a communiqué concerning last week's provisional takeover. "A thick cloud of bourgeois mystification has been hiding the truth from the paper and the paper from The People. On Tuesday night, The Provisional Revolutionary Authority took decisive action and we stand by that action. We say: let The People be the judge."

Just then the phone rang. "Unplug the fucker!" someone cursed, but George answered the phone anyway. "Yeah?" he barked into the receiver.

A voice screeched at him, "You assholes, I went to three clubs Saturday and every one of your fuckin' music listings was wrong. What's the use of your crummy paper if it can't even tell a guy where to boogie?"

"Wait a minute." George put his hand over the mouthpiece. "Ken," he said. "—it's for you. It's the People."

Just then Pastor Willie came in. "Which one is Ken Singleton?" he wheezed.

Sval pointed. "That's him."

The Pastor gave Ken a document. He called out four more names, the rest of the Solidarity Quintet, and gave each of them a document as well. "That's a court order barring you five from setting foot on church premises. I've called the police, Mr. Singleton. You can leave now or let the police escort you off the premises."

Ken glared at the minister. "Call off your dogs," he said finally. "We have no further use for this newspaper." He jerked his head at his cohorts and they rose and followed him out.

The Kiss

By some terrible oversight, Marica had forgotten to put on a dress before going downtown and now, clad only in bra and panties, she was hurrying from store to store, toughing out stares as she searched desperately for something to wear. But nothing on the racks quite took her to another level. It was just a whirl of merchandise speeding up. The luster broke into fragments of dirty sound as the crowds pressed closer and the stares turned to grabs.

Then the whole hurly-whirly vanished. She was in a warm, dark, cedar scented attic, on her knees in front of an old chest. Reverently she lifted the lid and there, neatly folded, were the clothes she'd been looking for: her grandmother's clothes.

She pulled out a long dress with hemstitched sleeves and ruffles around the bottom. But as she tried it against her body, her mother wandered into the room, shoveled the clothes into a basket, and wafted out again. Heartsick, Marica followed her, and found her mother on her hands and knees at the end of the hallway, gnawing on the telephone cord. "I washed them for you," said her mother. "They're in the basement, hanging out to dry."

The stairwell to the basement was cramped and dark. Marica picked her way down with growing dread. The basement ceiling was dank with pipes, all of them leaking. The only light came from one dim bulb at the far end of the room, where the clothes were vaguely visible, draped over a clothesline.

"No!" she shrieked. "I won't I won't wear them!"

Marica jumped awake: she had glimpsed a moment from WOMANLIFE. Had been immersed in it. Had been transformed into WOMANLIFE. How to re-enact that moment for an audience? The bed beside her was empty. George had gone, God only knew where. He was in one of his disappearing phases. She couldn't help him with whatever he was going through. She had her own hyenas to keep at bay. Everybody knew she'd quit the Ark to create a solo, one-woman show. She'd told them all. If she backed out now, they'd all know what a failure she was. But she couldn't play it safe. Life was risk. She had to plow into her project and have faith that the path ahead would open up.

She took a bath and sat in front of her dresser in her bathrobe, drying her hair and planning her day. The prospect of working on the show loomed faintly as a chore. That was a bad omen. Too late to call the whole thing off, though. Too late! She had already made arrangements to rent the theater space in the Comfort Zone. People who knew her were already asking casually, every time they met, "How's the show coming?"

She'd underestimated the need for privacy in the solo creative process. Early on, she'd let a few people watch her work—a mistake she had not repeated. She was giving birth to something here; a mother couldn't let other people's energy form her child. No one seemed to understand what a private experience this was: giving birth. It was a burden a woman couldn't share. She had to do it alone.

Marica sighed and from the closet took out a little knapsack into which she packed her tights, her leotard, her leg warmers. Chore or not, she had to sally into the teeth of it. This was her chosen Work. She couldn't shirk it.

After her workout, Marica took a long, long, bath. She counted this as part of the work: when her energy was low, she had to recharge. She luxuriated in the bubbles, relaxing her resistance to the cosmic flow, letting the energy seep through her pores. Afterward, however, she felt rather limp. "Well," she thought, "perhaps I've worked on the show enough for one day." She took the rest of the afternoon off and went shopping thrift stores.

By five o' clock, she was back in her apartment, hoping to find George. He wasn't there. Too bad. She could have used a little frivolous fun tonight. A dinner out, a tavern, a little dancing. Six nights a week, George was hammering at her to paint the town with him, but tonight of all nights he was off somewhere sulking.

Then came an idea. She pitched it to Martha. "Let's have a clothing exchange party! What do you think? Everyone brings something, everybody takes something. It'll be like exploring each other by swapping clothes—exploring what it's like to be someone else. What do you think?"

"How would it work? Everyone's not the same size, Marica."

"It could be anything," Marica said. "Hats, Scarves. Masks. Capes. Accessories. Jewelry. Anything a person wears to say This Is Me."

Zoe brought an outlandish hat and a hand-painted tie to the clothing exchange party. They were good accessories a few years back, closer to the sixties, when she was always eager to announce as boldly as she could to all the world, "Here I am." Now, five years later, she still didn't know who she was, so she felt less like shouting Here I am.

She dropped her items on a coffee table already mounded high with clothes. In the dining room, Marica had set out tea crackers, meringue cookies, hot tea, coffee, and Postum. On a side table was a gallon jug of Gallo burgundy. Maureen had brought a bottle of Wild Turkey, which some of the women were passing around. Others stood around at the table, picking at the food and waiting for Marica to finish rolling a joint. A general call had gone out, but only women had dropped in. Men could have come if they'd wanted, but none were interested in a clothing exchange party.

Zoe returned to the living room, where a dozen or so women were picking through items piled on the table, holding up particular pieces to gauge the fit. Clothes had never been of compelling interest to Zoe. Costumes, yes: costumes were a different matter. But clothes—meh.

Watching from a distance, she wondered who each of these women would be in ten years. How many would be mothers? Mothers! The mere word made Zoe feel claustrophobic. Being a tree, unable to move, reduced to doing nothing but providing shade and food. A preposterous choice, but the choice of billions. Or not, come to think of it. Not all mothers were mothers by choice. Maybe this Roe v Wade thing would change that. Maybe in years to come women would actually have choices.

Losing the prison project was a blow. Sval lavished her with sympathy about it, but Sval didn't get it. To him, you lose one project, you launch another, no big deal. But then, no one got it. She shouldn't hold Sval to a higher standard, she supposed. Sval did a lot of things right. There were still whole days when just being with him felt erotic, when she woke up spontaneously and mysteriously awake to his body and the world thrummed with arousal from sunup to sundown because Sval was there. On days like that she found herself able to believe. But those days always ended and the next day very often opened gray.

Zoe examined a large antique-looking shawl that someone had brought to the party. It was a clingy knit with faint gold threads woven in. It looked very fifties. She was reminded of the Ed Sullivan show. She draped it idly over her shoulder, liked the feel of it, and wondered about the look. She ambled toward the hall where she'd seen a full-length mirror. As she came around the corner, she saw Martha, in a derby hat and a hand-painted tie, mugging at herself in the mirror. The effect was comical but Martha was carrying it off as a costume and standing there all by herself, she was carrying it off strikingly well.

"Oh," she said to Zoe. "You caught me. And I see you found my shawl. You're Lady Astor now."

"You brought this shawl? It's hot, Martha."

"Hot!" Martha giggled. "Found it at St. Vincent De Paul. A dollar eighty-five."

"That's where I got the tie."

"So *you* brought the tie—"

"And the hat." They stood side by side, exchanging small laughter, gazing at themselves in the mirror, and obliquely studying each other.

Zoe remarked, "You look different. What have you done to yourself?"

"It's because of the tie," said Martha. "You've never seen me wearing a hand-painted Hawaiian tie before. I bet this is going to be worth a lot of money one day. Are you sure you want to give it away?"

"You're wearing it as a scarf. I never thought of that." Zoe pursed her lips. "It's not the tie. Have you been working out?"

"Swimming." Martha shrugged. "I use the pool at PSU. I have a card."

"How do you have a card? You're not enrolled there anymore."

"It's just paperwork," Martha winked. "I'm good at paperwork."

"Jovial sarcasm." Zoe snapped her fingers. "That's what's different! You didn't used to be this way. Honestly—when I think about it? Since we met? You've changed more than anyone I know."

"Me?"

"Yes, you. You've got a calm about you, like you know who you are and you're good with it. I wish I could have that."

"I have it because of the Ark."

"You do? How the Ark?"

"Because I'm needed there. I'm just as important as the rest of you. I've got something none of you crazy genius types have. The place would fall apart without me."

"I'm sure it would. What is this thing you have?"

"I know where everything is. I'm the queen of order. The empress of it really. George said that once to make fun of me, but it's true. People come to me when they can't find the keys."

Zoe looked into the twinkle of Martha's eyes. "You've got a lot of information like that stowed away, don't you?"

"About the Ark I sure do. Most people don't even suspect how much there is to know."

"Like what, for example?"

"Like when to order more toilet paper. Yeah," said Martha. "See?" She raised her eyebrow at Zoe with a cheerfully sarcastic smile. "Who thinks about toilet paper? But listen to them moaning when it runs out."

"I see what you mean." Zoe was tired of seeing herself in the mirror. "Let's go out and get some air."

"It's raining."

"But not cold. It feels good when it's warm and wet. You've got a hat."

Martha touched the brim, smiling. "Yes, I do, don't I?"

Outside, Martha asked Zoe a question. "Is Sval going to get with Marica, do you think? Marica acts like it's nothing, but she's always talking about him."

Zoe rubbed her cheek, bemused. "Marica's a goose, you know. She and Sval slink around like guilty children. I don't understand it."

"Well: like you wouldn't care? If Sval left you and went off with Marica? How would that feel to *you?*"

"Left and went off? Where would he go off to? We all live in Portland. We're all right here. And not just Portland. We all live in this little bubble of a so-called community in Portland. It's true. you know: you can't go anywhere in this town without running into twelve other people you know. And by the end of the day, every day, you've met fifty-thousand people, and they all know each other."

"You're changing the subject," Martha insisted. "You really wouldn't care? Really really? If him and Marica got together? Is that really really really true? Come on!"

"I don't *want* a commitment from him. I haven't committed to anything myself. Things have to stay in balance. Sval is fun to be with, sometimes, but I wish he *would* sleep with Marica or someone. I don't want to be his only girlfriend. It's too much pressure."

Zoe stopped speaking. Martha was strolling next to her, lost in thought. Zoe could just imagine what was going through her mind, and after a moment she said it out loud: "This is a big breakthrough for us, isn't it? Talking about Sval. This has been the elephant under the rug all these months. Let me ask you a personal question, Martha. Do you ever fantasize about sleeping with him?"

Martha emitted a short laugh. "Like Sval would be interested in me!"

"Why not? He's interested in me. I'll tell you something, Martha, the difference between you'n'me is, I don't give a damn. That's all it is. I don't care if men know what I want when I want it. And if they tell me

I can't have it, fine, I didn't want it that much anyway. Indifference is all you need. If you can turn that on and off, you're good to go."

"I don't want to feel indifferent all the time."

"Well, you have a point there. What's the opposite of indifferent? I do sometimes wish I could be like that, but I'm stuck being who I am— whatever that is. Aren't we all. Except you, Martha. You're not who you used to be. Why is that? It's the way you're carrying yourself maybe." Zoe paused for a moment, processing how she was going to describe it. "Not just your body, your everything. The way you're carrying your everything these days." Zoe paused to notice: the electricity of this moment felt good. "I'm thinking," she said, "what would you think about kissing right now? I'm wondering what you'd say. You and me. I would like to give you a kiss."

"A kiss? Oh, I don't know. A kiss-kiss, you mean? Zoe! I mean, I'm not a lesbian, if that's what you're asking. I mean it isn't you, it's me, I'm not gay."

"I'm not either, to my knowledge. But how can you really tell unless you try it? That's what I've been wondering. As Sval would say, a kiss is just a kiss, is my thinking. See how that feels. And then just see what *feels* like happening next. See what happens if we don't censor ourselves? If we don't plan what we're going to do next, just turn off that part of our brain and let whatever's going to happen, happen?"

Martha laughed a bit at that. "Why me? Why don't you want to see how it feels with… someone… you know. Like Marica, for example."

"Well, because I don't find her attractive in that way. You, on the other hand, I do."

"Me?" Spots of color rose into Martha's cheeks. "Attractive, huh. All right. Let's try the kiss thing."

She looked awkward, waiting for Zoe to lean in. Zoe edged in closer and felt the warmth of her lips sinking into Martha's lips, a warm sensation, like it was with men, not unpleasant, the opening of portals and the slick and wet slip and slide of tongues against tongues, pretty much like it was with men but somehow…more tender. The pressure of breasts against her breasts. The question was, of course: extended for eternity: was this really what she wanted? No more men? Just women?

She lifted away from Martha and fixed her with inquiring eyes. "What do you think? What comes next?"

Martha's laugh was embarrassed. "I still think I'm not gay."

"That was my takeaway too," said Zoe. "So now at least we know. Let's go back inside. There might be some brownies left."

"I hope there's still some wine," said Martha.

The Answer

"Marica! Whatchoo' doing here? Thought you quit the Ark!" Susie Sunbeam looked up at the figure suddenly filling the doorway: Marica, in a flower-print, yellow-and-black dress with a deep neck and a full skirt stood with her raincoat slung over one arm and a red scarf wrapped around her neck, surveying the room.

"I did," she replied to Susie, "but I was being too extreme. The Ark is part of my life too!" She stepped down into the room. "I have to maintain a balance. One day a week doing production at the Ark, I owe the community that much."

She waded into the bustle of the main room and deposited her belongings behind the light table as had been her habit in times past. Her appearance raised a gratifying stir. She protested that she was not here to party, she was here to work. She did however accept a cup of wine, because production night at the Ark was always so intense.

"Yes," she explained to Susie Sunbeam, once the fuss had died, "I was very depressed for a few days after I had to postpone my show. But then I decided, you know what? I was being OCD. That's not healthy!"

"I got that way about natural food once," Susie admitted.

"Nothing to excess! Not even moderation!" Marica proclaimed. "It's so true. That's why my performance piece wasn't coming together. The problem started with me. *I* wasn't together. I've rescheduled my performance for May 3. Don't you dare miss it, Susie. An artist is a— what's that word? Connector? Carrier? Channel?"

"Ditch?" Sval suggested.

"Sewer pipe?" George bellowed.

"Vessel," Raoul declared. "Artists are vessels."

"Thank you, Raoul! Exactly. Letting other people's voices flow through you and into the community, that's an artist's job. You *have* to stay connected. Look at me, running on like this—you have to understand, Susie, I've been so alone in my work. Dare-to-Juggle wanted me back, but doing street theater? While you're trying to invent a whole new art form? I don't think so. The Ark, though, takes a different kind of energy. In the end it's like Zoe Madigan's always saying. It's all about balance."

"We been wasting our time fighting racism and whatnot," George snorted. "All we need is woo woo. Gimme some yin yang someone."

"It's not either/or, Dumbo," she flung back at him. "Everybody needs to listen to what's inside them, all of us need to listen to what's around us too. Everyone has to do both. But what would you know about listening? You haven't heard a word anybody's said for years." She settled back in her seat, pleased to have met George gibe for gibe.

George frowned over his layout, struggling to think of a comeback. Susie cut in to defuse what she thought was a tense situation: "Of course the Ark isn't the same as when you left, Marica. We're one big happy family here now."

A random piece of somebody else's conversation floated to Marica's attention: "But mind you, I don't think organic carrots is the same thing as salvation. Not in the seventies. We're beyond that now." It set off a ripple of conversation about salvation and the seventies.

"Why doesn't someone do a feature about that for next week?" Sval suggested. "Salvation in the Seventies: Organic Carrots."

Bubba Sadhu looked up from his work. He was dressed in the loose-fitting clothes and blood red robe he had adopted ever since he had founded the new spiritual movement he called Cosmotherapy, which was temporarily headquartered at Bubba's own Truth and Light Vegetarian Pizza Retreat.

"Feature story," he scoffed with bulging eyes. "Salvation you say. All of you are looking for something and all you've found is a box."

"And what've you found?" Billy T. demanded.

"I," said Bubba, "have found The Answer."

"Well, what is it?" George barked at him. "Come on, Saddoo, don't leave us hanging. I could use an answer or two."

"Wait a minute, George—not so fast," Sval interpolated. "Let us first establish The Question."

"Bah! Questions are a dime a dozen," said George, "Let's get some answers." Cupping his hands for amplification, he broadcast to the room at large, "Listen up, everybody! Saddoo over here's got the answer."

"What's the question?" someone called.

"I nominate 'What's the meaning of Doo Wah Diddy'?" Sval said. "Or should we say *Sa-doo* Wah Diddy?"

"Mock on, ye doubters!" Sadhu smoldered. "Ye have ears and yet ye cannot see. The Question—" He peered around with a fierce gaze—"is life itself. Oh, how ignorant is he who would turn away from that precious blossom."

"Stop the presses!" George shouted. "Saddoo's got the Secret of Life Itself!"

"Precious Blossom Found!" cackled Sval.

Marica felt tension churning in her belly. Several people in the room were definitely not laughing—was she the only one to notice the glum, disapproving, tight-lipped look on the face of Zack, the Zen Buddhist bookkeeper? And the two women from the Ananda Marga House, who had turned their back resolutely on the howls of mirth? Marica could sense Susie Sunbeam's tension without even looking. And Sadhu himself seemed to be feeling real pain. Well, of course he was, poor dear. Everyone was laughing at the thing he held most dear. That wasn't kind. Although he did cut a slightly ridiculous figure, Marica had to admit. But was he not taking an immense risk, putting his deepest self on the table where anyone could laugh at it? He did not deserve this ridicule. No one did. If Sadhu could be sliced up this way, was Zack far behind? And then Susie? And then Marica herself?

Marica plucked up her courage, and though her throat felt shrunken, she said, "What is the answer, Bubba? I for one would like to hear."

To her surprise and delight, everyone quieted down. With two short sentences she had changed the whole chemistry of the situation. This was a power she'd forgotten she had. Almost without effort, she had transformed Sadhu from an unwilling clown into a man of dignity.

"The Secret of Life," he said, "is Breathing."

Howls of laughter exploded from every side. George actually jumped out of his chair and staggered around in a circle, holding his sides. "I think he's right. Oxygen!" he gasped. "Someone, gimme' some oxygen!"

"No, no," Sadhu cried out, his voice almost lost in the general hilarity. "Not like that, George. Follow me. Look!" He pressed his thumb against the side of his nose. "Breathe through the right nostril—everybody! Long slow breath! One. . .TWO—top off at the eight-count—THREE. . ." But as no one was following his example, Bubba Sadhu abandoned the lesson.

Zack the Zen Buddhist exchanged a glance of sympathy with him, as did the two women from Ananda Marga. Marica looked on with dismay. Here it was again, she thought, happening right before her eyes: could no one else see it? Another crack in the Ark?

Great winged beings had started to appear in Raoul's dreams, begging him to come away to their incalculably distant home planet, a place beyond space and time. As dreams, they would have been startling enough; but the truth was even more stunning.

"They're members of an alien race," Raoul explained to Marica that day as they left the Ark. "Of course, the actual creatures aren't in my head. I'm seeing images I've invented. That's how they do it. That's how they communicate with someone like me from a galaxy so far away: by entering my imagination. Apparently they're in some kind of jam, Marica. I haven't found out what it is yet, but they seem to think I'm the only one who can help."

Marica gave these remarks thoughtful consideration. "How did it start?" she asked, trying not to sound like a doctor inquiring about symptoms.

"In a stadium," he said. "I was in a stadium, there was a concert. I was just another nobody way up in the bleachers. There must've been a jillion fans. This place was HUGE. But I looked across the stadium and all the way on the other side—this was in a dream, mind you—incredibly far away, I spotted him."

"On the other side of the stadium."

"Yup. Out of a billion faces, I picked out one face right away and said to myself, whoo! That little bit there is not a dream. Everything else, yes, but not that little bit. You know how photographers have a painted background, and you stick your head through a hole like you're in the scene? It was like that. This alien had cut a little hole in my dream and stuck his head through. He was hoping to blend in, but no ma'am. Uh uh. Not a chance. I spotted him right off."

"And how could you tell he wasn't just another part of your dream?" Marica felt her cheeks' faint flush. After the hoots and jeers she'd witnessed at the Ark, she wasn't about to do the same to Raoul. "Don't dreams always feel real when you're in them?"

"Oh, I'm good at telling the difference between what's real and what's a dream," Raoul assured her, "especially when I'm asleep. This little piece was real."

They walked along toward Belmont, their sides brushing slightly. Marica was thinking about her performance piece: wasn't she actually saying much the same thing as Raoul? Dreams are where the myths live. The maiden. The woman-warrior. The mother. The mythic archetypes—they're what's real. Wasn't that what she was saying? "We're just shadows," she said, "of a real world that is all myth and metaphor. What sort of dream-work have you done, Raoul? I took a dreaming workshop once in Berkeley. My boyfriend back then, he woke me up whenever he saw my eyelids fluttering. That's when you can remember your dreams best, when you've just woken up from REM sleep. Those dreams, it's like they tap into another reality that's realer than real."

"I know what you mean," Raoul agreed. "Sval says the great winged beings exist only in my head. He says there's no distant civilization out there, sending me messages. He tells me I have to be *here* in this reality. I tell him, that's where I *am*. This reality is where I'm getting the messages."

"I've done a lot of dream-work," Marica told him, "but I still can't tell what's real. I feel like I'm groping through something in the shadows. I think about the stories in the Torah, though. Those aren't just stories. Judith … Joseph… Ruth… they're like messengers. From our own deepest selves."

"That's what I told Sval. The Winged Ones are real. I told Sval, you're the one that only exists in my head! You'd better hope I don't wake up because that'd be the end of you!"

Marica grinned. "I can picture what Sval would say to that. 'Could be, could be.' He'd nod like he's being perfectly objective, but pretty soon he's got a counterargument."

Raoul grinned too. "No. Not 'could be, could be'. For this, he'd say 'granted, granted.' "

She and Raoul laughed together then.

"Winged creatures from outer space. Who knows, Raoul? It makes a kind of sense," she allowed. "The Goddess, some people see her as a great winged being, so right there in a way you have a winged creature from outer space. It's a metaphor, but metaphors are part of reality."

Raoul pulled a fresh joint from a matchbox in his pocket and paused to light it. They ambled down the sidewalk trading tokes. Freshly stoned for the day, Marica found herself in a mood to have new experiences. Today's work, she decided, was to see the world afresh. What better way than to sign onto someone else's trip as a tourist and see what strange worlds she drifted through with him: places she herself might never think to go. Especially Raoul of all people: what kind of journey would she go on if she jumped on *his* starship?

Raoul's starship took them to a busy block just off Sandy Blvd that was bristling with used-car dealerships and low, junky storefronts. He had an errand to get done there, something about a shell shop.

The day felt pregnant and silent, overhung with the hush of low grey clouds that somehow muffled the roar of traffic. Hidden emotions were breathing within the bulges of clouds, yearning for life. Then, just as they parked on Powell Street, a sliver of light glinted between the banks of clouds.

"Sunlight in April," said Marica out loud.

Then the rain started again.

"It's an omen," said Raoul. "Something big is about to happen."

"I feel it," said Marica. "It's pushing against the sky. Pushing up from the earth. It's like something in a womb … trying to be born." She didn't usually spout stuff like this. Honestly, she knew how ridiculous it would sound. But you could say stuff like this around Raoul, it didn't matter, because this was Raoul after all. Around him, you didn't have to make sense. "And you have to ask yourself, what is trying to be born? Is it the angel or the beast?"

"It's the One," said Raoul, his face suddenly alert, like a field mouse sniffing something in the wind. "I'm about to meet the One."

Marica guarded a smile. She'd heard about Raoul's "the one" from Zoe. She didn't think the idea was entirely silly, as Zoe seemed to. There was something sweet about it, actually, about Raoul and this angel he was expecting to meet someday.

The sound of the street broke in on her again. A truck was parked at the curb and people were carting boxes and furnishings into an empty storefront. Raoul stopped dead, looking dumbfounded.

"What?" she said. "It's just a van. Someone's moving."

"This was Bart Sloan's office," he said. "Martha's landlord."

"Are you sure?"

"I was here with Sval, just last week. This was Sloan Construction Company just last week."

"I wonder if Martha knows about this." Marica stopped a young man carrying an armload of books about Atlantis, Lemuria, and Mu. "What happened to Sloan Construction Company?"

"Who?" The boy looked about 20 years old: an immature 20. His hair was blond and stringy, his eyes moist, his nose runny.

"The business that was here last week. The rental agent."

"Sloan Construction Company," said Raoul. "Bart Sloan."

"Never met him, but I hope he's having a nice day." The boy grinned and shook his head. "We just took the place yesterday. We're organizing for the coming of The One."

"What did you say?" Marica stammered.

"The One?" said Raoul.

"Yup. We're his exclusive agents in Portland. We're setting up for his arrival. Do you know Bubba Sadhu?"

"I know him well. Vegetarian Pizza?"

"Cosmotherapy," the boy reproved. "Bubba helped us find this place. He'll be on the ship, for sure. That's why the One got in touch with him in the first place. Bubba Sadhu's going to let people know the One is coming."

Marica walked to the door of the building and peered through the dusty windows. There were two storefronts situated on either side of a hall. The one on the left was a shell shop. The one on the right was empty.

"What do you mean, the One? Who's The One?" Raoul demanded.

"You ask, but I think you know. The One you have been waiting for. The One who will deliver the message. Didn't you know? Beings from another galaxy have been studying the earth. Yes, and they're going to come and take a few people back, just the ones who are spiritually ready: back to their own planet. They've got a vastly superior civilization up there. You should read the case histories—*case histories!* People who've been up there and have come back to tell about it. Some of them have a Third Eye!"

"Third Eye!"

Marica turned away from the windows. Bart Sloan's operation was not just gone, but gone overnight, it seemed. This felt big. This felt ominous. "Come on, Raoul. We have to tell Martha. Sval's going to want to know about this too."

"You go ahead," said Raoul. "I want to find out more about this man's cult. I might want to join."

Good and Valuable Considerations

"Yes, can I help you?" The woman at the desk was a middle-aged Germanic type. She had the typical squared-off look of minor clerks in large bureaucracies.

Sval set his hands on the desk and leaned forward a little. "I'm trying to find out who owns some properties in Portland. Is this the place?" He'd been going from office to office, looking for the one room with the records pertinent to his particular quest.

The clerk pushed her glasses up and reached out her hand "Do you have the addresses?"

Ah. He'd found the place. He made his way into the aisles of files. One set of cabinets had property cards organized by location. Another had property cards filed by owners' names. The cards in one set were filled numerically, by blocks. The cards in the other were arranged alphabetically by last name. They were for the same properties but had different information.

Sval found the records for Martha's neighborhood. He narrowed his search down to houses on her block. He started at the corner furthest from her house and worked his way east. Some of the houses belonged to individuals—a Lyle Anderson, a Jay Morton—some to companies: Forest Estates, the O'Kane Group. Sval copied down the names. He came to Bart Sloan's name and saw that yes, he was looking at the card for Martha's house—but then he felt a tremor of surprise. Not about Sloan owning this property. The surprise was the other name on the card. The previous owner of this house had been a man named Robert Brody.

Wasn't that…? Sval glanced through his notebook to make sure, and yes: this was the fellow Martha had mentioned. Brody was the man who collected rent from the people across the street. Apparently, at one time, he'd owned Martha's house. Then, apparently, he'd sold it and bought the equally decrepit house across the street. Why would he do that? The two houses were essentially identical.

Sval found the card for the house across the street, just to confirm that Brody owned it, and he did. But here, Sval saw another and even more startling piece of information. The previous owner of *this* house had been Bart Sloan. Yes, Brody had bought his house from Sloan, Sloan had bought his from Brody. The two men had swapped nearly identical houses. Sval recorded this information. He didn't expend pointless energy analyzing what it meant. Time enough for that later, right now his only job was to record, record, every piece of information that might be relevant: he was clearly on to something.

Money, for example. How much money changed hands in the course of all this house swapping? Not that he could fathom why this would matter, but money always did seem to matter. If there was a mystery here, money might well be the key to it.

The card he was looking at did not carry any information about money. Maybe the other set. Sval crossed the aisle and found that yes: these cards showed the purchase price of each house the last time it was sold. Sval located the card for Martha's house and read with interest what it said:

> Purchased for Ten Dollars ($10) and Other Good and Valuable Considerations October 10, 1969.

Hmm. Good and valuable considerations. What the hell were those? He found the card for Robert Brody's house across the street. This one read:

> Purchased for Ten Dollars ($10) and Other Good and Valuable Considerations. November 10, 1969.

Whoa. Sval looked again. The words were still there. Ten dollars and other good and valuable considerations. Two men had swapped houses right across the street from each other for ten dollars and "other good and valuable considerations?" Considerations? What were those? What were they worth in dollars and cents?

Sval wanted to throw his notebook in the air. He wanted to start dancing. He didn't know what he'd found, but he'd definitely found *something*. Oh yes, most definitely, *something*. He snapped the file drawer shut and prepared to leave. A few days ago, he remembered, he'd been telling Martha about journalism being like detective work. Well, she could appreciate what he meant, she'd dug up some crucial clues herself. If she and he were Woodward and Bernstein, which of them would be which? Then came a sobering thought. He couldn't keep this information to himself until he'd written his piece. He might be looking at a crime in progress. If you know a crime is happening, you have to report it to the authorities, even if it wrecks your scoop. He approached the woman at the desk. "Hi. I found something strange in the files, I think you might want to look into this."

The clerk listened to his account unperturbed. When he'd finished, she shrugged. "It's probably for the tax break."

"What tax break?"

The clerk shrugged. "You'd have to ask an accountant. All I take is the home mortgage deduction. I don't even have a second house."

"But is it legal, what they're doing? Swapping houses like that? For good and valuable considerations? How could that be legal? Why would the city even keep records if this is the kind of records they're keeping? These goons must be covering up something. Is that allowed—lying?"

"Prob'ly. You'd have to ask a lawyer. I just file them. No one's complained."

Sval didn't know what else to ask. He left the building, deep in thought. What he'd discovered was big. He knew that much. It was like the 18-minute gap in the Watergate tapes. It was the proverbial smoking gun, the unmistakable evidence. Unfortunately, in this case, the key question remained. Evidence of what? He'd have to run this past Zoe. She had a way of bringing things into focus just by the way she listened. She had a peculiar genius for listening: how he loved her for it. On the way, however, he stopped and called Martha. She would want to know about this. After all, this was her story too, in a sense.

"Wow," was Martha's reaction. "How strange. You want to talk about it? I could go for an avocado sandwich at Produce Row."

"Definitely," he said. "How about next Monday, after the meeting? We could steal away for an early dinner."

It didn't occur to him that Martha was wanting to get together right now. He was on his way to Zoe's house, after all, with questions burning holes in his brain. Sval took the bus back to the southeast, sprang off at Hawthorne, and headed for her house, hoping she'd be home and in the mood to help him unravel this mystery. He entered without knocking but stopped short at the door to the dining room. Zoe was sitting in there with a man he'd never seen.

"This is David," Zoe said. "He teaches biology at Lewis and Clark. I'm thinking of auditing his course next semester. The college has a way you can do that without enrolling."

"Ah," said Sval. He sat down at right angles to both of them. "Please continue."

"Yes. Go on." She turned back to David. "This is interesting."

"I was saying, reproduction and immortality are two opposite survival strategies. The cells could be immortal, but what's the use? In nature, most organisms don't die, they're killed. So, evolution works out another way to keep life going." He paused. And then: "Sexual reproduction."

"Hunh!" Zoe was holding the man's gaze. "So the swamis have something, huh? Sex and death. They're connected."

Sval understood that he was on notice not to interrupt.

"Yes. The swamis and also Freud. Sex and death are definitely connected." The professor's voice hinted that he'd said something salacious. He'd given just that slight hiss of emphasis to the word *sex*.

"At the cellular level," Zoe mused.

"At the cellular level, but you feel it everywhere," said the professor, "because your cells are what you are, they're *everything* you are. In a sense your entire body is made up of… sex."

Sval wanted to argue with that one, but he felt out of his element. He tried to work his way into the conversation so that he could steer it toward the mysteries of Portland real estate, but the jump from metaphysics was too daunting. Zoe humored him by seeming to listen whenever he intruded with a comment, but the professor clearly considered Sval a pest who wouldn't take a hint and go away: there was serious seduction going on here, Sval was in the way. And Sval couldn't fault him. The professor had no idea that Sval was Zoe's primary relationship, and Sval knew not to bring it up. He understood the rules. Zoe was engaged in a conversation she preferred to his company at this moment. He should do the right thing and remove himself.

Sval made his way to the kitchen, where he poured himself a glass of orange juice and chugged it down. The door to the utility space at the back of the house was ajar and a cold moist breeze was wafting in. The room was littered with discarded boxes that would later be cut up and recycled. Sval stepped through them to the darkness outside, where mist was turning into rain. The steady hiss muffled his footsteps.

At home, bedraggled and wet, he thought he might be coming down with something. He crawled into bed and pulled the covers up to his chin but couldn't fall asleep. He lay there in the deepening silence of a city sinking into darkness. The slight discomfort he felt, he recognized as guilt. He'd left abruptly without even telling Zoe, and he'd done it for unworthy reasons: to let her know she'd hurt him. No, not just *let* her know, *make* her know. He'd done it just to spoil whatever she was in the middle of. He wished he hadn't done that, but he couldn't undo it now. Calling her to apologize would only make things worse. For one thing she might be in bed with the professor by now. He got out of bed and looked for his bottle of Jack Daniels. He must resist the urge to call.

Men Getting Drunk

"We don't want you coming round no more." Carter sat with his hands clasped in front of him on the table, his back locked stiff.

George was incredulous. "You want us to stop coming? What've we done? Give me a hint."

"There's no 'us', George. It's you. We don't want *you* coming 'round no more. After what you did? No way brothers can trust you no more."

George stared for a moment. He let out a long breath. What started as a laugh ended in confusion. "Can't trust me? Christ, man. Loyalty's the only thing I believe in. Man-to-man loyalty, I'd never betray *that*, there'd be nothing left!"

"Loyalty, huh?" Carter folded his arms. His curt nod was only punctuation. "You called the pigs in, on Brother Singleton."

"The pastor got a court order."

"You asked him to."

"They came *at* us. What were we supposed to do, lie down for them? That ain't ever happening!"

"So you called in the pigs. You crossed a line. There's a line between you and me, George. You out there, we in here. You never in your whole life worried you might end up inside. I never in my whole life didn't. I was born knowing this is where they'd try to put me, and they sent those pigs after me and sent 'em after me till they got it done. My life, never a day went by I didn't worry. And that's a line. Between you and me? That's a line."

"Yes. It is," George agreed. His face had gone pale under his jungle of beard. "That's a line. Sure. We're free, you're in prison. That's a fact. But can't we still connect? At some level?"

"You even ask that question shows where you at, man. I don't want you in the trenches next to me when the shooting starts. You never been but a visitor to the ghetto. There's heavy shit coming down the road, and personal man-to-man loyalty won't mean shit once the shooting starts. We're talking about class struggle, George. Brother Ken helped me with that, he helped me *see*. When you and me pick up guns, we'll be shooting at each other. Ain't no helping that."

"So you're saying 'The Letter from Prison' is dead. That's all I could ever give you, was a chance to be heard, that's all. And you don't want it? What about the others? You speaking for all of them? Why aren't they here today? I want to hear it from them."

"Oh, they'll be heard. We'll all be heard. Brother Ken's starting up a paper. He's going to put that Letter from Prison on his page one."

"Ken Singleton?" George's face twisted into a dark scowl. "You trust him over me? Are you serious?"

"Believe it, George. Your world always been too safe."

"Too safe. Huh. Okay. If you say so. Go with Singleton, then. Go, see what he can do for you. If he flakes out, get in touch," said George, "the Ark'll still be there. George Lubick does not break a promise. That won't change, even if a war starts tomorrow and we're enemies."

"War started yesterday," Carter said, "and you *is* the enemy."

George came out of the prison bursting with an urge to laugh. The universe around him felt like a big pair of jaws. He sat in the cocoon of his car in the middle of the parking lot and laughed for a while. No one could hear him, surrounded as he was by parked cars. Well, he thought, another project comes to nothing. Here in the jaws of the giant.

"End of the line, buddy," the bus driver called out to his only remaining passenger. George, huddled in the furthest back corner of the bus, looked up through a fume of liquor. Rain was drumming on the bus. Nothing outside looked appetizing.

"I'll stay here," he growled. "Property is theft," he added.

"Goddamned it," said the bus driver. "This car's shutting down."

George threw up.

When the police arrived, they found him snoring. One officer tapped his shoe, the other clapped handcuffs on him. On the way to the station, George told the police officers. "You work for me, men. I'm John Q. Public. You're my servants." On the way into the station house he treated some invisible audience to a shouting rendition of Howling Wolf's Mad Dog Blues.

George woke up royally hung over. He was sharing a cell with four other disheveled drunks. As part of a human cattle drive, he was taken before a judge, who said, "Drunk and disorderly. How do you plead?"

George pressed his head, wherein a herd of six-year-olds were playing stickball. "I *plead* I'm human. We're both human. Right judge?"

"Guilty." The judge banged his gavel. "Pay the bailiff one hundred fifty dollars."

Sval came to the courthouse to pay George's fine and take him home, but he grumbled about having to do it. "I don't know why you didn't call Marica."

"I did," said George. "She wouldn't come." He wiped his hand across his mouth and cleared his nasal passages. "She was too depressed, she said, about her friggin' 'Performance Piece'."

"Oh! I heard. Yes. She had to cancel. She has my sympathy."

"Save your sympathy. It's not canceled, just postponed!" George let out a burst of derisive merriment. "You think our Marica might fail at something? You must be thinking of someone else."

Sval raised a quizzical eyebrow. "You two doing okay?"

"Yeah, sure. We give each other what we want."

"None of my business, you're saying. I hear you. Didn't mean to pry. Sorry."

"That's not what I'm saying. You ask if we're doing okay. Well, you tell me. You've seen us together, me and Marica. Are we a couple? We don't get along, but we still tool around together."

"That's the definition of A Couple, according to Zoe. Two people who go everywhere together and don't get along. You know something, George—no offense here but I actually can't fathom how you and Marica got together in the first place. You're such an unlikely couple. I mean no offense, George, but *you*! You are so not her type! It would seem. To the outside observer."

"What could she possibly dig about me, is what you're saying."

"Well—"

"You know what it is? I tell it like I see it. That's why she sticks with me. She knows I see her, and I'd never lie about it. I tell her she's a fool and she knows it's true. Plus, she thinks she can fix me."

"Okay. In that case, I guess the question would be: why do you stick with her? She won't even pick you up from jail."

"Well…" George gazed at some spot far up the road. "There's the sex."

"Ah, to be sure. To be sure. That aspect." Sval sucked from his cigarette in a professorial pause. The windshield wipers went on beating time as tediously as the bass and drums of the song on the AM radio station.

They arrived at George's house. Sval parked and followed his friend inside. They were in the middle of a conversation, they weren't going to quit now. The conversation had to wait however until George took a shower and changed his clothes. During that time, Sval did not go to the kitchen to look for beer. He was too hung over. He merely waited.

George came down, shaking water from his hair, and plopped into the overstuffed armchair facing Sval. "These days," he snorted, taking up their conversation as if there had been no interruption, "she says she has to 'conserve her sexual energy for her art.' Why the hell does she need sexual energy for this foolish thing she's putting together? Her art! This dance-thing or whatever the fuck—I've seen her practicing. There's nothing sexy about it. There's nothing anything about it. I don't even know what it is."

"Maybe, for her, the art and the sex are coming from the same energy place."

"Jesus, Sval. Whose side are you on? Let's change the subject." George sprang to his feet, paced restlessly to the kitchen door and back, and plopped into his chair again. "What about you and Zoe." His teeth gleamed in a wolfish smile. "How're you two doing?"

"Well, she's depressed." Sval sighed. "Getting kicked out of that prison project mattered to her. Almost too much, frankly. There's something unhealthy going on there. It's like a symptom, how she's taking it. She claims I don't get why it mattered to her so much. She's probably right. And maybe you agree with Zoe. *You* got the heave-ho too, *you* should talk to her. All I could offer her was my ignorant sympathy. Sorry."

George dismissed the sympathy. "I'm over it. I had to get stinking drunk and spend a night in jail, but I'm done. Relieved, actually. Now I won't have to grapple with doubt."

"What doubt? The letter from prison was a good idea. You were right to go after it."

"Naw. I wasn't. I think about what Carter said yesterday and it made me realize. What him and the others wanted from me was hope. There's no way I could give 'em that. I looked at them, I saw men who were never getting out of prison. Inside or out, didn't matter. I don't see how any of us can *ever* get out of this hellhole. I couldn't lie to them. They're better off with Brother Ken. He'll give them something to cling to. The Revolution, hooray!'"

"Give the devil his due. Singleton really believes in that shit."

"He tells himself he does. That's how he keeps despair at bay. That's his ploy. Everybody has a ploy except me. I wish I had one."

"Everyone??" Sval cocked his head. "What's my ploy, pray tell?"

"You believe in life after the apocalypse. That's your rock."

"Hmm."

"I'd even settle for what Marica has."

Sval studied his friend's forbidding face. "What's she got?"

"She's a narcissist, dude! She believes in her*self*." George let a beat go by. "I'd *even* settle for the God-ploy," he said. "The trouble is, you have to believe in that shit or it doesn't work. Right? That's where I always fuck up. I can't believe some lie. I just can't."

"Belief is not as cut and dried for me as you seem to think." Sval was not to be outdone in Angst. "I do ask myself occasionally. What if there is no Apocalypse? Where does that leave our preparations? But agonizing about such questions doesn't get you anywhere. Lately my strategy has been to just slog away at daily stuff. You have to know when to stop asking questions and just do the work. If I can see my feet walking, I must be making progress. It doesn't matter what you're doing, just make progress. That's what counts. Set small goals and inch toward them. That's the trick, George. Don't keep looking at the stars, look at your feet. Try not to trip."

George shrugged at this advice. "Progress on what, champ? What are you making progress on?"

Sval had an answer. "This story about Martha's roof, for example. I don't let myself ask what difference it makes if anyone reads whatever I end up writing. I just keep digging for the story, and you know what? I think I've got something. I just have to figure out what it is." Sval paused to let the memories of yesterday harden. "I went over to Zoe's to talk about it, she always has a way of clearing my head, but she was with some guy, and she wanted me gone. So I went home and got drunk. I lost 24 hours. That's why I'm hung over."

"Some guy. Another one?"

"At what level remains to be seen," Sval assured his friend. "He's not in the ring with Raoul and me. I would judge him to be a tourist passing through her life. You know how Zoe gloms onto new fields of knowledge through men. She might be taking this one as a short course in biology. But what she does with her sexuality is her own business. I don't presume to judge."

"Bullshit, Sval. You do presume to judge. And you should."

"I can't agree. Letting go is what keeps a relationship alive. We don't clip each other's wings, that's the prime directive. Zoe and me, we're not going to become that dreaded two-headed animal known to society as A Couple. It's the one goal we share. If we give up on that, I don't know what we have left."

"Letting-go, she seems to have down cold," George declared. "You want my advice, go out and have yourself a fling. Have two, in fact, they're small."

Sval laughed politely. "Flings are not my métier. I doubt I could sleep casually with any of the women in my sphere of life. The next day would be too weird. It wasn't weird with Zoe, but she's a special case."

"What do you mean, your sphere of life? Forget that sphere, bobo. Go to a bar and find some woman who's looking for a casual slice of something hot. Even at the Ark, there's strange women flowing through all the time, hit on one of them."

"At the Ark?" Sval was shocked. "Hit on? In front of everyone?"

"Is that a crime now? Looking for a zipless fuck? Putting out feelers? You afraid they're going to drag you to the Women's Center and have you whipped? Half the people at the Ark already think you're Casanova."

"They do?"

"Yes, if they don't actually know you. You've got a blistering reputation as a cocksman. What do you expect, Sval? You're always walking out of the office with gaggles of women."

"Friends and colleagues," Sval protested. "Fellow warriors in the fight for social justice."

George heaved an exasperated sigh. "I ain't accusing you of nothing, I'm just telling you to go fuck someone. Literally. It'll boost your morale. It'll make Zoe sit up. What's to lose?"

"I don't know. With a perfect stranger, you're saying? Meet for the first time at seven, in the clinches by ten?" Sval shook his head slowly back and forth. "It would be weird, but perhaps you're right. Perhaps what I need is, in fact, an affair of the species you describe."

Help

A sharp-featured flat-faced woman with teased hair and heavy black eye shadow walked up to Sval at the Ark. "What's this I hear?"

"You tell me. What have you heard?" Sval went on with his work.

"Cut the crap," said the woman. "I hear you're not going to print my restaurant review."

"Restaurant review?" Sval scratched through a pile of papers at his elbow and came up with a handwritten sheet torn from a spiral-bound notebook. "Is this one yours?" He read a sentence from the work out loud. " *'The waiter crawled up to us on his hands and knees to serve us our horse d'oeuvres while licking our shoes.'* " Sval cocked his head at the girl, posing no question but nonetheless waiting for an answer.

"It's a satire," she protested.

"Of what?"

"Of the restaurant!"

"Which restaurant?"

"Not any *particular* restaurant," she complained. "It's a place I made up."

"Well, that's your difficulty, right there," Sval counseled. "A satire has more bite if the object of your satire actually exists. Incidentally, its hors, not horse."

"Does everything that gets reviewed have to exist?"

"Pretty much. Yes: that would be a minimal requirement. Pretty much."

"Wait a minute—" the girl said suspiciously. "You get to decide? It's just up to you? You get to say if my piece goes in or not? Who the fuck are you?"

"Theoretically, no one. But in practice, I'm the one who's sitting here actually doing the work."

"Fucking A." The girl stuck her tongue out at him in disgust. "How are you different from Hitler?" She walked away, swinging her hips.

Marica, who was laying out a page nearby, murmured sympathetically, "The new barbarians."

"The young keep getting younger," said Sval,

"And look at the way she's dressed," Marica reproved. "Nothing but fishnet pantyhose and a man's shirt? Does she *want* to be looked at as a sex object?"

"Yes. I think she might," said Sval, thoughtfully.

Later that week, Sval and Raoul went to Music Millennium. Raoul had worn out his copy of Santana's *Welcome* album, but he thought he might score a cheap second-hand replacement copy that was in better shape. Inside the store a promotional display for the new Aerosmith dominated the front of the room. Albums were scattered on a table among broken doll parts. A poster sized blowup of the album cover announced that Aerosmith's new one was called *Toys in the Attic.*

"Somebody in marketing went to town," Sval remarked. He stepped around the poster and made his way to the back of the store, where the second-hand records were displayed. Raoul went rooting for Santana, Sval browsed for early Beatles, early Dylan, but didn't find any. Those things were starting to become collector's items, people who had them were holding onto them.

A sharp-featured, flat-faced woman with frantically teased, bleached-blond hair and heavy black eye makeup walked into the store. Sval recognized the girl who wanted to write satirical reviews of restaurants that didn't exist. He'd not seen her back at the Ark since that day, but this was definitely her, standing at the threshold of Music Millennium, peering around. She spotted Sval and picked her way toward him teetering on the very high spiked heels of the boots she weas wearing. "Hofby!" she rasped. You here for Aerosmith? Fuck, that band is so hot, I can't stand it! Steven Tyler, man, I'd fuck *him* in a minute. Did you buy it yet?

"I'm not really a heavy-metal fan," he said. "I lean more to … outlier fare."

"Weird stuff. I knew it!" She preened. "I nailed you for a Captain Beefheart motherfucker moment I set eyes on you. That's cool. That's cool."

"Your name. . .as I recall. . .?"

"Fuck you, sweetheart. You know my name. What's happening at the Ark?"

"The usual. I haven't seen you at the office since the day we spoke,"

"Oh, I've come by once or twice. I came by looking for you, but you weren't around, so I said fuck it. What's the fun if Mussolini's not there."

"I hope I didn't chase you away with my judgments," Sval offered. "I'm one guy, what are my judgments worth. You should get involved, push a little of your energy into the mix, it would be refreshing."

"It wasn't you, man. You're cool. I got tangled up with this stuck-up bitch named Zoe. You know her?"

"I do, actually. If it would ease yo*ur* mind, she doesn't come to the office much. It's safe to come back. What're you into these days?"

"Weird drugs. Aerosmith. Kiss. Women's movement. What about you?"

"Just the drugs."

"Ha!" She let out a squawk of laughter and slapped Raoul on the upper arm, "This man's funny. Your friend is funny! Hey, where you living, Hawf-bee?"

"I'm in a house on 42nd. Out in the boonies."

"What's your number? Let's get together sometime. I got another restaurant review to pitch, if you know what I mean. And a thirst that's jes' killing me."

"Yes, indeed, we should. By all means, drop by sometime, let's talk.

"You're not hearing me, Hofby. I said let's get it on, man. Bang a gong. If I give you my phone number, will you call me?"

"By all means."

"No you won't. I'll call you. You'd like that, wouldn't you? You'd like that, me calling you at the Ark. That's what I'll do. You'll be sitting at that big old typewriter, and I'll be talking to you on the phone."

Raoul meanwhile had found the Santana album he wanted, plus a rare Moby Grape as well. Sval turned to the girl whose name he still didn't know. "As I say, do call me any time you feel the urge. At this moment, alas, we have other places expecting us, or I'd stop and chat some more."

At first Marica had been adamant about doing every aspect of her show herself. She was hungry to put on stage the purest possible expression of her own vision, unsullied by political cross-currents and aesthetic compromises. Then she was adamant about having every aspect of her show at least done by women: that was the whole point, after all: *WOMANLIFE*. Candy Miller came in with some marvelous fabric art for her sets; and Beth Karensky agreed to work with her on lights, just as she did with Family Vaudeville. But now Marica wasn't sure. Her current work was all about finding a balance. The place between extremes, the center of the universe, the heart of the matter. As part of finding this balance, she decided to consult with Raoul on some of the visual aspects of her performance piece. Say what you would about the boy, he had an eye for color.

When she got to Yamhill House a gaggle of hippies of the bushiest type told her that Raoul was in his "laboratory." His laboratory! She smiled at the term and started down to the basement, hunching her shoulders, shrinking from the spiderwebs clogging the stairwell. Bugs scuttled away on every side. This place was even worse than it had been when George lived here—or had she simply not noticed it then? Not noticed it because she was so drenched in the guilty pleasure of being done-unto? Was it she who had changed? Was she becoming bourgeois? A naked light bulb hung down over a pair of cement laundry sinks.

Marica could hardly believe that she and George had shared their first moments of passion *there*—behind that furnace...

She knocked on Raoul's door. He pulled it open as if he had been lying in wait. His glasses gleamed in the sudden fluorescence. The room behind him was copiously equipped with high-powered gro-lights. A heavy perfume of marijuana smoke billowed out. She saw some dozen or so plants in the room, a greenhouse here in the heart of darkness. Odd that in all the times she'd been down here with George, she had never so much as peeked inside Raoul's studio. But then Raoul had never invited her in to look. He probably didn't realize she too was an artist.

"Marica!" he yelped. "What brings you here?"

"We're supposed to be having a meeting, remember? We talked about it at the Acme Lit Club brunch the other day."

"Oh, golly, yes! I forgot! Ouch! I guess I'm not ready."

"Ready for what? I just want to get your eye." She stepped inside. The room was dense with works in progress. There was no real place to sit down, so Marica got briskly to business standing up. "I was wondering if you might? I was hoping? How about looking at some color swatches with me and maybe even, I don't know. Brainstorm about some *artifacts* for my—what on earth is that?"

A jumble of bizarre shapes made out of glass had caught her eye. They looked randomly stacked in the corner at first glance, but then she saw that they were resting on a system of shelves.

"Oops. You're not supposed to see that." She started toward the corner, but Raoul jumped in front of her. "Not yet!" he shouted. "It's not ready. I'm going to assemble it in my room when it's done. You'll all be there. I'm going to serve wine and cheese. You're invited!"

"Oh, I see! So that is your—"

"—egg-zacklee: my aquarium!"

"Well, I do know how you feel about your aquarium, as a matter of fact. I'm an artist myself, you know. I feel the same way about my performance piece—not ready to share. These things have a life of their own. Mine is too unformed still, too fragile. You can't have people handling your baby before she's even born. I understand! Which is why I came to see you."

She was speaking in that breathless manner she had when she was nervous and excited, swallowing syllables and jumping halfway over her words, a mannerism she couldn't help, but that men for some reason found terribly attractive. She knew how they felt, but she wasn't going to stop doing this, she wasn't going to stop talking like this, because this was who she was. She wasn't going to let men change who she was, just because they were attracted to it.

And then sometimes, and she hated herself for it, she couldn't help doing it on purpose because the heat she felt from men wasn't always a bad feeling. No, she wouldn't blame herself for liking that heat. As for Raoul, she didn't know why he made her nervous. There wasn't any of *that* feeling in the room, nothing she would have to fend off. This was just Raoul. Maybe she was nervous because he was an *artist*, and here she was, about to share her vision of *WOMANLIFE* with him. As an artist, he might feel entitled to judge. Which made her angry. She didn't need his judgment! And yet she did. She wanted it. But…not if he was going to be critical. She wanted his admiration. That's what she wanted. His admiration.

"I was thinking," she said. "I wanted to ask. Would you consider making some things for my show? For the stage? Not props, exactly— part of the art is what I'm really talking about. What do you think? I've brought some sketches along. What would you need to see?"

She set her box down on a high table and opened it shyly. Raoul came scurrying up with the quick curiosity of a young cat. She took out sketches that showed wings and flaps and environmental shapes for the stage. With these she would conjure up WOMANLIFE. A mythic figure of many aspects. She would conjure her into visible form, bring to life her magic, her darkness. All her hope and joy and pain. Women would see her and feel their power, men would see her and know what it *meant* to be a woman. "I had a color scheme in mind, but I want to know what you think." She spread out for him swatches of fabric that suggested the colors she wanted people to see. She grouped them under the labels she had thought up for her mythic figures: the faces of WOMANLIFE. "What do you think?"

Raoul's eyes darted among the swatches. Marica could see that he was re-grouping them mentally, shifting them around, working them. She wondered if she looked like that when she was in the throes of creative work.

"I see what you mean." He began to read her labels out loud, as if to himself. "The Maiden. The Mother. The Crone. Aquamarine would be the color for Maiden. She grew up in water. And Mother would be earth tones probably…burnt sienna…umber…ochre…"

"Are you sure?" Marica sucked in some breath. "Earth tones for Mother, doesn't that feel a little cliché?"

"Hmm. You're right. First thing you think of is always a cliché. But if you tweak it a little maybe you get to mythic." Raoul studied the colors. "A hint of green with the earth tones, hmm? Some dark, some light, because Earth is where plants come from. Earth has life inside it. You could get some driftwood. Aha—and the Priestess! Good. This is good. I'm glad to see the priestess. I saw the priestess once. This is really good, except … something's missing."

"Oh?" She studied him studying her fabrics samples. "What's missing?" She got ready to cringe.

"It's a who, not a what. These are all different faces of a woman who lives in the astral plane," he mused. "These are just projections. She has a face for each of her different stories down here on Earth. That's what I see. The priestess has a story…The maiden has a story… it feels like one story's missing though."

Marica's heart was thumping. First of all because he got it. Second, because she knew what was missing. Third, because maybe he knew it too. Was it so obvious? Sexuality was missing and of course it left a glaring gap. Because sexuality was a part of WOMANLIFE. It *was.*

"The missing woman doesn't have a name," she sighed. "That's her problem. She has a hard time existing here on Earth, you see, because down here the only words for her are insulting ones. She's a wanton. She's a hussy. The only words for her down here are words that are meant to hurt! She's shameless. She's a whore, she's a slut. Shameless!" Marica fumed. "Why not just: unashamed?" Then she stopped. My goodness, had she said all those words out loud? She glanced at Raoul hoping she hadn't set him off.

But he was merely musing. Maybe he hadn't been listening. Oh, but he had been, it turned out.

"In the astral plane," he said, "Shame isn't one of the categories. So shameless and unashamed don't exist up there. Up there, she might be called Fire Dancer because she's pure joy. You've got some of that. Sometimes, when you're doing Dare to Juggle? You're just dancing up on that tightrope, except with all those balls in the air around you and none of them falling. Channeling the Fire Dancer would be like that. Maybe you could throw people a glimpse of her."

Marica smiled. "The astral plane does sound inviting."

"Inviting is not the word. In the astral plane, every color goes with every other. Nothing clashes except when it's fun. Up there, the air is iridescent like the insides of shells and the winds are visible. It's pretty cool."

"Sounds lovely." She wanted to get back to her performance piece but didn't mind letting Raoul run on a bit, he was such a character, him and his astral plane.

"In the astral plane," he went on to say, "you can change reality with your thoughts. Up there, if you want something different, you just imagine it that way and voila! It's done. Imagination, you see, is a very powerful tool up there. *It's the most powerful tool up there.* People with rich dream lives generally do very well."

"I have a rich dream life," Marica wanted him to know.

"Well, then," said Raoul, "up there you'd be a millionaire. So would I. While cheaters and hustlers and the kinds of people that run banks and whatnot down here—they're generally wretched, miserable failures up there. Street bums, a lot of them. A few get jobs with the circus, but that's about it. From what I've read anyhow. That's why I'd much rather live in the astral plane. But you have to meditate till your nose falls off to get there. I was starting to think I might not make it."

"What kind of talk is that! Of course you'll make it!" With warm fingers, Marica pinched his upper arm.

"My trouble is, you have to be pure."

"Aren't you pure? You're always eating bee pollen and stuff."

"Yeah, but I fell in love once," he reported, "and it wasn't good for me. I've been smoking cigarettes and eating meat ever since. I've been an animal. But that's going to change." His features brightened. "The One is coming."

Marica felt herself blanching slightly. "Oh Raoul. I hope you're not talking about those people on Sandy Boulevard."

"Not them, that's just the advance group. See, what had me flummoxed all this time, I thought the One was going to be a girl. I even thought the One was *you* for a moment, when we first met. But the One isn't a girl, it turns out! The One is a messenger from another galaxy. Now suddenly everything makes sense. Isn't that cool?"

"Hmm." Marica didn't like where this was going. "I think we're all going to get there, Raoul, because we're all seeking the same essence. It's the seeking that brings us together. When you seek hard enough, you start to merge with others on your path. You become one with them. That's what you mean when you talk about the One, really. The One is all of us, together as one. That's what I'm trying to say with WOMANLIFE. It only *seems* like there's men and there's women and never the twain shall meet. Really there's just the one. We're all human. That's what I'm trying to put out there, that's why I thought of you, Raoul, you're so good with the visual side. You want to help me with this? I had a few ideas about mirrors. You're the glass man, after all, right? Maybe you could help me with the mirrors."

"Sure," he said, "If I'm not on Arcturus by the time you need me to get started."

Money

About a year to the day after Martha Williams joined the Ark, she headed out with a bunch of people to a ranch near The Dalles for a tribal day in the country. Sval was there too, and Zoe, and half a dozen other people from the Ark. Marica couldn't make it, she was busy working on her performance piece, and Raoul stayed behind in the city to help her. But George came.

The ranch had been a real working ranch not too long ago. Now, it belonged to the Sunshine Clan who worked with Greenpeace and other save-the-Earth efforts. They had turned old ranch houses into offices of a sort. They still had a barn, which they had retrofitted into a dance space. One person lived there full time, taking care of two horses, which were kept in a corral. They had a herd of goats, which roamed the sparsely forested slopes around the buildings freely and roamed back to the pen every night, like chickens coming home to roost. Some people went climbing around on the slopes that day. It was raining lightly, but that only made everything more green. A group of Ark people were in the ranch house playing canasta for money against a group from KLOO, the community radio station. Most of the crowd was hanging out in the barn, where Street Stomp was jamming. Friends of the band sat in with banjos and guitars and flutes. Non-musicians were tapping on anything that looked or sounded like a drum.

Around sunset, Martha called Sval out to the horse pasture for a walk. She was wearing a pair of farmer's overalls that looked way too big on her except for the broad suspender straps that pressed against her shapely breasts.

"The paper's in trouble," she told him. "Were you aware?"

"I've heard stirrings," he said. "Factions again. Factions, factions. The policy committee has been thinking—"

"Not that kind of trouble," she said. "Money trouble."

"Oh boy." Sval put his hands in his pocket and walked in silence for a moment. "I was afraid that's what you'd say. It's been on my mind too."

"I think our bank account is sinking," she said. "Slowly but surely, it's sinking.

"I had a feeling. But I wasn't sure. The account goes up and down, so you can't tell where we stand from what it shows on any given day."

"I've been tracking it," said Martha. "On average, we used to have about 9200. Now it's down to 9000 or less."

"Doesn't that depend on when you check, though? Right after the paper comes out, before we deposit the sales money—"

"I've been tracking it, Sval. The sales money is deposited on the same day every week. It's the ads we have to worry about. That money comes in all week. It's a stream, and it's shrinking."

"What do you recommend? Raise the cover price? Cut expenses, somehow?"

"I don't know that raising the cover price will bring in enough. And it might hurt circulation, which will hurt ads. And I don't know about cutting expenses. We pull in three thousand a week from street sales, maybe thirty-five hundred at most, and that barely pays for printing and camera work."

"But that's what costs money, isn't it?"

"And supplies."

"And supplies, okay, we have to go outside for that. But everything else we do ourselves. Labor at least costs us nothing."

"Well, I wouldn't say 'nothing'."

"Okay, sure, we pay ourselves a little for this or that piece of work, but why shouldn't we? The collective has looked at it, the collective has said yes. It isn't much, after all. Ten dollars here, ten dollars there, that won't break us. And that's all we're taking out of the paper for ourselves.

None of us are depending on the Ark to put a roof over our heads. We all do some sort of indentured servitude to pay the rent. Don't we? So that we can do our real work in here? We could cut those little payments to ourselves and go back to being all-volunteer. We could do that."

"We were never really all-volunteer. Walter and Grace were full time. They were living on what the Ark could give them."

"I know, but they're gone. We're distributing their money throughout the collective. That's where the ten dollars here and there comes from. Basically, it amounts to nothing per person. None of us would notice if we stopped getting those little bits of money. Why don't we cut those payments and at least stop the hemorrhaging?"

"Some of us are living on the edge, Sval. We need those little bits of money. I know I need mine."

"Hmm." Sval pondered the problem. "Well—how's this: our policy could be: hardship cases get to keep what they're pulling, especially if they're doing something vital—something no one else can do. That would be you, Martha. You're the classic example. You're a hardship case, and you do so much for the paper, you're literally indispensable."

"I'm not the only one. Ten dollars here, ten dollars there, pretty soon you're talking about real money. The production team, for example—"

"The production "team" is whoever drops in to help with production on Thursday nights," Sval said grimly. "It's not just those four bonobos who are pulling a salary. I know the collective voted on it but that's been worrying me, frankly. Four of us are taking a salary just to be in the office all night on production nights, even though fifty or sixty of us are pitching in to get the job done. How is that fair? How much did we allot—"

"Forty dollars a week for each of them," said Martha.

"Okay. See? That's substantial. Everybody does production work, but only four of us get paid. That's troubling. Sooner or later, that's going to drive a wedge right down the middle of the collective. How much is our weekly shortfall, did you say?"

"I can't give you an exact number. Maybe $190 a week? Give or take?"

"A hundred and ninety."

"And I think circulation's dropping."

"A hundred and ninety is just about what those four production people take."

"Four times forty comes to a hundred and sixty, so yes, almost. But—"

"If we cut out those salaries, we'd only need to raise another thirty dollars a week to break even. We could probably get that much doing a few benefits. Let's say Street Stomp does one, or Five Sleazy Pieces. Euphoria would host it, I bet. We could charge four dollars at the door, raise a thousand easy. That'd cover our $30 gap for—I'm not good with numbers. How long? A year?"

"More like six months."

"After six months, we do another one. Two benefits a year is perfectly reasonable. It could be the Mudslingers next time."

"I don't know."

"What's to know?" Sval was puzzled.

"Well—that just seems so makeshift. We need a permanent solution. Get more money coming in or cut costs. And I don't know about cutting costs. Everything is getting more expensive these days. We could aim to sell one more half-page ad a week. That'd cover the gap and then some."

"And maybe we'd have to sell a piece of our soul to the devil. This is something the full collective will have to discuss. The thing is—tell me if I'm mistaken—those four production people never come to meetings. They come to the office, do the work, and leave. That's what we should talk about. Are they really part of this collective? I don't think they'd come if they weren't paid. So I repeat. Are they really here because they believe in what we're doing? And the thing is, we don't need them. We'd get the paper out fine without them. Lots of people know how to do layout, cut'n'paste, all of it. Marica's a whiz. And tons of people come in to help with production for no money at all."

"I just think we can't solve all our money problems by tightening our belts. Some belts can't be tightened. We'd be, like, cutting off our necks to spite our faces. I don't like it."

"So what are you proposing?"

She looked up at the sky, her taut cheeks rosy. Her hair was pulled back in a bun held together with some long wooden needles, but bits of it escaped here and there near the top, giving her just a touch of a frenzied look. The odd thought crossed his mind that Martha, more than anyone, had become the modern Grace. He remembered his childish early hope that he and Marica would inherit the roles of Walter and Grace. How differently reality had played out!

"Well, we're heading into a crisis," she said, "so maybe you're right, *freeze* salaries, but just at first. Let's deal with the crisis, but then—"

"Agreed. Freeze *all* salaries, not just those four production people, and just until we turn things around. And maybe that's when we separate the sheep from the goats. Anyone who won't come in unless they're paid, maybe they don't belong. Meanwhile we do some long-range planning. We have some big decisions ahead of us, Martha. Oy. This is going to take a lot of extra committee time."

Accelerated Depreciation

Art Oliver's law office was situated on the tenth floor of a sturdy older building across the street from a half-built glass-and-steel monstrosity. Martha sat gazing at the swarthy construction workers eating lunch on the high beam. Sval did all the talking this time, glancing occasionally at his notebook. Martha knew the whole story, she'd helped him rehearse. The story began with the disappearance of Bart Sloan and moved on to the mystery of the names and the property swaps, and then onto the strangest mystery of them all: a listed purchase price of ten dollars and other good and valuable considerations for properties two men were swapping back and forth. Only the steady vibration of Sval's knee betrayed his excitement as he moved through his byzantine story.

But just as he was approaching the climax, the phone rang. Oliver waved him silent and spent the next ten minutes nodding and muttering lawyer-talk into the receiver. "So." He hung up finally. "You were saying?"

A bit crestfallen, Sval resumed his narrative. "Martha looked up the card for Robert Brody—he owns a property on Webster Street, you see—"

The door opened and a woman in a store-bought blouse-and-slacks combo peeped in. "Excuse me for breaking in, Art, but could I get you to sign these now? I'm going to stop at the post office on my way to lunch." She set a sheaf of letters in front of Oliver and clip-clopped out on high heeled sandals.

"Go on," said Oliver. "I'm listening." But he hunched over his blotter and signed letters while Sval finished up his presentation. "Just a minute," he said then. He punched his intercom. "Sally? You want to come get these documents?" He gave the secretary the letters and some further instructions. "So," he said, turning to Sval again. "The real estate records? They're a tangle out of Alice in Wonderland, aren't they! Don't let the records distract you, you can't tell anything from those. Your case is about forcing the court to define this term 'habitability'—plus the new provisions on 'retaliation'—"

"Yes, I understand," Sval interjected, "Martha gets evicted and becomes a test case. But how do you explain all these curious phenomena? Sloan's office disappearing overnight?"

"Offices move."

"At this exact moment?" Sval demanded. "With these Moebius strips in the records? Just when we're closing in? Two people buying houses from each other for ten dollars! How do *you* account for that?"

"Accelerated depreciation. They get a tax write-off. Perfectly legal with investment property."

"Oh." Sval exchanged a look with Martha. Write-off? Accelerated? Depreciation? Investment property? He couldn't hold back: "But aren't they avoiding taxes? Isn't that what they're really doing?"

"Minimizing them. Sure." Oliver rubbed his face and glanced at his watch.

"Well, isn't that what they're always convicting big-time mobsters on? Isn't that what they got Capone on? Tax evasion?"

Oliver indulged in a chuckle. "Sloan is no Capone, believe me. He's a businessman, doing what businessmen do." He gave Sval a tolerant smile. "A tax attorney might find something there, but tax law isn't my area. If there's nothing else?"

Sval drove away from the meeting with a creased face. "Well," he said, "so much for the story."

"What do you mean?" Martha was alarmed.

"You heard the man. There's no crime here. Just some boring tax write-off that even he can't explain, even though he's a lawyer, so good luck me getting Joe Blow excited. No crime, no story."

"Oh pooh," Martha growled. "Something fishy is going on here. We just have to find out what it is. Mr. Oliver doesn't see a crime? Of course he doesn't, he's not looking for one! He wasn't even listening to you. He just wants to file his lawsuit and get famous."

"Well—"

"That's all he wants, Sval, trust me. And he has to get me evicted before he can do it, so that's all he wants to talk about, is how to get me evicted. And I don't *want* to be evicted. So what am I supposed to do? My roof leaks, it's been a shitty winter, who knows how much more rain we've got coming, and I've got nowhere to go if I'm evicted. The only thing I can do is help you drag him into the light and let everyone see what he's doing. So don't you dare say you're not going to write your story, Sval Hofby." She looked fierce, standing there, bouncing a bit on the balls of her feet.

"*Your* story," he said.

"Our story. You're the writer."

"You've dug up half the clues."

"See? Clues. You're saying it too. Something smells here. Who are these people? There's got to be some dirt. I'll try the library. Maybe I can at least find out who they are."

Sval gave her a wry smile. If Martha said she wasn't letting go, she wasn't letting go. She was a terrier, this woman. "Tell you what, you hit the library, I'll get someone to explain accelerated depreciation to me. I know just who to ask."

"Who's that?"

"I was thinking about—don't laugh: Robert Brody. Can we get a number for him, do you think? I'll tell him I'm interviewing experts for a piece about real estate in Portland. How to spot bargains, that kind of thing. What do you think?"

Her eyes brightened. "It might work. You'd have to look a little different."

"What's wrong with how I look?" Sval glanced down at himself and saw his hair brushing his belt. "Oh. I see what you mean.." Then he heard himself say momentous words. "I could get a haircut, I suppose."

No bolt of lightning unzipped the heavens, no clap of thunder followed this pronouncement. Cutting his hair wasn't actually that momentous. It was simply the next practical move, if he wanted this story.

"Maybe we could find you a tie too," was all Martha said.

Robert Brody's "office" mystified Sval. It was a small space inside a warehouse, set off from the rest of the space by Formica room dividers. Sval had to pick his way around boxes and dollies to get to it. Brody was a man in his early sixties. His blunt chin jutted out, his jowls hung down in bulldog slabs, the creases on either side so deep his cheeks looked detachable. He wore a green suit and perforated white plastic golf shoes. His tie was pulled loose, and his top button was unbuttoned. He was on the phone.

"Soybeans?" he clacked. "At 31? Pick me up a coupla' hundred, wouldja', Mike? Thanks."

Sval waited at the door, feeling overdressed and alienated. He was wearing creased slacks, a tweed jacket, a white shirt, and a tie he'd borrowed from the maître d' at the Genoa. He wondered what a dealer in real estate would want with a couple of hundred soybeans. He felt a draft on his skull. Shorn of hair, Sval's head felt as light as a helium balloon pulling at his neck. Even his shoulders felt weightless

Brody set down the phone and herded Sval to a chair, crowding and jostling him with his attention, like an encyclopedia salesman. "So what's this all about? A newspaper, you say. Real estate? What newspaper?"

"The Rose City Ark. We're doing—"

"Rose City hoo-ha'?"

"The Rose City Ark. It's a weekly—"

"Never heard of it. Where are you published?"

"Here in Portland. We're a community newspaper."

"What community's that?"

Sval was stumped. He started to fidget with his hair, but his hair wasn't there to fidget with. "In the southeast, mainly?"

"A shopper! Don't apologize, young fellow. I like shoppers. What can I do you for?"

"Well, I'm working on a story about real estate in Portland—"

"News stories in a shopper. That's smart! Pull them in, then sell 'em. Here's what I have to say about Portland real estate, mister—great time to buy. Tell your readers, prices have never been this good compared to the economy. And there's a boom coming, mark my words. Buy now and you'll get rich, I *guarantee* it! But don't quote me on that. Heh."

"We were thinking more along the lines of an analytical look at—"

"Ana-la-hoowah-wich-ha? Run that by me again, son!"

"Just at how real estate works. How to pick a property. What to look for—how to make money in real estate—things like that. We figured, with your many years of experience in the field, Mr. Brody—"

"Bottom line? I'll tell you what. A house is worth exactly what someone is willing to pay for it. So, look at the market first." He let out a dry cackle. His slabs of cheek jerked up and down. "Rule of thumb? If you have to sell in a hurry, don't buy that house in the first place."

"A maxim worthy of Le Rochefoucauld, sir." Sval repeated the epigram with relish: "If you have to sell in a hurry, don't buy in the first place. That's what you tell sellers. What do you tell buyers?"

"'Get yourself a good, professional real estate man. You married, Hofby?"

"Well, no—"

"But you got someone in your sights."

"I do, although whether the opposite be true remains a matter for speculation."

"Whatever you say. You own a home?"

"No." And then, Sval's tongue leapt ahead of his mind: "But I'm looking. My fiancée says she'll marry me if I can just find us a good house."

The words opened up Brody's face. "You came to the right place, son. Real estate is an art, my boy. Do not try to do it on your own."

"How does an artist like yourself decide if a property is worth buying? I'm thinking about the story now."

"I'll give it to you in three words: location, location, and location." He congratulated himself with a chuckle. "Always think resale. Pick a neighborhood on its way up and when it's time to sell, set your price, and don't let some bargain-hunter Jew you down."

Sval tried to simply look studious and pretend he had not heard the slur. "How can you tell if a neighborhood's on its way up?"

"Look at the ads, see what houses are going for. That's why you need a realtor. Realtors—they've been looking at the ads all along."

Ten dollars, thought Sval, and other Good and Valuable Considerations. There'd be no way of telling how much Martha's house actually sold for the last time it changed hands. They'd sold the houses to each other, there was no way anyone else could know what good and valuable considerations were involved. Not from the records on file.

"And then drive around," Brody was telling him. "Use your eyes. Are people keeping their grass cut, their houses painted? What about Negroes, hippies? Fastest way to run down a neighborhood, don't quote me, but it's true, heh heh. You take my advice, young fellow? Get yourself a fixer-upper in a nice neighborhood on its way up, pump a few bucks into it and watch the money grow. You'll beat hell out of the bank rates, son. Write off the interest, which is nine-tenths of your payments first years, and by the time you're cutting into the principle, sell it and plow the profit back into another property."

"Wow," Sval said, and took a surreptitious breath. "Not to mention the depreciation."

"Well, that's another story."

"What is that story, though? How does depreciation work, exactly? I think our readers would be interested. And especially in '*accelerated* depreciation.'"

Brody looked puzzled "That's only for income property. If you're renting the house, you can take a fraction of the wear and tear off your taxes."

"You mean because the house is wearing out? You're making money from it but you're also losing money?"

"Exactly. Every year, that wear-and-tear is part of your cost of doing business, so you can subtract it from your taxable income. But that's only if you're renting. If you're living in the house, it isn't a business. For a fellow in your bracket," Brody said, "—hell, what do reporters make on the little papers? Ten, twelve thou' a year? Income property couldn't get you enough of a break to bother with. What you want is a nice fixer-upper, pump $2,000 into it, sell it in a couple of three years. pull $6,000 out. Find me a bank that pays 300 per cent. What kind of house you scouting for, Hofby? What's your price range?"

Sval managed not to drop his pose. "Twenty-five thousand," he deadpanned.

"Twenty-five'll buy you two bedrooms in Albina. That's niggertown now but the darkies are moving out. Twenty-five will buy you two bedrooms and a yard in Albina and believe me, if you buy right now, you'll make a buck when you sell. What kind of down you figuring?"

"Actually—" Sval checked his watch. Brody's language had his stomach churning. "I think that covers it, I'd better get back to the office and write this up while it's still fresh in my mind."

"Glad to do it. Call me when you're ready, I'll get you into something nice." Brody walked him to the door, steering him by the elbow. On the way out, he stopped abruptly and pointed to a stack of boxes. "Interested in a candle business, son? Wax, molds, wicks, dyes, everything you need to get started. It's just taking up space. I'll give it to you for two hundred dollars, put fifteen down, you can walk out with it right now. Use one of these dollies here."

Sval shook his head. "I'm not a craftsman," he stammered.

"You'd pick up a dollar if you saw one sitting on the sidewalk, wouldn't you? This is a four-hundred-dollar value, I'm letting it go for two hundred, you could sell it tomorrow for three hundred, pick up a C-bill. A hundred dollars just sitting on the sidewalk here. Interested?"

Sval shook his head, and Brody dropped the matter without rancor.

The Date

Sval was directing traffic at the Ark when the phone rang. "Sval," someone called out. "It's for you." On a Thursday night, there was always lots of traffic to direct, and Sval was reluctant to relinquish his command post, but he took the phone because a phone call might always be important. "Sval?" said a voice. He recognized that voice: the girl from Music Millennium. Rings, tattoos, frizzy hair.

"Speaking," he admitted. He dropped his voice slightly to continue the call. By the time George had gravitated to his elbow, the conversation was over

George nudged him. "One casual fling coming up?"

Sval glanced around the office in embarrassment. "Let us not write this off as casual beforehand, George. I'll meet with her, we might or might not make a real connection—"

"Don't give me that meaningful connection crap, Hofby. You've got a live one here, call her back and say yes!"

"Well, if you must know, I already said yes," Sval replied with dignity. "I agreed to meet with her tomorrow night. Just for a beer and a sandwich, though. It's not a date, George. It's a discussion. About her restaurant reviews."

The next morning, he woke up wracked with angst. How was he going to handle this upcoming appointment? Or "date", as George insisted on calling it. He'd have to distract himself somehow while waiting for the evening. Well, God knows, he had plenty on his plate. Lots to do and not enough hours in the day. And that's how he liked it.

These days, *The Adventure of The Leaking Roof* claimed most of his attention, and on this project, he could make actual progress. In fact, today, he had to tell Martha what he'd gotten from Robert Brody. She didn't even know he'd talked to the man already. They needed to sift the information Sval had gleaned. If anyone could cut through Brody's jargon about "depreciation," it was Martha.

He called her from the Ark after scheduling his non-date.

"You talked to Brody?" said Martha. "When?"

"Day before yesterday. I was tied up at the Ark yesterday or I would have called. I think I learned something from him, Martha. The trouble is, I don't know what I learned."

"Come on over," she said. "Let's brainstorm. I found out something, too."

"What did you find out?"

"It's better if I show you."

"Two heads are better than one," he agreed.

When he arrived, sunset was already dimming the apartment. She had a candle burning, which gave the air an aroma. She pointed to several stacks of papers on her sitting-room table.

Sval reached for them, but she stopped his hand, wanting to prepare him first. "The library's wonderful," she declared.

"Seems like you have spent months buried in there."

"Nice try. Not even one month. And yet I got the whole history of Robert Brody, going back to 1949—that's the first year his name showed up in the City Directory. I've got who he's worked for since then. I know when he moved, where he moved to, when he changed jobs, when he got married, when he got promoted—it's all there. It's creepy, really, how much you can find out about somebody, once you start looking. From public records, then you cross-check the newspaper archives— and sometimes there are yearbooks…and then club membership rosters that you can get…"

"You've built up quite an impressive kit of research tools, Citizen Martha. One must ask though: to what end, this skeletal outline of a man's life?" Sval strolled to the table and thumbed through her sheets full of notes. "In the end, what does it really tell us?"

"Well, you find out things," she said. "Sometimes, they're important. Like, for example, Brody knows Sloan."

"That's good to know. But that much, didn't we pretty much suspect already? After all, they've bought and sold property from each other. Of course they've met."

"I'm not talking about 'met'. I'm talking about way back. They've known each other for years. He's an older man, but their paths keep crossing. And that's not all. You know what else I did? When I was looking into Robert Brody's life? Every club or company he was connected to, I looked to see who else was in there, and I wrote down *their* names."

"I see the strategy. And I like it. By all means, let's pursue that line. People who knew people who knew people. The trouble is, a list like that can ripple out forever. You might end up very plausibly connecting Robert Brody to Chairman Mao, but how useful would that be? I am not trying to be negative here. I'm just playing devil's advocate."

"That's the thing, though, Sval. This list didn't just keep rippling out and out." Her eyes were dark and serious. "Once I started keeping track, the same few names kept bobbing up. It didn't ripple out, it rippled *in*."

She offered him a diagram: a complicated web of names connected by arrows. She started tracing the connections, her forefinger moving over the paper from name to name. "In 1952, see this? Ronald Beale…" Sval tried followed her moving fingertip. "…and then in 1957, see this? Brody and Bart Sloan…and then in 1963—are you following this?"

"Trying," Sval frowned. "These people have been in and out of each other's lives for years, you're saying. That's the gist of it, right?"

"Yes, but not because they work for the same company or anything. Just from buying and selling and trading stuff to each other. Look: in 1969," Martha said, "This Mr. Martinello—remember he was working as a salesman for the same company as Mr. Brody six years earlier—he *sold* a house to—you've got to love this: Bart Sloan."

"Who later sold it to Brody, shows here. Interesting."

"But what's really interesting," Martha said, "Mr. Martinello *bought* that same house from Bart Sloan in 1966— three years earlier!"

"Who sold it to Brody the next year. Jesus! I don't follow, but it sure as hell sounds like Woodward and Bernstein territory. What the hell are they doing?" Sval let out a histrionic sigh. "Where is Deep Throat when we need him?"

"We might not need Deep Throat." Martha handed him more papers. "I bet we've got enough here to figure it out on our own."

Sval sank into Martha's armchair and went through her notes and charts and diagrams, frowning and muttering. "Thick," he kept muttering. "Granted. Suspiciously thick." Finally, he stacked the papers back on the table. "It's like I'm looking at one guy jumping in and out of disguises. Here's a crazy thought. Maybe that's what they're hiding, Martha. Maybe it's really just one guy."

"Well, it is, in a way. That *is* what they're hiding. They all know each other. They're one single *something*." She leaned back and let herself be washed in Sval's gaze for a long moment. "What?" she said.

"It just dawned on me. Accelerated depreciation."

A quizzical look was her only response.

"It's what I talked about with Brody. I think I know what this property swapping is all about. It's about accelerated depreciation."

"Explain."

"Well, it's complicated, but bear with me."

"I want to hear it."

"I want to explain it. If only to help me understand it myself. You ready?" He set his hand on hers for emphasis. "Lend me thine ears."

Her hand stirred but didn't pull away. "Do go on."

"If you're making a hundred thousand dollars—"

"I wish!"

"—and you own a house you're renting out, you can tell the government you only made ninety thousand. Why? Because some of your money came from rent, and the house is wearing out. Every year, you can tell the government, you've lost five percent of its value."

"Every year for twenty years. Okay. I get that."

"Twenty or whatever. The point is, you get to subtract a percentage of your money from your income every year. That's depreciation. If you sell the place in ten years, though, and make a profit, you have to give some of it back. You understand why?"

"Sure. Because you weren't losing money after all. The house was going up in value."

"Right. That's capital gains. Okay?"

"I'm with you."

"Now *these* guys! They're taking *accelerated* depreciation. I'll hazard they're taking the whole twenty years of depreciation the first year they own it. Basically, they're saying they think this house is going to wear out in a single year. One year later, they sell the house for ten dollars. Presto! Their prediction came true. The house lost all its value. So, the depreciation they took was legal after all. That's what they're doing, Martha. And God help me—whatever it is, whatever their exact motive might be…they all do stuff like this. All the real-estate wheeler-dealers out there. Bam—there goes our story."

"Why? I still think it's a story."

"There's no crime to expose here. What's happening here is perfectly legal, apparently: it's normal. Dog-bites-man, as Niles would say. All you've got here is fodder for another blistering critique of capitalist society. I've done so many of those."

"Well, I don't know." Martha's determination was that of a terrier with a bone. "You can't sell a house to yourself for ten dollars and say you lost money."

"Well, no." Sval smiled. "You can't do that. But who says that's what they're doing?"

"If you're selling it to yourself, you can't just change your name and say you're a different person. You're still your own self."

This drew a chuckle from Sval. "True enough, that."

"If they're a group," she said, "that's who's doing this. Some group. And what that group is doing is, it's buying and selling to itself. And these people—look." She handed him a sheet of paper with twelve names on it. "Don't tell me that's not a group."

"These are…?"

"The most connected ones. Five or six different ways, all of them. Same school here. Bought and sold there. Lived next door. One of 'em's married to one of 'em's sister. This is a group. They pay taxes as twelve separate individuals, but they make plans as if they were one person."

Sval's pulse quickened. "These twelve people, huh?"

"The spider at the center of the web," she said.

"The Cabal," he murmured.

"If that's what you want to call 'em."

"The Sinister Twelve," he suggested.

"Just as good." She spread out two more sheets. "Here's all their fictitious business names."

"Fictitious? Whoa! These are all fictitious? Does the city know?"

It was Martha's turn to chuckle. "That's not the illegal part. Fictitious-business-names is some kind of legal term. Every business *has* to have one of those."

Sval relapsed into his chair with a groan. "What does a man have to do to go to jail around here?"

"Even if it's not a go-to-jail kind of thing, it might be a story," Martha said.

"No. That's exactly my point. If they're doing something everybody does and everybody knows about, even if we disapprove, we look like idiots 'breaking it' like we're cracking Watergate. Unless they're hiding something, we don't have a story."

"A man might have other things to hide besides a crime."

"Granted. A politician might want to hide an affair, for example. But these people aren't politicians."

"Let's order a pizza," said Martha. "We're just getting started. Let's keep at this till we crack it. We're close."

"Very close," he sighed.

"So, what do you say? Ring for a pizza? I've got some more stuff to show you. It's really interesting."

"Man, I wish I could." He glanced at his watch. "I wish I could stay here and just keep doing this until we break on through, because you're right, Martha, we're this close to cracking it. But tonight? Alack. . ."

"You've got a meeting."

"Tonight, yes," he said. "In a sense. Someone wants to write restaurant reviews for the Ark. I promised I'd sit down with her. Believe me, I'd cancel if I could."

"We're getting warm, though. Right? Can you feel it?"

"The heat is palpable. But alas…" And he said it again. "I committed to this…meeting." He began his preparations to leave. "I'll call you." He touched her shoulder in a gesture of goodbye. And then he wanted to squeeze because her body felt so supple under his fingers. But he didn't.

The next day George bashed into Sval's flat without knocking. "Look at this!" He waved a copy of the Oregonian. "Page four. Prison Authorities Cancel Writing Program. Singleton, that dickhead. I don't know what the fuck he was thinking. He did something so stupid. They kicked him out. They caught him trying to smuggle a gun into those prisoners. That's the buzz, anyway. I wouldn't put it past him, that stupid asshole! In the name of the revolution, no doubt."

"Reprehensible." Sval yawned. He was sipping coffee in his bathrobe.

"Repre*hensible*? Fuck no, Sval! Inexcusable!" George shouted. "They didn't just kick *him* out. They cancelled the whole fucking project. No more writing program. We're out too."

"Ouch. That sucks."

"No more workshops. No letter from prison. Not ever. Thanks Comrade Singleton. You just boarded up the only window those poor guys had. Nobody'll hear a peep out of them now. They don't even exist now. Out of sight, out of mind. Unbelievable!"

George lapsed into silence. Sval continued to sip from his cup. The silence lingered but the mood gradually turned reflective, even though neither of them had spoken. It was Sval who broke the silence. "Unbelievable," he said, as if testing the word for its flavor. "Just the word I'd use for my date last night."

"Oh! Hey, I forgot." George pulled up a chair. He leaned forward, getting cozy for an expected story. "Your albino. So! What was it, then: a date or a discussion?"

"She's not an albino, she bleaches her hair. She calls herself Blondie. How'd it go, you ask? Well, let me tell you. I took her to Reuben's, I thought maybe we'd have a pitcher or two and get to know each other. But the moment she gets into the car, she pulls out *pills*."

"Pills?" George grinned.

"I wasn't into them," Sval growled, failing to see the humor

"What kinda' pills? Downers? Uppers?"

"That kind. Yes. I said no thank you, but she popped a couple. Downers, uppers, I don't know which, maybe both. Then we stopped for a light, the streetlight's shining into the car, and she pulls up her shirt."

"Good—"

"No. Not good. She wants to show me she's got a ring in her nipple. She said the last guy she was with pulled on it and it was, as she put it, 'hot'."

"What did you say?"

"Well, I mean, what *could* I say, George? I said, Hmm, interesting. And let out the clutch. Drive on, Jeeves, was my thinking. But then we got to Reuben's, we had sandwiches, we talked about the Velvet Underground, and she was like, nothing weird had happened. Like, we were just two people talking, the talk was normal, everything felt normal. I'm thinking, I must have got something wrong. So when we're done, Blondie wants to keep on keeping on, and I'm thinking, why not? Everything's normal, right? So we end up at her house, because that's where she wants to go, and once we're there, she asks if I'm into games. I say, well, an occasional game of chess—but she says no: 'role-playing'—and there's no mistaking she means some kind of sex game. But what the hell kind of sex game is role-playing? I'll be Louis the XIV, you be his mistress? Is that it?"

"Beats me," said George. "Which of you played Louis?"

"Ha ha. Such a wit. Listen. So we're standing there and the bald roommate comes home. Suddenly, uh oh. Back to Not-So-Normal." Sval shook his head. "Bald Girl is wearing chains. Minimal amenities exchanged, Bald Girl goes into her room and shuts the door. Blondie starts giving me the elbow. She's tittering. Go in there, she's waiting, you'll enjoy it. I don't even want to ask what she thinks we'll be enjoying. I decline of course, not without a certain bristling discomfort. And it's like *I'm* the one who's committed a faux pax!"

"They don't teach you nuthin'," George agreed.

"Well, what do you want then, she says? A little wearily. Like: okay, she's going to make one last effort to please the impossible guy. Do you want to tie me up? That was it. Red alert! Evacuate! Evacuate! I started edging toward the door. She followed me halfway down the sidewalk, yelling, 'What about clothespins?' Goddamn it, George, what role could clothespins possibly play in the sex act?"

George pursed his lips. "I don't know. Bleached hair? Ring in her nipple? I could be interested." He grinned as if speaking in jest, but also as if he wasn't entirely jesting.

Sval looked away. He didn't really want to be sitting here with clueless George, talking about sex. This wasn't what he wanted to do. He didn't like where this conversation might be going. What he wanted was a different listener. What he wanted was Zoe, but it couldn't be her. Not for this. This could not be one of the topics they shared.

"Hate to bust in on you like this," Sval called up the stairs at the bar of light where Martha stood silhouetted in her doorway. "I'm a little jangled. I wonder if there's any such thing as 'normal' to be found up there."

"You came to the right place," Martha giggled. "I'm as normal as can be. Come on up. We were right in the middle of something yesterday, weren't we?"

"I'm eager to get back into it," he said. "Right back into the middle of it, hopefully."

"Well, like I told you, I've got a lot more to show you. I was saving the best for last," she said. "Get up here."

He took the steps two at a time, long-legged Sval, his palms flat against the banister. Entering Martha's flat drew a sigh of relief out of him. Her roof still leaked but somehow this place felt cozy.

"What kind of normal are you looking for?" she asked. "A Mickey's Bigmouth Ale, of course, but what else?"

"A slice of cherry pie would not be unwelcome," he said. "I know, I know, this isn't a restaurant, but a man can dream."

"Here," she said, "a dream like that can come true. I made a cherry pie just yesterday. Most of it's still left."

"Mother of God," he exclaimed. "Where is Raoul when we have mystical portents to marvel over? Bring it out and let's get cracking. One breakthrough coming up."

"The way you talk. Get cracking." The phrase seemed to touch her funny bone. "Let me get you that pie.

He watched her leave the room, her long brown skirt swishing against her calves as she walked. She was barefoot. His muscles were starting to unclench. If she was going to be barefoot, he wanted to be unshod as well. He took his shoes off and placed them carefully next to the chair, where they would not be in the way. He noticed the leak pans situated here and there. They'd been empty cans before, but now they were ceramic artifacts Martha had found in thrift stores around town, making it seem as if the leaks were all part of a decorating plan. There was something luxurious about lolling in the heart of someone else's decorating plan.

"Where were we?" Sval accepted his pie and his beer and dug into both with satisfaction. "The Sinister Twelve, you were saying?"

"*You* were saying. You're the writer. I was just calling them the spider at the center of the web."

"Well, whatever you call 'em. That's what we got to, right? There's a cabal of some sort, buying and selling to itself. But it has no official existence, this was our difficulty, right? Because what's our story in this case? Legally, this is just a bunch of separate individuals buying and selling property to people they know. Depreciation is in there somewhere, but who wants to read about depreciation? That's not a story. Even if they're out and out swapping houses, what's the crime? And yet they're hiding something, Martha. They are hiding something."

"You're damn right they're hiding something. I keep trying to tell you."

"I hear you loud and clear. I'm on tenterhooks. What've you got? Tell me."

"I can't *tell* you, I have to show you. It's in my bedroom. Come."

Her bed was neatly covered with a lavender quilt. All her possessions were in place, her clothes were out of sight. Here in her bedroom, there were no leaks. On one wall of the room was tacked an enormous map of Portland, some four feet high and at least six feet wide. It was covered with colored pins, some red, some blue.

"The pins?" he said. The air felt redolent, as if electricity was coursing through it invisibly.

"Yes. Each pin is for something they've bought. Blue pins for what they've sold, red for what they're holding, still, right now." Standing next to him, she was a glowing presence in the light of this small, warm, yellow room. All curves and cunning was this woman Martha Williams.

"This is what the cabal owns?"

"This is everything they've bought. Some of these properties they've already sold. Look at which ones."

He gazed at the map and the light dawned. "I see it."

"You do, right?"

"It's obvious, once you put it all on the same map. Whoever they are, they buy in clusters, these people." They were both leaning forward, intent on the map. He barely registered her body pressing lightly against his. That was just part of the complicated flavor of this moment, when the story was finally coming into view. When he saw that indeed they had something real. "This is just north of Corbett-Terwilliger ..." he murmured, his fingers hovering over a forest of blue pins.

"Right where you come off the Ross Island Bridge," she noted.

"This all used to be houses," he said.

"Now it's where all those big office buildings are going up."

Sval felt the moment sucking him in. Progress was pleasure, but this was better than mere progress: this was breaking into the light and not alone: with a partner. "They used to call this area here Goose Hollow. In the sixties, this is where you could get cheap rent. The houses were full of rats, but the rent was cheap. I think the Ark started in here somewhere."

"Right here." She brought the point of her pencil to rest on the intersection of Columbia and Third Street. "On Walter and Grace's kitchen table. This is where they lived." She peered over his shoulder, her breasts pressing against his back.

"They buy up whole blocks in run-down neighborhoods," he said, "and sell them to developers."

"Is that what you're seeing? I think it's more than that. I think they run neighborhoods down on purpose so they can buy them up cheap. I've seen it up close. I've been part of it. They buy the cheapest house on a block, rent it out cheap, and refuse to make any repairs. The house falls apart, and it makes the whole block look a little shabbier, and the house next door loses value, and they buy up that one, and rent it out cheap, and do it again. If anyone knew that there was a single buyer after the whole block, they wouldn't get away with it. Never. Prices would go up. The last holdout would be holding—what's that hand called? In poker? The one you can't beat?"

"A royal flush."

"That's it. That's why they buy the houses under a lot of different names. Maybe it's not illegal, but it's still a story, isn't it?"

Sval was nodding. "They couldn't pull it off if everyone knew what they were doing. Wherever there's a secret, there's a story. What they're doing isn't a crime but you're right: it is a story: clever legal business practices and the people it hurts. We dramatize it by putting you at the center. A real human being living without heat, living in the rain, just so these guys can make a buck."

"No. Not me. There's a better angle, Sval. Look at the map. Look at my block and the ones next to it. That's what they're after right now. Something is coming to these blocks, and they know it's coming. They're trying to get two whole blocks so they can sell it for millions when the time comes. And look what they've already got."

"All of your block, pretty much. All of the next one too."

"Pretty much, but not all. Look what they don't have, Sval."

"There are still a few." Sval scrutinized the map. "The house right next to yours."

"Mrs. Harney," said Martha.

"Holey moley, what if she's the last holdout? She'd have them by the balls, and she doesn't even know it. There it is! That's the story! An elderly black woman, living on fixed funds, clinging to her house in a block some secret group has targeted for development, too poor to move but too poor to hang on. In the end, she'd have to sell her house and by that time, thanks to the Sinister Twelve, the house would be worthless. Except—at the last moment—she reads the story in the Ark and realizes she could just refuse to sell. They'd have to give her whatever she's asking. That's the sequel! Man, this is going to be good!"

"You put Mrs. Harney on page three," said Martha. "You make that story super human-interest You make people cry, you make people angry. Then—"

"I know. Then—jump to page seven for the story behind the story. The Sinister Twelve: how they operate, what they've done, what they're doing right now—"

"No, not page seven. Page Five," Martha argued. "That's where we usually put hard facts and big picture stuff. Page five, show Mrs. Harney's house on a map—"

"With a sidebar explaining why it is so critical to their scheme. And then—ooh. Ooh. I've got it. We finish with a half page box—thick border. Make it jump out at readers. That's where we tell the readers about her being the last holdout. About how she has them by the balls. We'll explain the whole thing. How they need the whole block or they've got nothing. How, if she won't sell to them, they'll have *nothing*."

"She has them." Martha's eyes gleamed. "Like you said. *That's* our story."

In one twinkle, many months of dogged digging morphed into a memory of many months of making steady progress. Brainstorming together, taking off on separate scents, coming together to share notes, making progress that led at last to this aurora borealis of a moment.

"We did it, Sval."

He felt a flush of gratitude and warmth. "We make a helluva team, woman." He put out his arms, inviting a chaste hug of celebration. She came to him and it was companionable, their arms around each other, letting their bodies get to know each other like this, the curves and cushions and hard spots and soft spots. At first, they were jostling against each other in a pool of one emotion: pride in what they'd done. But gradually, there were other emotions and sensations sloshing around in the mix. Affection was in there with the pride. And in there with pride and affection was desire… He wondered how he had managed never to notice the intelligence in this capacious woman's umber eyes.

"I told you there was a story." They relinquished the hug just before it could move them across a risky threshold where decisions would have to be made and words would have to be spoken.

"We make a helluva' team," Sval repeated. "You and me." And then he couldn't hold back, he rested his head on her shoulder, just for a moment, merely to bask in the satisfaction of this moment: just to make a tasty moment last. The basking was indistinguishable from arousal. "You and me." He could smell her perfume. It struck him that Zoe was in North Carolina, visiting friends. And anyway, it didn't matter, did it, where Zoe was right now. They had an open relationship? He didn't need Zoe's permission, only Martha's.

It was she, however, who stepped across the border first. "You're tired and hungry." She put her arms around him and pulled him close. "You want some of my cherry pie?"

"Yes," he said. "Can I stay here tonight."

"It gets cold," she warned him.

"We could keep each other warm."

The arms around him neither tightened nor loosened. They were both waiting for the tension to drain away so that this would feel normal. Already he could feel the easy comfort of normalcy. The striking part was how achievable it felt, here in Martha's flat. This ease felt like the default condition of life. Somehow, the impossible seemed, not just plausible but possible. Not just possible but desirable. And not just desirable but intoxicating. Irresistible.

"Sval," she said. "Um."

"Hmm?"

"What are we doing?"

"You tell me. You're the one with your arms around me."

"You're the one with your head on my shoulders."

"I like what we're doing. Whatever this is."

"Me too. What is this? What are we doing?"

"We're feeling our way forward," he said, "into our relationship."

A silent moment added punctuation to the flow of time. "Go on," she said. "Keep feeling your way forward. I want you to."

"Here?" he said.

"There," she said. "Uh huh. Right there. Yes."

Smith Rocks

The Coordinating Committee for the Coming of The One, which consisted chiefly of Cosmotherapists, regarded Raoul as a pest. He came to their office full of enthusiasm but never did any work. And there was plenty of work to be done. No one on the Coordinating Committee knew exactly when or where The One would appear, which made advance work ten-fold more difficult. The Cosmotherapists labored around the clock generating leaflets and cranking the rumor mill to accumulate a vast mailing list. Their labors were rewarded. When details of time and place did at last come in, they were able to put 10,000 announcements in the mail overnight.

Zoe received one of those postcards. She was in North Carolina when it arrived, but she saw it first thing when she got home, and it made her gulp.

The Coming of the One
Smith Rocks
April 13, 2 PM
Be there.

"Shit," she exclaimed. "That's today."

She called Sval and told him about the postcard, then read it to him over the phone. "It's that thing Raoul's been talking about. He's going, Sval. I bet you anything he's going!"

"Quite probably. Bubba Sadhu's been promoting it around the community. He's been pressing the Ark to give it more publicity. I find the whole thing distasteful. What's it got to do with you or me?"

"I might go. I was thinking we should both go."

"To a convention of quasi-religious sci-fi kooks? I think not."

"I'm worried that Raoul might be there now."

"I wouldn't be surprised." Sval's voice was perfectly neutral. "To each his own. Zoe, listen. I have something important I need to discuss with you. Let's get brunch today, shall we? Original Pancake House, I was thinking. It's about Martha."

"Let's do that tomorrow, Sval. I have to go to Smith Rocks today. Raoul might be getting into trouble there."

A silence ensued. "Let me see if I understand." Sval paused as if giving cadence to a speech. "I'm saying we have something to discuss, it's important to me. You're saying you have a commitment to Raoul, you're going to Smith Rocks to be with him today."

"Not *with* him. He might have left already, Sval. I have a bad feeling about this Coming-of-the-One thing. Raoul is so susceptible. I'm worried he's about to join a cult."

"Raoul's needs come first. I see. Okay then, go, I guess. My issue can wait."

"Come with me! Raoul is *your* friend too. You don't care if he gets sucked into some stupid cult?"

"Him and me, we've talked about this One-business. I do consider it a cult, but we don't see eye to eye. It's not my place to talk him out of his beliefs. He's a grown man, he's made a choice. Now, you have a choice to make. Come to the Pancake House with me? Or go to Smith Rocks with Raoul."

"For God's sake, Sval."

"For God's sake yourself, Zoe. Every time you face a choice like this, what you choose has a meaning. But then ... maybe...." He subsided into melancholy. "Maybe we're drifting apart, you and me. Are we?"

"Oh stop it! Drifting apart. Over pancakes? Please!"

"This isn't about pancakes, Zo. Not really."

"You just woke up, Sval, you're grumpy. Have some coffee, maybe you'll change your mind. If you do, I'll see you at Smith Rocks. Otherwise, I'll see you tomorrow. We can talk then. I promise I'll give your issues all my attention then."

She hung up. Sval waited several minutes, then went to his porch, half expecting to see Zoe driving up. But the street remained empty. The neighbor's Dalmatian was out of control. As always. Clouds were scudding across the sky, and a hard breeze rocked the trees. High in the air, birds were being tossed and swirled by the wind.

Sval stared at the figs that had fallen off the tree in the back yard. He could gather up a basketful for Martha. She'd stripped the tree outside her window, she might appreciate some fresh figs.

Then he decided, no. He had an obligation to go to Smith Rocks and see what this "Coming of The One" was all about. His going had nothing to do with Zoe or Raoul. Someone needed to cover this event for the Ark. If it was bullshit, as was more than likely, the Community needed to know

Unfortunately, Sval's car wouldn't start. He had to call around for a ride. Unfortunately, most who might be going had already gone. The only ride he could get at this point was with Bubba Sadhu. And Bubba agreed to give him a ride on one condition only: Sval must promise not to write anything about the Coming of the One. This was Bubba's story. He'd be covering this one for the Ark.

"Okay," said Sval, "if it's so important to you, Bubba. I promise. Not one word." He got into Bubba's car. He was going to Smith Rocks. Not because Raoul had gone. Not because Zoe would be there. He was going for another reason. He'd think of the reason when he got there.

Raoul didn't drive to the Rocks, he hitched a ride. He figured if the One was coming, he wouldn't need a car to get back. He'd be on the mothership, headed to Arcturus. It was noon exactly when Smith Rocks came into view. From a distance, the spires barely broke the plane of the desert. They were hundreds of feet tall but rising from the floor of a canyon hundreds of feet deep. From close up, from the rim of the parking lot, the rocks looked like other-worldly orange cathedrals.

Raoul started down the path to the canyon floor. In his pocket, he had a half-tab of killer acid. He'd taken the first half of this very tab five years ago, just before his draft physical. He'd been saving the second half for a day he knew would come.

A crowd had accumulated in the canyon. It strung along both sides of the river, which looped around the clusters of enormous orange rocks that stretched in both directions. The One was nowhere to be seen, but the air felt electric, so charged was it with hidden forces. Raoul felt thirsty and just when he noticed this, a man appeared beside him with a chilled canteen. A sign from the Universe?

The canteen held iced tea but it was laced with some sort of hard liquor, so Raoul took only two swallows. Then it was time to drop the acid. Or was it? Yes, if he was going to do it today, now was the time. *Or was it?*

He took the little pillbox out of his pocket, opened it, and studied the half-tab of LSD nestled there, on a scrap of purple velvet: five years ago, the first half of this tablet had ripped a hole in reality and the Void had sucked him through the hole. He'd always known there was only one way back. Someday, he'd have to buckle up his courage and take the other half.

Was today that "someday"? Raoul needed a sign. He strained to listen to the Universe. He thought he heard it whispering. What was it whispering?

Not today.

Not today. You have to listen to those voices. Raoul shut the box and put it back in his pocket. It was then that he saw the Sunlight Man. There could be no other name for what he was seeing. The Sunlight Man was standing on a rock at the northern end of the canyon in a suit so golden, so bright, it must be made of sunlight. Words were crackling out of him through a cone.

PEOPLE OF EARTH!

GREETINGS FROM THE GREAT SCIENTIFIC
CIVILIZATION OF ARCTURUS!
THE PROTECTOR OF THE GALAXY HAS CHOSEN
ONE AMONG YOU TO DELIVER A MESSAGE.
MEN AND WOMEN OF EARTH, I AM THIS ONE!

Smith Rocks Canyon was an illusion, of course. This was all in Raoul's mind, a beautiful stage-set he himself was creating. With the power of his awesome imagination, he was holding this world together and what a beautiful world it was, what a testament to his prowess. But like the aliens that visited his dreams, there was one figure in this scene that had come from outside. The Sunlight Man was not a creation of Raoul's mind. The Sunlight Man was real. He was The One.

AND I SAY TO YOU, MEN AND WOMEN OF
EARTH!
WITHIN THIS YEAR, A MOTHER SHIP WILL
COME.

Raoul glanced around and saw that in addition to creating a canyon and a river and these wonderful rocks, he had to keep the people looking like people. Because some of them weren't really people, was the thing, they were bat-like creatures from a galaxy incalculably far away. You could tell from their wings, which shimmered into view from time to time, then winked out, leaving the illusion of a crowd of people intact.

He was creating this illusion of a world with such tremendous mental strength, it was acquiring a life of its own. When he let go, the illusion remained intact. The man with the megaphone jumped off the rock and went running up into the narrowing canyon. It wasn't what Raoul would have had him do, but the illusion was running on automatic now. A surge of people followed The One. Raoul thought they should slow down, but he couldn't slow them down. The surge of the crowd was happening on its own. That's when it hit him. This was no illusion after all: this was *all* real. He wasn't inventing this crowd. This crowd was inventing him. It was a human river flowing, he was just a drop of that river. Where it went, he went. What it was, he was.

The One stopped atop another rock and the crowd stopped too. *That's* when Raoul realized he was not a drop of the river after all, because he did not stop. He had a will of his own. The crowd stopped but he kept going, picking his way on into the canyon, picking his way up among the boulders, clambering up and up. No one noticed him because they were all so focused on the Sunlight Man, who was moving back continuously now, receding faster than the crowd could follow. But Raoul was moving back faster than the One, staying behind him and above him. Why? Because he could. That's all. Just because he could.

> …WHERE SCIENCE HAS WIPED OUT DISEASE
> … SOLVED THE AGE OLD PROBLEM OF SEX…

The One didn't see Raoul observing him. The One was focused entirely on the people in front of him. In that windy open space his words were reaching them as disconnected fragments now, mingled with static.

> … FREE CONCERTS …THERE … FREE …
> SCIENCE OF BREATH . . . SECRET EACHINGS …
> RECORD NUMBERS. . .

The canyon was so narrow at this end, the crowd was strung out almost single file. The Sunlight Man had stopped moving. The crowd was catching up to him. Soon they'd surround him.

> ABANDON … EARTHLY POSSESSIONS …
> MOTHER SHIP … COMING … MONEY IS A ROCK
> IN YOUR POCKET . . . DROWN WHEN THE
> WATERS RISE. … YOUR BANK ACCOUNTS …
> ABANDON POSSESSIONS … PURE HEART . . .
> THE MOTHER SHIP …

The man stepped back between two tall rocks. For just a moment no one in the crowd could see him. Raoul, however, was behind him and above him. Raoul saw what happened in that moment. The One yanked his shining suit off like a sheet of spray-painted plastic wrap. It *was* a sheet of spray-painted plastic! In one blink of an eye, he balled it up and stuffed it into a backpack that someone had already placed behind the rock and almost in the same motion hoisted the backpack onto his shoulder and the Sunlight Man was gone. In his place stood an ordinary bumbling fellow in khaki pants and an army surplus jacket, just another bit of the crowd lapping around the corner, lapping from every direction. Nothing set this man apart from anyone else in the crowd. They were all trying to catch up to the Sunlight Man. The crowd didn't know the man they were following was in their midst, was just another one of them now, just as baffled as any of them, peering and craning like everyone else to see where that man in the suit made of sunlight might have gone.

The crowd stopped flowing, started milling, searching among the boulders for The One, but in vain. Surrounded by hundreds of eye witnesses, The One had simply vanished. The crowd had witnessed a miracle.

Raoul's head felt full of broken glass. He'd witnessed something too, but not a miracle: a magic trick. A brilliant one, but in the end, still, a trick. And once you know how a trick is done, it's not magic anymore.

Something strange *was* happening though. Was he losing weight? Was the ground dissolving? A chilly wind had started to blow. He was tripping. On acid. How could that be? He'd not taken that leftover half-tab of Orange Sunburst. It was still in his pocket. How could he be tripping? Yet the signs were unmistakable. He was not *in* the world. The world was *in* him. The sky was not a sky but a painting of a sky on the inner surface of an egg.

And he was that egg.

Koo koo ka choo. I am the eggman.

A spiderweb of hairline cracks were forming along the whole inner surface of the egg. He noticed this. *Something was outside, trying to get in.*

The eggshell crumbled and Raoul's whole life so far proved to have been a dream. From that dream he was waking now, not up but down, waking down into a deeper realm of dreaming. Waking down into a world where bat-creatures swooped and sliced every which way in the eternal twilight of a bottomless abyss.

"Are you flying?" one of them said.

That question popped the last illusion—that he could fly. Stripped of illusion he began to drop down between two endless parallel walls of stone.

"I can't fly!" he shrieked at those bat creatures. "I'm not one of you! I don't belong here. I'm not one of you!"

Something broke his fall. One of the bat-creatures had caught him. He looked into that leathery bat-face and saw human eyes. He knew who it was, looking back at him through those eye-shaped windows: it was Marica. The jolt brought him smack dab to the here and now. Instantly he knew what had just happened. He'd stumbled over rocks, and tumbled among boulders, hit a path in motion and went careening toward another edge but she stepped into his way, and he crashed into her. But instead of getting knocking over, she brought him to a dead halt. She was holding onto him. She was saying, "Don't be silly, Raoul, of course you're one of us. We *cherish* you! Ever since you came to the Ark that day with those pictures…"

"I'm human," he realized. "You and me, we're not bat-creatures! We're both humans!" The wonderful discovery bloomed inside him like a sunflower. He felt like a fresh loaf of bread coming out of an oven.

Marica wasn't sure she was going to go to Smith Rocks until she saw the note from Raoul pinned to her door. "Today's the day." She knew what day, of course. She was there when Raoul found out about the Coming of the One. He'd talked about it a few times while they were working on her performance piece. The things he said sometimes had made her uneasy. *I might want to join this man's cult.* She called Raoul to check if he was going but was told he'd already gone. That's when she decided.

She drove through heavy mist up the west slope of Mt. Hood. The traffic seemed heavier than normal. She started down into eastern Oregon where wet, blue forests gave way to stands of pine trees dotting dry yellow fields. The air was pleasantly warm and dry. But the traffic still seemed unusually heavy.

Marica turned off Highway 26, into the small town of Terrebonne. A lot of the traffic behind her was turning too. She found the little country road that led to Smith Rocks State Park. Scores of cars ahead of her had turned at the same place.

A single Terrebonne policeman and one park ranger were halting cars up ahead. The parking lot was full, they said. People should park where they could along the road, and walk the rest of the way. Marica slipped a jacket over her sweat shirt and started marching.

On the path down into the canyon, a man came weaving up to Marica and offered her a canteen. "Tea?" he said.

She took a polite sip. It was iced tea laced with whiskey, and it hit the back of her throat pleasantly, but she handed it back after two sips. She didn't want to encourage the man and have to spend the rest of the afternoon fending off his advances.

Along the river, people were milling about, waiting for something to happen, but nothing much was happening. A few started to drift downstream and Marica drifted with them. Then the crowd changed its mind and started drifting upstream, and Marica let the crowd set her course too. Then she began to realize that the tea she'd drunk earlier had been laced with more than whiskey. Her eyes were pulling the world out of shape, and the streaks on the rock were drooling. She was high on acid. The crush of bodies made her uneasy. She climbed out of the crowd, she climbed up from the crowd, away from men's greedy groping fingers.

She got onto a narrow path that followed the contour of the hillside, high above the river, along the western slope. Down on the canyon floor, the crowd would have obstructed her view. From up here, she could see that a man was standing on a rock upstream. That was why people were moving upstream now. He was wearing some sort of gold-colored outfit that gleamed in the sunlight. Standing on that big rock, he looked like a statue of a Greek god. He was preaching through a megaphone. Marica was too far away to hear what he was saying, but she saw him jump down from one rock, move up the canyon, and hop onto another rock and from there he preached some more. Then he hopped off that rock and moved on, and the crowd followed him, into the ever narrowing canyon.

Suddenly he disappeared. Maybe she'd looked away for a moment. Marica rubbed her eyes and looked again. There was nowhere he could have gone, but he was gone. It wasn't the acid playing tricks on her. The whole crowd was confused. The whole crowd was looking around for him, looking between rocks, peering around trees. With no one to follow, the crowd didn't know what to do, which way to go. A broad murmur came rising out of the crowd's collective bafflement. And now, as it spread out to search for the man who had disappeared, the crowd was dispersing back down the length of the canyon.

Marica heard a strangled cry. She saw Raoul climbing down toward her from among the craggy boulders that formed the slope of the canyon wall, picking his way carefully because the slope was steep and he was still quite a fair distance above the path, high enough to hurt himself if he fell. Maybe badly.

"Raoul," she called out.

He kept clambering down, his gaze fixed on her face. And now she saw that he was looking frightened. It struck her that he too might be tripping. The man with the flask had been offering sips to everyone he met. Poor Raoul. The last thing this boy needed was acid.

"How are you doing?" she asked without inflection. She didn't want to freak him out. She knew what one was supposed to do for a man in his condition. She had to treat him like she didn't suspect he was freaking out, help him feel everything was normal, there was nothing to worry about. The trouble was, she detected in herself a mist of grey anxiety. She must not let him see the fear rising within her own self. She had to present him with a smile, a warm smile.

"The One," he announced, "doesn't exist. He's a fraud."

She couldn't process what he said. She was too busy watching him negotiate his way down that rocky slope. He couldn't climb down safely if he was in the astral plane. She had to be ready to catch him if he fell. She wanted to tell him he wasn't alone. She wanted him to know she was tripping too but doing fine with it, doing fine, he'd be fine too, this was just normal fun, they were having fun. "I'm flying," she said as gleefully as she could. "Are you flying?"

He looked down at his feet. "Yikes!" he yelped. "I can't fly!" His shoes slipped out from under him and he pitched forward. Fell forward. "I can't fly!" He was sliding feet first toward the path. He hit the path and pitched further forward, toward the edge. He would have gone staggering and stumbling over that second edge and rolled a long way down the steep hillside, maybe to his death, except that Marica shifted left, blocked his way, let him crash into her, held position, wrapping her arms around his body, securing them both in place. Like a rock they stood planted, locked together, face to face, so gravitationally correct, nothing could have knocked him over. It was then that he whispered, "I'm not one of you. I don't belong here. I'm not one of you."

The words chilled Marica. The ground beneath her seemed to open like a trapdoor. She didn't have to look down to know the emptiness that stretched forever downward from her feet. She knew then what Raoul felt, not just now but all the time. "Of course, you're one of us," she growled. "You belong here, Raoul. We cherish you. Ever since that day you brought your pictures to the Ark…"

She wasn't sure how many of those words actually got out, but she was thinking them. And holding onto him the whole time with her eyes, holding him to the here and now. She was saving him, but she'd been trembling on the edge of trouble for a moment there herself: he was saving her. They held each other to the here and now with their eyes until the moment passed and it was safe to let go.

"You ran into him too." Marica breathed. "Oh that asshole! Woo! I got a little *too* tripped out. I'm still tripping a little! Woo! That man with the flask?"

"Iced tea," Raoul choked out. "Lucky I didn't take the tab."

"I didn't see any tabs, just the tea. Are you coming down? Don't you dare say you don't belong here. We adore you, Raoul. Oh, look at me, mother hen—cluck cluck. I should add that to WOMANLIFE huh. Mother Hen. What do you mean, you're not one of us!"

His eyes had looked like pinwheels but not anymore. He was safe now, he'd be okay. Marica waited to feel embarrassed, but the feeling didn't come. People should help each other if they could: there was nothing to feel embarrassed about here. He rubbed his face. "I'm human!" he exulted. "You and me, we're not bat-creatures! We're humans!"

Marica smiled at the joy Raoul was getting from this revelation. They weren't bat-creatures. They were humans. Well, yes. Must be good to know if it wasn't obvious already.

It's the World

Hours later, or perhaps only minutes, Raoul found Sval. Both had hitched to Smith Rocks and both now needed a ride home. Marica had a car, but she'd gotten separated from Raoul in the course of the long afternoon. Sval and Raoul set to work looking for her. But the canyon was big and she might have left already. Then Zoe came ambling upstream. She'd gone to the wrong end of the canyon and missed the "miracle".

"You guys!" she called out. "You need a ride?"

They did. In the car, however, the conversation was a little stilted. The three-way relationship and its complications did not come up. They talked instead about the Coming of the One. Raoul told the others what he'd seen. Zoe was not surprised. "It's like something Houdini did one time. I read about it when I was studying magic."

Sval fulminated about Bubba Sadhu. "He asked me not to write about what happened here today."

"And you said yes?" Zoe gave him a skeptical look.

"I had to. He was giving me a ride. Why don't you write something, Zoe? We could run your piece next to Bubba Sadhu's. Two views of the same event and let the readers be the judge."

Zoe gave a half-hearted shrug and changed the subject. She wanted to stop for dinner on the way back, at Forest Inn, a famous gourmet restaurant about 40 miles from Portland. It was not cheap, but Zoe wanted this and implied that she had the money to cover it. So they stopped.

Over dinner, Raoul fleshed out his account of the One's disappearance, and Zoe elaborated on the Houdini trick it resembled. Something about a horse onstage and outfits made of paper. Sval thought she could build her story for the Ark around the Houdini anecdote. Nobody brought up their three-way relationship.

"Even if The One is fake, though, something did happen today," Raoul said. "Just for a moment the sky was cracking and I saw *something*. And don't tell me I'm crazy, you guys. I'm not just paranoid. There is *something* out there, and it's trying to get in."

"No one's calling you crazy," Sval assured his friend. "You might be the sanest of us all. At this moment, however, if I'm not mistaken, you are somewhat under the influence of hallucinogens. And even if you weren't, in my opinion, crazy is not a useful term—"

Zoe had heard Sval's theory of crazy. More than once. This, she decided, would be a good time to visit the restroom. When she came back, she stopped in the darkness just beyond the doorway to the dining room. She watched the two men, illuminated by their candle, leaning toward each other across the table, a study in intensity framed against the darkness, like some dramatic moment from religious history caught by Tintoretto.

"On my first trip," Raoul was saying, "I realized everything is in my head. That's big, Sval. I mean, science'll back me up. The only thing we ever see are the nerves of our own eyeballs tingling. The only thing we ever hear is the nerves in our own ears vibrating. When we dream it's just our own brain cells going ape. This is not my head." He clutched between his hands what anyone else would have called his head. He flung his arms out in a gesture that encompassed the entire room, perhaps the entire universe. "THIS," he declared, "is my head."

How long had it been, Zoe wondered, since she had seen the two of them together this way? And the minute she returned to the table the dynamics would change again. One day, it was her and Raoul together, Sval was the outsider. Another day, it was her and Sval closing ranks against Raoul. Triads always broke into two against one; but why did it always have to be her and one of the men against the other man? What this triad needed was balance, that elusive thing that Marica was always going on about. An inspiration came to Zoe. She signaled to the waiter.

"But what I saw today was even bigger," Raoul was saying. "The thing is, Sval, for five years now I've been saying, this is my head and nothing's outside it. Nothing's out there. What is out there? Nothingness itself. That's what I've been saying. But I was wrong. Today I saw *somethingness*. Just for a flash, but I could sense it. There is something outside my head—"

"Raoul." Sval reached out and stopped Raoul from saying more. "Of *course* there's something outside your head. Don't you know what it is?"

"Well, I've been thinking about it. I know it's big, I know that much—"

"Yes. Big. Ineffable. Ubiquitous … infinite—it's out there. But what is it?"

"You act like you know. Tell me."

"It's the world."

Raoul sat back. "Whew!" he whistled. "You're saying the world might *actually* exist? Whether or not I'm here to see it?"

"I'd wager cash on it." Sval pursed his lips thoughtfully. "Of course, maybe we're not so different, you and I. You say you've been looking out and seeing nothing but the inside of your head. I can tell you, I've been looking out and seeing nothing but the inside of this bubble we're all living in. This microcosm, this community. What you're calling 'your head'—this community might be my version of it."

"Most everyone lives in a head," Raoul stated. "They think they see the sky when they look up, but really they're just looking at a ceiling."

"Point taken," said Sval. "but when your bubble is an ideology, it's not so obvious. I mean, consider a person like me. I have all kinds of references to an outside world in my kit. I say words like Angola and Mozambique like they really exist. I say Mobil Oil and Senator Frank Church like I've seen them with my own eyes. How can a person know he's not just juggling bits and pieces of his interior world? The same *words* might exist in someone else's 'head', but *mean* entirely different things. Still, it's not an inescapable phenomenon, is it? After all, Raoul, today you saw cracks in the sky. You saw an outside world. And my 'sky'? That's been cracking lately too. I too have been catching glimpses of true sky."

"Or," said Raoul, "the ceiling of the next bubble."

"Ah, you rascally rhetorician. Yes, perhaps just the ceiling of the next bubble."

Raoul grinned. "Rascally rhetorician." The moniker pleased him. He attacked his food with gusto and then just as suddenly abandoned the attack. "Boy," he said. "The world might actually exist! What an idea! That would explain everything, wouldn't it?"

Sval smiled and shook his head. "I suspect it opens up more mysteries than it solves."

"Like what?"

Sval was silent for a moment. "Well," he said finally, "consider what happened today. Zoe went to Smith Rocks. Not to see The One. Not to get on the Mother Ship. She went because she thought *you* might be in trouble, and she wanted to be there in case *you* needed help. If the world exists, then she's not you. If she's not you, then why should she give a damn? In theory, I mean. But she does. In theory and in fact, she came here for you. She came because she wanted to be there for you if you needed help. That right there, that's an illuminating mystery to plumb and ponder. How is it that when the odds are not too great, and nothing awful is at stake, most human beings are capable of at least small decencies?"

"Why did you come to the Rocks?"

"Well, that's the other mystery," Sval admitted. "Human beings are also capable of mean jealousies. I'm the living proof."

"What are you saying? Jealous? Of who, of me? Over Zoe? But you're Sval Hofby!"

"Aye, and what is Sval Hofby?" Without seeming to quote, Sval went on, "No, I am not Lord Hamlet, nor was meant to be. Am an attendant lord, as it turns out. An easy tool, full of high sentence but a bit obtuse. At times almost ridiculous. At times indeed the fool."

"Oh come on. What she feels for me is sorry, mostly. And you know something, no one has to feel sorry for me. You all think I'm this hopeless case, like I can't even pay the rent, but I pay my rent! I make plenty of moolah cleaning those skyscraper windows. You couldn't even do what I do, sit on a shelf a hundred feet up from the street with a squeegee and a pail. To me, it's just work. Yeah, that's right, I'm out there working, like the rest of you. I just don't let it stop me from dreaming. Why should Zoe feel sorry for me? I'm the lucky one. I *can* still dream."

"No, Raoul. You've got her wrong. She doesn't hang out with you out of pity. With you, she has fun. With me—well, we've lost the capacity for fun. I'd rather work, frankly. You're Zoe's type more than I ever was. I only caution you. Don't ever imagine you can possess her. Zoe Madigan has fun in lots of ways but no one can ever possess her."

"Are you in love with Zoe?"

Sval looked discomfited. "In-love is not a term with which I'm comfortable. She's been my best friend and my primary relationship, that's been the assumption, but I'm starting to see that eventually she'll be a perfect stranger to me. I accept that. Not without some sorrow, but I accept it." His attention jerked away from Raoul. "Where is she, anyway? She's been gone a long time."

"She went to the bathroom, I think."

"For half an hour? What's she doing in there?" Sval turned in his chair and searched the dark recesses of the hallway with his gaze.

The waiter noticed him looking and shuffled over with a bill in one hand and a note in the other. "She left this for you, sir."

Sval frowned as he read the note. Then he handed it to Raoul. "Do you have any cash on you?"

The note read:

Dear Men:

You were having such an intense discussion I couldn't bear to interrupt you. Besides, you've been estranged from each other and it's really my fault. The two of you need some time together without me around to complicate matters. You may hate me for a few hours, until you get out of this predicament, but I've always thought sharing an adventure is healthy medicine for any relationship. So I've taken the car and gone back to Portland, leaving the two of you stranded late at night, miles from home.

Love,
Zoe

P.S. I didn't pay the bill. I hope you're carrying enough money between the two of you to take care of it. I'll pay you back, of course, when I see you in Portland. Have a wonderful adventure, boys!

The Story

Zoe sound chipper and well-rested the next day, when she called Sval. "You're back!" she chirped.

"In spite of your best efforts," he responded coldly.

"Oh please, Sval, do have a sense of humor," she laughed. "You had an adventure, didn't you? And you're back. You're both back, safe and sound. I knew you'd figure it out—you're so resourceful. So, what happened? Tell me the story. I can't wait—"

"I see. I'm so resourceful. So actually, this was a vote of confidence. A tribute to me and my resourcefulness. Thank you, Zoe. For the vote of confidence."

"Didn't you read my note? Didn't you understand what I said? You and Raoul needed to have an adventure together, and I thought—"

"I read your note. Here's my note: you owe us nine dollars for your share of dinner at Forest Inn. A dinner you insisted on, incidentally."

"All right. It backfired. I blew it. I thought you were going to have this great story to tell. I thought you'd see it as a funny story you'd be telling for years. I thought you'd have a sense of humor."

"Being dumped penniless miles from home for no apparent reason late at night with a fat bill to pay—pardon me while I die laughing, my dear."

"I *told* you the reason: so that you and Raoul could share—"

"Me and Raoul don't want to be manipulated, Zoe. We both—"

"Aha—see? You *both*! Why shouldn't there be a you-both? Why shouldn't you and Raoul be the Couple for once, you and him against me? I was just trying to balance the triangle."

"There was no excuse for it."

"I did it for the relationship," she protested,

"What relationship?" He thrust the words at her like a rapier. "This, what we've got? You call this a 'relationship'?"

"Is it over?" she cut in bluntly, suddenly. "Is it over between us? Is that what you're saying?"

He caught his breath. "Is that what I said? Come on! Did I say those words?"

"No," she said, "but if it is, we should say those words. And if it isn't, we should say *those* words. Whatever it is, we should say it. Are we done with each other?"

He wanted to say yes. Last night's abandonment had filled him with too much unreasoning rage and pain. Long after he was safe in bed, it had festered and battened, sucking up meaning from all the other times she had left him dangling. Right now, he didn't want to be in the same room with her.

"Well?" she said. "Is that what you're saying? We're finished?"

And yet he couldn't bring himself to say yes. He bit his lips. He could never possess her, but for that very reason he could never willingly let her go. He turned the question around. "What do you think?"

A brief moment of hesitation and then she said, "Yes. I think we might be."

And that was that. The "yes" hung in the silence for a few long seconds. Sval let it. A dim ringing in his ears sounded like some distant conversation between strangers. An almost two-year relationship terminated in one second with one word. It felt unreal. Then a tumult of awakened memories caught him like a wave. He knew what he couldn't do. He couldn't withdraw his question, placate, apologize, or plunge into another round of criticism/self-criticism followed by cathartic mutual forgiveness and sex.

"Okay," he said. "In that case, we understand each other."

"We do?" she said. "That's all you have to say?"

They stayed on the phone, listening to each other breathe. "I'm all talked out," he said. "Let's get on with what we were doing."

"What were we doing? I thought there would be more to say, Sval. After all this time? Get on with what we were doing? What were we doing?"

He forced himself to adopt a brisk tone. "Well, you said you'd write something about the fiasco at Smith Rocks for the paper. If you don't, Bubba Saddhu will have the story all to himself. His version would be THE version. I really need someone to write an alternative narrative. You're the one who could do it, the only one I trust." Sval managed to speak as if they had done nothing more than settle a pesky debt just now. He managed that much.

"You can do that?" said Zoe. "Just set it aside like that? Everything we've been to each other?"

"What have we been to each other?"

"Whatever we've been. We never needed a term for it. That's what we always said. Two different people and yet we're a single *something* together. Why can't we be both? Together and apart. A relationship like that has to exist in the world. We've come so close, Sval. Can you just abandon the quest?"

"I can if you can. The soap opera is over, you say? Fair enough. I see what you mean. This is a way of agreeing. It's nice to agree with each other about something. We haven't done that in a while. This is a positive step forward for our friendship. Which endures, right? Now we're free to focus on the story. The story is what matters right now."

"All right." She accepted the new terms with maddening ease. "I'll call Raoul and get to work on this. We'll do it for you, Sval. Raoul and me."

No one tried to hide Zoe's article from Bubba, but circumstances conspired to keep him ignorant. The copy meeting at which it should have been discussed got swamped by Martha's grim report. The paper was losing money steadily and would very soon be broke. Someone proposed that the wages paid to the production people be reduced. It raised a storm. Sval brought up the idea of doing two benefits a year to pay the production people, but also organizing a committee to re-think how money was distributed among those getting money from the paper.

On Wednesday, as Zoe's piece was creeping through the approval system, one of the Cosmotherapists read it. Sval had laid out Bubba Sadhu's report and Zoe's side-by-side in parallel columns, under a single head for the page as a whole: *Yes We Have No Nirvanas.*

That Friday, when the paper came out, Bubba Sadhu stormed angrily into the Ark to confront Sval. What happened to the promise he'd made on the way to Smith Rocks? That he wouldn't write about the event? Sval met Sadhu's histrionics with cool indifference. Yes, he remembered his promise, and he'd honored it. The piece Bubba found so offensive was not his but Zoe's. The information in it came from Raoul, not Sval. Yes, Sval had encouraged Zoe to write about her experience that day, but he himself had expressed no opinions, not even in a letter to the editor.

Besides, Sval pointed out, no one was trying to censor Bubba's version of the events. His story was right there too, typeset and laid out on page three under the headline, "WHO IS THE ONE?" By what right then was Bubba trying to censor a competing version of the same events running alongside his article under the headline, "WHO NEEDS THE ONE?"

Sadhu glowered but kept his silence. He had nothing to complain about. Everything Sval said was true. He nonetheless tried to bring up his grievances the following Monday, but without success. At that meeting financial wrangling swamped all other discussion. And the same thing happened at the next meeting: squabbles about the money crisis crowded out trivial complaints about what the Ark had published many weeks ago.

And then another drama upstaged the Cosmotherapists and their complaints. Sval launched his real-estate series. What had begun with the leak in Martha's roof was now centered on Mrs. Harney. The Ark agreed to run the profile of Mrs. Harney on page 3, and then provide a jump to page 5, where they could read a full-on essay about the Sinister Twelve.

The piece itself was not the drama. The Ark hit the stands on Friday; lots of people read it over the next few days. Sval got some complimentary letters but nothing out of the ordinary. The drama broke a full week later when a phone call interrupted Monday Meeting. Sally Feinberg, who answered the phone, informed Sval that some businessman wanted to talk to him. It sounded important, she said. Sval urged the meeting to go on without him and took the call in the next room.

The meeting was breaking up by the time he got back, but when he said "That was Tom Leonard," everybody settled right back into their seats. They all knew who Tom Leonard was: Whitaker's friend, the man who owned Your Mama deli down in Gold Town: what did *he* want? This the collective wanted to hear.

Sval frowned the whole time he was telling his comrades about the phone call. Tom Leonard had seen his article about Mrs. Harney and the Sinister Twelve. He wanted to meet with Sval.

"About what?" several people asked simultaneously.

"I don't know," Sval admitted. "He spent most of the phone call..." He paused then, blushing slightly. "Going on and on about how great my piece was. Don't worry. I wasn't taken in. He wants something. He implied that he might have a story for me."

"Yeah? He probably wants us to run that kiss-ass profile of him that Whitaker was going to publish. I say no."

"Agreed," Sval assured the collective. "If that's what he wants, I too say no. We're not resurrecting the profile—so say we all. But he didn't bring up the profile. He implied that he had something else for us. Should I meet with him? I leave it to the group. I want to do it, but you guys decide. No promises involved, just meet with him and find out what he wants. What do you think?"

The group had no objection to that proposal. Meet with the guy and see what he wants. No harm in that. George might have protested on principle, but George wasn't at the meeting.

Sval put on his jogging shoes and stuffed his boots, books, and papers into a knapsack. His obsession with jogging had been burgeoning lately. He liked to insist that no significant part of Portland was more than 45 minutes away by jog, and that no one needed to get anywhere in less than 45 minutes, a dictum he had repeated so often so publicly that now in conscience he could never use a car except in the most dire weather. And today the weather was not dire, only misty.

He smoked a joint to fortify himself for the meeting, put the roach in his pocket, and took off. Soon the exercise was pumping cannabis into his every cell, and he felt alive with sensation. Crossing Belmont, he saw two teenage boys, glowing with young lust, questioning an attractive young female passerby "No," Sval heard her say, as he came slap-slapping toward the group.

"Well, good-bye then," one boy bubbled to the girl and followed her up the sidewalk, reluctant to let the connection break.

The other boy stepped into Sval's path and stretched out an arm. "Dude!" he pleaded. "Spare a joint?"

Sval kept running. A joint! He'd assumed they were looking for an older guy to buy them a six-pack. What was the world coming to? As he pulled away, he heard one of the boys jeer at his back: "Jog old man! Jog!"

Leonard's office looked more like a luxury apartment than a place of business. It was a split level, and the lower level was furnished with lush modern furniture—soft cushions heaped in spare metal frames. An expensive quadrophonic sound system emitted fine cool jazz with perfect clarity at a volume just loud enough to color the atmosphere without inhibiting conversation. Tom Leonard himself was dressed in perfectly faded Levis, a velour shirt, and running shoes. He greeted Sval cordially, shaking his hand with both of his own, and guided him to one of three chairs around a glass-topped coffee table. "What would you like?" he asked. "Some coffee?" Sval nodded and Leonard pressed a button unobtrusively located on a sculpture that looked African. "Erika, could you get us a couple of coffees?"

A gazelle of a woman brought the coffee from the next room. She too was dressed in casual though unpretentiously fashionable clothes—slacks, a loose white blouse, a scarf. The coffee was freshly ground French roast.

"Robert Brody," Leonard said with a smile. "Bart Sloan. Those rascals sure know how to cover their tracks. This 23rd-street scheme of theirs? Oh man, you blew the lid off that one just in time, Mr. Hofby. We had no idea it was those two blocks they were after, but the moment I read your piece it all came together for me. I called Mrs. Harney that day, we got together and we made a deal. That very day. I want to thank you for that."

"A deal? What kind of deal?"

"She agreed to sell me her house, and I agreed to sell her a better house in a nicer neighborhood. For the same price."

"You swapped houses." Sval thought about it, and then just had to add: "Let me guess: The purchase price was ten dollars and other good and valuable considerations?"

Leonard chuckled. "The price doesn't matter. Let's just say we came to a private agreement. She has a decent place to live and a furnace that works and no mortgage to pay. We've got the property on Webster. With that purchase we can block what the Sinister Twelve was trying to do. I like that name, incidentally. The Sinister Twelve!"

"When you say 'we', who's this 'we'?"

"Just a number of like-minded individuals. Nothing official. Developers like myself who have, let's say, a very different vision of Portland than Mr. Brody and his … associates." Leonard stood up and walked to the wall. He pulled a string and down rolled an enormous map not unlike the one Sval and Martha had been using to track the activities of the Sloan-Brody cabal. "You say this was their next target. They had the whole block minus this one house." Leonard pointed to Mrs. Harney's former property. "You said they were in touch with a corporate development outfit, but you didn't know exactly which one. I can tell you which one. It was Neptune Global Management LLC. They own the Starbright motel chain, the Big Burgers franchise, Charley Dogs—a basket of other fast food brands. And what they had in mind—as you speculated—was a motel complex surrounded by these fast-food joints. It was based on their projection that if the state decides to connect Highway 26 to the Fremont Bridge the freeway extension will be coming through this neighborhood. They wanted to turn North Portland into 82nd Street."

"Have you already. . .?"

"Filed the paperwork? Yes, it's all under way, there's nothing they can do to stop us. This property turns us into players. I don't mind telling you," Leonard continued, "your column tipped us into some big decisions. You see, Sval, we're not ultimately interested in buying and selling real estate, me and my partners. We care about the direction that Portland takes as a city. And when a Robert Brody comes along, rips out a fine old neighborhood and puts in a twenty-story motel and a string of fast food joints, we don't feel that's an improvement. They just about had these two blocks. Well thanks to you, now they don't. We got that property, and we can box them out. Their motel project is history, and without the motel, the fast food joints won't fly. And the way we'll change that neighborhood, people with political connections will be moving in, people who'll fight back against any freeway extension coming through *this* area. We're looking at acquiring six houses here, and we have a plan to interconnect them. The idea is to make one whole quarter of a block here into a recreation complex. We're not going to knock down any of the existing buildings. Don't replace, renovate, that's our operating philosophy. Something tells me you and I see eye to eye on this. We'll join up six back yards into one larger garden, Japanese sort of thing with a Zen atmosphere. And then a small cafe, hot tubs, massage facilities—"

"And the other houses on the block?"

"Will be bought and renovated. Some of them as residences. Some as businesses. The market will be hot here. That's how things get done. I see coffeehouses, I see organic groceries, bookstores…With Xanadu in the neighborhood—"

"Xanadu?"

"A tentative name. 'In Xanadu did Kublai Khan a stately pleasure dome decree…' What do you think?"

Sval shrugged, feeling blank and stunned. "I've never been good at names."

"About the project, I mean. We believe it'll have an upgrading effect on the whole northwest part of town. In fact, we already have some investors eager to buy and renovate properties in the several block area."

"Do you mean this Xanadu, as you call it, would be a neighborhood facility?"

"Yes, essentially."

"And it would be run as a … collective?"

Tom Leonard laughed mildly. "Well, no. Not quite that. But as a membership cooperative. Like a health club. You'd pay a membership fee of, say, $500 a year after which—"

Sval could not restrain a slight gasp. "Five-hundred!"

"That's not unreasonable, considering. Think of the Esalen Institute. There, it's a two- or three-week workshop you get for five-hundred bucks a pop, here it's a one-year membership. We've done the research, Hofby, there's a market for this. A $500 membership fee would be quite feasible while at the same time—in conjunction with a proper advertising strategy—it would keep its connection to the neighborhood. It would be inclusive. If you live here and you can pay the fee, you're qualified to join. Period."

"I see." Sval's head was whirling. "And what about the Mrs. Harneys of the world? People who can't pay the fee? All the poor people who will not be able to afford to live in these neighborhoods, once they've been renovated, where will they go?"

"I told you how it worked out with Mrs. Harney. Believe me, she's happy. This was win/win, Hofby. How often does life give you one of those?"

"Win/win for her. But there are a lot of Mrs. Harneys."

"Well, that's what city politics is about. You can't save the whole world at once. You have to save it one Mrs. Harney at a time."

"I see. And what did you want from me?"

"I just wanted to let you know what we have in mind. 'You may say I'm a dreamer, but I'm not the only one.' I think you're a dreamer too, Mr. Hofby. May I call you Sval? You write about development, this could make a perfect series for you. We'd loop you in, you'd have the inside track on how these projects are moving along. Stories about lifestyle changes in the neighborhood. You'd be giving your readers an inside view of how a city works, how it changes: right down to the bones, gristle, and muscle. I like your feel for what's happening in Portland. I like your writing style. If you're interested, I could give you an exclusive interview the week before we send our press release to the Oregonian. You'd scoop them. And if you want to go after it, you could turn the Ark into a player in this city. Information is a sword, my friend. What do you think?"

Sval leaned back in his seat and studied Tom Leonard. The developer exuded ease and charm. He didn't look like a corporate capitalist. He didn't seem culturally foreign. He looked like a better dressed—a much better dressed—version of Sval and his friends.

"I can't say yes or no," said Sval. "It's not my decision. I have to take it to the collective. If the Ark approves, I'm probably interested, but I have to tell you. I won't be writing any puff pieces, I won't hold back from asking tough questions. If you sit down with me, be forewarned. I'm always looking for the story behind the story."

"Hit me with your best shot, sport. I've got nothing to hide," said Tom Leonard.

"Okay," said Sval. "Well, I'll take it to the collective and then we'll see."

At the next Monday Meeting, Sval was the first to admit that this interview raised policy questions. Could the Ark run a positive piece about a business developer, no matter how benign his plans? Sval was the first to admit the collective needed to talk about this.

But the discussion proved to be quite short. The collective was pretty much unanimous. Interview Leonard? Why not? As long as it wasn't some kiss-ass profile. What Leonard was proposing sounded like news. Wasn't a newspaper supposed to give the news, good or bad? The community deserved to know. That's what a newspaper was supposed to do, tell the community what was going on.

"That's still our mission as a newspaper." Sval was summing up his sense of the group consensus. "The community's not just the people in this room. We have to think in terms of the whole community. Our community is Portland itself, in a sense. Not just people we could see getting stoned with. It's all the people of Portland."

George might have objected, but George wasn't coming to Monday Meetings anymore.

Performance Piece

The great and terrible day had arrived. When Marica opened her eyes, she couldn't call it waking up, for she'd hardly slept. The whole night had been a cocktail of light dreams and sharp anxieties. All morning, doing her substitute-teacher stint at Ross Elementary, Marica could scarcely pay attention to the children, much less control them, preoccupied as she was with thoughts and fears about her upcoming show.

No turning back now. The too-late-to-turn-back moment had come and gone weeks ago. She had rented the theatre-space at the Comfort Zone, the community center around the corner from the Pythian Ballroom. In one stroke, she'd used up half of her life's savings: non-refundable. Raoul had designed a poster for her and diligently made all the props she had asked of him. George had tacked up copies of Raoul's poster all over town. Marica had spread the word through her own networks. Thousands of people must have read Sval's interview with her in the Ark by now. She'd jumped out of the plane and all she could do was hope her parachute would open.

How could she have known, when she re-scheduled her show, that the Vietnam War would end that very week? And she certainly couldn't fault the Portland Coalition of the Left for throwing a big, public bash to celebrate the great event. The end of the Vietnam War deserved no less.

And of course they'd have it on the first Saturday after the fall of Saigon. The timing made total sense. But there went most of her potential audience. Under the circumstances, she probably should have been proud to draw as many people as she did. But all she could feel when the lights went up was the booming emptiness of the room. She had put out enough seats for 300 people and filled at best 75 of them, the worst possible number. Twenty would have been nothing but family. A hundred and fifty would have been mostly strangers. Either of those, she could have handled. Seventy-five meant this whole audience knew her just well enough to know exactly who was up there on stage. If she blew it, they'd know exactly who was up there making a fool of herself.

And then the lights went up, and she was performing her piece, and nothing else existed or mattered. She couldn't see or hear anyone over her lights and soundtrack, she didn't know if they were bored or rivetted, she didn't know if they were seeing what she was showing them, she had her performance to deliver. She was the witch, she was the earth opening up, she was the child, she was the vengeful Judith. There was no Marica on stage to witness what she was doing.

At intermission she hid in the bathroom and tried to relax. But she couldn't relax. Letting go of tension brought tears to her eyes, but she couldn't afford tears now. She had to tense up again deliberately, because she needed adrenaline to finish her show. One whole half remained, one whole hour, and right now, nothing existed but that one hour.

George fell asleep toward the middle of the first half. When his snores became audible, Martha slapped his arm and he woke up with a start, clearing his throat and looking all about with startled eyes. Then he remembered where he was and dutifully turned his face to the stage. But there, on a slightly raised platform, Marica was running about in circles, trailing a white gauze behind her, while the sound of running water bubbled out of hidden speakers. Random motion against random images to the tune of random noise—the very thing that George dreaded most: a work of art even more meaningless than life.

His fingers were itching to draw from his pocket the story he had clipped from the Oregonian that morning. A prisoner at the Oregon State Penitentiary had somehow acquired a gun and fired it at another prisoner before the guards shot them both dead. The guards would face no consequences; the shooting was justified, the authorities said. One of the prisoners had a gun. His name was JJ. His intended victim was a man named Duane. George kept staring at the stage but couldn't tear his mind away from the clipping in his pocket.

Zoe had read the news too. JJ dead. How he'd gotten the gun remained a mystery. The authorities had not charged anyone yet, but Zoe suspected Solidarity involvement. She focused on the stage to escape her brooding thoughts about a book she'd now never write. Marica was up there dancing amidst props and sets. Voices were chanting and music was playing. Marica kept changing masks and costumes. Zoe couldn't stop thinking about JJ.

Sval focused on the show, but it was hard, in part because Zoe was sitting right next to him. Why she'd chosen that seat, he could not fathom. Their breakup was a fait accompli. There were plenty of empty seats in the hall, she could have sat anywhere. Then, again, they'd agreed they would still be friends, so why should she not sit next to him? Marica's show was all myth and metaphor, and Sval found himself wanting more narrative. But who was he to criticize?

Martha was proud of her friend and clapped at intermission. Well, everyone did, to some extent. The clapping lasted a few minutes and it wasn't just polite applause. Some people were looking puzzled, but some were clapping pretty hard. Someone even whistled. Well, they should: the show was full of deep ideas. Martha wasn't sure what they were but the show felt deep. Toward the end, Marica started taking off costumes, but each time there was another costume underneath it. How she could have been wearing so many layers of clothes at the beginning and not look fat? This was magic. Finally, she got down to no clothes at all, which was sort of a shock because suddenly there she was, bare-naked, just standing there in front of everybody. Well with a body like hers, Martha thought, why not? But it wasn't sexy or anything. Just standing there, like that, she was just some body. Anyway, it was only a glimpse. One or two seconds, then the stage went black.

☼

The moment Marica's performance began, Raoul was transfixed. He couldn't take his eyes off the stage. He saw artifacts he himself had crafted and only now was he seeing what they meant. He was half responsible for the luminous egg she used in her opening scene, but he had no idea Marica was going to be inside it when the lights went up, and he sure as hell couldn't see how she managed to look like she was floating when her feet had to be touching the ground the whole time. With dance alone, she seemed to be liberating herself from gravity.

And then the chanting began. The egg gave way to mysterious sheets of see-through fabrics. Images of war and violence and destruction appeared, rendered ghostly by the screens of fishnet and cheesecloth upon which they were projected. Gazing at those eerie shifting layers of color, Raoul found himself craving forgiveness, though he didn't know for what. And all the while, Marica danced and danced.

By the time intermission came around, Raoul didn't want to leave his seat: the spell must not be broken. The room he was in had become deep woods. His eyes were tiny windows looking into a scented garden, like the fairy-tale about the woodchopper's son, who gets lost in a forest, and the air turns sweet and the flowers grow big, and he runs away frightened by the vastness of it all, only later to realize he'd strayed into the outskirts of paradise and now, because he'd lacked the courage to stay, he was shut out of it forever.

As soon as her show ended, as soon as the lights were out, as soon as the room went dark, Marica groped her way backstage. The last two hours stretched behind her like a dream. She didn't know what she'd done. She had not seen the show herself—nor heard it, nor felt it, nor tasted it. Marica had put every drop of herself into the performance. The performer cannot also be an observer. Others would have to tell her what she'd done. Behind her, the lights came up on an empty stage. Marica dressed quickly, huddling backstage, listening to the applause. She couldn't tell if it was long or short: tension had warped her sense of time. She couldn't bring herself to go out and face that audience, but she did. She faced the inscrutable darkness and the darkness applauded and the darkness went on applauding, and then the applause turned into scattered clapping, and then it stopped and she wasn't sure if it had gone on for a good long time or a humiliatingly short time. For better or for worse, it was over. She'd put her vision out there, and that was all she could do. She let go of breath. Very soon she would be shedding tears.

She knew her friends would seek her out. They'd let her know how she'd done. She wanted them to be honest, but she hoped they wouldn't be honest. She could take it, but she couldn't take it. They came in one at a time and murmured words of congratulation. They sounded sincere. But Marica longed for something more than "sincere." Images flashed into her mind of the post-performance scenes of her fantasies. Flowers, champagne corks, rambunctious toasts.

They weren't all her friends. Some strangers came by too. A woman in balloon trousers and a strappy t-shirt, short hair, mid-thirties, stepped up. "Hi." Her horn-rimmed spectacles announced that she was an intellectual. She proffered her hand for a mannish handshake. "Linn Bennet. Just visiting from New York. Marvelous! Who ever dreamed of seeing such a thing in Portland, Oregon!"

"Thank you," said Marica. Had she just heard a compliment? Or was that just New York insulting Portland? She didn't know. The woman thrust a card at her, and she took it; but then, before she could really glance at it, Maureen and her entourage were jostling Bennet out of the way. Call me, said the woman from New York, but Marica didn't have time to digest what had just happened. She had to give the women of the Athena Collective her full attention. Their judgment mattered more than anyone's. And they showered her with kudos, they did. And yet… did she detect some whiff of disapproval? After a bit, they moved on, leaving Marica roiled with doubt.

Then Sval was standing in the doorway, his lanky frame making several angles that added up to a look of repose.

"Won't you come in," she said.

He was holding a rose but didn't offer it to her. Instead, he got busy setting it on the table and puttering about for a vase. He was rummaging for words. Praise would have been easy. Apparently, he had something more complicated to say. Finally, she gave him a break by letting out a squirt of nervous laughter. "Don't be shy, Sval. I feel a little fragile, okay? But be honest. What did you think?"

Sval deliberated for a moment. "My God, Marica," he said at last. "That took a lot of courage."

Took a lot of courage? Was that good or bad? Marica swallowed. "What does that mean?"

"It means … my respect for you soars."

"Which means?"

"You packed so much into that piece. So much thought and emotion. I'll be deconstructing it for weeks. Bravo, Marica. Bravo."

His words were devoid of content. Those words he could have said even if he'd never seen the show. She knew not to press him. Sval had been in the house, occupying a seat, but he hadn't really seen what she was doing up there. Et tu, Sval? She suppressed the pang and tried her best to receive his words as a compliment. It was the right thing to do. He meant well. After he left, Marica felt bereft.

And then came George.

"Well," he said, "that sucked. I bet you're glad it's over. Listen, get dressed and let's get a beer. You gotta' hear what Singleton's done now." Or at least that's how she remembered his words in the thunderclap of her own subsequent silence. Then she told him to get lost—she didn't lose her temper, she said it quietly, calmly. And he didn't seem surprised When she told him not to come to her tonight, or ever again, not to even think about it, he didn't seem disappointed. And she didn't care if he didn't care. She really didn't.

She thought she was alone then. But one more person came, and she spent her fury on whoever it happened to be, and it happened to be Raoul. She didn't even realize he'd come in. She had her back to him when he spoke and she had no idea what he was trying to say. Something Raoul-ish. It was only after he darted away that she realized what she had said to him in response. "Go away!" That's what she'd said, that was all she remembered saying. What was wrong with her? Marica was alone with her feelings at last, and all she could remember from the whole night now were the words Raoul had spoken to her back, "As long as there was light, I could see you there." And she'd turned on him like some Hollywood star brushing off some inappropriate fan. Go away, she'd spat, and she cringed at the venom she remembered in her cry.

She finished getting dressed, but Raoul's words kept buzzing in her head. As long as there was light, he'd said, she was there. Who said such things? Who *said* such things? And yet—wasn't that exactly the sort of thing she'd been longing to hear all night from all the other people who trooped in to offer tepid compliments?

Maybe Raoul was the only one in the house who had actually *seen* her performance piece. And that mattered. Because if even one person saw it, then she'd actually created something. And all she could think to do was shout *Go away!*

She had to make this right. She had to let him know she wasn't the kind of person who'd say a thing like she'd just said. She had to make this right. She was on her way out of the building when the woman with the horn-rimmed glasses stepped into her path. "So. You've got my card, right? I'm going back to New York tomorrow, but you've got my number, it's on the card." Marica felt the woman beaming some sort of attitude at her, and she could not at this moment get a fix on what it was. Criticism? She wasn't in the mood. "Yes, yes," she muttered. "I will." She skirted the woman from New York and hurried on. She had one last thing to do tonight and no time to waste. Only a mean spiteful person would treat Raoul the way she had just done, and she wasn't that person. She had to let him see: she wasn't that person.

Fire

When Raoul arrived backstage, he saw that Marica was surrounded by her friends and fans. He didn't want to push in ahead of people who knew her better… a cluster of women from the Athena coffeehouse… some of her Dare to Juggle mates, they certainly took precedence… Sval…. George … He waited until all of them were gone.

Only then did he approach her. She didn't see him coming, she had her back to the door, and the door was open. She didn't notice he was there until he started speaking. "Marica," he said. "I am speechless. What you did tonight? I saw you up there right through all the costumes. I saw *you*."

She turned. "Oh, for heaven's sake, Raoul. What did you say? What is that supposed to mean?" He saw tears in her eyes and fury on her face and melancholy deep inside.

"You were calling out from across a stadium like those creatures from another galaxy but I heard you. And you're right. It's all masks and costumes out there in the world. You're right. Even when you're down to wearing nothing, it's still a costume. There's still a you inside. You made me see that tonight. As long as there was light, I could see *you*."

Marica stared at him for a moment. "I can't deal with this," she snapped. "I have no idea what you're saying. Look: you made some wonderful things for me, Raoul, I'm sure I let you down, I know what you must think of me. You don't have to be nice. I can handle this. I just have to be alone right now. Would you honor that wish? Please?

Just go away. I can't deal with this right now. I need to be alone. *Go away!*"

Raoul's next words wouldn't come out. He didn't even know what they would have been. It didn't matter. Words couldn't change the fact that he was stranded in the real world. Ever since Smith Rocks, there was nowhere else to be. But he didn't have to hang around here feeling sorry for himself. He had an aquarium to finish making. A few last adjustments and it would be done. Marica wasn't the only one in town who could create a masterpiece. She'd see. They'd all see. Tomorrow they'd see. Tomorrow he'd show them all *his* masterpiece.

On the way home from Marica's show, Raoul heard the sirens. They were coming from the northeast but getting closer. At first, he thought they were police sirens, but then a red truck appeared behind him. He pulled over and let it zoom past him. "Gosh," he thought, "the fire must be in my very neighborhood."

Then he came around the corner and saw the red truck on *his* street and the crowd on the sidewalk and the flames licking out of *his* own bedroom window. Several of his roommates stood on the sidewalk in a tense clump. Further back was Stan the Man, chewing his fleshy lip. Firemen were scurrying busily here and there, dragging hoses.

Raoul parked in the neighboring laundromat lot and jumped the fence to the back yard of Yamhill House. One of the firemen spotted him and yelled, "Hey!" but Raoul had already dashed up the back steps and banged his way into the kitchen. The ground floor looked perfectly normal, but the house smelled of smoke. Raoul bounded upstairs to the second floor and saw wisps of smoke twisting down the stairwell. The fire was on the third floor. He took the next flight, and now he was in the hall that served as the antechamber to his own room and to Zak's. His own door was framed by the smoke leaking out around it. The fire was in there, all right. Leaning against the wall was a two-by-four left over from another art project. Raoul grabbed it, sucked in a breath, and put his hand on his doorknob. And stood there for a moment. Knowing what he must do.

From below came dim shouts. Somewhere a woman's voice sounded. Raoul snatched his door open and steeled himself and then leapt inside—into the room where just this week he had finally installed his aquarium. He could see the red flames in the corner where he'd left some painters' rags, soaked in turpentine: next to the heat vent. His fault. The rug was on fire, the books were catching, the box with the letters from Zara were already aflame, and the hoses weren't going to get up here in time. If the house burned down, it would be his fault. But he knew what to do. There was plenty of water in the room. His aquarium filled the entire space, wall-to-wall, floor-to-ceiling, like a huge tinker toy construction made of glass. Everywhere in the room, there was water.

No one had ever seen it. And now, no one ever would. He started swinging. It took a few whacks before anything broke. He'd built sturdy! Then something cracked and something crashed and water roared. Raoul kept swinging, blindly swinging, covering his face with his arm. Amid an explosion of glass and water, he heard the hiss of fire dying, felt the hot breath of steam coming up from the floor. The sound of some woman's voice turned into sharp cries. They were coming from Marica Margolis. She'd followed him up the stairs and was standing in his doorway, ankle-deep in water and exotic guppies.

Marica got to Yamhill House just in time to see Raoul jump the fence from the laundromat parking lot. She saw a space next to his, and pulled into it. She tumbled out of her car and chased after him. The firemen were on the back porch, clumsily uncoiling a big hose. When she vaulted the fence, one of them grabbed for her. "Ma'am! It's dangerous!"

But she wrenched free of his grip and was in the house and running to the third floor, where she knew Raoul would be. And there he was, all right, at his bedroom door, his hands on the knob, about to rush into a burning room. She wasn't close enough to stop him, couldn't stop him. He pulled his door open and she saw threads of flame. Yes: the fire was in Raoul's bedroom.

And then she saw.

In that room was something besides the fire: In that room was an artifact of glass woven entirely into the space; yet every part of the room was accessible. She could see in one glimpse that if this was your room, you could get to the closet, sit at the desk, climb into bed. You could live a human life in here, surrounded by water, living among fishes. "Oh my God," burst from her lips. "It's real."

Her view of Raoul's aquarium probably lasted a few seconds at most. Then he'd waded into it, wielding a club. She was frozen in place, watching in horror. Then the fire was out. The whole room was still hissing and panting, but the fire was out. And his aquarium, his masterpiece, was just shrapnel littering a steaming floor.

She rushed to him, across shards of glass. "Oh my God, Raoul!"

"I broke it.

"You put out the fire!"

"I had to." He dragged his sleeve across his runny nose. "I had to." The air still smelled thickly of smoke.

"The whole house could have burned down! My God, Raoul, the room was on fire. You saved the house."

"I broke my aquarium."

"I know."

"It was almost done. I wish *someone* had seen it."

"I saw it."

She would have said more, but then the firemen were rushing up the stairs. Hubbub filled the room as the firemen confirmed that the fire was out and identified the cause and issued some stern warnings, and with much clatter and confusion, assembled their gear and departed. The hubbub continued for a while longer, as excited roommates came through and surveyed the damage and berated Raoul and expressed sympathy and wished him solace. But eventually they too all departed and Marica was alone with Raoul again.

She could not leave now. She was needed here. She stepped into him, put her arms around him, held him close. "I'm so sorry."

"It was almost done," he whispered into her shoulder. "I was going to have a party. You were all going to be invited. There was going to be wine and cheese. There was going to be dancing. Balloons."

"Champagne," she whispered. "I know."

They held each other and went on holding each other. Marica could absorb Raoul's grief, she knew this flavor of grief. After a while, he disengaged. "Tomorrow might be bad," he said. "It might catch up to me, but tonight? I just feel numb. You saw it, huh?"

"I did."

"Just for a second though."

"Long enough, Raoul. It got right into my head. I can still see it, right now, if I close my eyes."

"Wow." He gazed at her, and she liked the feeling of his eyes on her. "I kept telling people it was real."

"And no one would believe you. Humans and fish living in the same world—maybe there's hope for men and women," said Marica. "Raoul, I really, really am so sorry. I really am."

"Don't be." He looked around at the ruins of his aquarium. "One person saw it. That's all it takes, you know, to make it real. One person makes all the difference, Marica." His gaze continued to rove over the wreckage in the room. "You know what? This thing wasn't my masterpiece. It was my ball-and-chain. I feel released. I can finally stop being the guy who's building an aquarium no one else can see. I'm free to do anything now." His voice wound down. He peered at her, then, puzzled. "What are you doing here, Marica?"

"I came to apologize," she admitted. "I snapped at you earlier tonight. That was just so wrong of me. What you said was beautiful. I was waiting all night to hear something like that, and then when you came along and said it, all I could do was snap at you. Honestly, what's wrong with me?"

"Nothing's wrong with you, Marica. What the lips say is just the body talking. The body's only something you're wearing. You said it yourself, tonight, in your show. That's what you were telling us. I don't care what your lips say. I hear *you*."

He was looking into her eyes. She waited for his gaze to drift down, to her breasts, and further, but his gaze remained on her eyes. Which made her uncomfortable. She wanted him to look away. Eyes were too intimate, too private. It wasn't what men mostly looked at. Any moment now, she was going to feel violated. But any moment didn't come. She let him look. She gave him unqualified permission to look. She wanted him to look at the woman she was, because she was looking too, and he was nice to look at, this man-child with his tight black curls. Raoul was not a boy, she realized; no, no, this was a man. He had a universe inside him just like she did. And for now, they didn't have to do or say anything, they could just look through their windows at this world they were imagining together. Being seen would take some getting used to, but the tension was draining. There was no reason to hurry now. Nothing was waiting for them up ahead except time and more time.

"You saw my show," she said finally. "You really saw it." And then, recklessly, she added, "And we're all so fond of you, Raoul, the things you say. We really are. What I said up there at Smith Rocks, I wasn't just blowing smoke, I meant every word of it. You're precious to me, Raoul my dear. I love you."

Then her throat closed. What had she just said?

His radiance turned to warmth. "I love you too. Is it okay to say that? Well, too late, I've gone and said it." And then he laughed as if there was nothing dangerous or awkward about saying I-love-you to her face. As if speaking such words was just innocent delight.

She hugged him for that, laughing a little, and humorously kissed him for that, affectionately, still laughing somewhat, because only with Raoul could one say such things and not worry about it, and then she kissed him some more. And was surprised to realize he was kissing too, kissing her back. And was more surprised to realize she wanted him to kiss her more deeply. They moved apart for a moment, both panting a little. The smoke had dissipated, the air felt clear and cool, but Marica couldn't get her breath back. Rising inside her was a thrill of longing and desire. She wanted to open her heart to this man and let him in like the tide. She would show him the fire dancer. They were kissing again now, only kissing, just his tongue seeking hers so delicately, the two of them pressed together, body to body, on a floor littered with shattered glass and dying guppies. How unlikely this was, and yet she wanted more. She sought between his legs and what she found made her feel adored.

"Raoul," she said. "Not here in all this water and glass. Come home with me."

"George?" he said.

"No longer exists," she said.

He didn't ask her what she meant by that. He knew what she meant by that. It was settled then, wasn't it? They were going to go to her house and make love through all the hours of darkness left in this dramatic night. She moved toward the stairwell, fumbling in her coat pocket for her keys. But when she pulled them out, a card came out too.

"You dropped something." Raoul picked it up from the floor.

"Oh—some woman gave me that tonight after my show. She wanted to talk but I was in a hurry—I needed to catch up with you." Warm with arousal, Marica was still in a hurry, to be naked, to surround him with herself and be filled with him.

But Raoul was still examining the card. "Elizabeth Bennet," he said. "What a strange name. Culture Shock. She's with *Culture Shock?*"

"I don't know. What's *Culture Shock?*"

"It's an arts mag out of New York. The cutting edge is what they cover. They did this piece about Christos. You know the one? He's building a fence in California?"

"A fence." Marica shook her head and reached for the card.

"She wrote something on the back," he said.

She turned the card over and read the words out loud. "*Want to interview you. Call me.* Oh my God, Raoul! Maybe *two* people saw what I was doing."

"I was first," he said. "You can call her tomorrow."

"I'll drive," Marica panted.

Strike

The financial crisis began to heat up. Everybody knew a day of reckoning was coming. One day, the paper would not have enough money to pay both the printer and its core production people, the four who were drawing small weekly stipends. The printer was the outside world, so them you had to pay. The production salaries would therefore have to be suspended until the money crisis was resolved.

The volunteers saw no ethical issues there. Why should four people draw salaries when dozens of people were doing the work? The paid production people should do the right thing and stop taking money out of the paper for now. The paid production crew didn't agree. Those four never came to Monday Meeting anymore. They sent in a message telling the collective they were not going to take no stinkin' pay cut. If their payments were reduced, there would be consequences. How could the money be raised? They had no idea, not their problem. They were production people.

Bubba was good friends with the production people. He delivered a message to them from the collective. The message told them the collective would discuss the issue at the next Monday meeting. They were part of the collective, they should come to meeting and be part of the decision-making process. With or without them, however, the issue would be discussed the following Monday, and whatever the collective decided at that meeting would be final.

On Monday, the four people who were taking salaries made an appearance, but only to present their terms. They would not take a pay cut, that was number one. Second, they demanded that on production

Thursday, the radio be tuned to KSAN, the AM pop-schlock station all day—*not* to KLOO, the community station that delivered non-stop left-wing political analysis and cultural programming. Then they stalked out.

The discussion that flared up then was fierce. The collective splintered into three factions. One wanted to leave the salaries alone. Another faction, led by Sval, proposed that the collective appoint a committee to plan a benefit that would keep the paper afloat for a few months while the issue was discussed further. A third group felt the money-grubbing paid production crew should be ousted from the Ark. Who needed the greedy motherfuckers?

Zack the Zen Buddhist bookkeeper folded his hands. "We can't take wages away from a brother."

Calumnies were hurled at Zack. He of all people should have known the Ark was sinking. Was he not the bookkeeper? "I did know," he protested. "I didn't want to put out negative vibes." Then came the shocking revelation. Zack had been paying himself fifty dollars a week for months. He'd never brought the matter up to the collective, he'd just cut himself a check. "Bookkeepers always get paid!" he cried,

"Buddhistgate!" came the howls. "Buddhistgate!"

Bubba Sadhu sprang to Zack's defense. "The brother's wages are holy!" he shouted.

"Not when the brother's wages are stolen!"

And so it went, deep into the night, three camps hardening their positions, until at last, at nine o' clock, the shrunken collective agreed to forget about consensus and settle the matter with a simple majority vote.

They decided that from now on any profits realized by the Ark would be distributed among all who had put time and effort into the paper that month. Each person's share would reflect how much time they'd put in as a percentage of the whole. In times of no profit, no one would be paid. As soon as the paper's fortunes improved, the collective would revisit the issue of stipends and salaries. Until then, the Ark would be a labor of love, produced entirely by volunteers—like in the good old days.

The arguments about the money-crisis had consumed so much of Monday Meeting that copy for the next issue had been left more or less to chance. There was no shortage of copy however. For one thing, letters reacting to the incident at Smith Rocks were still pouring in. That week, Zoe brought in a follow-up to her own original article about the incident. Now that hordes of people were selling all their possessions and abandoning their homes and leaving their jobs and heading to the Oregon coast, hoping to get on the Mother Ship when it arrived, the matter had become a news item that even the Oregonian was covering. For once, the Ark had gotten the jump on the city's biggest newspaper. Zoe's follow-up wasn't a news story but an opinion piece, an interview with Sval. She wanted him to tell the readership *his* stance on the Coming of the One. Sval declared it part of a larger pattern, the rising tide of cults in American society. Yes, cults. He would not shrink from the word. Cults.

The Ark decided to devote two whole page-spreads to letters from readers this week, on both sides of the Smith Rocks controversy. Sval laid them out in parallel columns, for and against. He added no editorial judgment. It wasn't his fault if one side sounded smart and the other sounded stupid. He didn't write the letters, he just chose them.

On Thursday morning, Bubba called the office to pronounce that after a harrowing night of meditation and reflection he had decided he and the Cosmotherapists could no longer in conscience contribute to the Godless Ark. The message was taken by a volunteer high school student who tacked it on a crowded bulletin board that no one looked at anymore.

At seven o' clock Thursday night, when Marica came into the office she noticed that the paper was looking a great deal less full than usual. "What's holding up the copy?" she asked.

"Nothing," said Martha. "Look." She reached over the composer, keeping her breasts away from the keys with one hand while with the other picking up a stack of typeset copy from the box. "That's all ready to proofread."

"Where's Kale, then? She's not here? Someone else could proof a little copy, for heaven's sake." Marica walked up to Ryan, who was slouched over a layout in the corner, stroking his big handlebar moustache. "What gives?"

He lit a cigarette and took a long puff. "You got complaints? Boss?"

"Don't call me boss. I'm asking about the layout. We're three hours behind. I'm concerned. Aren't you concerned?"

"Not my problem. When you decide to pay me, I'll care. Till then, I'm going at my own pace."

"It's not me that pays you or doesn't pay you. What's happened to you, Ryan? You didn't used to be like this. This is a collective. Everybody else is busting their butts right now, working for nothing. And you're feeling sorry for yourself because the collective isn't paying you enough!"

They veered apart from each other, both sullen.

At eight-thirty Kale the proofreader walked in.

"You decided to wander back?" Marica said.

"If I'm working for nothing, I figure I deserve a two-hour dinner break."

Marica made no reply. Hostility hung thick in the air. Martha was her only ally in the room, two against four: they were losing the battle of vibes. Where were all the usual Thursday night volunteers? They should have started pouring in half an hour ago. The room felt like a tomb.

Then, to her relief, George and Sval arrived in a whirlwind of energy. They must have been in a tavern; they both looked bright around the gills. At this moment she loved them both, even though she was with Raoul now, whom she loved best of all, her best decision of the year so far.

"Hi, sugar cookie. What chew doing?" George sprawled in the chair next to Marica. "Proofing copy, huh? I'd help, but you know me: Mister-Never-Does-His-Share-of-Shitwork. I got a rep to maintain. How's the paper?" He jumped to his feet and did two quick circuits of the layout boards. "Holy hell," he spluttered, "what the be-Jesus, am I drunker than

I look? What time is it? Almost nine! We should be way more done by now! Ryan. Buddy! You're falling down on the job!"

Ryan made no response to George. Instead, he snatched at Sval's elbow. "Got a minute?"

Sval's jaw muscles bulged. "Dial it down, Ryan. What did you want to talk about?"

"I'm done talking. We get paid tonight or we walk. End of story."

"We?"

Ryan tilted his head toward his clump of friends. "Martha's here, she could write us our checks *now*. We get the money or we walk. You hear me, Kemo Sabe? Deal with it."

"And if you walk, what? The paper was coming out before your time, it'll keep coming out after you're gone. None of us is essential except all of us."

"That's deep, Plato. But I'm warning you. Give us our money tonight or—"

"Ryan! It's not mine to give, it's not yours to take." Sval dropped his voice to a mutter. "There *is* no money. Don't you get it? That's the problem. Pitch in and help us solve it. Be part of the solution." He spoke quietly, but Marica had never seen him so furious.

"Yowzah, Mr. Rockefeller." Ryan turned and plucked his jacket off the back of a chair and said, "All right, boys. The Man says he don't need us. Let's see if he's right. Good night."

He nodded and the other three members of the so-called production crew stood up.

Marica turned from the layout table. Her face had gone pale. "Ryan. Please. At this hour? You can't. You'll leave us in the lurch."

"That's the point, boss. We're on strike. Let's see how you do without us. We *are* the paper. You'll see." The paid production crew marched out.

For a few moments, no one made a sound. Then Marica sighed. "We'd better get on the phone," she said. "Round up some help."

"If he could only have given us a few days' warning," Martha groaned. "Even a day's worth. But nine o'clock Thursday night?"

"That was rather the point, I imagine," Sval said. "Leaving us in the lurch was not an unexpected side effect of what they did. They intended injury."

"We're in trouble now." Martha began fiercely cutting typeset copy into long strips, ready for pasteup.

"It's not the end of the world," Marica laughed. "We don't need that crew. Remember the old days? One time, we got all the women from the Mt Hood Collective to come in on a Thursday night. Oh, and Yamhill House pretty much always turned out a crew at some point. I tell you what, I'll call Anita, and I'll tell her to bring some guacamole when she comes."

"And some chips would be nice," Martha agreed.

"I'll get on the horn to Yamhill House," George boomed, and he plopped himself down in a seat to dial. "Hello? Yeah—who's this? Raoul? Get your ass down here, the Ark has another king-size crisis going. Tell everyone, okay? Okay. Your turn." He thrust the phone at Marica. She dialed a number and talked into the phone softly for a few minutes, then dialed another number and another, conversing for a couple of minutes each time. Finally, she put the phone down.

"Well?" said Sval. "How many?"

"Well, Anita's not there…she went out dancing…Charlotte says she's coming down with something—and it's true. She looked pretty dragged out when I—"

"We're not looking for doctor's notes. Who's coming from your neck-of-the-woods?"

"No one."

"No one? Not . . . any? None?"

"They're all busy. Or else burned out. Melody says she's sick of saving the Ark."

"What about the coffeehouse, did you call?"

"They said they'd put out the word. We should get two or three from there."

"But no commitments?"

"Nothing definite. How about you, Sval?"

"Well, I called the Taylor Street House, but I'm afraid they're sour about the Smith Rocks brouhaha. They're somewhat Ananda Marga connected. And then I called the bookstore, but you know they're still a little hostile to the Ark after what happened with Singleton and they're still—"

"So they're not coming either? What about Chuck Ridley and—"

"I called them. Apparently, they—I wasn't aware of this before—but they were partial to the Whitaker faction and so—"

"I get it. They're not coming either. So, who's coming?" Martha demanded.

Sval took a deep breath. "From my connections? Nobody."

A despairing silence descended, broken only when Raoul and Zoe walked in, looking bright-eyed.

"My God, a sight for sore eyes," Sval cried, "Where are the others?"

"I brought my rapidograph set," Raoul announced. "What others?"

"We need layout," George exploded. "I told you to bring a crowd. Is this all you could scrape up? You and your rapidograph?"

"Stan the Man was meeting a woman at the White Eagle. He said if you saw her, you'd see why he was meeting her instead of coming to the Ark. He said he doesn't know anything about putting together a newspaper anyhow. And Melanie was angry because of Zack. And the others, I don't know. They were mostly going to the White Eagle—The Rounders are playing tonight. In fact, I was kinda' thinking I—"

Sval uttered a cry of despair. "Did you tell them it was a crisis?"

"They said the Ark is always in some kind of crisis."

For a moment, the six stood shuffling their feet, and occasionally clearing their throats.

Then Martha slapped her palms together. "Well," she said. "If this is it, this is it. Let's get to work. Zoe, why don't you proof? You too, Sval. I'll keep setting type. George and Marica, you two …"

Parceling out tasks took only a few minutes and then the meager crew set to work. At midnight Raoul made a run for provisions and came back with soda pop and coffee. At three o' clock George and Marica went for more coffee and corn chips from the all-night grocery on Lombard Street. At five a.m. George broke out a supply of cross tops and everybody took half a tab. By seven a.m. the sense of camaraderie was as thick as glue. By eight o' clock—only six hours later than usual—the layout was substantially finished. Martha cut the boards apart and rearranged them as signatures. Sval checked page numbers, corrected the staff roster, and put together the package for the printer.

At that moment, with sunlight gleaming into the devastated office, exhilaration was the mood. The group agreed to disperse to their various homes, get some well-earned sleep, and meet that night at Marica's house for dinner. George and Raoul then guzzled some more coffee and headed off in George's red truck to deliver the paper to the printer.

The Wake

The following evening a bedraggled sextet assembled in Marica's living room, looking hung over and mauled. Sval had brought a six-pack, but only he drank from it. Raoul had brought two joints but only he was smoking. Everybody spoke in disjointed fragments if at all.

"Well!" said Martha, with false vigor. "What's for dinner?"

Marica hung her head. "I forgot to cook."

"Never mind," growled Sval. "We'll go out. What about Stannich's Ten-to-One?"

"Monster-burgers?" Martha frowned her distaste. "Couldn't we go someplace nicer?"

"Oh sure. Why not." Sval let out a hollow laugh. "We just sank the Ark. Break out the champagne, this calls for a celebration."

"What about the Genoa?" said Zoe.

"The Genoa!" Martha broke into a laugh. The Genoa was a tiny, artsy gourmet northern Italian restaurant staffed entirely by student dropouts and former professors from Reed College. It was also one of the most expensive restaurants in the city.

But Zoe explained: "Sval and I piled up some credit there, washing dishes last year. Between the two of us, we've got six free dinners coming. I made reservations, just in case. Table for six. It's free except we have to pay for wine and tips."

"Table for six," said George. "Huh. The Rose City Six."

The Genoa had only ten tables and only one that seated six. The room was dimly lit by four globes that seemed to hover in the darkness above the tables. The walls, a nondescript brown, blended in with the darkness, giving an impression of limitless space. One end of the room was dominated by an enormous, polished burl table laden with fruits and succulent-looking desserts. Across from it hung a wall-sized back-lit abstract expressionist batik through which seeped a warm glow of interwoven crimsons and cinnamon yellows. Here and there along the other two walls, antique blond furniture functioned as discrete sideboards.

A long-haired pony-tailed waiter shepherded the Rose City Six to their corner table. Sitting there, they were enclosed in a bubble of private light. Irritation melted from their bones, and words began to flow.

"Ah," Sval sighed, "now that the Ark is dead, I regret we didn't get Raoul to do a proper, good-bye cover. The Ark going down with all of us animals on it, waving good-bye. Or at least a picture of me with a pickaxe bashing holes in the boat, with a caption that read Sval Hofby, The Man Who Sank the Ark."

"You!" Marica shook her head vigorously. "If anyone sank the Ark it was me."

George stared moodily into his wine glass. "Forget it. I killed that sucker. I'm the one."

"That's ridiculous!" Marica hooted. "You couldn't sink a paper bag! I sank the Ark by leaving when I did."

"*I'm* the troublemaker. Always have been!" George insisted. "No one can take that from me."

"You're talking prehistory," Sval barked. "Before Whitaker you were the Prince of Trouble. In modern times, I think I can lay undisputed claim to the title of chief saboteur—no, no—please!" He raised his hands to quell objections. "Allow me the luxury of my mea culpa. I sank the Ark."

"Or I did maybe?" Raoul suggested. "I sank the Ark? Somehow?"

"Raoul," said Sval, "you're the only of us who comes out of this innocent."

The waiter arrived then, with the antipasto, a rich anchovy and cream fondue, with fresh vegetables. Martha dipped a celery stick into the heavenly concoction and closed her eyes to fully savor the first bite.

"What we needed was more criticism/self-criticism," said Marica.

"What we needed was less goddamn criticism/fucking-self-criticism," George scoffed.

Sval shook his head. "I don't know, George. Every time you looked around this past year it seemed like some different fulminating, flea-bitten, single-minded little group of nutjobs was trying to take control of the Ark. And we the sensible majority, it always seemed to me, we were always fighting them and defeating them and saving the Ark. But now? When there's just the six of us left? How the hell can we say we're the sensible majority and not just another flea-bitten fulminating little group, the toughest of the lot? How can we say we saved the Ark when the Ark is dead and we're standing over its corpse with blood dripping from our teeth?"

Sval's statement was greeted with mild laughter and shrugs, except by Martha who looked thoughtful. The group had finished one full bottle of Suave Bolla and now agreed unanimously to order another and hang the expense. By the time the fish arrived they had fallen into a boozy sentimental cheer. Sval told an anecdote about the first time he ever came to the paper, how he thought Marica was one of the founders of the paper only to discover that she had joined the staff only three weeks before he had.

Marica smiled and related her own fond first impressions of Sval. "I asked myself, is this man really here, or am I just talking to his ambassador?" Then came a flurry of first impressions, lasting to the brink of the entree, whereupon the group decided to order two bottles of red wine and hang the expense. Barolo was the full-bodied red recommended by the waiter, a lanky long-haired guy from (improbably enough) Afghanistan. Over breasts of chicken stuffed with capers and pine nuts the streams of discourse flowed and branched into the nooks and crannies of the Golden Age, those electric months before Niles Whitaker set in motion the events that had led to this sorry moment, six bedraggled survivors reminiscing at a wake.

"What's a wake?" Martha asked.

"An Irish funeral custom. Partying like there's no tomorrow when someone dies. May the Ark be in heaven half an hour before the devil hears it's dead." Sval lifted his glass.

"Why do you keep saying the Ark is dead?" Martha demanded. "What did we do last night? We got the paper out. It's on the stands right now. People are reading it all over town."

Sval made a clucking noise. "Let's not be sentimental. In the old days we never had fewer than 30 people working on the paper. Now we have six. Q.E.D."

"I don't see what's so blankety-blanking Q.E.D. about it," Martha protested, "if QED means what I think. Six people got the paper out last night, we're the six who did it, and we're still here. What else counts?"

"We did the tail end of production was all. You know damn well there's a lot more to getting that paper out week after week," said Sval.

"So what?" Martha spooned up the last of her Béarnaise sauce and leaned back. "There's six other days of the week to get all that other stuff done."

"It's still just the six of us, Martha. Between the six of us, we just don't have the nuts-and-bolts know-how. Whitaker was right. We're nothing but a bunch of effete intellectuals, good at sitting around quibbling about ideology all day, but we're helpless when it comes to nuts and bolts—"

"Speak for yourself," Martha huffed "What nuts and bolts are you talking about?"

"You name it. Take bookkeeping, for example."

"Fooey. I can handle bookkeeping better than that stupid Buddhist any day. What else you got?"

"Well, managing the ad accounts—"

"I can do that, it's nothing. Easy macheesi. What else?"

"Ah, but who amongst us has actually ever gone out and sold an ad?"

"None amongst us has to," said Martha. "Freelance salespeople sell the ads, they're self-starters working on commission, and they didn't quit. Why should they? As long as there's a paper coming out and ten thousand subscribers, they can keep selling ads and making money. They'd never want the Ark to fold. As long as we keep putting a product out there, they'll keep their end going. For their own sakes, not for ours, but so what. They'll keep selling ads. What else?"

"Well. . . I don't know. There's a whole rash of piddly stuff. . . isn't there?"

"Inventory?" said Martha. "Sure. Contracts? Sure. Keeping the office together, making up a dummy, organizing story assignments, I can do all that, Sval, I've been doing some of it all along. All I need is people to write and edit and do graphics. And production, of course. As long as I can hold onto my salespeople, the Ark is alive."

There was a moment of silence around the table. Finally, Sval said, "What are we discussing here? One more superhuman effort like last night? One grand final issue? Or tomorrow and tomorrow and tomorrow?"

"I'm just not ready to say the paper's dead is all." Martha folded her hands in her lap primly, and sat staring at her silverware which she had neatly arranged on the table cloth in front of her in their original positions.

"You got a plan?" George demanded. "Spit it out."

"Okay. I think six full-time people can produce the Ark. I'm saying let's try it that way. No more volunteers. Just six people working full-time, all of us getting paid."

"Paid with what?" Sval cried. "There isn't any money for wages or whatever! That's what the whole fandango's been about!"

"Not at first. Not for a few weeks," Martha admitted. "But if we keep the paper going, just keep putting it out week after week, just keep the ads coming in—see, that's where you and me've never agreed, Sval. You've always said, cut salaries, I've always said, get more money coming in. I still say, get more money coming in. I know I could *get* more money coming in. Like I said, the people selling ads are not going anywhere as long as we're giving them a paper to run the ads in, but it has to be a paper people want. That's our part. That's what helps them sell ads. Us putting out a paper people want."

"Easy to say," said Sval. "The devil's in the details."

"Details is just what I'm good at. Here's what I want. I want you five to keep working on the Ark—full time. Help me get it rolling again. No one gets paid for a couple of three weeks till we get through the crunch but after that, if my plan works, we can start squeezing out forty, fifty, maybe even sixty dollars a week for each of us. And keep building up from there."

"Well," said Zoe. "I can live on fifty a week. Count me in, Martha. What am I doing with my life anyway? You want to try, I'll try to help. At least for a while. I've got something else in mind for the fall, but I'm yours for now."

"I've got some bucks saved," said Raoul. "I could quit my job. Does this mean I get to do all the graphics from now on?"

"That's the idea. Each of us does whatever we do best. You handle all the art. George does all the photos and some of the writing—"

"Well, but I do have my own art to think about," said Marica. "I'm not giving up my own art just to save the Ark. That woman from New York gave me her card, she's the dance critic for *Culture Shock*. I might be moving to New York one of these days. But for now—"

"Give me six months," said Martha. "What I need from you, Marica, is production. How about you give us three days a week full-time, Tuesday, Wednesday, Thursday. And we'll be looking for someone who can take your place when the time comes."

"Well, of course I could do *that*. Three days a week. But not more," Marica warned.

"Sval?"

All eyes turned to the lanky man. He was sitting with head bowed, his hands clenched in his lap. When he looked up, his eyes were glistening. "If the Ark dies now," he said, "a lot of people will say I killed it. And they'll be right. If there's a chance to save it, I can't say no. What do you need from me, Martha?"

"I need you to commit to this one hundred percent. And to me. I can't do it without you. It has to be both of us doing this."

As his friends watched, Sval then took both of her hands in both of his. "I'm all in," he said.

Martha blushed. "And I promise, Sval. I swear. I'll keep the Ark living long enough for you to finish your whole series about the Sinister Twelve and Tom Leonard's project and everything else you might ever want to write and publish."

"Wait a minute," George spluttered. "I don't get it. Sval writes, Sval edits, I write, I take photos, Marica does production Raoul does what he does, all of us pitch in with grunt work—I get it. But you, Martha? Where do you fit in? You keep saying 'our paper' 'our paper'. What'll *you* be doing?"

"I'll be the publisher," Martha told him pleasantly. "I'll be the one telling all the rest of you what to do."

The Rose City Six sat silently, sunk in their thoughts, absorbing this new reality: Martha would be head honcho. No one objected. Oddly enough, this made a crazy sort of sense.

September 10, 2001

Zoe Madigan's second book tour took her through Portland, which she hadn't visited in years. She stopped for candy at a magazine store in the airport and saw that the Ark *was on sale there, right next to* Willamette Week *and* Oregon Times. *Except, it wasn't spelled "Ark" anymore. It was now the* Rose City Arc. *Under its name, the masthead carried a well-known quote from Martin Luther King: "The arc of the moral universe is long, but it bends toward justice."*

Zoe bought a copy and skimmed it in the cab on the way into town. It was still a weekly but a fat one now, at least 64 pages. The cover was still a cover, as it had been in Zoe's day. It smacked somewhat of the New York Review of Books. *Everything about the paper's design let readers know this was lively material for serious people who were not afraid to think deeply.*

As in the old days, the content started on page 3. The facing page was still reserved for letters to the editor and a sidebar that now listed Martha Williams as the publisher and Sval Hofby as the managing editor. Below them came a list of names that Zoe didn't recognize.

The book she was touring was her second one on the politics of prison reform. Like the first book, it was a quick read, because Zoe used anecdotes and case studies and inventive language to make her grim points; plus it was peppered with prisoners' own stories as-told-to-Zoe Madigan. Her edited transcripts somehow managed to deliver a sense of their own unedited voices. Zoe's reading was at Powell's, which had been a tiny one-room bookstore in the southeast in her day. Now it straddled an entire city block in the northwest and was several stories tall, the biggest bookstore in the world, supposedly. She drew a very modest crowd, but that did not surprise her or even disappoint. Her job was just to reach the ones who came. If she did that, they might tell others who might tell others. That was how the world really worked. She understood that now.

Sval and Martha came to the reading, of course, and that was so nice. Afterwards, the three of them went to the Wood Stove to have a drink and catch up. They'd heard the sad news about George dying in Lebanon the year before, killed by a car bomb. He'd been there taking pictures for the Washington Post. *The pictures ran posthumously. Sval and Martha offered gracious sympathy to Zoe. They knew she and George had stayed in touch after Portland and the two of them had remained close, right to the very end. Marica and Raoul came up in the conversation, too, but none of them had much recent news of those two. Martha was pretty sure they were still together and living in New York somewhere, but not in the city. Upstate New York was her impression. She had a number for them somewhere. She'd been meaning to call. Sval said he'd heard they were still doing art and having some success. He thought they might have gotten married, but he wasn't sure.*

The End

9 780999 826232